BEHIND THE
FRONT FENCE

BEHIND THE FRONT FENCE

30 Modern Australian Short Stories

Edited by **Barry Oakley**

The Five Mile Press

Cover image:
Howard Arkley
Family Home – suburban exterior 1993 (detail)
Synthetic polymer paint on canvas
203.0 x 254.0 cm
Monash University Collection
Purchased 1994
©The Estate of Howard Arkley
Licensed by Kalli Rolfe Contemporary Art

The Five Mile Press Pty Ltd
950 Stud Road
Rowville Victoria 3178 Australia

Phone: +61 3 8756 5500
Email: publishing@fivemile.com.au

First published 2004

Introduction and chapter openers © Barry Oakley
Stories copyright © individual authors

Designed by Zoë Murphy
Printed in Australia by Griffin Press

National Library of Australia Cataloguing-in-Publication data

Behind the front fence: 30 modern Australian short stories.

ISBN 1 74124 431 5.

1. Short stories, Australian. I. Oakley, Barry,

A823.0108

CONTENTS

INTRODUCTION 8

MYSTERIES

Sandtrap — Liam Davison 13

Our Own Little Kakadu — Janette Turner Hospital 22

The Argument — Anthony Lynch 41

Who's Afraid of Rupert Bunny? — Desmond O'Grady 49

DIFFICULTIES

The Girl Next Door — Steve J. Spears 57

Green — Nick Earls 67

Diwai Meri — Gretta Beveridge 82

The Drill Sergeant — John Gascoigne 91

SECRECIES

Southern Skies — David Malouf 105

A Pitch Too High for the Human Ear — Cate Kennedy 130

The Taxman's Mango — David Astle 140

Dreams as a form of travel — Sari Wawn 155

MEMORIES

My Father's Axe — Tim Winton 167

A Kind of Peace — Marshall Browne 180

Word from Stan — Bill Collopy 190

DISUNITIES

A Mixed Marriage — Lily Brett 201

The Milk — Jessica Anderson 212

Rocks — Miles Hitchcock 240

Home — Larissa Behrendt 253

ETHNICITIES

My Mother-in-Law in the Family Tree — Paddy O'Reilly 275

The Hafli — Eva Sallis 285

Padre Nostro, Who Art in Heaven — Josephine Vraca 293

HOSTILITIES

Dingle the Fool — Elizabeth Jolley 301

The Hair and the Teeth — Carmel Bird 318

The Vampire's Assistant at the 157 Steps — Michael Wilding 326

The Death of Sardanapalus — Barry Oakley 338

MORTALITIES

Nails of Love, Nails of Death — James McQueen 349

The Wheelbarrow — Patrick Cullen 367

A Pawpaw All the Way from Queensland — Beverley Farmer 374

The Car Keys — Peter Goldsworthy 385

NOTES ON THE AUTHORS 398

INTRODUCTION

People like reading stories because people like telling them. In a sense, our entire day consists of moving from one story to another. First, news stories in the papers or on the radio. Then gossip around the tea-urn or in the canteen. Home again, we will exchange stories with our partner about how our day has been. Finally, at bedtime, children insist on having tales told to them. One could almost say that if there's no story to our life, there's no life.

In our day-to-day domestic storytelling, a series of facts has to be shaped and given an ending. We tell these factual stories using the methods of fiction, and if we do it well enough we reward our listeners with something greater than the sum of its parts: truth.

Though the stories in *Behind the Front Fence* are purely imaginative (with one exception: Steve J. Spears' 'The Girl Next Door' is fact-based), their techniques are the ones we all use to make sense of our lives, only here they are applied more intensively – to embody characters and actions in a narrative that seems, ideally, to unfold of its own accord.

Stories like the ones chosen here create imaginative spaces, which they invite us to inhabit and vivify. The words lie in black rows on the white page, waiting for the reader to resurrect them. Their imaginings can only be released by ours. Films and television tell stories too, but their noisiness and wall-to-wall visualness leave the imagination with nowhere to go: we lie back in front of a big or small screen and the stories run right over us. Imagination is flattened. Movies capture us. Prose fictions set us free.

The overall theme of the stories collected here is domestic, but not in the sense of domesticity. They move behind the front fence, past the tidiness of the front garden and into the secrecies of the house. Pressures build, and when they erupt, are all the more powerful because of their confinement within four walls.

So what you will find here are insights into what the writer Kenneth McLeish called 'the gaps, hinges, holes, awkwardnesses, uncertainties and epiphanies' of everyday life. What you'll also find, as well as impressive work by a number of well-known Australian authors, is compelling fiction by new writers. The arrangement of the material is somewhat loose. Most, but not all, organised themselves conveniently into thematic groups. A few could have fitted into a number of categories, but seem to fit most comfortably in the one chosen for them.

We begin with *Mysteries*, because that describes some of the most teasing stories. They range from the unnerving crying in the middle of the night in Liam Davison's 'Sandtrap', through the neighbours whose secret is never discovered in Anthony Lynch's 'The Argument' and the nursing-home mother in Desmond O'Grady's story who clings so determinedly to her fantasy, to the visions of the patriarch in his overgrown Darwin garden in Janette Turner Hospital's 'Our Own Little Kakadu'.

The next section offers a variety of *Difficulties*. Steve J. Spears applies his dramatist's skills to 'The Girl Next Door'. The comedy is not quite so black in Nick Earls's 'Green', where the ultimate nerd triumphs over his nerdiness, and then lightens further in John Gascoigne's 'The Drill Sergeant', where gentle ironies expose the great Australian sports obsession. But there's nothing amusing in the beleaguered mother's plight in Gretta Beveridge's 'Diwai Meri'. Though Papua New Guinea is an exotic place of wonder for her daughter, it seems barbarous and threatening to her.

David Malouf opens *Secrecies* with a typically subtle study of an adolescent boy's discovery of someone else's secret, which in turn releases something deep within himself. More secrecies are explored by the other trio of writers: Cate Kennedy's basketballer goes for nocturnal runs to relieve his sense of familial entrapment; David Astle's taxman preserves the memory of one blissful week to sustain him through his marriage, and in Sari Wawn's fable a mother nourishes her deprived spirit by moving more and more into fantasy.

The next grouping opens with Tim Winton's exploration of the power of *Memories*. A stolen axe recalls the father who once so powerfully used it, provoking disturbingly violent dreams in the son. Something equally troubling lies deep within Julia's memories in Marshall Browne's 'A Kind of Peace', and it takes a visit to her childhood home to release them. But for Bill Collopy's Stan, whiling away his remaining days on the front verandah of his house, recollections are all that he has.

Disunities probes the consequences of separations. In both Lily Brett's and Jessica Anderson's stories, a wife leaves a husband. In the first, briskly and plainly told, Lola outrages her Jewish parents by going off to live with another man. In the second, Anderson shows her novelist's skills in tracing the twists and turns in Marjorie's late-in-life attempt to gain independence. Larissa Behrendt's 'Home' concerns a young

Aboriginal girl who is taken from her family and put into domestic service which is close to slavery, and Miles Hitchcock's 'Rocks' plunges us into the noisome underside of ordinary day-to-day existence.

The alienation theme continues in *Ethnicities*, where Asian, Arab and Italian attempts at accommodation to a sometimes bewildering Australian reality are dramatised. In Paddy O'Reilly's story, Dorothy's Asian mother-in-law is a forceful character who is determined to impose her traditional culture on the local suburban one. The girl in Josephine Vraca's 'Padre Nostro, Who Art In Heaven' rebels against her mother's Italian pieties by refusing to say the rosary any more. In Eva Sallis's 'The Hafli', a refugee from Iraq has to endure bereavement as well as exile.

Hostilities takes us deep into the region of domestic disturbance. In 'Dingle the Fool', two sisters quarrel over the fate of their disabled brother, with Elizabeth Jolley's distinctive quirkiness taking the edge off the grimness. The other three in the section depict violations. Carmel Bird's 'The Hair And The Teeth' perfectly catches the flattened tone of voice of a battling single mother whose house has been broken into. An unwelcome visitor in Michael Wilding's story exacerbates the paranoia of a neurotic living alone in an uncomfortable fibro cottage, and 'The Death of Sardanapalus' takes us back to the heady nineteen-seventies, when rebellion against suburban conventions was in the air – and, to one housewife at least, disastrously irresistible.

We end, logically enough, with *Mortalities*. Death is a tricky subject for writers, with the danger of melodrama beforehand and sentimentality after. In James McQueen's and Beverley Farmer's stories, the victim is inconsequential and anonymous in one and a burden to the family in the other. Both, in their different ways, seem to court death, as if they know it's waiting for them. In Patrick Cullen's 'The Wheelbarrow', death's grimness is leavened by the attitude of the father, who shows a farmer's stoicism and defiance as the moment approaches. And Peter Goldsworthy, in the final story, artfully poises mortality between comedy and awfulness – avoiding, like the others, the twin dangers mentioned above.

Every kind of emotion lurks behind the front fence, as these 30 stories show. I invite you to step inside them, and share their imaginative spaces.

Barry Oakley
2004

MYSTERIES

Sandtrap

LIAM DAVISON

Ross McLennan has a neighbour who's a golf pro, and to whom he rarely speaks. One night, near dawn, he hears someone crying. Is it his son? Or is it his neighbour? He investigates and finds its source, but the reason behind it remains a mystery. The art in 'Sandtrap' lies in what is left unsaid.

Ross McLennan wakes to the sound of crying. It is 4.21 in the morning and he waits for his wife to stir. She is curled away from him on the far side of the bed and by the time he accepts that she had not heard and won't be attending to the sound, he has realised that the time has long since passed when their children cried in the night. His daughter no longer lives in the same house. Her room – it is still her room – is filled with things they no longer need. The old computer is there, and the boxes the new one came in. There is a leather coat, hardly worn. The crying doesn't stop.

His son is eighteen years old now. He works late at the Caltex to fund his studies. It worries Ross McLennan that his son is crying at 4.21 in the morning and he gets out of bed and walks down the hallway to his bedroom door. He leaves the light out so as not to disturb his wife, though why she's not awake already to hear their son crying he can't say. The moon is nearly full and the bathroom, when he passes it, is filled with cold light coming through the frosted window glass. He wraps his arms about himself.

He pushes open his son's bedroom door and sees him lying – a man now, almost as big as himself – on the single bed. It occurs to him that he doesn't know what to say. Or do. It's been a long time since he has held his son. He looks at his broad back and his man's arms hanging over the edge of the bed. Then he realises that the sound of crying is not coming from his son's room at all but from somewhere else. And it frightens him, he doesn't mind admitting. There is no one else in the house except his wife still sleeping in his own bed. He closes the door on his son's breathing and sees how the whole inside of the house now is bathed with the pale light shining through the windows. He stops outside the door to his daughter's room.

She is not here anymore. He reminds himself of this. She is on the other side of the country working with people he doesn't know, living in a house he has never seen. His beautiful daughter. He leans closer to the door. The crying sounds like something breaking. How, he wonders, can people sleep through such a noise. He pushes open his daughter's bedroom door and sees, in the wash of moonlight that fills the room, the old computer at the foot of her empty bed, the empty boxes piled as he had left them. Even her smell has gone. The leather coat is folded on her chair.

From her window he can see the trampoline on the back lawn and the square of yellow sand beside it, still there after all these years. There is, he knows, an identical square of yellow sand in the garden of the house next door, not visible now even with the light of the moon. He had assumed children when they'd first moved in. Expected them. Their own children, even then, were too old for sand.

'We'll move it,' they had said. 'Cats.'

Yet here it is, still here. The same as next door.

The crying comes from nowhere in particular. It is neither soft nor loud. It seems to be both inside the house and out and he peers through the glass to see if there is any sign of movement in the backyard or in the trees that separate the houses from each other. He should wake his wife, he thinks, and talk to her. But instead he stays there at the window, looking out into the night, listening.

His neighbour is a man who plays golf for a living. He has seen him standing in the yellow sand on his side of the fence practising his swing. Chipping balls. Not children then, he'd thought. Golf. He makes his living teaching people the correct way to strike a golf ball. There is a demand for this. He makes a good living from it, his wife had said, which had surprised him. Then, when he'd thought about it, it made as much sense as anything else people might do with their lives. He had taught also, many years ago, in a school for boys and he supposed there might now be one or two of them – grown men – who thought of him occasionally and remembered something that he'd taught. Perhaps.

In the eight years since they moved here he has never exchanged more than twenty words with his neighbour. Which is fine. They wave or nod. Once, he returned a golf ball that had strayed.

His neighbour used to live in the house they live in now. Their home. He knows this because of the sand, but also because his wife has spoken to him about it and discovered that he used to rent their house when he still lived with his own wife, but that is a long time ago now. A long time. They spoke about the sand and golf and about the cats which he admitted were a problem.

'If I had my way,' he'd said, 'they'd all be trapped and killed.'

Sometimes he thinks of his neighbour living in his house, standing in the bathroom where he stands in the morning to shave and clean his teeth, looking out the same windows he looks out now. He thinks of his neighbour's clothes hanging in his wardrobe.

One night he thought he saw him sitting at the kitchen table in the half-dark, leaning forward on his elbows as though to speak. It scared him then, like the crying scares him. There is no explaining it. Noise travels, but this was something different.

He wonders, did he use his daughter's room to store his clubs?

He leaves her room and closes the door behind him. From where he stands, he can see the humped shape of his sleeping wife in their bed and hear his son's breathing at the other end of the hallway. And from somewhere else, the crying. He walks to the back door, opens it and steps out into the night.

The crying is louder now, still from no particular direction. The backyard slopes away from the house to what used to be a creek and is now a gully of reclaimed land. Sounds carry along it from a long way off. There have been times when he has heard whole conversations as though people were talking in his own yard. Once, he remembers, he heard his daughter's voice calling out, only to find she was visiting two blocks away.

The moon is almost full. He walks to the back of the yard and looks back at the house from beside the trampoline. The windows now are dark squares and he sees the door he has left standing open like an invitation. He should walk back up and close it he thinks but instead he stays standing beside the trampoline listening to the sound of crying. It is punctuated, he realises now, by soft sobs and could be coming from the house itself or from as far away as the end of the gully which runs for a mile at least before opening to the bay. He's heard that sound carries over water.

. . . . .

He remembers, years ago, when he was half the age his son is now, travelling in his father's car at dusk. They drove past the dockyards and customs houses at the top end of the bay along roads that have long since vanished and between long rows of windowless railway sheds built of corrugated iron. On the far side of a cyclone fence was a steel wall streaked with rust. It loomed above the car, blocking his view of the night sky so it felt they were driving through a darkening tunnel. Ahead, he could see the skeleton frame of a black gasometer. He can't remember if they spoke or what time of year it was. He remembers his father had bought two bottles of beer and wrapped them in newspaper and the sound they made as they clinked together on the back seat of the car. Suddenly, the steel wall came to a stop and his view opened to the black water of the docks and beyond it a wasteland of disused warehouses. He realised the wall hadn't been a wall at all but the side of a ship and when he looked back he saw the word GDANSK in white letters through the rear window of the car.

They travelled on past the gasworks and the seamen's mission – a squat, dank-looking building with wire mesh windows – and across a single-lane bridge. Once across it, the dockyards slipped away and they drove past paddocks filled with weeds and thistles and the occasional pool of still water that caught the last light of the fading day. He sensed they were still following the curve of the bay, though when they arrived at the weatherboard house where his father would drink his beer with a man and woman who were not quite his uncle and aunt, he couldn't say for certain which way it was. There were no children at the house and he sat out on the front porch by himself looking back in the direction they had come. The street was lit with yellow light and there was a smell his father told him came from the abattoirs and tannery further along the road.

He sat there for a long time listening to the sound of a man singing. At first, he'd thought it came from inside the house and had thought how strange it was that his father would sing. Then he realised it was not his father or the man who was not quite his uncle but someone else a long way off in the night singing in a language he didn't understand. There was no music, just his singing. Then there was a shriek and the singing stopped.

When his father finished his beer and came out onto the porch, he placed his hand on his shoulder and said 'Alright then?'

He didn't know what to say but he remembers his father left his hand there on his shoulder longer than he expected him to do and he didn't know whether to put his own hand there or to move away. Later, on their way back home, his father told him that sound carried a long way over water and the singing might have come from anywhere. The other sound, he said, would have come from the abattoir.

After all these years, he can still feel the weight of his father's hand on his shoulder.

. . . . .

He leaves the trampoline and walks up the side of the house that faces away from the gully. The crying is clearer now. It is so close it might be coming from himself. Through the trees he can see his neighbour sitting in the half-dark on the far side of the square of sand. He is leaning forward in a plastic garden chair, nursing his head in his hands and crying. Ross McLennan doesn't know what to do. He stands there watching. He should go back inside and shut the door.

His neighbour stops crying to take a breath then starts again. It is open and unashamed. Then he lifts his head and looks through the trees to where he stands. There is enough light from the moon for both men to see each other clearly. Ross McLennan doesn't move or avert his eyes. He holds his neighbour's gaze and sees his face streaked with tears, his wet lips trembling. They look at each other for what seems like minutes, saying nothing. Then Ross McLennan walks back the way he came. He goes inside and shuts the door.

He goes back into his son's bedroom where his boy is still sleeping with his arms hanging over the edge of the bed. He sits beside him and listens to him breathe. He stays there for a long time then places his hand on his shoulder and feels it rise and fall, rise and fall and wonders, would he wake if he took him in his arms and held him?

His wife stirs when he crawls back into bed.

'What time is it?' she says.

'It's early. 5.21.'

'Did you hear something?'

'Nothing,' he says. 'Go back to sleep.'

. . . . .

His son is still in his bed when he leaves for work. He has showered and shaved. He has eaten breakfast with his wife. The morning is cold but the day promises to be fine. Already, the ti-tree is coming into flower and he can smell the salt smell coming off the bay.

'Leave the back door open,' his wife says.

He walks up the side of the house and sees the plastic garden chair where his neighbour left it. The sand is raked smooth as though it's been freshly done, with the rake laid flat beside it.

He puts his bag on the back seat of the car and is about to get in when he sees his neighbour. He is walking towards his own car on the opposite side of the fence carrying his clubs. Ross McLennan could be in his car and backing out the driveway before his neighbour sees him. It would be safer, he thinks. But he waits. He watches his neighbour sling his clubs into the boot of his car. Waits for him to turn and see him. Their eyes meet through the painted trellis. Neither of them looks away.

'Alright?' Ross McLennan says.

'Alright.'

. . . .

Our Own Little Kakadu

JANETTE TURNER HOSPITAL

The Wilkins's Darwin garden has become a jungle because Jug, the patriarch, has turned against pruning and penning things in. Jug, the tough road-builder, is having visions out in his derelict bus. Is he mad, or has he been 'sung' by the Aboriginal people whose sacred places he once despoiled? There are mythic depths to Hospital's narrative: it works on a number of levels.

There must be, by Maggie's reckoning, upwards of fifty chooks running loose, but who would know? When she steps carefully between pineapple rows to test the fruit cones, she puts her foot on at least a dozen eggs. First comes the soft crunch, then the streaky corona-squirt of ochre and snot, then the ooze between her toes. The soles of her feet squelch against her sandals, she is practically skating on slick. Hah, she thinks. Walking on water, tiptoeing on eggshells, what's new?

'He took an axe to the chook house months ago,' her mother said on the drive from the airport. At the stoplight, her mother had lifted both hands from the wheel, palms up, and raised them toward the roof of the car, beseeching someone, something, to bear witness.

'Jug's violent again?' Maggie was startled. 'I mean, *physically* violent?'

'Not toward me, no, no. Not at people. Not even at your brother. But there's something ... he *feels* violent, yes. He's against anything being penned in now. Against pruning. You should just see the passionfruit. I could rip miles of it off the laundry shed if I thought I'd get away with it. It's taking up all the clothes line space, I have to hang half our underwear on trees.' She clasped her hands together, the interlaced fingers pressing the knuckles white. 'Well, he's never done anything by halves, has he?'

'Juggernaut by name,' Maggie said.

'You can say that again. I never know what it's going to be next. I'm terrified he'll decide *mowing's* forbidden. We've had two pythons on the verandah already, and god knows what's living out there in the bus with him.

'Mum, the light's green.'

'What? Oh.' The car leaped forward, stalled, rallied. 'You don't know what it's been like, Maggie. Chooks roosting in the laundry, in the bananas, in the vegetables, in the –'

'Mum, mind the –! Would you like me to drive?'

'I had a smashed egg in my hair last week. They're laying on the rafters in all the sheds, you never know what's going to fall on you. Not to mention chicks hatching wherever you happen –'

'Mum, pull over. You're upset. Let me drive.'

'I'm not upset, I'm scared. He won't talk to me, he won't talk to your brother, he's started drinking again, he does say things to his mates at the pub when he's pissed, and there's *talk*, there's plenty of talk, but nobody can make sense of it. Nobody knows what happened. That's why you had to come back, I'm counting on you.'

'Oh yes,' Maggie said drily. 'We're famous for getting on famously, me and Jug.'

'That's the point. You'll strike sparks. If he gets mad enough he might blurt out some clue.'

'Doesn't Ben strike enough sparks?'

'It's weird. They're totally silent with each other. Anyway I can't get your brother near the place now, I have to go to him and Liz. And this is a taboo subject with them. Look, I wouldn't have dragged you back from Melbourne for nothing.'

'I think I was looking for an excuse to come back anyway.'

'Yeah? The girl who couldn't wait to get out, couldn't wait to shake the dust –'

'Yeah, well.'

'Melbourne people are so up themselves, I did warn you.'

'Yeah,' Maggie laughed. 'Made a bet with myself you'd say "I told you so" before we got home.'

'And wasn't I right? Didn't they give you the pip?'

'Yeah. Well, you know, there's all kinds. I've got some good friends. It's just … I don't know … You can't even talk about Darwin down there. You might as well announce you've come from Mars.'

'They give me the pip.'

'Whew, I'd forgotten how sticky –' Maggie eased her damp shirt away from her skin and leaned out the window. She wouldn't forgive her body if it had switched allegiance, adjusted to Melbourne chill, lost the knack for wet heat.

And then they passed under the familiar tangle of mango, frangipani, bougainvillea, and she cried, 'Hey! You can't see the house *at all*.'

'I told you. Pruning's not allowed, no cutting back, nothing. What we've got here is five acres of new-growth jungle with room to walk sideways round the house. Our own little Kakadu.'

. . . . .

Between the half acre of pineapple rows and the house, Maggie can see flashes of yellow, bits and pieces of the bus. It is almost entirely covered by passionfruit vine, though at the four points where its axles rest in the earth, pawpaw trees rise in thick spiky clumps. He must dump the seeds there, Maggie thinks; it's some new geometric ritual, the compass points of whatever this latest obsession is. He could live on pawpaw and passionfruit without leaving his rusty cocoon, she thinks. He could just reach out through the windows and pick. The light inside must be green now, like under water. He'd love that, Jug would, odd fish in his tank (shark in angelfish clothing? dolphin in sharkskin?), jugging it down, *jug jug*, tanking up in his tank, probably having a whale of a time, driving them all round the bend. As usual.

She sees now what was impossible about Melbourne. It was having to explain this, him, Darwin, all of it, any of it; trying to explain it without having to endure *how quaint, how awful, how bizarre, how exotic, how horrible, how –*. She couldn't bear to expose her perfectly ordinary strangeness, her loony family's ordinary Darwin madness, to people who knew so very little. *Everyone's a bit troppo up there, aren't they?* they would laugh, nudge. *The Top End's a bit over the top, wouldn't you say?* I could scratch you, she would think, and you wouldn't be one sweat layer thick. But she'd learned to do it herself, play the clown, betray a memory here, the self there, one drink, two, it was easy, pile the accent on thick, get the laughs. Besides, only two years earlier, let's admit it, she'd been frantic to flee, *frantic*, indecently keen to put as much distance as possible between herself and her own little haywired Top End bubble.

I can't *breathe* here, she'd said.

She breathes the damp air, sluggish with pineapple musk, frangipani, white gingerflower. I'll drown here, she thinks. I'll never get away. I'm just part of this blissed-out vegetable world, slumping into the Arafura Sea. We're all drugged. We're all troppo.

Hallelujah! as Jug would have said.

She steps on another egg.

The whole bloody garden must be protein-enriched, she thinks. It seems to be doing wonders for the pineapples. Almost every plant has a plumed cone at some stage of ripening, and when she looks down the throats of not-yet-fruited clumps, she sees the telltale blush of things underway. How sexually blatant plants are, she marvels. She twists four ripe fruits from their serrated nests and cradles them in her arms. Squashing eggs as she goes, scratching her legs on the pineapple swords, she makes for the bus.

'Jug?' she calls tentatively from the door.

It was a school bus once, long ago put out to pasture, deregistered, bought at auction, on whim, for a song. Maggie thinks the most telling census question in Darwin might be this: how many deregistered, de-wheeled vehicles are slowly listing into your five-acre lot? The Darwin average, she suspects, would be three. Beyond the pineapples, beyond the bananas, the mangos, the vast overgrown lawn, the avocados, somewhere down among the compost heaps, there are, she surmises, four earlier family cars now all but invisible, bleeding rust into jasmine that has run amok.

In Jug's bus, all the seats have been removed. There's a galley kitchen in the driver's niche, a bunk where the back seat used to be, a chemical lav in one corner, a hinged lift-up table along the side, a couple of armchairs spilling stuffing. Everywhere there are cobwebs with watchful spiders as large as poached eggs at their hubs. Chickens, eggs, ants: the floor seems busy. A harmless carpet snake, thick as a forearm, has coiled itself neatly into a chair.

'Jug?' There's no answer so she climbs in. She sees him lying on his back on the bunk at the rear of the bus, arms folded behind his head, staring at the ceiling. He is wearing khaki boxer shorts and a singlet, nothing else, and the bus is ripe with the smell of unwashed male. Light comes through the passionfruit leaves, amber green. 'Four pineapples,' she says brightly. 'Real beauties.' She puts them into the miniature stainless steel sink. 'Mum says you've given up on roads and bridges and gone into vegies and fruit. The marketman, the green-fingered genius, she says.'

Speak, you stubborn old bastard, she wills him. She can feel the usual dual pull of rage and protectiveness. For a big blustering man, he looks unexpectedly frail, and she is alarmed by the sight of his skinny legs and bare feet. His face and shoulders and arms are like old leather, but the legs and feet – trousered and shod throughout his respectable years as civil engineer – are as pale as the skin of young children. She feels embarrassed to see her father this way. It's like seeing some soft creature with its shell peeled off. Improper. She lifts the lid off his icebox and takes out two cans of beer, watching him. She peels the tab off one can. It makes a slight hiss, and brackish foam bubbles out and spills over her hand. She sees his eyes swivel in her direction and she walks down the bus: 'Mum tell you I was coming home?'

'Nope. But I reckoned you would, sooner or later.' He accepts a beer and swings himself upright. 'Told you I was bonkers, did she?'

Maggie sits cross-legged on the floor in front of him. 'Didn't need Mum to tell me that,' she says, cuffing him on the leg. Tactful, she makes no comment about the beer, which he had so dramatically renounced ten years ago. Maggie had been fifteen at the time, her brother Ben, eighteen. 'The Lord has delivered me,' Jug told them. 'I've been born again, pure as the driven snow.'

'Not much call for snow round here,' Ben said, asking for it. But there had been no oath, no swipe at Ben, no bash across the side of his son's head, so that they had marvelled and had known something eerie had occurred. Only the rigging in his neck, corded tight, told them the old Jug was still down there somewhere, inside the new one.

'It's funny,' Jug says meditatively now, looking around the bus. 'Well, not bloody funny at all. Something plays bad jokes on us, eh? I lived in the back of a truck when I first ran away to Darwin, fourteen years old. Jeez, jeez, jeez. I hate the way stuff comes back. Like bloody spiders crawling into your head.'

He never speaks of his childhood unless he's drunk, and it's a bad sign when he does. They know almost nothing about it. He began brand new on his wedding day, no baggage, no past, except for the bits that sometimes leaked out of beer-soaked cracks, or showed up, mangled, in rage. He was a famously hot-tempered boss on the road gangs, a short-fused husband and father, a weekend roisterer and larrikin of note.

And then the Lord spoke to him from a Gospel Hall pulpit. It was a steamy Sunday night, and Jug, guzzling from a large Darwin stubby of tarblack bitter, was weaving by the chapel's open door on the esplanade when the Lord shouted at the top of His Almighty lungs: 'Jug Wilkins, it is required of you this night to be a juggernaut for God.' Jug broke his teeth on the neck of the bottle in shock, and cut his lip, a potent sign. Blood streaming from his mouth, unnerved but belligerent, he staggered into the chapel and walked down its central aisle. 'Who the fuck do you think you are?' he demanded, teetering on his feet. 'I am the Lord your God, Jug Wilkins.' God fixed him with His pulpit eye, and Jug just stood there, confused – like a kangaroo in truck lights, people said later, swaying at the lip of some steeply pitched gully.

d. And Jug did. He jumped. He crossed
enforcer for the Lord, a role that not
put him into collision with his rebel
resisting son. Bible in hand – his surveyor's
– he would chapter and verse them, laying down markers, calling the shots, mapping everyone's road to Eternity.

'Watch out,' he tells Maggie, now, fretfully. 'I'm infectious. I got these old dreams, bad dreams, coming back.' He bats vaguely at the air and she sees mosquito swarms of nightmares buzzing him, giving him no quarter. 'Western Queensland somewhere,' he says, ducking. 'Must've been. Between Charleville and the Territory border, I reckon. I'd just nicked off, me old man didn't believe I'd ever do it. I hid in the back of a roadtrain, see.' He is not so much talking to *her*, Maggie thinks, as talking in a waking sleep. His voice seems very far away, inside a bubble in his head. 'It was cold as the bloody South Pole, that's the way it is out there, nights, June, July, cold as the bloody South Pole. You wouldn't believe the difference between night and day, she's an oven by day (you could fry an egg on the road), and deep freeze after dark. If you tripped over your foot in the dark, it'd snap right off, you'd get ice in your eye. Blimey, it's cold, it's cold.' He huddles into himself and begins to shake. 'I'm shivering under this tarp, which, let me tell you, stinks of bloody cowshit, *stinks*, and me old man steps out of nowhere with his whip in his hand. Steps out of the air, *abra*-bloody-*ca-dabra*, and into the back of the truck and rips off the tarp. He's got horns on his head.' Jug drops the beer and puts his arms in front of his face, warding off blows. He is trembling violently.

'Jug!' Maggie says, alarmed. 'Jug, you're drinking too much'.

'*Gotcha,*' he says. '*Gotcha, gotcha, gotcha.* You'll never get away from me, you little bugger, you little twerp.'

'Jug, it's okay, it's all right.' Maggie takes hold of his hands, which are clammy. He's sweating like a pig, but feels dangerously cold to the touch.

'He *laughs* when he does it.' Jug says. 'And I never did, I never did, he was right about that, I never got away from him.' He's shivering, curled into himself, barricaded behind his arms. 'He's back again,' he says. 'He's back. He's showing up after dark.'

Maggie can't bear it. 'Dad,' she says, hugging him. 'Oh Dad, you've got the DTs again.'

But it's the wrong thing to say. Wrong word. A sort of spasm passes through his body, and lucidity, like a brilliant tropical bird, swoops down on him. He leans toward her and takes her chin in his hand. 'I do not have the DTs,' he says distinctly. He repeats himself intensely, enunciating each word as only challenged drunks can, exaggerating syllables to such a degree that Maggie, helplessly, thinks of stepping on eggshells, thinks of his chook-mad garden, thinks of the crusted goo on her feet.

'*Take my yolk upon you,*' she splutters, on the edge of something, anxiety, compassion, hilarity, fearful hysteria. But this does not help.

'That's cheap, Maggie, cheap. Is that what they taught you in Melbourne? Cheap blasphemy? Blasphemy is cheap. Making fun of the Bible is cheap, making fun of your father is cheap.' His grip on her jaw is tighter, tighter. 'Your father does not have the DTs. Can you get that into your fucking head? I do not have the DTs. I know what's fucking real and what's not.' Any second now, Maggie thinks, my jaw will crack. 'This world,' he says furiously, 'is full of fucking people who don't know what's real and what's not. DTs, they say. Visions, they say. Bonkers, they say.' For emphasis, he bears down on her face with rhythmic force as he makes each point. Because she *cannot* speak, quite literally cannot speak – she can feel her bones giving way – Maggie focuses her outrage in her eyes, and he glares right back. 'Don't you look at me like that, young lady, with the devil between your eyes, and between your legs too, I reckon. Honour thy father, young lady, and fucking remember this: I fucking well know what I've seen and what I haven't, don't you fucking forget it.'

. . . . .

'If I ever kill anyone,' Maggie tells Ben and Liz. She's still crying. 'If I ever kill anyone,' she sobs.

'Yeah,' Ben says, 'I know. Hey, it's okay, kid. It's okay. We won't. I've thought it a thousand times, but we won't. We love the old bastard, and we won't.'

'But I would've,' she says. 'If I'd had a gun or a knife in my hand, I would've aimed straight for his gut. I *wanted* to.'

'Yeah, well you didn't, and you won't.'

'Ben came close once, though,' Liz says. 'In high school, remember?' Ben frowns, a warning, but Liz barrels on. 'The night he kicked Ben out. I nearly killed him myself that night.'

'Yeah,' Maggie says. 'I remember.'

She remembers the two of them standing there, Ben and Liz, and Jug screaming at Ben: 'The beginning of the end, that's what it is. A man starts fucking *boongs*, that's it, he's into the sewer, mate, and it's all downhill, all fucking downhill from there.' This was before God had grabbed Jug by the scruff of the neck. Weeks before. 'No son of mine,'

Jug had roared, 'is going to screw around with some black fucking gin. You wanna fuck *boongs*, go and live in their stinking camps.'

There had been fists and blood and mayhem.

'Get out,' Jug had yelled. 'Get out, and take your black slut with you, and don't ever come back.'

'Too bloody right,' Ben yelled. 'You can count on it, mate.'

Weeks of storm weather had prevailed, weeks of walking on eggshells.

And then God had spoken.

And then Jug had pulled in his horns.

'She's all right,' he'd say gruffly of Liz. *For a boong:* you could hear him refuse to think the thought. 'Red and yellow, black and white, All are precious in His sight,' he'd say. In fact, Liz got on better with the born-again Jug than his son or his daughter did. It's my Mission School background, she'd say. I know that country.

'How long's he been like this again?' Maggie asks.

'Didn't Mum tell you?'

'No. She never said a word in letters till the chooks got her down. So how long has it been?'

'Since the new road from Jabiru,' Ben says.

'Mum says nobody knows what happened.'

Ben says nothing.

'Well?' she says, watching him closely. 'Is that true?'

'Yes and no,' he says. 'I don't want to comment. I can't comment.'

'I can,' Liz says. 'He's been sung.'

'What?' Maggie blinks at her. 'By who?'

'By my mob,' Liz says. 'By the elders of the tribe.'

'Why?'

'The road,' Ben says. 'The mining company. The new road through Kakadu. It runs through sacred sites.'

'He knew that,' Liz says. 'We made depositions. The press refused to cover it, per usual, but everyone knew. I faced him one day, with the demonstrators. Nose to nose.'

'So that's it,' Ben says. 'You never told me.'

'No.'

'What'd he do?'

'We just stood there staring at each other. And he said: "What can I do, Liz? I'm a working man, I build roads, what else can I do?" And I said: 'You can cross the line, Jug.' And he said: 'Easy to say, Liz. Easy for you.' And I said: 'Don't do this, Jug, please. It's our land, it's our Dreaming, it's our old people, you're tearing us up, it's our country.' And we just kept standing there, looking at each other, eye to eye, people pushing and shoving, but it was just us two, him and me.'

She is staring at the backs of her hands.

'Yes?' Ben prompts.

'I don't know,' she says. I felt he was standing right on the line, I felt he was thinking about it, I thought maybe he just might step over and join me, he just wanted a nudge, so I said …'

Maggie pictures the scene: the graders, the steamrollers, the tiptrucks of crushed stone, the sharp smell of tar, the demonstrators, the workmen in their heavy boots and singlets, the heat. She watches Liz remember it. She watches Ben watching Liz. *This is a taboo subject with them*, she hears her mother say.

'What happened?' Ben nudges.

'I said something …'

They wait. Liz studies her hands. '*What?*' Ben says.

'What did you say?'

Liz sighs heavily. 'I said the wrong thing, I reckon.'

'What was it?'

But she's back at that line, nose to nose with Jug, her mob and his mob, stalemate.

'What, dammit! What did you say?'

'I said: 'You've got a grandchild coming, Jug. It's his Dreaming you're messing up. It's his place, it's his country, your own *grandchild's*. You're desecrating his birthright, Jug.'

Maggie watches Liz breathing, she knows the way of it, how the ragged tempo takes you over, it's like a weather pattern that you enter when you get too close to Jug. 'What did he say?' she asks.

'He said: "You fucking manipulative *boong*".'

Ben puts a hand over his face.

'And I told him, I hissed it at him. I said, 'You're being sung, Jug Wilkins. You'd better make arrangements, because you're gonna be sung.' She starts collecting dishes with extraordinary vehemence and banging them into the sink. 'Fucking boong-hater,' she keeps saying. 'Fucking boong-haters, all of you, deep down.'

When she passes by him, Ben lifts a hand to touch her, but drops it again. Maggie has a sudden lurch of panic: they'll fight, she thinks; they'll say things they can't take back; he'll turn into Dad. Maggie wants a lightning bolt, she wants to point the bone somewhere, she wants someone to unsing the country, she wants to stop all of this. She gets up and puts her arms around Liz, but Liz pushes her away, furious. 'Don't you bloody *touch* me!' Liz yells, but the words puncture her rage which leaves her in a sudden rush, half sob. She looks deflated and unutterably weary. 'Oh shit,' she says helplessly to Ben: 'I'm sorry, mate. I really thought, you know, he was going to cross the line. I was so fucking *disappointed*.'

She says to Maggie: 'Anyway, they did. Sing him, I mean. They did it. He's been sung, and he knows it.'

. . . . .

Maggie is standing at the very back edge of their lot. It's night, still stiflingly hot and humid, but there's a full moon and just the suggestion of a breeze beginning to snuffle in off the sea. Around her rise the burial mounds of old cars. What would an archaeologist make of this? she wonders, this humpy terrain of rusted frames and compost heaps, all smothered and choked with jasmine, allamander, bougainvillea, and the ever rapacious morning glory, all of it sliding back into bush. Who knows where the boundary lies? What mad surveyor ever tried to mark such a thing?

'So wha'd'ya reckon, Maggie?' His voice is slurred, rising from somewhere in the smothered heaps of junk.

'Oh god, Jug, don't *do that*, you nearly gave me a heart attack. Where are you?'

'Where you gonna place your bet, Maggie?' He knocks on a creeper-clothed mound, and it gives back a hollow note, faintly metallic. 'The Earth our Mum? Or the cars? Wha'd'ya reckon?'

She's still too angry with him for patience, she wants to hurt. 'I've been to Ben and Liz's,' she says. 'You shouldn't've worked on the road. I know why you've gone loco, you've been sung.'

'On the road to Ka-ka-du-uu,' he sings drunkenly, 'where the crocs and the jabiru play –'

She will make him bleed. She will. 'They've turned you into the fruit and vegie man,' she says.

But he's not listening to her. He's not paying attention. He comes crawling out of the undergrowth on all fours, his head cocked to one side. He's listening for something else. She thinks of the cats watching invisible birds in the bush, that fixed intensity, his concentration focused at the point where the car humps merge into impenetrable wetland scrub. She peers into the moonwashed darkness, curious. 'What are you looking for?'

He gives no reaction, no sign, she might as well have ceased to exist.

'Jug,' she says, irritable. She wades through ground cover, creepers, rotting matter, she crunches sticks and eggs as she goes.

'What are you looking at?' And when he ignores her, she pummels his shoulders with her fists. He yelps, and throws her a brief startled glance, but whirls back again as though he dare not waver in his attentiveness. She has the creepy sensation that they are both being watched.

'What are you looking at, for god's sake?'

'Them,' he says.

'Who?' She batters him with her fists, years of rage, anxiety, helpless compassion all shouting through her white tight knuckles. 'Wha'd'ya mean, *them*, you bloody loony?'

He catches hold of her wrists. She can see he's snapped out of it now. He's with her again. He's just Jug. 'You see, Maggie,' he says quietly, 'that's why I can't tell you. I can't tell anyone. You'll say drunk, loony, the DTs. It's too big for that. It's too – .' He can't even find a word.

But she knows suddenly, intuitively, what he's talking about. She has a sharp vision of a Melbourne dinner party, the usual little terrace house, cast-iron lace balconies, North Carlton candlelit table, a whole roomful of elegance, brittle wit, and glibness. Maggie's in mid-flight, and all eyes are upon her, waiting. They are waiting for the laugh. *And as for Jug ...?* someone prompts, but Maggie has fallen silent. There's a line she won't cross. She has bumped into sacrilege and recognised it in time. I forget, she says politely. I forget what I was going to say.

'Except maybe Liz,' Jug says. 'I could tell Liz, but I won't give her the satisfaction, me pride won't let me. And I can't tell anyone else.'

'It's okay, Dad,' Maggie says. 'I know what you're talking about.'

He puts out a hand to steady himself. 'I got vertigo,' he says. 'Comes and goes. Ever stood over a crack into nothing?'

'Yeah,' she sighs.

He holds his two hands up against the moon and brings them slowly together. He matches them carefully, palm to palm, finger to finger, thumb to thumb. 'There's two worlds,' he says, trying to explain something to himself. 'They're both as real as can be. They match exactly, so you can only see one at a time.' They both study his hands against the moon, a single dark silhouette. He could be someone praying, Maggie thinks. He sighs heavily. 'They match exactly,' he says, 'but they don't fit.'

'Yeah,' she says. 'I know.'

He looks at her warily and she gestures with her hands, palms up. Who has answers? her shrug implies.

He is assessing something. He reads her gestures and her eyes. He makes a decision. 'I saw something,' he says.

She nods.

'But I can't tell you. It's too –'

'I know,' she says. 'It's okay.'

They watch each other for a long time in silence. Then

she raises her hands, palms facing him, and he brings his up to meet hers. They sit there like two children, fingertip to fingertip, palm pushing lightly against palm, an imperfect fit.

'If I told you...' he says gruffly.

'You don't have to tell me. It's okay.'

'If I tell you, you gotta promise –'

'Cross my heart.' She licks an index finger and gestures over her breast.

'It was before they sung me anyway,' he says. 'It was just after me and Liz – well, I blew me top.'

'Yeah, she told us.'

'Didn't mean to. And then afterwards, I just wanted to smash something. I climbed up on the steamroller. We had the first bed of gravel down, I wanted to crush it meself. I wanted to mash it in, flatten it. I saw Liz leave with her mob. Good riddance, I thought, and I moved 'er up to full throttle. You could hear the road crunching into dirt, it's a good sound that. I was up there behind the wheel, and I suddenly had this giddy feeling I was on the spine of a razorback. Each side of me there was nothing. *Nothing.* I mean, if I moved, I could've fallen right off the world. And then I got this funny feeling on the back of me neck, this prickle, like when you know someone's watching you.'

He opens his eyes very wide, the pupils dilated. The moon, bright orange, sits behind his head like a plate. Maggie sees herself, twice over, in his eyes.

'I turned around,' he says, whispering now, 'and there were hundreds and hundreds of them, thousands maybe, just standing there with their spears in their hands, watching me. They didn't make a sound. They were naked except for those little things they wear, and white bodypaint.'

He clutches at his heart, a sharp pain grabbing him

again. 'It spooked me,' he whispers. 'The way they just stood there watching. They never made a sound, but I knew what they were waiting for.'

He looks at Maggie intently. 'They are *with* us,' he says. 'I never realised before, but they're with us.'

Maggie swallows.

'I climbed down off the steamroller,' he says. 'And I walked away. I never went back.'

'Dad,' Maggie says gently. 'Let's go back to the house.'

But he doesn't want to. He stands there staring into the wetlands. 'Alpha and Omega,' he murmurs. He seems to be sifting through clutter in his mind. 'The first and the last,' he says. 'The First Ones. *The last shall be first.*'

Maggie tugs at his hand. 'Dad,' she says.

'*Seeing we also are compassed about with so great a cloud of witnesses,*' he says, pulling at a creeper from the scrub of his Gospel Hall decade. He thinks he's got hold of something. 'And in those days, the last shall be the First Ones, and they shall be with us in the land.'

'Dad, you're mixing things up.'

'Nothing fits,' he says, turning to offer his puzzled benediction. 'That's the problem, Maggie. Nothing fits. But I know what's real and what's not, and they are with us.'

. . . .

From *Janet Turner Hospital: Collected Stories*, UQP, 1995

The Argument

ANTHONY LYNCH

A couple in one anonymous flat overhear a couple in another, quarrelling. Lynch's view of modern life is bleak – relationships fragment, lives are tangents never finding a centre. We learn tantalisingly little about the characters in 'The Argument'.

A voice moved along the balcony, bounced off a wall at the far end and took a sidestep through our doorway. The voice was neither loud nor close but it was hard and persistent.

'Something's going on outside,' I said to Kate.

Kate unscrunched the top half of her body. She sat next to me on the couch, one we'd bought from a furniture stall at Camberwell market. Her legs stayed folded against the green vinyl underneath her backside. She shifted her eyes from the TV and listened with her right ear and eye.

'It's the people below, that's all. They're loud people.'

'I know they're loud but they're louder than normal,' I said.

'Maybe they're happy,' she said. I listened, not to the words, I couldn't really catch the words, but to the tone.

'I don't think they're happy,' I said.

I sat some more and watched the TV. It was a British show about a police officer working in a small town in Scotland. I liked the show but found the accents hard to follow, and the voices outside got louder.

'Okay, you might be right,' Kate said.

A commercial break came on and she muted the TV. 'Which flat's it coming from?'

'I can't tell,' I said. 'I can't tell from here.'

'Stick your head out the door.'

Our door was already open so I stood up and stuck my head out. I heard a woman say, 'You've always got an answer, haven't you? You've always got an answer.'

'It's the flat below and across one,' I called back through the door.

'What're they saying?'

'There's a woman telling someone that they've always got an answer.'

Kate came over and put her head out too. It was a warm night with no one about, so we stepped onto the balcony. Kate brushed back her hair as if that would clear her ears.

'Any answers I've got are lost on you', a man said.

'You never trust me with the car,' the woman replied. 'I can tell you don't trust me. I wonder if you think I'm competent at anything.'

'I've never said I don't trust you with the car,' said the man.

I looked over the balcony. A light shone out from the flat and sometimes a shadow moved but there was nothing distinct. A moth slapped at the balcony light above me.

'Living with you I start wondering why I bother. I mean what am I supposed to be doing here anyhow?' The woman's words came as if she spat in the man's face.

'I never said I don't trust you with the car,' repeated the man. 'I never said that.'

'You don't have to say it out loud. I know. I *know*. There're more things said than what comes out of people's mouths. You stand at the window when I back the thing out. Half the time you're still there when I drive it back in.'

'If I am it's not the car I'm looking out at,' he replied. It was a good shift in tack by the man but perhaps it wasn't enough. The woman took a moment to form her next sentence.

'The thing's a tin can anyhow. I don't know why you spend so much time working on a tin can that's an embarrassment to drive.'

Their voices came clearly now. They echoed up the staircase to the side of our block; the concrete stairs and balcony floor seemed to vibrate with their words.

'I'm not worried about the car,' said the man.

'Well you give an awful lot of time to something you're not worried about,' said the woman. 'An awful lot of time. I mean what are your priorities? Your mother is a bigger priority than I am. When your mother rings the world turns on a different axis. It's plain she hates me.'

'She doesn't hate you.'

'She hates me. She *hates* me. I can see it in her eyes. I can't pour a coffee without her watching me do it. She's got a son who's the same.'

'Jesus, I can't believe this,' the man said.

I saw the shadow of a figure with arms outstretched. The arms moved suddenly down and a window thumped. The man said something else but his voice was muffled.

The commercial break finished and we moved back inside.

'Typical,' said Kate. 'The guy can't part with his favourite toy or his mother. Men never grow up.'

'All men?' I asked. 'That's inverted sexism.' I sat down on the couch and folded my arms.

'Yeah, the whole lot. It's something in the male psyche. Can't survive without props.'

'But if he didn't care about his mother you'd call him a hard bastard. When he *does* care he's too wet. Well, I suppose you can't judge people from one conversation anyhow.' With the remote propped inside my elbow I reignited the TV.

'Hell, I'm only teasing,' said Kate. 'You're so cute when you're concerned about something. You're a sweet guy,' she laughed.

A friend once told me that you only ever know five per cent of what goes on between a couple. He said it as if the five per cent was the absolute proven limit, and the figure stuck in my mind and put a shroud over something ordinary, something unshakeably common. I wondered now if for neighbours you ever got a higher return, whether you ever got more than five per cent of knowledge. Probably not.

At the next commercial break we quickly silenced the TV and stood outside. The neighbours' voices hadn't softened but with their window still closed their words were muted. We followed who had the better of the argument by judging whose voice we heard most and loudest.

'All balls and no ballet,' the woman said, or something like that. Then she said some other words, building up to finish with 'Well I don't! I don't!'

'You're throwing rocks in the dark,' I think the man said. 'Just rocks in the dark.'

The woman said more but I picked just one word for sure. Mother. She said it long and loud as if to make sure we'd hear. 'Maaatheeerrr!'

'Rubbish,' shouted the man.

The woman continued but I made little of it. Kate turned and said, 'She's giving it to him, but her words sound slurred. I reckon she's been drinking, or it's drugs.'

'I don't know,' I said. 'Maybe it's just the closed window.'

'Rubbish,' said the man again, but it wasn't enough, he

was losing ground. When the commercial break finished we lingered, guiltily, where we were. I felt uneasy but I stayed.

'It's a hopeless situation,' the woman said, then added something about a part-time relationship. She said 'relationship' again.

'That's just bloody astonishing,' the man responded. He found voice and now he shouted it once more.

'I'm stuffed if it's my doing,' said the woman. She swore at him. The man swore back. They didn't wait for each other to finish and it was as if they were shouting in tunnels that echoed up and down.

The door swung open and the shadow of the man moved through the doorway. We ducked inside as he walked out. The woman said it was a piss-poor reaction and the man asked her what reaction she'd prefer. The door slammed and the man walked from the flat. His footsteps headed out to the car.

We returned to the couch and sat in silence. I looked out the door, and the moth from the balcony light flew inside. We put the sound back on the TV even though there were more commercials on now.

A few minutes later came a knock at the door below. The knocking was firm but not very loud. We turned our heads to listen. The door opened, grating as it caught on its frame. The man paused before he spoke.

'I forgot my keys,' he said. He said it flatly, without anger. As if he were saying that earlier it had been day and now it was night. He must have stood in the dark until he came back to the door because he had no keys. He couldn't drive anywhere without a key.

'That's a first,' said the woman. But she'd softened her tone.

'I was leaving in a hurry,' said the man. He must have walked inside after that.

'I don't feel right about listening to another couple's unhappiness,' I said to Kate. I shut the door softly, using both hands so it made no noise.

'Yeah, right,' she said. 'I hope they sort it out. Sometimes confrontation helps people sort problems out.' She scooped her legs back underneath her on the couch, but at a different angle now.

'I don't like it when people argue.' I said. 'I hope we never have to do much sorting out. I hate that kind of thing.'

'You're a softie, you are,' she said. She wound her arm around me. I tried to watch the TV but I'd lost the plot. It took me a minute to realise the British police show was over and we were watching something else.

A week later they argued again, and a month after that they moved out. They left quietly and I never knew if that was because they'd made their peace or because everything was over and they had nothing more to argue about.

I thought again about the five per cent rule, and I wondered what one hundred per cent would mean and whether you could know everything about yourselves, much less about others. But then your one hundred per cent might prove different to that of another person anyhow.

A fortnight later a pair of students moved in. They were from Malaysia and I said hello to them when I took out the rubbish.

'With any luck they'll be quieter than the last couple,' I told Kate.

We never found out, though, because soon after we moved on ourselves. We went our own ways. After lots of talking we sorted everything out. We packed our belongings and left in separate vans, but a few books, a lamp and the green vinyl couch we sold at Camberwell market. It took a Sunday morning's work but I think we got our money back on the couch. I suppose that's all you can ask for.

. . . .

First published in *Island*, No. 95, 2003

Who's Afraid of Rupert Bunny?

DESMOND O'GRADY

Was his mother, now in a nursing home, really once painted by Rupert Bunny, as she claims? Her son, briefly back in Melbourne from Rome, tries to find out, but his mother is more than a match for him. A shrewdly affectionate character study.

He was somewhat disappointed by the Rupert Bunny exhibition but admired the self-portrait mistakenly described, in a note beside it, as one in which the artist's hand masked his face. People writing on painting, he thought, rarely see what is before their eyes; Bunny was not hiding his face at all, his fingers were merely holding a cigarette while he observed coolly. The visitor, who so far had spent 30 years in Italy, wondered how Bunny had sized up Melbourne on his return in 1932 after 46 years in Europe.

And he wondered also whether Bunny had sized up his mother. Years before she had claimed more than once that Bunny had painted her when she was a young woman, adding that he had been struck by her beautiful blue eyes. His mother had often reported that people expressed admiration for her beauty but he had suspected these reports may simply have illustrated her dictum: praise yourself if nobody else does.

Crosshatched creases marked all her face except her nose. But even now, in an old people's home, she would hitch up her skirt to seek confirmation from him that she had shapely legs. Moreover she said that the visiting doctor had told her he had never seen such clear eyes as hers. Exceptionally clear, she added, which was all the more defiant because as a result of a botched cataract operation, one pupil was enlarged and askew.

Although she had a fertile imagination, he doubted she would have invented the story that Rupert Bunny had painted her. He had been surprised that she had even heard of Bunny.

. . . . .

During his fortnight in Melbourne, which included a daily visit to his mother, he wanted to clear up the mystery. She would introduce him to other inmates at lunch or in the television room and lament, in the privacy of her bedroom, that they were not lively enough. Although she had made friends with several, she had a keen eye for the foibles of all. She complained that nurses stole clothes from her wardrobe; however, his brother said nothing had disappeared, indeed that she had somehow obtained a nurse's brooch. Her face had changed: formerly heart-shaped, it was leaner, which made her nose seem longer. Her hair, only now greying, and which used to be permanently waved was a side-parted helmet. He was reminded of a Plantagenet royal on the silk cigarette cards he had played with as a child. She was grieving for the loss of her husband but also of their East Malvern home where, after his death, it had become too dangerous for her to continue living alone.

'Well-furnished and comfortable,' she said as if to herself. 'Go and take a look – I'm told they've added two rooms at the back. See if the garage door is still blue – remember I wanted it the same colour as the lounge ceiling.'

Like other inmates, she was wearied by the bleak wait for her own death. At times this ultimate destination was forgotten but occasional deaths of inmates were chilling reminders in case anyone felt comfortable. There were gradations among them: some slept as they sat before the television screen in the common room, some watched it without understanding, but others had opinions about the programs.

His mother's bones seemed chicken-thin when he took her arm and he was afraid she would fall while scuttling along because she talked over her shoulder to passersby. But at least she was better off than those who had to work their way forward on walking frames.

She had always loved being taken to restaurants but now was not confident enough to accept his invitation. At times she confused which day was which or relatives' ages and complained that her mind was 'all a fuddle.' He encouraged her to obtain window plants in order to see things grow and have a sense of the future, but she was not interested; it seemed a weak idea even to him. He asked about the priest who visited her.

'He says God's not ready for me yet. I'm ready though: I'd like to die and be done with it, go to sleep and not wake up. And I don't want this tired old body at the Resurrection.'

She sought reassurance about her husband: 'He loved me, don't you think?' One thing she was sure of: he had a terrific will.

· · · · ·

At the end of one visit, she said: 'It's a pity you were so clever, otherwise you mightn't have gone away. The family broke up after that.' She was dispassionate but her words thudded home. She added – not for the first time – 'Couldn't you take me back to Rome in your luggage?'

After a pause, she said, 'When you're useless nobody

wants you – not even the police.' She reached out, a wafer-ish hand corded with veins, to caress his fingers.

'Your nails are like mine, well curved. They're called Filbert nails, like Filbert the Gilbert, the colonel of the Nuts. Remember?' A pause.

'Do you take any notice of the twaddle about the royal family? They're just German upstarts really – that's what Dad used to say.' Another pause.

'I'm not for a Republic,' she croaked, then waited as if for effect. 'Instead, I want an Irish Queen and an Irish Pope.'

She was striving for the outrageous. He savoured in anticipation the laugh this would bring from his brother when he recounted it. Her lifelong lesson was that it was worth doing anything to get a laugh.

Protesting that she could not remember, she supplied sparse information about Bunny, saying only that she had met him while living in Middle Park and that Bunny had asked to paint her. His persistent questions irritated her and even more now that she was frustrated by an unsatisfactory hearing aid.

Her claim became more probable once he looked into Bunny's life. Bunny had worked in the Middle Park area and drew many attractive women, not only society dames but anyone who interested him. But if Bunny had met his mother in Middle Park, where was the portrait now?

On his last day in Melbourne he lunched with his mother who, true to form, was capricious about the food.

'That's a stringy old fowl,' she commented after polishing off a chicken. 'Of course, if they bought decent food, they'd make less of a profit out of us. Next time you come – if there's ever a next time – bring me a lobster. These days I find oysters too salty.'

One nurse had said of her, 'She's spoilt rotten – she demands it.' And a Filipino girl, Cecilia, waiting on the table, was upset by the comments about the chicken.

'It's really beautiful material, dear.' His mother mollified Cecilia by fingering the girl's lilac blouse and bringing her cataract-afflicted eyes close to it.

'Why don't you get it made up into a blouse?'

She laughed at what she knew was a corny line. 'Don't take any notice of me.' She added, 'It's beautifully cut.'

Afterwards, while he napped in her room, she went to the weekly sing-a-long in the lounge, which consisted of a visiting pianist playing through a medley of old favourites. Thinking unhappily of leaving his mother again for at least a year and perhaps for ever, he heard, *My father was born in Dublin, my mother was born in Cork, and I've been taught to love the Irish ever since I could walk*; 'Try a Little Tenderness'; 'It's Easy to Remember'; 'Just One More Chance'; 'Oh No, It Isn't a Dream', 'Tea for Two', 'Is It True What They Say About Dixie'; 'I Don't Want To Live Without You …'

'Gawd,' said his mother on her return, 'The old folks at home again! Doesn't he know any other tunes? You can smell the mothballs. I told him to play something that's not out of the Ark.'

Perhaps she had. She talked about items from the newspapers, which she still read avidly with her eyes pushed against the print, and about his brother in whose house she spent a day each week. But mostly, in this his last conversation, she talked about his friends: she had always lived partly through them and recalled arcane details of their lives. But now when she managed to hear a detail, such as that one of his friend's sons was ill, she added others.

It was too difficult to correct all these surmises, to which she confidently added others. The world beyond the old people's home was becoming a fable. He did not tell her that he had lost touch with many of the friends she had known. Some of the ties with his mother were becoming tenuous.

· · · · ·

Even though he feared it might anger her, before leaving he made a last attempt to find the truth about Bunny. She hung her head, not willing to answer, and took refuge in deafness. Then he coaxed her, delivering the message directly into her left, still partially functioning ear.

'Come on, at least you must remember what he was like.' After long seconds, as if giving a considered judgment, she said, "A bit rough.' Then, as if sensing his disbelief, she doubled the dose. 'Yes, likeable but a bit of a roughneck.'

It seemed wholly unlikely that those elegant fingers, the handsome face with its fine features and observant eyes, could be those of a roughneck from Paris.

When he stopped over in Sydney on his way back to Italy, he mentioned the Rupert Bunny exhibition to a friend from his school days whose mother was a crony of his mother. The friend said that one of his eventual assets would be a Rupert Bunny portrait of *his* mother.

'A Rupert Bunny portrait? Are you sure of that?' he asked.

'Yes,' the friend replied. 'It hangs above her bed, it's signed and mentioned in books on Bunny.

It was more than a hint of an explanation. A bit of a liar inventing a bit of a larrikin. If it had been otherwise, he would not have written this story or – perhaps, others.

· · · · · · · · · · · · · · ·

DIFFICULTIES

The Girl Next Door

STEVE J. SPEARS

She might be only fifteen, but she has twin babies. He's only a boy, but he's also the father. They turn out to be the neighbours from hell, damaging everything they touch – including kindly, well-meaning Steve Spears, who brings a dramatist's skills to this sad and funny story.

*And they shall beat their swords into ploughshares,
and their spears into pruning hooks:
nation shall not lift up sword against nation,
neither shall they study war any more.*

                                      Isaiah 2:4

She was a cute little thing. Autumn. Big dark eyes, just 15, and she had given birth to twin girls when she was 14. Her boyfriend, Lenny, aka 'Lurch', was a strapping, IQ-60, 15-year-old of the baseball-cap-backwards, the pants-around-the groin type. He never smiled. He had terrified eyes – as though he suspected every stranger was either a cop or otherwise out to get him.

A year previously I had left tired, noisy, pointless Kings Cross and, *comme on dit*, downsized. I moved into one of three cheap beach shack units 30 metres from the water, in a NSW South Coast town. It was as close to paradise as I had ever found. I looked out my window and saw the sea. At night it shhh-ed me to sleep, I took up swimming again after 40 years and went from 20 metres nonstop to 20 minutes nonstop. Joined the local club. Mixed in with the old-timers at the pub. Volunteered for Meals on Wheels. Wrote like a man possessed. Boy, was I happy!

Then Autumn, the twins and Lurch moved in next door. Excellent! I could be a good guy! I could help! Come, my fellows! Share paradise! 'If you guys want to borrow the proverbial cup of sugar,' I say to Autumn, 'just bang on the door.'

She smiles prettily. 'Thanks.' What a sweet kid. What gorgeous babies. *What a saint I am!*

And tiny Tony the landlord, 60 – what a saint he was. He lived in the front unit and never, but never, interfered with me and my long-dreamed-of sea change. Tony's great joy in life was to come home from work in Wollongong and to fish at sunset. In shorts, Bonds singlet, sandals and hairy Sicilian back, he'd stand placidly at water's edge, fishing rod in hand till well after the sun set and then say, in his ethnically non-PC accent, 'No-a fish. Never mind-a. Tomorra. Tomorra.'

. . . . .

Tony's a bit doubtful at first about leasing Unit 3 to smiling little Autumn and big grim Lurch. The rent isn't much but, when you're on a single mum's pension, everything's much, I guess. 'Wha' ya gonna do? The babies a' so beautiful. The kids a' so young to be parent. Wha'ya gonna do?'

I know what Tony's going through because I am the same. We both feel like honorary grandpas helping out the star-crossed lovers and their innocent offspring. He gives them a three-month trial lease. 'Is-a be fine.'

Little Autumn comes to the door several times most days, usually with one of the twins on her hip. 'Steve … I hate to bother you, but we don't have a phone yet?' Or …' Steve, I wonder if you could loan me the vacuum cleaner?' Or … 'Steve, this is really embarrassing but payday's tomorrow and I'm broke and I need to borrow 10 bucks for the babies' formula.'

But of course! *A phone? A vacuum cleaner? Ten measly bucks?* Are you kidding me? 'Who steals my purse steals trash/ 'tis something, nothing;/ t'was mine, 'tis his, and has been slave to thousands …' And without me, these babies might die of starvation in a non-vacuumed unit! O happy day that I was sent to this earth to help the unfortunate!

Boy, am I happy!

. . . . .

The first tiny beep on Grandpa Steve and Tony's radar comes a week later. One lovely evening as Tony is heading for his beloved beach, little Autumn fronts him right outside my sea-view study window. Somehow or other, her sweet young face has hardened into an ugly 100-year-old's and her voice into that of an LA gangsta-ette.

'EXCUSE ME, where's our washing machine?'

Tony looks puzzled. 'Is-a no wash machine.'

'Excuse ME! The agent told me there'd be a washing machine!'

'That-a wrong. You must-a bring your own.'

'DIDN'T YOU HEAR WHAT I JUST SAID? The AGENT told me there'd be a WASHING machine.'

I can't see Tony's face but I bet he's at least discomfited. Even though I'm out of her line of fire, she scares the shit out of me. Anyway, Tony digs up a washing machine for her.

'She got the babies. Wha'ya gonna do? They need-a clean clothes.'

Lurch breaks the machine two days later (overload, sand). Tony gets it fixed. He also digs up a TV set for them. Lurch,

I notice, stays in the background when the missus does her negotiating with Tony or me.

. . . . .

Fuck you motherfucker/This nigger's no punk/Gonna shove ma dick in your bitch's cunt!

As far as I can gather from the high-decibel music blasting from Unit 3's state-of-the-art sound system, these are the words of Lurch's favourite song. I hear it several times a day – 7am, midnight, anything – as long as Autumn isn't around. I do some negotiating with Lurch. I knock on his door, invite him outside for a man-to-man chat.

'Golly, man,' I break it on down to the dude, 'I'm no square. I still think Sex Pistols are the last great rock band.' Lurch looks at me, terrified. His mind is working overtime. Do I want sex? Do I have a pistol? What the fuck am I talking about? I try again. 'Gee – when I play those rockin' cats on my stereo, I like it good and loud! It's just … ain't no thang but …. we're neighbours and maybe you wanna think about keeping it down a little and maybe playing it during daylight hours, ya know?'

It takes a while but finally I see a glimmer of understanding flicker in Lurch's eyes.

'Oh. Yeah. Sorry.' He goes inside, turns it down. To my horror, I see the twins are in the room. Jesus! They'll be deaf by the time they're five. The rapper chap has moved on from his desire for sex to his desire to kill many, many police officers, have anal sex with their corpses and also to kill his rival and his rival's children. With the volume now down to shouting level, the song does have a certain Greek tragedy or even Shakespearian grandeur.

. . . . .

Alas, Lurch's conversion to good-neighbourly behaviour lasts only half a day. It takes me a few days to learn that the only way *Fuck you motherfucker/This nigger's ...* is going to be stilled is by little Autumn herself.

'Lenny! You turn that shit off right now!'

'What?'

'You heard!' Lurch always does what he's told. I know now why the fear is in his eyes. Autumn has bullied the poor bastard into a quivering jellyback Harvey Milquetoast. No wonder he plays gangsta rap when the missus isn't home. For a brief few hours he's Killa Monsta Lurch, the baddest dude in Compton – a gun in either hand and a bitch on every corner making the Benjamins with their nappy dugouts – not some hapless kid who's fathered twins, has no education or skills and will live on the dole as soon as They let him. The liberal in me wants to believe he'll find a way to make a good life. My realist heart thinks. 'No way. He's doomed. They both are.'

. . . . .

Two months pass. They're two months behind in the rent.

Tony: 'Autumn. You gotta pay the rent. Ever' fort-a-night.'

Autumn: 'EXCUSE ME! IT'S NOT MY FAULT! I GAVE THE MONEY TO MY MOTHER! SHE SPENT IT, THE SILLY COW! SHE'S FUCKING HOPELESS!'

The 'silly hopeless cow' was right there. A worn but still beautiful woman who had seemingly lost all hope. It was normal Autumnal abuse. The mother, too, had fear in her eyes – but, more, she had deep despair. Life is like this. Brutal, violent, impoverished and finally, happily, over.

. . . . .

'Excuse me, Steve,' says Autumn sweetly.

'Payday's tomorrow and I need baby formula. I think it's 10 dollars and 90 cents. Can I borrow it?'

'No.' $10.90. That's what a pack of her favourite ciggies – Lung Winds or some such – costs. I know her fave brand because there are butts and packets all over the yard.

'Why not?'

'No.'

Her sweet face turns 100 years old.

'Why NOT?'

'If you and Lur – er Lenny stopped smoking you'd have 10 dollars and 90 cents.'

'What do you mean?'

'Don't play me. You know what I mean.'

'EXCUSE ME! It's none of your BUSINESS if I smoke.'

'Can I have my vacuum cleaner back?'

Big mistake. I've surrendered the high ground to the enemy. 'Sorry. Can't find it right now.'

'Sure you can, sweetheart. It's a tiny unit. You've had it a week. Give it back.'

'EXCUSE ME! WHAT DID I JUST SAY? I CAN'T FIND IT!'

I change my battle plan. 'Okay, okay. I'll lend you 11 bucks. Just get the vacuum cleaner.'

Her eyes light up with the joy of victory.

'You promise?'

'I promise.'

She gets the vacuum cleaner. 'Now, where's the money?'

'I lied.' I slam the door. I do a victory dance. Steve J. – sophisticated world traveller, multi-award winner and minor footnote in Oz theatre history – has just scammed a 15 year-old! *Am I any good or what?*

A month passes. All bets are off now and, even as the bodies fall in Iraq and Israel, war has broken out between the forces of Unit 2 and Unit 3. She loads her household rubbish in my bin. I put it back in hers. She moves her bin to just outside my kitchen window and never, ever takes it out. I swallow my pride and take the stinking mess out. She wins the Battle of the Bins.

I concoct a cunning – no, brilliant! – plan. Autumn's main source of joy is washing clothes. Hers, the babies', her poor mum's. So, what I do is, I get an extension cord the exact shade of the washing machine cord and I unplug the machine, stick the useless cord in the socket and hide the real cord under the machine. It's a brilliant example of deception in the art of war. Sun Tzu would be proud.

And guess what? It works!

For a whole 12 hours, I hear Autumn complain to the heavens and the three dogs that have moved in about her luck. The machine won't start! Why me, Lord, why me? I am appalled at the glee I feel at her anguish but the rising fascist beast thrills to the battle-ness of it all. Then she cottons on and, every time I open my creaky door, a cry of 'Poofter!' or 'Faggot!' or 'Wait till Lenny gets home! He's gonna beat youse up!' rises from the enemy encampment.

I phone the pigs – er, police. I need the other side to know I'm just that much of a wuss. Cops come. Autumn denies. Cops shrug, give me a 'What a girly man!' look and go away. Autumn thinks she's won the Cop Skirmish. Pah and piffle! What she doesn't know is that I know some of her visitors are 'persons of interest' to the law. Meet threat with threat, says the master. The threats stop.

. . . . .

In all this Current Affair warfare, there's only one constant that shines with its own special beauty. Every time Autumn or Lurch leave each other, she says, 'Love ya', and he always replies, 'Love ya.'

. . . . .

I lie awake thinking of new tactics. I obsess. I have terrible dreams. One recurs. Autumn is mowed down by a bus but she gets up only to fall off a tall building and smash onto the pavement. She's in mortal agony but, in the dream, I don't care. The terrible part is that, when I wake up, I still don't care.

. . . . .

Poor Tony suffers a double blow. First (and, gentle reader, I am ashamed to confess this) he witnesses the Mother Of All Trash Talk.

Her: 'You're a poofter! Look at ya!'
Me: 'What's it like to be born a loser, sweetheart?'
Her: 'DON'T CALL ME SWEETHEART!'
Me: 'What's it like to know that all you're gonna do with your life is shit out a few more kids, then die?'
Her: 'Least I'm not a poofter!'
Tony: 'Please-a. Both of you. Please-a.' His face is a picture of stress. He sees two maniacs screeching hate at each other right there in paradise. Autumn and I walk away, both, I think, ashamed.

The second blow is worse. Tony learns that, even though the real estate agent issued an eviction notice way back, it's going to take a month for the Tenancy Tribunal to hear the case.

'What-a case? They tree month behind!' They never pay-a once!' He's petrified that if he does anything at all to Autumn and Lurch, the tribunal might find a way to let them keep living on his property. He's scared that anything I do might produce bad results, too. They break a window or two. They steal some tools. He calls the cops. The star-crossed lovers deny. The cops shrug and leave.

Tony is adamant. 'Please-a Steve. No more the yell. Please-a.' I promise Tony that I shall study war no more. I'll leave the Trash Talking to the *Jerry Springer* show.

Finally they front (or rather, ignore) the Tenancy Tribunal and one early spring morning – as in the best westerns – the sheriff runs the varmints out of Tony's unit.

We won.

I guess.

. . . . .

A few months pass. Tony comes to my door one evening and tells me about this new worker at his Wollongong job. He's a friend of Autumn's family. Lurch had finally split. Autumn was pregnant again. Autumn was very depressed and had taken to slashing at her arms and legs. Her mother was very worried. 'He say it-a like the poor girl is-a broken.'

. . . . .

One thing globalisation has made abundantly clear is, the closer different nations get, the more they loathe each other. I never really understood it. Now I do. I had broken something inside myself – something kind, something sane – and tossed it into Autumn's rubbish tin. I had to see if I could find it again. I had to see if I could mend it.

. . . .

Green

NICK EARLS

Phil is a nerd, and he knows it – a naif, a bumbler, the one from whom girls take flight. How will he cope when Frank Green, the student smoothie, invites him to the pub with the boys? Phil turns out to be a very funny man, and he tells a great story against himself.

In our year at uni, Frank Green is it. The style council, the big man on campus, the born leader. From day one, Frank Green has been the definition of cool. Frank Green, frank in all colours, shameless and sure as a peacock. Peach jeans, pink jeans, Frank Green.

Queensland Uni, Medicine, 1981. Nothing counts here if Frank's not a part of it.

Frank Green juggles so many girls he's nearly juggling all of them. He juggles so many girls they all know. They all know and don't care. It's the price to pay, if it's a price at all. Frank Green has magic in his hands, the poise of a matador, the patter of a witless, irresistible charm.

I juggle girls the same way possums juggle Ford Cortinas. I'm road-kill out there, bitumen paté, seriously unsought-after. Quiet, dull-dressed, lurking without impact on the faculty peripheries. Lurking like some lame trap, like a trap baited with turd and I'm not catching much.

I have – my mother says I have – a confidence problem.

Frank Green has bad bum-parted hair, mild facial asymmetry and teeth like two rows of dazzling white runes, but he ducked the confidence problem like a limbo dancer.

Frank Green makes entrances. I turn up. When Frank is the last to leave I'm still there, but no-one's noticed. Frank

Green dances like a thick liquid being poured out of something. I dance like I'm made of Lego, like I'm a glued-up Airfix model of something that dances. Better still, I don't dance. I retreat quite imperceptibly like a shadow in bad clothes.

My mother says I have lovely eyes, and just wait, they'll all get sick of Frank Green. My mother thinks he has no staying power, but I beg to differ. Frank, those pants and Countdown, I've told her, are three things that are here to stay. And she says, If you say so Philby, if you say so.

And I've told her there's no more *Philby* now, but does she listen? I've told her I'm Phil. And I'm sure I was only even Phillip for about five minutes before Philby surfaced in Moscow loaded up with Orders of Lenin. Philby the Russian spy. Philby the Third Man. Philby the bug-eyed, black-haired baby just born in London. Me. Seventeen years of Philby now. And what chance does a philby have? Philbies sound so pathetic you shouldn't let them out. Philby: a soft, hopeless marsupial that without a great deal of molly-coddling will drift into irrelevant extinction. A philby. A long-nosed, droop-eared wimp of a marsupial with lovely eyes, destined to die. Inevitably nocturnal, and very afraid.

Outside the house you don't call me that, I tell her. Okay? Outside the house, no Philby.

On weekends I lie on my back with my physics book open over my head and I dream of girls. Girls who come up and talk to me at faculty functions. Who approach quite deliberately and talk to me with a calculating seductiveness. Glamorous, desirable girls who tell me quite openly that they crave me with a painful urgency, that Frank is all style and no substance, that they hope they're not making fools of themselves, but they know what they want. And in the dream under the physics book I don't shake with fear and lose the grip of my burger, I maintain calm, I sip at my plastic cup of Coke, I let them have their say and I acquiesce to their outrageous desires. In my dreams, I am a peach-jeaned man of cool. I am lithe and quite elegant. I am all they could want, I am highly supportive of their expectation of orgasm and I treat them kindly.

And unlike Frank, I'd be happy with one, though admittedly any one of several. I have a list, a list of four girls I would be quite unlikely to turn down, should I figure in their desires. I have spoken to one on three occasions and another once. Other than that, nothing happens. But that's okay, I've got six years for this degree.

Chemistry pracs begin on Fridays, and this is where things get weird. I'm in Frank's group (alphabetically) and his friends aren't. Week Two and the group divides to do titrations and I'm standing next to Frank and a little behind him when the division occurs so I'm his partner.

I learn things about Frank. Close-up things. Unglamourous things, but quite okay things just the same. Frank twiddles his pencil when he doesn't know much. Frank says Hey several times whenever he has an idea, or had something he thinks is an idea. Frank is very distractable and has no great interest in organic chemistry. In the first prac we talk a lot about bands we like. Frank sings like someone with terrible sinuses and fills beakers up with varying amounts of water and plays them with his pencil with no concession to the dual concepts of rhythm and melody. Our titration goes very poorly. Our tutor takes us aside and says, Listen guys, I'm worried about your attitude, that prac was piss easy. Frank sings several lines of 'The

Long and Winding Road' but all on one note, and the tutor doesn't know what to do.

Frank says hi to me three times over the next four uni days. Frank actually says hi to me, and people notice every time. People look at me and I can see them thinking, Hey, he's Frank's friend.

Friday in the chem lab, Frank says, I think I can get it right this time, and sings 'The Long and Winding Road' again, but still all on one note. We spend the first forty minutes of the prac (Caffeine Extraction from a Measured Sample of Instant Coffee) discussing how profoundly the death of John Lennon has affected both of us as individuals, and society as a whole. The tutor asks if we could please do the chem prac and I tell him he should treat Frank's deeply held feelings about the death of John Lennon with respect. The tutor says he feels really bad about the death of John Lennon too, and agrees that the implications are undeniably global, but could we please do the chem prac. And he says 'The Long and Winding Road' is actually one of his favourite songs and could Frank please possibly never, ever sing it again, because Frank's version makes him very angry. Frank starts to sing 'Hey Jude', all on one note (the same note as that used for 'The Long and Winding Road'), and then thinks better of it.

We take a look at the chem prac. Frank admits he's done none of the prep we're supposed to and apologises to me, saying he's not really doing his bit for the partnership. I tell him I spent a few minutes on it last night, and as I see it we have two options. The first is to do the prac the way the book says, bearing in mind that this involved several titrations and the result will be very bad. The second option has two parts, which I explain to Frank quietly. The first part is the maths. I have done the maths, and I know exactly what our yield should be. The second part is the extra instant coffee in my pocket.

Frank chooses option two. We end up with 120 per cent of the caffeine we are supposed to, and we tip just enough down the sink to give us an impressive but subtle 96 per cent yield.

After the prac Frank asks me if I'm doing anything tonight, not realising how unnecessary the question is. He says, we're going down the pub if you want to join us. I say, sure, but I try so hard to be cool when I say it that I gag slightly. I try to disguise it as a cough, but that only makes things worse. Frank looks at me. It seems I have to say something, so I say mucus, and he says, sure, I've got these sinuses, you know? So I get away with it. When Frank's not looking I take my pulse. It's 154. I hate the confidence problem.

So I go home after the chem prac. I have to think about this and I can't do that in lectures. This is it. This is a big moment. This is tribal. This is right out of our anthropology subject, not out of my life. This is the bit where the anthropology lecturer said, all tribes have rituals, and if you don't know them you're not in the tribe.

There are problems with this. It took me seconds to realise I'd never had a drink in a pub before (and this is where the gritty issues of ritual will come into play), but it wasn't till I was in the backyard thrashing the guts out of the Totem Tennis ball at 4.20 that I realised I didn't know which pub to go to. With the *Yellow Pages* and a map I work out the half-dozen pubs nearest uni. At some point this evening I will enter one nonchalantly, and probably fashionably late (if late's still fashionable), and say hi to Frank and whoever he drinks with, and I won't say a word about the other pubs I've been to first. I understand ritual. Step one – appear to know which pub.

I shower and put on a lime green shirt with a yachting motif and regular jeans. Will there be girls? I wish my teeth were straighter, my lips more full. I lace up my white canvas shoes and my mother stands me in front of the body length mirror and I just can't believe this is as good as it gets. I don't know what she expected, standing me here. I don't know if she thought I could still go out after seeing this.

I think I'll tell Frank I came down with something, some bug. If I was a real contender I could tell him I got a better offer. Sorry I didn't make it Friday, Frank: girl trouble, you know? I'll go with the bug. I'll see him Monday morning and affect some queasy face that suggests a whole weekend of gastric discontent, and this'll all be fine. And no prep for chem pracs in future, that's where this trouble started.

My mother will have none of this. She's seen the map and tells me I'll need a driver. I'll drive you round till we find the right place, and I'll give you the money for a cab home, she says. And even though I'm protesting and telling her I'm really not feeling well, we seem to be having this conversation in her car and I seem to be taking ten bucks from her when we're stopped at a traffic light.

This is really bad, this whole thing. I'm aware of that. Imagine if Frank sees me, being dropped off by my mother, my mother fussing over me before I'm allowed out of the car. I say none of this, but she knows it, anyway. This is the plan, she says, slipping on sunglasses even though it's early evening, driving faster than she needs to, braking late, talking with maybe just a hint of an accent. And I think it's a hint of the accent she used sporadically but to good comic effect in a minor role in the Arts Theatre's recent production of *Uncle Vanya*.

I'm hating this.

At the Royal Exchange I'll park in the back car park, she says, going on in that damn accent. There appears to be a lane leading south-west from there, between two shops. You will walk down that lane. You will then turn right and walk along Toowong High Street until you arrive at the hotel, as though from the bus stop. I shall wait ten minutes, during which time I shall be reading this book. She holds up a Robert Ludlum novel she has borrowed from the library. If you are not back in ten minutes, I shall assume you have been successful. I shall drive down the lane, turn left and be gone.

My mother, when she takes the piss, really takes the piss. I am hating this evening even more. Hating this evening, hating Uncle Vanya and his whole family, hating Chekhov, hating my parents whose abiding strangeness means I don't have a chance out there. You've damaged me, I want to tell her. You've given me no idea of normal, damn you. If I die like a philby in there it's all because of you.

She parks in the most secluded spot in the car park. I do the lane thing as she has directed. The Royal Exchange, it seems, has several different parts to it. I hadn't expected that. (What had I expected? A barn? How could I not expect rooms?) It's amazing how relaxed the people are in here, all of them, how conversant with ritual in a way that seems innate. How none of them has white canvas shoes, but maybe Frank won't notice. I'm running round working up a sweat, running down my ten minutes, finding new bits of the Royal Exchange Hotel, not finding Frank Green.

I run back to the car park, to the secluded spot where my mother has opened her Robert Ludlum novel but is only pretending to read.

He's not there, he's not there, I tell her, and I don't like this slightly desperate tone I use.

Calm now, Philby, she says. The mission has just begun. All will be well.

She guns the car out onto the High Street, loops back and parks in front of a panel beater's shop round the corner from the Regatta.

Usual drill, she says, and reaches for Robert Ludlum.

I run to the Regatta, telling myself not to run. Telling myself Frank Green wouldn't run. I'm sweating quite a lot now. I'm smelling like a wet dog, I'm sure of it. And I don't see Frank Green, despite copious amounts of stupid looking. Everyone here is so relaxed. No-one's wearing a shirt like mine. No-one's wearing white canvas shoes. I feel sick, some bug, maybe.

Hey, Phil, Frank says from behind, tapping me on the shoulder and catching me quite unprepared. We're outside, on the verandah.

Pink Floyd *Dark Side of the Moon* T-shirt, peach jeans tonight. White canvas shoes. Frank Green is wearing white canvas shoes.

I just came in to buy a round, he says, and we walk to the bar. So what do you want?

I'm not prepared for this moment. Damn it, I didn't think this through. I'm an anthropological idiot. What do I want? My palms sweat, my tongue rattles round in my mouth like a cricket ball. What do I want? I'm thinking all those beer words, but I have to pick the right one. I've never done this before. Do I want a pot? A schooner? A middy? Do I have to say which beer? What are the names of beers? I'm dying here. How many Xs was it? Or something involving spirits, spirits mixed with something. Frank's waiting. Frank's becoming confused. But Frank isn't dizzy. Frank's heart rate is well short of 200. Frank isn't about to throw up and get frog-marched out of the tribe on his first day. I'm visualising my parents' drinks cabinet. Damn them. Damn them and their stupid English people's drink cabinet. You amateur theatre-loving bloody G and T drinking British colonial bloody bastards, I'm thinking when Frank says, What do you want? again.

I tell him beer, Fourex, a pot. In my head this is what I tell him, but my mouthparts are against me and say, crème de menthe.

Frank looks as though I've slapped him. Creme de menthe, he says. You want creme de menthe?

Yeah. I say yeah, because what else could I say now?

Righto, he says and shrugs his shoulders. You want ice?

Yeah.

So he orders three pots and a crème de menthe with ice.

He carries two pots out to the verandah. I carry one pot and the crème de menthe. And I visualise my parents' drink cabinet and I curse the bright green bottle at the front. I see my father pouring it, offering me a glass with a con man's smile and a white linen napkin over his arm, saying, And do we want it *frappé*, sir?

The others, Vince and Greg, friends of Frank's from our year, stare at my drink from some distance away. I am about to begin a long journey into the wilderness. The urge to apologise for my drink choice is almost irresistible. I want to start again. I want a pot. I want to go outside and pay a cabbie ten bucks to drive over my head.

What's that? Vince says, pointing to my drink (as if there's any need to point).

I tell him and he nods, nods like he knew but he hoped he'd been wrong. He wants to ask why. He wants to ask why, but he doesn't.

And I want to tell him. I want to say Look, it's not my fault. My parents are so northern hemisphere, so insufferably strange. They drink this. They've made me drink it three times in company, but you shouldn't think I'm one of them. I meant to get a pot.

We drink quickly.

My shout, Greg says, and goes inside. He's back in a few minutes with three beers and a crème de menthe with ice.

And I can't change now. I know I can't change now. To say no, I'll have a pot would be to admit a gross error of judgement, so I sit in my lonely, soft cloud of mint, sipping away. I take the next shout. Three beers and a crème de menthe with ice.

Frank is looking comfortable, leaning back in the white plastic seat and crapping on about uni, specifically about the chem prac and the coffee in my pocket, pinging a fingernail repeatedly against the rim of his beer glass and grinning at me while singing 'The Long and Winding Road' with the aid of no actual notes at all.

Shit, 96 per cent yield, Vince says, shaking his head. We got 88 and we thought that was okay.

I'm smiling, laughing with Frank about Vince who doesn't quite get it and thinks we're champion titrators, laughing with him about the coffee in my pocket, about how we wouldn't have got 50 per cent without the coffee in my pocket. I'm sweating peppermint. I'm stinking of sweet mint and many parts of me are starting to relax, starting to become loose and less interested in direction. I'm laughing at almost anything now, just thinking about turning up at the chem prac with coffee in my pocket and laughing heaps.

This is very refreshing, I'm saying. Very refreshing with a little ice, you know. But I think I'm only saying this in my head, doing a secret ad for Crème de Menthe, turning to the camera with a James Bond smile and saying, Damn refreshing, and giving a little tilt of the head.

Vince says, Hey, what's that like, that creme de menthe? And he takes a sip from my glass. He scrunches up his eyes and thinks hard. He passes it to Greg and says, What do you reckon?

It's not great with beer, Greg says. It's not great after ten beers, but maybe it's not the best time, you know? Jeez, it's strong though. I reckon if you wanted to get pissed, you'd get pissed pretty quick on this. What do you reckon, Phil? Get pissed pretty quick on this, do you?

I want to say, shit yeah. I really want to say shit, yeah, but I can't work out with any confidence which order the words go in, and while I'm thinking about it, while I'm trying really hard not to say, Yeah, shit, he says, I reckon Phil's pissed on this, you know?

Well he would be, wouldn't he? Frank says.

I can't get up when it's my shout any more, so I just hand Vince the money and he automatically comes back with three beers and a crème de menthe with ice.

My sinuses feel very clear, I say to Frank. Very, very clear.

And Frank says, Good on you.

I tell him it must be the mint. The mint clears the sinuses, I say quite loudly. I can recommend it. And Frank thinks I am recommending it, in an immediate and personal way and, aware that he has a problem with his sinuses, orders himself two crème de menthes with his next beer, taking them both quickly and earnestly, like medicine.

I am now feeling hot all over, and there is a ringing in my head coming from a long way off. I want to warn Frank about this, to say there might be side effects, but I can't possibly be heard over his singing, particularly while Vince is shouting, Yeah I think they're a bit clearer, your sinuses. Yeah. That's sounding bloody good, mate.

So he joins in.

Hey, how about some Five Hundred, Greg says, pulling a deck of cards from his pocket. Just for small stuff, for ones, twos and fives, hey?

First I think he means dollars and I wonder what I've let myself in for, and then he scoops a handful of small change onto the table and organises it into three wobbly piles. So I say, sure, and then realise I've never played Five Hundred before.

And just when I think I'm about to be thwarted by the tribal problem, I remember the Solo my father taught me to play. The Solo he had played when with the British Armed Forces in India. No-one in the Punjab could touch me lad, when I had a bit of form going, he told me once. And he's always said that Five Hundred was an inferior version of the great game, and that anyone who mastered Solo could make the best Five Hundred player in the world look like a fool.

So, after a brief clarification of house rules, we play. We play, and I hear myself shouting, but, I hope, not ungenerously as I take hand after hand. Boldly, flamboyantly, elegantly, like an impresario, like a hussar, feeling nothing below the waist, watching the table sway in from of me and rise on one occasion only to strike me softly in the face. And I feel nothing, nothing at all but mint and victory. And there are times when I'm sure my brain is resting and my arms play on without me, flourishing strategies that haven't been seen outside the British Armed Forces in India since the late nineteenth century, passing Crème de Menthe to my shouting mouth, raking money across the table.

From this point, my recollections are non-linear.

I lie on my bed with my room full of well-established daylight and stinking of old mint. Crusty green debris around my nostrils, hidden crème de menthe oozing from my sinuses whenever I roll over. There is a bucket on the floor near the bed. A blue bucket with a slick of bubbly green swill on the bottom.

We sang 'Across the Universe', I recall. Sang it, or at least shouted it at the cars on Coro Drive, and they honked their horns, and I think I saluted. I recall myself shouting at all stages of the card game, loudly and in a ridiculous English accent, and saying very pukka things that today mean little. I remember giving the anthropology lecturer the bagging of a lifetime in his absence. At least, I assume it was in his absence. I can see him rearing up through my rickety dreams saying, You just got lucky kid, but I don't think he did.

And some of my large pile of small-change winnings went on a bottle of Crème de Menthe and we toasted many things, including the way the game is, or was, played in the Punjab, back when it was played by experts and the sun had yet to set on the long twilight of the empire.

And I took the pack and started ripping out card tricks at high speed, just the way my father showed me, shouting at the others in a private parody of his voice, Come on then Charlie, pick a card, any card. And I fooled them every time, baffled them, and I can hear Vince's voice saying, The man's a genius, a genius.

And I'm still in the middle of this slow, green, glorious death, heaving up some more unnecessary gastric juices into the blue bucket when my mother comes in.

Your friend Frank's called a couple of times, she says. He said to tell you that there's a barbecue at his place tonight, and that three of the four girls you mentioned last night will be turning up. He said to tell you that it's BYO – but don't worry, he'll have plenty of ice.

She watches me nod and lose a little more gastric juice.

You're doin' well, Philby, she says, perhaps in the accent she used to try out (unsuccessfully) for the part of Blanche in *A Streetcar Named Desire*. Doin' fine.

. . . .

Diwai Meri

GRETTA BEVERIDGE

'They know our every move.' Isabel's mother is deeply uneasy in Papua New Guinea, and stays indoors, away from the locals, who come to her door with offerings, hoping for money in return. But for Isabel it's a land of marvels. The two views are deftly caught and contrasted.

'MISSUS, Missus.' The man is outside again, calling up the wooden steps, through the bent wire screen into our house. 'Missus, Missus.' He never walks up. Mum bangs her big straw hat on her head and unlocks the flyscreen door. I won't wear my hat. I want the kingfisher to know it's me. 'Hold on,' Mum says, and waits until my hand is on the rail. When she moves away I pull my fingers down the wire netting that Dad got his coffee boys to put on the sides. It stops me falling through.

The kingfisher's watching, from his tree next to our driveway. He sees my hair. 'Strawberry blonde,' Dad told me. The bird sees my arm, my feet in my sandals, and my face when I show it to him.

The man's waiting. I stand on the second-last step to see his feet. They're flat, spread out with big twisted toes. There's mud stuck on them, and his toenails are long and yellow. Mine are sparkly pink. Mum painted them when she did hers. She's on the last step, looking down at the brown bag the man is holding out.

'What is it this time?' she says to the man, and he grins a big red smile and spits *buai* onto the gravel on our drive. Mum turns her head the other way. '*Pisin*, Missus,' the man says, and puts his hand into the bag.

What does the kingfisher think of that, when the man drags out a big pile of speckled feathers? *Pisin* means bird. I know some of his words.

Then the speckled feathers open two round yellow eyes and a big, big mouth, with a white tongue inside. '*Gutpela*, Missus.' Mum puts out one finger and strokes the bird's wing. 'Look, Isabel,' she says, 'it's a tawny frogmouth. A baby.' She takes my hand, spreads my fingers and presses them onto the soft feathers. The bird's beak is sharp so I take my hand away.

'*Pikinini meri em I laikim pisin*,' the man says. 'No she doesn't,' Mum says, 'she doesn't like it and neither do I.' She grabs my hand and makes me walk quickly up the steps. I watch the man through the flywire. He pushes the bird back into the bag and sits down on our driveway. He takes a cigarette out of his curly hair and smokes. The kingfisher watches too.

. . . . .

Mum tells Dad when he comes home. 'But if I bought it, Roger, just let it go, he'd only bring more.'

Dad says, 'You did the right thing, Angela.' He's reading. I can tell by the way he's talking. He isn't really listening. Mum tells him so much about our day. Every little thing Maini our house *meri* did wrong. She washes our windows with dirty water so I can't see out of them and puts the filthy mop into the kitchen sink after she's washed the floor. But if we didn't have Maini, all day Mum would be at the door, telling everyone we haven't got a job for them. That's how it was before, but when we got Maini, people stopped knocking. 'They know our every move,' Mum says.

. . . . .

Kee, kee, kee. First I hear the kingfisher, calling from his favourite tree, then I hear 'Missus, Missus.' Mum bashes the top of her sun hat. She unlocks the screen door and we go out of the dark house into the light. I look for the kingfisher, up in the big tree. Even with my hand over my eyes, like Dad, the sun stings and I can't see. I stand on the verandah and blink until the spots go away. People are walking on the main road past the corner of our little road. People, people, all the time. Men with hats, women bent over with *bilums* on their backs, kids running, a pig with a rope on its leg, skinny dogs. It's better to see than through the wire door, and I can hear them singing and shouting.

The kingfisher is quiet. Down the steps, Mum's got plants in her hands, turning them over and pulling at their leaves. The man calls out '*Apinun, pikinini meri.*' I wave to him. 'If he eats *buai* all the time, so his mouth is always red, all his teeth will go black and fall out,' Mum said. She doesn't let Maini chew *buai*. 'Imagine,' she said to Dad. 'Red spit all over the floor, like walking in blood.'

'*Gutpela,*' the man says. He's got his nose stick in. Sometimes he hasn't and I can see right through the end of his nose if I'm close. Today he's got a straight bit of wood stuck through the hole. One day he had his cigarette there. 'Then he puts it in his mouth,' Mum said. 'These people.'

'Stay there,' she says to me now, and goes inside. The man grins up at me from the yard, then bends over his bag and pulls out more plants. They're lying on our steps, green leaves and brown roots, drying in the sun. Mum picks up some of them and gives the man money. He puts the rest away in his bag.

The kingfisher sees it all, in between hunting for lizards in our yard. The man walks off down our street and onto the main road. I can't tell him from all the other people then. He looks the same.

Mum sweeps the dirt off our steps. That's Maini's job, but the bag man only comes after Maini goes home. 'He knows she'd *raus* him,' Mum tells Dad.

'Probably her father,' Dad says.

'More orchids,' Mum tells him. 'I couldn't resist.'

· · · · ·

Mum ties the plants up with all the others in the red flower tree. I hold the string for her. Our yard is full of trees. Even our fence is trees, growing together so people can't see in. Dad told me the names, but I can't remember them, except banana. The kingfisher likes the big grevillea tree, I remember that one, because grevilleas come from Australia, and the kingfisher comes from Australia too. 'He comes for a holiday every year,' Dad said, 'a long working holiday like you and Mum and me.'

We've got a guava tree, I know that, and kids come into our yard to get them. They try to whisper, but they laugh too much and I hear them when I'm playing in my room. I climb onto my bed and look out of the window, down onto the branches. The leaves shake and I can see the kids' arms. They crawl back through the fence with yellow guavas in their hands, two boys and a girl in a dress that's falling off. Mum can't hear them. She's sewing.

They're laughing and shouting, those kids from next door, so I stand on my bed again and watch over our tree fence. They're digging a hole in their yard, their mother and father and lots of others with big bushy hair and red and yellow and blue clothes with flower patterns. Their black and white dog is lying on the ground, not moving. The people dig a big hole and light a fire in it. They cut down banana leaves with their bush knives and wrap the dog in them. They put the dog on the smoking hole and cover it with dirt. They wake me up in the night, having a party, screaming and laughing and eating their dog.

These people, Mum would say, but I don't tell her.

'Missus, Missus.' It's raining loud on our roof, so the man is shouting at the bottom of our steps. Mum unlocks the screen door and puts her head out. I go next to her big blue skirt and put my head out too. The man's got a bag over him to keep off the rain and something big in the bag in his hand. I want a baby pig to be in his bag.

'*Gutpela tru*, Missus,' he says, '*Diwai meri*.' He's smiling red and his shorts and bare legs have got water running down them. 'Come up,' Mum says. 'Stay inside,' she says to me, and pushes my shoulder with her hand. Then she goes out to the verandah. The house wobbles when the man walks up the steps.

'Our house is on stilts like an emu,' Dad said, so in *gurias*, when everything shakes and Mum screams, our house wobbles from side to side but it doesn't fall down. 'Remember the three little pigs,' Dad said. 'Our house is built to stay up.'

'The wolves will still be waiting,' Mum said. But Dad said 'Sshh, Angela, try to be positive for God's sake.' Then he pretended to be an earthquake and shake me off his lap, but I stayed on.

'*Diwai meri*,' the man says again, and unwraps his bag. He puts a big wood thing on the boards. I have to look through the flywire. 'Oh,' Mum says. I open the door and she doesn't stop me.

It's a wooden person, nearly as big as me. A *meri*, you can tell from the *bilum* on her head. She's got shell eyes, no hair and a face like Maini. There are orange beads around her neck and a blue plastic grass skirt around her middle.

'What's her name?' I say to the man, but he says *diwai meri* again and laughs. 'Wooden lady,' mum says. 'You know *meri* is the same as Mary, like Mary had a little lamb.' I can smell the man next to me. Smoke and water, mixed together.

I pick up the *diwai meri* and carry her in through the door. She isn't heavy, just big. I go right down into my bedroom and put her on the floor. Her beads click when I touch them and her skirt is soft. She smells like the bag man, right in my room.

'Why do you want a big ugly thing like that?' Mum says. 'Oh, look at your clothes.' My top is black, like my hands. Mum picks up the *meri* with just her fingertips holding onto her wooden ears. 'Take off those clothes,' she calls back to me. 'You'll have to have another shower.'

. . . . .

'She just took off with it, Roger, I had to buy it. Ten kina for that smelly old man to buy buai with. It's filthy. She got covered in black.'

'Shoe polish, that's all. They polish it with Nugget to colour the wood. It won't hurt her, Ange,' says Dad.

'It stinks, but she wants it in her room.'

Dad is rustling paper. he doesn't want to listen. 'Let her have it. It won't hurt her,' he says.

'It's so black and ugly, she'll have nightmares.' Mum's talking fast.

'She's not the one who's afraid, Angela, face it.' Dad's talking louder. I can't hear anything for a while.

Then Mum shouts 'I want to go home.' She's crying again.

Dad's footsteps are coming, so I put my head under the sheet. He closes my bedroom door and all I can hear is the raindrops plopping onto the banana leaves. Where does the kingfisher go when it rains? I wanted to see under the house one night, but Mum wouldn't let me. I thought he might be there, sitting on one of the big wooden bits that hold up our house. Dad was away. He would have taken me down the steps in the rain to find that little bird, dry and warm.

. . . . .

When I wake up I ask Mum where *diwai meri* is, but she doesn't answer. She goes into the toilet so I get a chair and push it over to the high cupboard. I can reach the door knob but I can't get it open.

. . . . .

Kee, kee, kee. The kingfisher is in his tree. I can see his long beak and blue feathers through the flyscreen, then he moves higher. I press my nose against the door, but I can't see him. Mum's in the shower so I push the chair over and unlock the door. It's sunny outside. The man is walking down our driveway with his bag over his shoulder. He stops at the bottom of the steps.

'*Apinun,*' he says, and holds out his bag. Something is wriggling in the bottom of it. 'Come up,' I say, like Mum did on the rainy day. He puts his big feet on the steps and wobbles the house. I look but Mum isn't coming.

The man sits on our verandah. I can see through the hole in his nose and smell him. He unties a string at the top of his bag and tips it up. '*Pikinini pusi,*' he says. He says it again, and shakes the bag until a grey and white baby cat falls out onto the boards. It opens its mouth and all its little teeth are there, then it runs around my legs and into the house.

The man laughs and stands up at the door. '*Kisim I kam*,' he says to me. I want the kitten. I want Mum to pay the man, give him money to keep his teeth red. I call 'Snap! Snap!' but the kitten is running around the room and she doesn't know her name yet.

Mum comes out of the bathroom wrapped in a towel with her hair wet and bare legs. She starts screaming 'Isabel! Isabel!' She grabs me and drags me into the bathroom and locks the door. We sit on the floor in there and Mum won't talk to me. I comb her wet hair and do it up in pigtails. I put glitter on her arms and feet and I put lipstick and eyeshadow on me. If Mum wasn't there, I'd get the chair and unlock the door, but she is.

. . . . .

'Nothing stolen,' Dad says when he comes home, 'but a bloody kitten pissing all over the floor. Get a grip Angela.'

He shuts my door as soon as I go to bed. The kingfisher might be sleeping in the guava tree, but I can't see him in the dark so I get under the sheet.

There's a chair in my room and I'm big enough to open the door. I won't now. Dad's home.

But I can.

. . . .

First published in *Meanjin*, Vol. 62, No. 3, 2003

The Drill Sergeant

JOHN GASCOIGNE

The narrator is a cricket umpire, at a lowly level of the game. Above him is Alf, the autocratic umpires' adviser, and below him is Robert, the foul-mouthed bowler, whom he reports for his language. A comedy of petty officialdom and an insight into the Australian sporting obsession.

Alf wasn't quite the same after his stroke. His speech and general movement didn't appear altered. But the umpires who had borne the brunt of his withering, sergeant-major's eye and understated, sometimes sarcastic, criticism were certainly altered. We started to relax a little.

For the myriad watchers of the game who insist its standards have slipped – they tend to be into their retirement years or counting down – Alf would have been their man. Had the International Cricket Council chosen him to clean up the world game and granted him the necessary budget and sweeping powers, we'd have had none of this malarky of relaxed dress codes and manners, surly send-offs by bowlers, none of the gimmickry of stump cams and cameras at square leg to usurp the traditional role of the umpire. There'd have been no bribery, no 'Johns' offering cash or sex to swing matches for the bookies. Corruption would have gone no further than a quick draw on a Craven A in the tea break. Or whatever brand it was that Alf used to clog his lungs.

When afforded the luxury of a partner in matches, and that was rare in the association for which Alf was umpires' adviser, I'd use the alternate overs spent at square leg relaxing. The two-to-four minutes' duration of delivering these balls before my gaze at ninety degrees to their linear path was a time for studying cloud formations, their wonderful woolly forms, reshapings and mergings, expansions, contractions and colour changes. All the while, the week's toil and stress ebbed and flowed away.

And the tree tops, remembered from previous years standing in the same park; I saw how they had altered, enjoyed the way the English deciduous types, swaying metronomically for the steady march of white cumuli, would transport me to the lands of their provenance and into the literary settings of Thomas Hardy, the Brontës, Jane Austen and E.M. Forster. A church steeple in the vicinity would invoke reveries almost of rapid-eye-movement depth. Then, alas, my ball-counting responsibilities would be abandoned, presumably to the annoyance of my partner behind the stumps. Transfixed in concentration by his position central to the action, he would be counting dutifully the balls bowled, awaiting in vain the returned signal that just one was left, when it would be my turn to officiate on the core of the action, that twenty-two yards between stumps.

Such reveries were out of the question if Alf had announced at the previous meeting that he would be scouting the parks, checking on all he had told/warned us about: neatness of dress, general bearing, clearness of signals, stillness behind the stumps, clean shoes, possession of all the paraphernalia that goes with starting and sustaining a match, even to checking that the stumps were correctly aligned and the creases clearly marked to the correct spacing and lengths.

Alf had bought himself a big shiny Landcruiser with bullbar, and he would drive it quietly into the park, stop it and watch. I would see the vehicle crawling along a roadway or parked beyond the boundary and my stomach muscles would tighten. I'd check myself out in the imagined mirror of Alf's gaze. Like Papa Doc Duvalier's Tonton Macoute, the deadly civilian militia described in Graham Green's *The Comedians*, whose members hid behind their dark shades, Alf would watch us, for over after suspenseful over, behind the slightly tinted glass of his Black Maria. Then, at the next drinks or tea break, would walk onto the field to confront his victim.

And he would hedge. 'Lovely day, John,' he'd say as an en garde. 'Warm. Not over 30 degrees, though, I'd say.' Then the thrusts began. 'So, the tie. It's not done up; in fact I thought I saw you loosening the top button. The rule is, if it's really hot – over 30 – you don't have to wear a tie. You know that – I say it often enough at the meetings. But it's nowhere near 30, you know that too, and have a look at yourself – your tie's half-mast and crooked. And look at your shoes. When was the last time you put a whitener on them? Not this year, I'd say. I won't hold you up, but when you get in there for your break, check yourself out if they've got a mirror. It's not a good sight. The other thing, try and keep still when you're at square leg, 'specially when the bowler's actually delivering; you're like a bloody cat on a hot tin roof. I'd better have a chat to Jimmy. Anyway, have a good match.' And he'd stroll off for a friendly word with my colleague, Jim, who has headed to the pavilion, fumbling as he goes at his tie, shirt buttons, fly, and pausing to rub his uppers on the backs of alternate trouser legs.

Alf is what they call a stickler. I try to please him, but if I ever succeed, it's to be gleaned only by an absence of this overt displeasure.

A few seasons of this go by. I enjoy umpiring in this particular association. Its purview takes in my home suburb of Brunswick, an ethnically diverse proletariat of colourful, complementary cultures and cuisines (pity about the KFC on the corner of my street and Sydney Road though). The matches assigned me often steer me west, to cross the Maribyrnong River to parks whose features I remember years after I've departed, and to teams whose company I mostly enjoy.

However, the disquieting feature is an awareness that each year our umpire numbers are declining. A bigger umpires' association to our north has been making overtures. They are to be our saviour by act of takeover. Or, as some of the leaders of our association insist it will be, a merger of equal partners. The meeting at which the permanent get-together is mooted is protracted, acrimonious and, at times, bigoted. The season is nearing its end and the takeover/merger question has to be resolved. We are in no bargaining position. The steering committee, representatives of each body, will make its recommendation, and we all know it will be a takeover with the Darwinian inevitability that the victor – the bigger – will retain its gene pool, untainted by our own motley molecules, and keep its name, insignia, colours, etc.

But will Alf retain his status as umpires' adviser?

Given that the northern lads have their own, and a universally popular chap whose reputation reaches frontiers beyond Alf's range, this question, too, will surely be settled in the northerners' favour. Alf is one of the fierier of our members advocating a 'No' vote to the act of takeover. For that's what it will be, insist Alf and ten of his mates who have been propping up this outfit for decades, first as players, then as umpires. And damned Alf will be if he'll shake hands with, and make concessions to, one of their leaders who's a queer; a poof. And, by all he implies in an ugly tirade, *ipso facto* not to be trusted.

I hear on the winter grapevine that the takeover has gone through, approved by the Victorian Cricket Association, and we'll begin the new season with a new name (our saviour's), new insignia (theirs) and a new umpires' adviser. It isn't Alf.

Months of not seeing him pass by, then I hear of Alf's stroke. He's come through it well, though, and is about to make his return to umpiring just as soon as he's strong enough.

Then I hear Alf has been appointed to the expanded association's tribunal, which hears and rules on cases of misbehaviour. An appropriate role, I figure, imposing standards and meting out discipline, all while sitting down.

But I hadn't planned on standing, even as leading prosecution witness, before Alf and his two colleagues, quite so soon. If at all.

Bustling, bad-mouthed trundler Robert is the medium that takes me there. It is a calm, still day when voices carry as though on a mountain top where the beating of an eagle's wings moves the air and is audible. Robert uses the 'f' word at regular intervals when his labours bear no fruit and the runs mount up, and I am sure the expletives can be heard beyond the boundary – the auditory standard summoning an umpire to issue warnings. I issue one, then a second, reasoning that like excessive bumpers hurled at a tail-end, helmetless batsman, two warnings will be sufficient before taking decisive action.

And when Robert tacks a 'c' word to his favourite 'f' upon my turning down another of his appeals for l.b.w., the warnings and their number become irrelevant. Particularly as this time he's locked eyes with me as he invokes the ruddy Anglo-Saxon couple, or coupling.

It's usually been the case with me that as I unhook the writing papers and stub-pencils from the shirt pocket and begin my walk to the captain to tell him of my intentions, I feel a rush of blood to my face and my heart pounding; and always in the aftermath there's a regret that my involuntary response is an immediate leap to anger – personalising the particular, when all I am in reality is a random, at-hand pressure valve for a bowler's frustration. My father was a part-time sign-writer and an expert marksman with a rifle, but none of this steadiness was inherited and, as I make my notes (time of offence, circumstances and quotations), the game is held up longer than it should be because an overheated mind, my anger, is making the task of wielding wood-encased graphite as difficult as though I were chilled to the bone and clasping it in Sir Edmund Hillary's gloves.

On Wednesday night, as I pull into the car park, there are too few people. Alf is there with a tribunal mate, but we're short of their chairman. He's late, and no one else has thought to bring a key to the clubrooms. An association chap knows someone who will have one, and takes off in his car.

For me, reminiscence has started to kick in. Robert is standing next to a club official and his own three-year-old daughter. He's where I should have been, I tell myself, but I was never comfortable as a player, mouthing 'f's and 'c's. That was a habit I was to pick up a little later in life, somewhere in my thirties, I believe, and nowadays I give way to it too often.

What I remember is that, at Robert's age, my swearing was done internally, silently, and that the most satisfying wicket I took as an opening bowler in my teens and early twenties was with a ball that reared at the batsman's throat, driving him back and into his stumps. The fact is, that as a bowler who tried to bowl fast and never realised that of which he dreamed (deliveries at the pace of Lillee and Thommo, who came along a few years later), I converted this frustration over lack of anatomical wherewithal to frighten batsmen into an intense dislike of them.

Later, a sports commentator coined the term 'white line fever' for even-tempered men who become potential killing machines when they cross the line and run onto the field of football battle. Well, I had a strain of that disease, because for five years I experienced the maddening imbalance of running fifteen to twenty yards to the wicket in order to have my energies and hoped-for irresistible force – packed into a bone-jarring effort beside the stumps – nullified by an over-padded, lazy-arsed, immovable object, rocking forward on to his left leg to kill the missile stone-dead with a bat angled at 45 degrees. How much effort does that take? On hot days it was especially maddening. And as the opening bowler in a team like Marlborough College Old Boys, you did this for as long as it took to tire and for the batsman to reverse the balance of aggressions.

Yes, I detested batsmen, and as a young adult I saw in the angry, rampaging Dennis Lillee a fellow traveller. There was no doubt, in his early years especially, that D.K. Lillee had a rabid dislike of willow wielders and an intense desire to dismiss them from his presence.

Such thoughts go through my mind as we wait for the man to bring the key to the rooms where justice will be dispensed. The umpire who made the booking with shaky anger four days ago was a hanging judge. But if I was

Redmond Barry, who sentenced Ned Kelly, then, I am the beatified Mary MacKillop, defender of the oppressed, now.

As we (umpires and alleged miscreants) stand waiting in our two camps on the bitumen outside the clubrooms for the key-fetcher, my mind goes back to an earlier time, to another association at which Alf was umpires' adviser. It was to be a standard meeting of the men in white, but, as no key was to be found to give us entry to our rooms, we strolled across to a power pole and gathered round it. Bathed in the light from above, we listened while the secretary read the correspondence and Alf gave his usual sound advice to round out a seven-minute meeting. If only they could all be like that. (Power poles have always been funny buggers, ever since a night of the 'wide games' our Scout troop used to play in Blenheim, New Zealand. On this night, we had embarked on a tracking exercise, and the trail-maker of our patrol made it easy for us by using an onion. What wasn't easy was that the sadist laid his 'trail' at the base of power poles through the heart of the town on a late-shopping night. As, on all fours, we sniffed the poles along High Street and out into the suburbs like savvy wolf cubs, our tender, virgin ears picked up crudities and oaths from passing cars that would have spun Baden Powell in his grave.)

Eventually, in Australia, our key, and the tribunal chairman, arrive and we file into the clubrooms where plastic bins are filled to the brim with Saturday's emptied cans and the floor is unwelcoming concrete. As Alf and his mate sit on either side of chairman Harold at a trestle table, we make our own seating arrangements, pulling up plastic chairs before the tribunal.

Clearly, we'd all rather be home watching *Cheers*, so Harold tries to make this a relaxed, informal occasion. It's not a court, rules of law don't apply here, we'll simply be expected to tell the truth, and he has no doubt that will happen. But it's not a kangaroo court either, and the normal procedures will be adhered to.

Now the chair turns its attention to me, telling me that 'we've all' had a chance to read my written statement of events, but, regardless of that, will I please read it for the convenience of the tribunal. This seems reasonable, except for a couple of things. Robert's daughter is playing on the floor in front of us. At one point she makes a grab for one of my shoes. It makes me uncomfortable. Is she grovelling on her father's behalf? Involuntarily, I draw my foot back. I feel like a Roundhead. Robert is a Cavalier.

Chairman Harold is concerned that my statement is larded with the 'f' word. He leans towards me, looking secretively left and right, as though someone might overhear him.

'It may be a good idea, as the 'f' word appears throughout your statement, to use another word in its place,' he suggests. 'Why don't we say … 'major' instead?

So I begin, spelling out times and places, the state of the match, and Robert's mounting anger. 'When he was bowling to (player named), I heard him say major, but it was said quietly and he could have been talking to himself. However, the batsman drove the next ball for a single and (Robert) said slightly louder, 'You major! Major it'. I then asked (Robert) to tone down his language as he might be heard by people on the boundary. The next over he used the expressions 'major shit', 'major hell' and then just 'major' on its own. In his next over again, at 2.40p.m., when I rejected his l.b.w. appeal, he looked at me and called me a major, and then added …'

My testimony now is interrupted. Alf leans forward and

his expression suggests he had just trodden on a dog turd. But what he has to say suggests he's been off with the fairies.

'Excuse me,' he says, 'but what are you talking about? What ... what's all this hogwash about major?'

I look to Harold for assistance, but he has turned to his left to stare, disbelievingly, at Alf.

However, this benign courtroom won't be hardened, especially against its own, and patiently the chairman explains our euphemism as a protection of Robert's cute moppet who is now dragging a plastic chair across the concrete, creating a sound like an untuned tuba.

Embarrassment is triggered in Alf's nervous system. Blood rushes to his face and, somewhere in the left hemisphere of his cranium, corpuscles jostle and fight for limited space, bumping into nerves as a consequence, knocking one towards another so that an electric charge is able to leap across the reduced space between nerve endings, so producing a spark that appears as a light in Alf's previously closed eyes.

The chairman's explanation has been the switch. Alf, now alert, a half smile on his lips, looks at me, then at Harold, and says: 'Well, I'll be majored.'

When the mirth subsides, Harold and his adjudicators listen to the evidence of Robert (he was only talking to himself when he used the magic words, and apologises for any offence he caused) and the pleas of his club official (Robert's out of work and the opportunity to play cricket with his mates is an important part of his support network and self-esteem). Then Harold thanks us all and asks us to step outside while he and his colleagues make their decision. 'Verdict' being eschewed; this isn't a court, remember.

In the warm night air, I gravitate to a group of umpires surrounding Don, who will lead the evidence in the next case to be heard. Don tells us a ripping yarn of wrong-doing, and as he rehearses its relatively complex details to the group, my own 'case', by contrast, appears stunted, increasingly tacky, brought by a thin-skin against a good, honest, working-class man (with a loving, dependent daughter).

Perhaps I'm an innocent instigator who's just been doing his job, but I am now wearing the black cap of Redmond Barry and I turn away from my peers to look for Robert. He is standing by his car, with just two supports: a cigarette between his index and middle fingers and his little girl clasped tightly to his left leg. I feel a strong urge to join his group, to be third pillar of the support team. I walk over to him and the words come spontaneously: 'G'day, Rob.' (Note the solidarity implied by the diminutive.) 'Just want you to know, whatever happens, there's no hard feelings as far as I'm concerned.'

He clasps my proffered hand, shakes it, and says, 'Yeah mate, no sweat.'

This is a little disappointing, especially the bit about 'no sweat', which could have come from the speechwriter who gave us 'Aussie, Aussie, oi, oi, oi'.

We talk about his daughter, curled into his leg, looking up plaintively at me, about our respective cars which are parked as companionably close as their owners, about our work, actual and hoped-for … about anything but cricket. The pauses are excruciating.

Then mercifully, the call to judgement comes and we file to the change rooms, all returning to our previous positions. That is, except for Robert, who stands before the tribune in the middle (Harold) as though programmed to do so by generations of forebears who adopted the same supplicant position, awaiting sentence.

'Thank you, gentlemen,' says Harold. 'We've listened to both sides in this matter and we congratulate you both in giving evidence succinctly and, we believe, honestly. But in considering all the evidence, we have felt inclined to believe that given by (our lot). Robert, we hope you have learned from this experience and will return to the competition with a better understanding of what you can and cannot do in this game. However, in this case we believe your behaviour breached the standards that all players must adhere to. We have found you guilty of the charge brought against you, and we are suspending you for the next ten match days.'

There will be no standing around, no more awkward moments between accused and accuser. Robert pivots, heads straight for, and out, the door. Several of us walk after him. I see him gather up his daughter and put her on the front seat beside him. No time for seat belts. The car is gunned to life, and as it heads down the car park towards the road it swerves, sending up showers of gravel, then lurches through the opening onto the bitumen and roars off into the night.

I feel stunned, empty; but manage the silly, random thought: I'd hate to be his wife, pet dog or cat when he gets home.

As I drive towards my own home, the Mary MacKillop rises in me, forming a notion that I will write to his club – no, make that the association and the tribunal – appealing the severity of the sentence, saying that I regret the outcome and am asking clemency on Robert's behalf. But this notion is like those ambitions and actions we dream in the ephemeral, twilight world of pre-sleep when best courses are clear and anything is possible – the dreams that melt away in the cold, hard light of day.

Somewhere on Sydney Road, dodging the tram tracks so the wheels won't slip and slide on them, I think of my 'adviser', the old pre-stroke Alf, and what a damned silly idea he would have deemed this appeal to be… not clemency, but weakness. And silently I fall in beside him, hoping that mute inertia is the better part of valour.

. . . .

SECRECIES

Southern Skies

DAVID MALOUF

The professor, the distinguished friend of the family, shares their nostalgia for the old world, as they struggle to adapt to the raw new one in Brisbane. And the adolescent boy, aware of his youthful attractiveness. The Professor's passion is his telescope, but it's not always turned upwards ... Malouf's study of a boy's self-discovery proceeds in subtle steps to a final illumination.

From the beginning he was a stumbling-block, the Professor. I had always thought of him as an old man, as one thinks of one's parents as old, but he can't in those days have been more than fifty. Squat, powerful, with a good deal of black hair on his wrists, he was what was called a 'ladies' man' – though that must have been far in the past and in another country. What he practised now was a formal courtliness, a clicking of heels and kissing of plump fingers that was the extreme form of a set of manners that our parents clung to because it belonged, along with much else, to the Old Country, and which we young people, for the same reason, found it imperative to reject. The Professor had a 'position' – taught mathematics to apprentices on day-release. He was proof that a breakthrough into the new world was not only possible, it was a fact. Our parents, having come to a place where their qualifications in medicine or law were unacceptable, had been forced to take work as labourers or factory-hands or to keep dingy shops; but we, their clever sons and daughters, would find our way back to the safe professional classes. For our parents there was deep sorrow in all this, and the Professor offered hope. We were invited to see in him both the embodiment of a noble past and a glimpse of what, with hard work and a little luck or grace, we might claim from the future.

He was always the special guest.

'Here, pass the Professor this slice of Torte,' my mother would say, choosing the largest piece and piling it with cream, or 'Here, take the Professor a nice cold Pils, and see you hand it to him proper now and don't spill none on the way': this on one of those community outings we used to go to in the early years, when half a dozen families would gather at Suttons Beach with a crate of beer bottles in straw jackets and a spread of homemade sausage and cabbage rolls. Aged six or seven, in my knitted bathing briefs, and watching out in my bare feet for bindy-eye, I would set out over the grass to where the great man and my father, easy now in shirtsleeves and braces, would be pursuing one of their interminable arguments. My father had been a lawyer in the Old Country but worked now at the Vulcan Can Factory. He was passionately interested in philosophy, and the professor was his only companion on those breathless flights that were, along with the music of Beethoven and Mahler, his sole consolation on the raw and desolate shore where he was marooned. Seeing me come wobbling towards them with the Pils – which I had slopped a little – held breast-high before me, all golden in the sun, he would look startled, as if I were a spirit of the place he had failed to allow for. It was the Professor who recognised the nature of my errand. 'Ah, how kind,' he would say. 'Thank you, my dear. And thank the good mama too. Anton, you are a lucky man.' And my father, reconciled to the earth again, would smile and lay his hand very gently on the nape of my neck while I blushed and squirmed.

The Professor had no family – or not in Australia. He lived alone in a house he had built to his own design. It was of pinewood, as in the Old Country, and in defiance of local custom was surrounded by trees – natives. There was also a swimming pool where he exercised twice a day. I went there occasionally with my father to collect him for an outing, and had sometimes peered at it through a glass door; but we were never formally invited. The bachelor did not entertain. He was always the guest, and what his visits meant to me, as to the children of a dozen other families, was that I must be especially careful of my manners, see that my shoes were properly polished, my nails clean, my hair combed, my tie straight, my socks pulled up, and that when questioned about school or about the games I played I should give my answers clearly, precisely, and without making faces.

So there he was all through my childhood, an intimidating presence, and a heavy reminder of that previous world; where his family owned a castle, and where he had been, my mother insisted, a real scholar.

Time passed and as the few close-knit families of our community moved to distant suburbs and lost contact with one another, we children were released from restriction. It was easy for our parents to give in to new ways now that others were not watching. Younger brothers failed to inherit our confirmation suits with their stiff white collars and cuffs. We no longer went to examinations weighed down with holy medals, or silently invoked, before putting pen to paper, the good offices of the Infant of Prague – whose influence, I decided, did not extend to Brisbane, Queensland. Only the Professor remained as a last link.

'I wish, when the Professor comes,' my mother would complain, 'that you try to speak better. The vowels! For my sake, darling, but also for your father, because we want to be proud of you,' and she would try to detain me as, barefoot, in khaki shorts and an old T-shirt, already thirteen, I wriggled from her embrace. 'And put shoes on, or sandals at least, and a nice clean shirt. I don't want that the Professor think we got an Arab for a son. And your Scout belt! And comb your hair a little, my darling – please!'

She kissed me before I could pull away. She was shocked, now that she saw me through the Professor's eyes, at how far I had grown from the little gentleman I might have been, all neatly suited and shod and brushed and polished, if they had never left the Old Country, or if she and my father had been stricter with me in this new one.

The fact is, I had succeeded, almost beyond my own expectations, in making myself indistinguishable from the roughest of my mates at school. My mother must have wondered at times if I could ever be smoothed out and civilised again, with my broad accent, my slang, my feet toughened and splayed from going barefoot. I was spoiled and wilful and ashamed of my parents. My mother knew it, and now, in front of the Professor, it was her turn to be ashamed. To assert my independence, or to show them that I did not care, I was never so loutish, I never slouched or mumbled or scowled so darkly as when the Professor appeared. Even my father, who was too dreamily involved with his own thoughts to notice me on most occasions, was aware of it and shocked. He complained to my mother, who shook her head and cried. I felt magnificently justified, and the next time the Professor made his appearance I swaggered even more outrageously and gave every indication of being an incorrigible tough.

The result was not at all what I had had in mind. Far from being repelled by my roughness the Professor seemed charmed. The more I showed off and embarrassed my parents, the more he encouraged me. My excesses delighted him. He was entranced.

He really was, as we younger people had always thought, a caricature of a man. You could barely look at him without laughing, and we had all become expert, even the girls, at imitating his hunched stance, his accent (which was at once terribly foreign and terribly English) and the way he held his stubby fingers when, at the end of a meal, he dipped sweet biscuits into wine and popped them whole into his mouth. My own imitations were designed to torment my mother.

'Oh you shouldn't!' she would whine, suppressing another explosion of giggles. 'You mustn't! Oh stop it now, your father will see – he would be offended. The Professor is a fine man. May you have such a head on your shoulders one day, and such a position.'

'Such a head on my shoulders,' I mimicked, hunching my back like a stork so that I had no neck, and she would try to cuff me, and miss as I ducked away.

I was fifteen and beginning to spring up out of pudgy childhood into clean-limbed, tumultuous adolescence. By staring for long hours into mirrors behind locked doors, by taking stock of myself in shop windows, and from the looks of some of the girls at school, I had discovered that I wasn't at all bad-looking, might even be good-looking, and was already tall and well-made. I had chestnut hair like my mother and my skin didn't freckle in the sun but turned heavy gold. There was a whole year between fifteen and sixteen when I was fascinated by the image of myself I could get back from people simply by playing up to them – it scarcely mattered whom: teachers, girls, visitors to the house like the Professor, passers-by in the street. I was obsessed with myself, and lost no opportunity of putting my powers to the test.

Once or twice in earlier days, when I was playing football on Saturday afternoon, my father and the Professor had appeared on the sidelines, looking in after a walk. Now, as if by accident, the Professor came alone. When I came trotting in to collect my bike, dishevelled, still spattered and streaked from the game, he would be waiting. He just happened, yet again, to be passing, and had a book for me to take home, or a message: he would be calling for my father at eight and could I please remind him, or yes, he would be coming next night to play Solo. He was very formal on these occasions, but I felt his interest; and sometimes, without thinking of anything more than the warm sense of myself it gave me to command his attention, I would walk part of the way home with him, wheeling my bike and chatting about nothing very important: the game, or what I had done with my holiday, or since he was a dedicated star-gazer, the new comet that had appeared. As these meetings increased I got to be more familiar with him. Sometimes, when two or three of the others were there (they had come to recognise him and teased me a little, making faces and jerking their heads as he made his way, hunched and short-sighted, to where we were towelling ourselves at the tap) I would for their benefit show off a little, without at first realising, in my reckless passion to be admired, that I was exceeding all bounds and that they now included me as well as the Professor in their humorous contempt. I was mortified. To ease myself back into their good opinion I passed him off as a family nuisance, whose attentions I knew were comic but whom I was leading on for my own amusement. This was acceptable enough and I was soon restored to popularity, but felt doubly treacherous. He was, after all, my father's closest friend, and there was as well that larger question of the Old Country. I burned with shame, but was too cowardly to do more than brazen things out.

For all my crudeness and arrogance I had a great desire to act nobly, and in this business of the Professor I had miserably failed. I decided to cut my losses. As soon as he appeared now, and had announced his message, I would mount my bike, sling my football boots over my shoulder and pedal away. My one fear was that he might enquire what the trouble was, but of course he did not. Instead he broke off his visits altogether or passed the field without stopping, and I found myself regretting something I had come to depend on – his familiar figure hunched like a bird on the sidelines, our talks, some fuller sense of my own presence to add at the end of the game to the immediacy of my limbs after violent exercise.

Looking back on those days I see myself as a kind of centaur, half-boy, half-bike, forever wheeling down suburban streets under the poincianas, on my way to football practice or the library or to a meeting of the little group of us, boys and girls, that came together on someone's verandah in the evenings after tea.

I might come across the Professor then on his after-dinner stroll, and as often as not he would be accompanied by my father, who would stop me and demand (partly, I thought, to impress the Professor) where I was off to or where I had been; insisting, with more than his usual force, that I come home right away, with no argument.

On other occasions, pedalling past his house among the trees, I would catch a glimpse of him with his telescope on the roof. He might raise a hand and wave if he recognised me; and sprinting away, crouched low over the handlebars, I would feel, or imagine I felt, that the telescope had been lowered and was following me to the end of the street, losing me for a time, then picking me up again two streets further on as I flashed away under the bunchy leaves.

I spent long hours cycling back and forth between our house and my girlfriend Helen's or to Ross McDowell or Jimmy Larwood's, my friends from school, and the Professor's house was always on the route.

I think of those days now as being all alike, and the nights also: the days warmish, still, endlessly without event, and the nights quivering with expectancy but also uneventful, heavy with the scent of jasmine and honeysuckle and lighted by enormous stars. But what I am describing, of course, is neither a time nor a place but the mood of my own bored, expectant, uneventful adolescence. I was always abroad and waiting for something significant to occur, for life somehow to declare itself and catch me up. I rode my bike in slow circles or figures-of-eight, took it for sprints across the gravel of the park, or simply hung motionless in the saddle, balanced and waiting.

Nothing ever happened. In the dark of front verandahs we lounged and swapped stories, heard gossip, told jokes, or played show-poker and smoked. One night each week I went to Helen's and we sat a little scared of one another in her garden-swing, touching in the dark. Helen liked me better, I thought, than I liked her – I had that power over her – and it was this more than anything else that attracted me, though I found it scary as well. For fear of losing me she might have gone to any one of the numbers that in those days marked the stages of sexual progress and could be boasted about, in a way that seemed shameful afterwards, in locker-rooms or round the edge of the pool. I could have taken us both to 6, 8, 10 but what then? The numbers were not infinite.

I rode around watching my shadow flare off gravel; sprinted, hung motionless, took the rush of warm air into my shirt; afraid that when the declaration came, it too, like the numbers, might be less than infinite. I didn't want to discover the limits of the world. Restlessly impelled towards some future that would at least offer me my real self, I nevertheless drew back, happy for the moment, even in my unhappiness, to be half-boy, half-bike, half aimless energy and half a machine that could hurtle off at a moment's notice in any one of a hundred directions. Away from things – but away, most of all, from myself. My own presence had begun to be a source of deep dissatisfaction to me, my vanity, my charm, my falseness, my preoccupation with sex. I was sick of myself and longed for the world to free me by making its own rigorous demands and declaring at last what I must be.

. . . . .

One night, in our warm late winter, I was riding home past the Professor's house when I saw him hunched as usual beside his telescope, but too absorbed on this occasion to be aware of me.

I paused at the end of the drive, wondering what it was that he saw on clear nights like this, that was invisible to me when I leaned my head back and filled my gaze with the sky.

The stars seemed palpably close. In the high September blueness it was as if the odour of jasmine blossoms had gathered there in a single shower of white. You might have been able to catch the essence of it floating down, as sailors, they say, can smell new land whole days before they first catch sight of it.

What I was catching, in fact, was the first breath of change – a change of season. From the heights I fell suddenly into deep depression, one of those sweet-sad glooms of adolescence that are like a bodiless drifting out of yourself into the immensity of things, when you are aware as never again – or never so poignantly – that time is moving swiftly on, that a school year is very nearly over and childhood finished, that you will have to move up a grade at football into a tougher class – shifts that against the vastness of space are minute, insignificant, but at that age solemnly felt.

I was standing astride the bike, staring upwards, when I became aware that my name was being called, and for the second or third time. I turned my bike into the drive with its border of big-leafed saxifrage and came to where the Professor, his hand on the telescope, was leaning out over the roof.

'I have some books for your father,' he called. 'Just come to the gate and I will get them for you.'

The gate was wooden, and the fence, which made me think of a stockade, was of raw slabs eight feet high, stained reddish-brown. He leaned over the low parapet and dropped a set of keys.

'It's the thin one,' he told me. 'You can leave your bike in the yard.' He meant the paved courtyard inside, where I rested it easily against the wall. Beyond, and to the left of the pine-framed house, which was stained the same colour as the fence, was a garden taken up almost entirely by the pool. It was overgrown with dark tropical plants, monstera, hibiscus, banana-palms with their big purplish flowers, glossily pendulous on stalks, and fixed to the paling-fence like trophies in wads of bark, elkhorn, tree-orchids, showers of delicate maidenhair. It was too cold for swimming, but the pool was filled and covered with a shifting scum of jacaranda leaves that had blown in from the street, where the big trees were stripping to bloom.

I went round the edge of the pool and a light came on, reddish, in one of the inner rooms. A moment later the Professor himself appeared, tapping for attention at a glass door.

'I have the books right here,' he said briskly; but when I stood hesitating in the dark beyond the threshold, he shifted his feet and added: 'But maybe you would like to come in a moment and have a drink. Coffee. I could make some. Or beer. Or a Coke if you prefer it. I have Coke.'

I had never been here alone, and never, even with my father, to this side of the house. When we came to collect the Professor for an outing we had always waited in the tiled hallway while he rushed about with one arm in the sleeve of his overcoat laying out saucers for cats, and it was to the front door, in later years, that I had delivered bowls of gingerbread fish that my mother had made specially because she knew he liked it, or cabbage rolls or herring. I had never been much interested in what lay beyond the hallway, with its fierce New Guinea masks, all tufted hair and boar's tusks, and the Old Country chest that was just like our own. Now, with the books already in my hands, I hesitated and looked past him into the room.

'All right. If it's no trouble.'

'No no, no trouble at all!' He grinned, showing his teeth with their extravagant caps. 'I am delighted. Really! Just leave the books there. You see they are tied with string, quite easy for you I'm sure, even on the bike. Sit where you like. Anywhere. I'll get the drink.'

'Beer then,' I said boldly, and my voice cracked, destroying what I had hoped might be the setting of our relationship on a clear, man-to-man basis that would wipe out the follies of the previous year. I coughed, cleared my throat, and said again, 'Beer, thanks,' and sat abruptly on a sofa that was too low and left me prone and sprawling.

He stopped a moment and considered, as if I had surprised him by crossing a second threshold.

'Well then, if it's to be beer, I shall join you. Maybe you are also hungry. I could make a sandwich.'

'No, no thank you, they're expecting me. Just the beer.'

He went out, his slippers shushing over the tiles, and I shifted immediately to a straight-backed chair opposite and took the opportunity to look around.

There were rugs on the floor, old threadbare Persians, and low down, all round the walls, stacks of the heavy seventy-eights I carried home when my father borrowed them: sonatas by Beethoven, symphonies by Sibelius and Mahler. Made easy by the Professor's absence, I got up and wandered round. On every open surface, the glass table-top, the sideboard, the long mantel of the fireplace, were odd bits and pieces that he must have collected in his travels: lumps of coloured quartz, a desert rose, slabs of clay with fern or fish fossils in them, glass paperweights, snuff-boxes, meerschaum pipes of fantastic shape – one a Saracen's head, another the torso of a woman like a ship's figurehead with full breasts and gold nipples – bits of Baltic amber, decorated shards of pottery, black on terracotta, and one unbroken object, a little earthenware lamp that when I examined it more closely turned out to be a phallic grotesque. I had just discovered what it actually was when the Professor stepped into the room. Turning swiftly to a framed photograph on the wall above, I found myself peering into a stretch of the Old Country, a foggy, sepia world that I recognised immediately from similar photographs at home.

'Ah,' he said, setting the tray down on an empty chair,

'you have discovered my weakness.' He switched on another lamp. 'I have tried, but I am too sentimental. I cannot part with them.'

The photograph, I now observed, was one of three. They were all discoloured with foxing on the passe-partout mounts, and the glass of one was shattered, but so neatly that not a single splinter had shifted in the frame.

The one I was staring at was of half a dozen young men in military uniform. It might have been from the last century, but there was a date in copperplate: 1921. Splendidly booted and sashed and frogged, and hieratically stiff, with casque helmets under their arms, swords tilted at the thigh, white gloves tucked into braided epaulettes, they were a chorus line from a Ruritanian operetta. They were also, as I knew, the heroes of a lost but unforgotten war.

'You recognise me?' the Professor asked.

I looked again. It was difficult. All the young men strained upright with the same martial hauteur, wore the same little clipped moustaches, had the same flat hair parted in the middle and combed in wings over their ears. Figures from the past can be as foreign, as difficult to identify individually, as the members of another race. I took the plunge, set my forefinger against the frame, and turned to the Professor for confirmation. He came to my side and peered.

'No,' he said sorrowfully. 'But the mistake is entirely understandable. he was my great friend, almost a brother. I am here. This is me. On the left.'

He considered himself, the slim assured figure, chin slightly tilted, eyes fixed ahead, looking squarely out of a class whose privileges – inherent in every point of the stance, the uniform, the polished accoutrements – were not to be questioned, and from the ranks of an army that was invincible. The proud caste no longer existed. Neither did the army nor the country it was meant to defend, except in the memory of people like the Professor and my parents and, in a ghostly way, half a century off in another hemisphere, my own.

He shook his head and made a clucking sound. 'Well,' he said firmly, 'it's a long time ago. It is foolish of me to keep such things. We should live for the present. Or like you younger people,' bringing the conversation back to me, 'for the future.'

I found it easier to pass to the other photographs.

In one, the unsmiling officer appeared as an even younger man, caught in an informal, carefully posed moment with a group of ladies. He was clean-shaven and lounging on the grass in a striped blazer; beside him a discarded boater – very English. The ladies, more decorously disposed, wore long dresses with hats and ribbons. Neat little slippers peeped out under their skirts.

'Yes, yes,' he muttered, almost impatient now, 'that too. Summer holidays – who can remember where? And the other a walking trip.'

I looked deep into a high meadow, with broken cloud-drift in the dip below. Three young men in shorts, maybe schoolboys, were climbing on the far side of the wars. There were flowers in the foreground, glowingly out of focus, and it was this picture whose glass was shattered; it was like looking through a brilliant spider's web into a picturebook landscape that was utterly familiar, though I could never have been there. *That is the place*, I thought. *That is the land my parents mean when they say 'the Old Country': the country of childhood and first love that they go back to in their sleep and which I have no memory of, though I was born there.*

Those flowers are the ones, precisely those, that blossom in the songs they sing. And immediately I was back in my mood of just a few minutes ago, when I had stood out there gazing up at the stars. *What is it,* I asked myself, *that I will remember and want to preserve, when in years to come I think of the Past? What will be important enough?* For what the photographs had led me back to, once again, was myself. It was always the same. No matter how hard I tried to think my way out into other people's lives, into the world beyond me, the feelings I discovered were my own.

'Come. Sit,' the Professor said, 'and drink your beer. And do eat one of these sandwiches. It's very good rye bread, from the only shop. I go all the way to South Brisbane for it. And Gürken. I seem to remember you like them.'

'What do you do up on the roof?' I asked, my mouth full of bread and beer, feeling uneasy again now that we were sitting with nothing to fix on.

'I make observations, you know. The sky, which looks so still, is always in motion, full of drama if you understand how to read it. Like looking into a pond. Hundreds of events happening right under your eyes, except the most of what we see is already finished by the time we see it – ages ago – but important just the same. Such large events. Huge! Bigger even than we can imagine. And beautiful, since they unfold, you know, to a kind of music, to numbers of infinite dimensions like the ones you deal with in equations at school, but more complex, and entirely visible.'

He was moved as he spoke by an emotion that I could not identify, touched by occasions a million light-years off and still unfolding towards him, in no way personal. The room for a moment lost its tension. I no longer felt myself to be the focus of his interest, or even of my own. I felt liberated, and for the first time the Professor was interesting in his own right, quite apart from the attention he paid me or the importance my parents attached to him.

'Maybe I could come again,' I found myself saying. 'I'd like to see.'

'But of course,' he said, 'any time. Tonight is not good – there is a little haze, but tomorrow if you like. Or any time.'

I nodded. But the moment of easiness had passed. My suggestion, which might have seemed like another move in a game, had brought me back into focus for him and his look was quizzical, defensive. I felt it and was embarrassed, and at the same time saddened. Some truer vision of myself had been in the room for a moment. I had almost grasped it. Now I felt it slipping away as I moved back into my purely physical self.

I put the glass down, not quite empty.

'No thanks, really,' I told him when he indicated the half-finished bottle on the tray. 'I should have been home nearly an hour ago. My mother, you know.'

'Ah yes, of course. Well, just call whenever you wish, no need to be formal. Most nights I am observing. It is a very interesting time. Here – let me open the door for you. The books, I see, are a little awkward, but you are so expert on the bicycle I am sure it will be OK.'

I followed him round the side of the pool into the courtyard and there was my bike at its easy angle to the wall, my other familiar and streamlined self. I wheeled it out while he held the gate.

. . . . .

Among my parents' oldest friends were a couple who had recently moved to a new house on the other side of the park, and at the end of winter, in the year I turned seventeen, I sometimes rode over on Sundays to help John clear the big overgrown garden. All afternoon we grubbed out citrus trees that had gone wild, hacked down morning-glory that had grown all over the lower part of the yard, and cut the knee-high grass with a sickle to prepare it for mowing. I enjoyed the work. Stripped down to shorts in the strong sunlight, I slashed and tore at the weeds till my hands blistered, and in a trancelike preoccupation with tough green things that clung to the earth with a fierce tenacity, forgot for a time my own turmoil and lack of roots. It was something to *do*.

John, who worked up ahead, was a dentist. He paid me ten shillings a day for the work, and this, along with my pocket-money, would take Helen and me to the pictures on Saturday night, or to a flash meal at one of the city hotels. We worked all afternoon, while the children who were four and seven, watched and got in the way. Then about five-thirty Mary would call us for tea.

Mary had been at school with my mother and was the same age, though I could never quite believe it; she had children a whole ten years younger than I was, and I had always called her Mary. She wore bright bangles on her arm, liked to dance at parties, never gave me presents like handkerchiefs or socks, and had always treated me, I thought, as a grown-up. When she called us for tea I went to the garden tap, washed my feet, splashed water over my back that was streaked with soil and sweat and stuck all over with little grass clippings, and was about to buckle on my loose sandals when she said from the doorway where she had been watching: 'Don't bother to get dressed. John hasn't.' She stood there smiling, and I turned away, aware suddenly of how little I had on; and had to use my V-necked sweater to cover an excitement that might otherwise have been immediately apparent in the khaki shorts I was wearing – without underpants because of the heat.

As I came up the steps towards her she stood back to let me pass, and her hand, very lightly, brushed the skin between my shoulder-blades.

'You're still wet,' she said.

It seemed odd somehow to be sitting at the table in their elegant dining room without a shirt; though John was doing it, and was already engaged like the children in demolishing a pile of neat little sandwiches.

I sat at the head of the table with the children noisily grabbing at my left and John on my right drinking tea and slurping it a little, while Mary plied me with raisin bread and Old Country cookies. I felt red, swollen, confused every time she turned to me, and for some reason it was the children's presence rather than John's that embarrassed me, especially the boy's.

Almost immediately we were finished John got up.

'I'll just go,' he said, 'and do another twenty minutes before it's dark.' It was dark already, but light enough perhaps to go on raking the grass we had cut and were carting to the incinerator. I made to follow. 'It's all right,' he told me. 'I'll finish off. You've earned your money for today.'

'Come and see our animals!' the children yelled, dragging me down the hall to their bedroom, and for ten minutes or so I sat on the floor with them, setting out farm animals and making fences, till Mary, who had been clearing the table, appeared in the doorway.

'Come on now, that's enough, it's bathtime, you kids. Off you go!'

They ran off, already half-stripped, leaving her to pick up their clothes and fold them while I continued to sit cross-legged among the toys, and her white legs, in their green sandals, moved back and forth at eye-level. When she went out I too got up, and stood watching at the bathroom door.

She was sitting on the edge of the bath, soaping the little boy's neck, as I remembered my mother doing, while the children splashed and shouted. Then she dried her hands on a towel, very carefully, and I followed her into the unlighted lounge. Beyond the glass wall, in the depths of the garden, John was stooping to gather armfuls of the grass we had cut, and staggering with it to the incinerator.

She sat and patted the place beside her. I followed as in a dream. The children's voices at the end of the hallway were complaining, quarrelling, shrilling. I was sure John could see us through the glass as he came back for another load.

Nothing was said. Her hand moved over my shoulder, down my spine, brushed very lightly, without lingering, over the place where my shorts tented; then rested easily on my thigh. When John came in he seemed unsurprised to find us sitting close in the dark. He went right past us to the drinks cabinet, which suddenly lighted up. I felt exposed and certain now that he must see where her hand was and say something.

All he said was: 'Something to drink, darling?'

Without hurry she got up to help him and they passed back and forth in front of the blazing cabinet, with its mirrors and its rows of bottles and cut-crystal glasses. I was sweating worse than when I had worked in the garden, and began, self-consciously, to haul on the sweater.

I pedalled furiously away, glad to have the cooling air pour over me and to feel free again.

Back there I had been scared – but of what? Of a game in which I might, for once, be the victim – not passive, but with no power to control the moves. I slowed down and considered that, and was, without realising it, at the edge of something. I rode on in the softening dark. It was good to have the wheels of the bike roll away under me as I rose on the pedals, to feel on my cheeks the warm scent of jasmine that was invisible all round. It was a brilliant night verging on spring. I didn't want it to be over; I wanted to slow things down. I dismounted and walked a little, leading my bike along the grassy edge in the shadow of the trees, and without precisely intending it, came on foot to the entrance to the Professor's drive and paused, looking up beyond the treetops to where he might be installed with his telescope – observing what? What events up there in the infinite sky?

I leaned far back to see. A frozen waterfall it might have been, falling slowly towards me, sending out blown spray that would take centuries, light-years, to break in thunder over my head. Time. What did one moment, one night, a lifespan mean in relation to all that?

'Hullo there!'

It was the Professor. I could see him now, in the moonlight beside the telescope, which he leaned on and which pointed not upward to the heavens but down to where I was standing. It occurred to me, as on previous occasions, that in the few moments of my standing there with my head flung back to the stars, what he might have been observing was *me*. I hesitated, made no decision. Then, out of a state of passive expectancy, willing nothing but waiting poised for my own life to occur; out of a state of being open to the spring night and to the emptiness of the hours between seven and ten when I was expected to be in, or thirteen, or whatever age I would be when manhood finally came to me, out of my simply being there with my hand on the saddle of the machine, bare-legged, loose-sandalled, going nowhere, I turned into the drive, led my bike up to the stockade gate and waited for him to throw down the keys.

'You know which one it is,' he said, letting them fall. 'Just use the other to come in by the poolside.'

I unlocked the gate, rested my bike against the wall of the courtyard and went round along the edge of the pool. It was clean now but heavy with shadows. I turned the key in the glass door, found my way (though this part of the house was new to me) to the stairs, and climbed to where another door opened straight on to the roof.

'Ah,' he said, smiling. 'So at last! You are here.'

The roof was unwalled but set so deep among trees that it was as if I had stepped out of the city altogether into some earlier, more darkly-wooded era. Only lighted windows, hanging detached in the dark, showed where houses, where neighbours were.

He fixed the telescope for me and I moved into position. 'There,' he said, 'what you can see now is Jupiter with its four moons – you see? – all in line, and with the hands across its face.'

I saw. Later it was Saturn with its rings and the lower of the two pointers to the cross, Alpha Centauri, which was not one star but two. It was miraculous. From that moment below when I had looked up at a cascade of light that was still ages off, I might have been catapulted twenty thousand years into the nearer past, or into my own future. Solid spheres hovered above me, tiny balls of matter moving in concert like the atoms we drew in chemistry, held together by invisible lines of force and I thought oddly that if I were to lower the telescope now to where I had been standing at the entrance to the drive I would see my own puzzled, upturned face, but as a self I had already outgrown and abandoned, not minutes but aeons back. He shifted the telescope and I caught my breath. One after another, constellations I had known since childhood as points of light to be joined up in the mind (like those picture-puzzles children make, pencilling in the scattered dots till Snow White and the Seven Dwarfs appear, or an old jalopy), came together now, not as an imaginary panhandle or bull's head or belt and sword, but at some depth of vision I hadn't known I possessed, as blossoming abstractions, equations luminously exploding out of their own depths, brilliantly solving themselves and playing the results in my head as a real and visible music. I felt a power in myself that might actually burst out at my ears, and at the same time saw myself, from out there, as just a figure with his eye to a lens. I had a clear sense of being one more hard little point in the immensity – but part of it, a source of light like all those others – and was aware for the first time of the grainy reality of my own life, and then, a fact of no large significance, of the certainty of my death; but in some dimension where those terms were too vague to be relevant. It was at the point where my self ended and the rest of it began that Time, or Space, showed its richness to me. I was overwhelmed.

Slowly, from so far out, I drew back, re-entered the present and was aware again of the close suburban dark – of its moving now in the shape of a hand. I must have known all along that it was there, working from the small of my back to my belly, up the inside of my thigh, but it was of no importance, I was too far off. Too many larger events were unfolding for me to break away and ask, as I might have, 'What are you doing?'

I must have come immediately. But when the stars blurred in my eyes it was with tears, and it was the welling of this deeper salt, filling my eyes and rolling down my cheeks, that was the real overflow of the occasion. I raised my hand to brush them away and it was only then that I was aware, once again, of the Professor. I looked at him as from a distance. He was getting to his feet, and his babble of concern, alarm, self-pity, sentimental recrimination, was incomprehensible to me. I couldn't see what he meant.

'No no, it's nothing,' I assured him, turning aside to button my shorts. 'It was nothing. Honestly.' I was unwilling to say more in case he misunderstood what I did not understand myself.

We stood on opposite sides of the occasion. Nothing of what he had done could make the slightest difference to me, I was untouched: youth is too physical to accord very much to that side of things. But what I had seen – what he had led me to see – my bursting into the life of things – I would look back on that as the real beginning of my existence, as the entry into a vocation, and nothing could diminish the gratitude I felt for it. I wanted, in the immense seriousness and humility of this moment, to tell him so, but I lacked the words, and silence was fraught with all the wrong ones.

'I have to go now,' was what I said.

'Very well. Of course.'

He looked hopeless. He might have been waiting for me to strike him a blow – not a physical one. He stood quietly at the gateway while I wheeled out the bike.

I turned then and faced him, and without speaking, offered him, very formally, my hand. He took it and we shook – as if, in the magnanimity of my youth, I had agreed to overlook his misdemeanour or forgive him. That misapprehension too was a weight I would have to bear.

Carrying it with me, a heavy counterpoise to the extraordinary lightness that was my whole life, I bounced unsteadily over the dark tufts of the driveway and out onto the road.

. . . .

A Pitch Too High for the Human Ear

CATE KENNEDY

Andrew the ex-basketballer and his wife Vicki, who's forever complaining. He too feels trapped, but he hasn't the words to describe what it's like. Andrew escapes the claustrophobia by running, secretly, in the middle of the night, with his best friend, his dog, for company. Kennedy penetrates to the silent heart of inarticulacy, yielding insights into those who 'swim in the sea of the unsayable'.

If I signed off at 4.50 I could take the 5.00 pm bus and be home in time to help Matthew with his maths and peel the potatoes while Vicki moved around the kitchen doing everything else. We'd turn the TV round on its console, like one of those things in a Chinese restaurant, and watch the 6.00 o'clock news together, hardly ever commenting on it. Baths and a story. Another beer at 9.00 and I'd already be thinking of tomorrow. It was that kind of tiredness you get from doing nothing all day, the exhaustion of sitting. When I married I was a fairly handy forward with the Cougars – B Grade, scored 174 baskets one season. Now I drove my kids to sports, stood on windy sidelines hearing parents scream at their eight-year-olds to get in and kill him. Sometimes I'd still be awake at 3.00 am or so, usually Sunday nights, lying there unstretched, cramped up and watching the smooth outline of my wife dreaming something else nearby.

This is how you slide from a bed – move your foot out and over the edge, find the floor, slide sideways supporting yourself on the bedside table, your fingers touching the fake antique lamp your parents gave you a pair of for a wedding present. Haul out from under the doona. Carry your runners out and put them on outside the back door, with your dog already leaping with the thought of what's ahead, way down at the gate. You can just see, in the moonlight, that strange red-gold glint, like road reflectors, from the dog's eyes. Ecstatic to be out, to be marauding, to be running.

When I was in training, before I was married, I used to run four or five kilometres a night sometimes, around the deserted cul-de-sacs in the suburbs when they were so new there were no streetlights. I'd learned to drive in the same streets, reverse parking down battle-axe driveways of barely finished houses, doing hill starts up in the high parts of the new residential zone. Look out beyond the landscaping of roads then and there were paddocks full of agisted horses. Now the shrubs were higher than your head, there were cars in every drive, ten buses a day, a new health centre. Five kilometres then, with a sense I could have kept going out past the cleared blocks and sewer trenches and run straight into the hills. Now I was flagging after three, barely making it to the service station on the corner of the expressway, looking at the yellow neon of the 24-hour drive-through McDonalds where the horses used to be. Fourteen years – what's that? Two kids, a wedding photo where you can't believe the suit you wore, and the golden arches.

We'd got Kelly when he was two years old from a workmate who said he needed a lot of exercise, whose relief I could feel as he brushed dog hair off his car's upholstery and declined a beer.

He was a sucker for the dead-of-night runs, Kelly. Heeler-cross, and I never saw him tire. On Sunday nights when Disneyland was on Kelly would be pressing himself to the back door, staring inside with such longing that Louise and Matthew would beg Vicki until she'd relent, and they'd slide open the glass door and Kelly would be allowed to come in, so abject and grateful he'd be practically crawling, licking our hands, cramming himself between the kids and

Vicki saying *look just leave him alone and he'll calm down, kids, just relax and stop mucking round with him*, but finally something would be overturned and Kelly would be outside again, and *OK now, time for bed, school tomorrow*, the dog staring in through the glass with desperate remorse. You could hear him, sometimes, this barely audible high whine, still as a statue, only a muscle in his throat giving him away.

Half past three in the morning, though, and Kelly was beautiful to watch, down across the footy oval and up the hill, turning back to recover the ground back to me, a long shape in the moonlight. He'd streak past me and out of the darkness I'd feel him nudge my hand in passing as he came forward again, he could have gone all night, barrelling into the sleeping suburbs. I'd pound up those streets with my chest hurting, my feet feeling like sinkers, knowing I'd never score 174 again. Catching my breath at the servo, Kelly would go round behind the 7-11 and root through the weekend garbage, and nobody was there to give a shit.

. . . . .

Here's how you get into a bed without waking the other person – flush the toilet and come back in as if you're practically sleepwalking, fold back the sheet so that it doesn't disturb them, slowly straighten out your legs under it, and watch the red digital numbers change from 5.15 to 5.16, to 5.17. They're so silent they're eerie, digital clocks – it's as if time is not passing after all, just kind of rolling.

. . . . .

Why don't we talk more, after the kids are in bed, is what Vicki used to say. Then it became *why don't you talk more*, then *oh, Andrew, he never talks*. *Don't bother*, Vicki would say at the barbecues we went to, to other women drinking wine on the folding chairs. I married a non-talker.

When she stopped talking, though, when she got so jack of it she closed up and just worked silently in the kitchen like a black cloud, I could hardly stand it. I would rather have her filling in the blank spots, even complaining, even shouting, than silent. Spreading butter on bread, on the eighteen rows of sandwiches she was going to put in the freezer so that you'd know for a week it was going to be devon and tomato sauce, then cheese and ham, things that froze well, so careful with placing the squares against the crust of the bread, saying *Andrew this is just crazy, I'm going to have to do a night course or something to get out of the house.* Tucking the corners back on the baggies, wiping the back of her hand against her eyes like she thought the kids wouldn't notice. Watching her, a hundred things came into my mind to say which I discarded, everything staying unsaid, like when Matt was born and we just sat there looking at each other. The difference was then it didn't seem to matter, me being something which she used to call inarticulate and she now called withholding. Ham and cheese, ham and cheese, ham and cheese, seed mustard on Dad's, chutney on the kids'. I couldn't take my eyes from her hands, remembered them squeezing mine on our wedding day as I'd stood up to make my speech, the culmination of four days of nervous diarrhoea. I married a non-talker, Vicki saying with a tight smile at parties, or silently flicking through the channels with the remote as I wracked my brain for something to say that would make her talk again. *How can you just STAND there?* Vicki said now, sawing the sandwiches with the knife.

I don't know, I answered, which was the honest truth.

. . . . .

Twelve years of night running, working the bolt open silently on the back gate, watching Kelly let it rip.

When we started the oval had opened out to empty land, now it was a maze of clotheslines, fences, paved patios. When the dog disappeared up the incline on the other side he'd pause and turn, waiting for me. I could whistle so softly it was barely audible and he'd instantly race back like a rocket. Incredible hearing, turning towards the sound like a dish picking up radar. Outside the back door, ears straining through the glass, he'd hear his name and start shaking with excitement, picking up his front feet like they were hot, trying to sit up straight like a kid waiting to be let out of school. *Oh please, Mum*, Louise would plead. *Please let him.* My soft-hearted Lou.

I got promoted. Matthew got taller and sat hunched over his Nintendo GameBoy instead of practising soccer. Vicki did two nights a week at TAFE: 'Write Your Life Story', 'Crystal Healing', 'Thai Cooking', 'Start Your Own Small Business', 'The Tarot and You', 'Stretch Sewing'.

One year I was opening and unfolding the Christmas tree and remembered that I'd meant to fix the two broken branches with fishing line a few months before. No – it had been a year ago. It couldn't be a year since Christmas but it was – the same jammed aisles of $2 crap, worrying what Vicki would like, 36 shopping hours to go, going crazy with the musak. If you'd have asked me what I'd wanted, I couldn't have said.

It had been different, I was sure it had been, when the kids believed in Santa, and Vicki and I had drunk port together and eaten the shortbread, scattered the grass clippings Louise had arranged in little piles for the reindeer, listened to the carols on TV, gone into the bedrooms and looked at our kids sleeping, feeling sentimental and exhausted from setting up train sets and fairy outfits in the lounge-room. Kids believe in Santa, adults believe in childhood.

· · · · ·

Then it was January the second of a New Year we didn't stay up for, and I was back to work on the twelfth, and in that time would be a week at the coast, and in the middle of the night I'm watching the digital numbers shift like blinking and I get up and get my runners. Kelly's curled up on the back mat, wakes up from a deep sleep when I touch him and looks surprised. He stands and stretches, runs a bit stiffly down to the gate to wait, and it seems like the same kind of strange joke that only such a short time ago you couldn't keep him down, he leapt from that guy's car into our front yard with so much energy. Now he takes off down the street and I stop at the end to rest a stitch that feels like a deep knot in my gut pulling upwards, and I jog to the oval and see Kelly trotting slowly to the incline on the far side. I am forty-two years old and the kind of guy who once scored 174 baskets in a season but now gives his wife a StaySharp Knife for Christmas, who can barely jog two kilometres, who can never think of what to say, and none of it really hits me until I whistle to watch Kelly bolting back down across the grass and he doesn't come. He is turned towards me and seems to be waiting, he seems to pick me out in the darkness and know what has always happened before, but he shakes his head, gives a nervous yawn and I realise he can't hear me, he's deaf.

· · · · ·

It seems a little extreme, the vet said to me, *lots of dogs with impaired hearing continue to enjoy a good quality of life.*

Kelly lying there, looking at nothing. Not impaired, silent. I watched the vet click his fingers behind the dog, clap, whistle. *Sometimes,* he said, *this kind of thing's hereditary.* He got out a kind of tuning fork and struck it against his desk and tried again. *This is at a pitch too high for the human ear,* he said, telling me about frequency range and how maybe it was only partial, how I'd have to watch out now for traffic and keep him on a leash, how often heelers live to a ripe old age, and Kelly, deaf, stiff and fifteen years old – it suddenly struck me like a train – didn't stir once. *But you're going to have to start thinking soon ...* said the vet, and I interrupted him.

Do it now, I said. Driving home, it felt like something was strangling me, a muscle tight as a wire in my throat, giving me away, a sound escaping like one long word. The only word.

. . . . .

God, how could you, how could you, Vicki kept saying, rocking Louise on the couch. I couldn't open my mouth, for fear of what might come out. The compression of unsaid things filling my chest, lungs hurting for air. *Don't you have any feelings at all,* she said. It was Matthew that had the nightmares after that, in the week we didn't go to the coast. We both jumped to get up to him, both grimly solicitous, comforting, heating milk, suddenly keen to outdo each other as the better parent, as if we both knew what was ahead. Passing each other in the hall we might as well have been two strangers on the bus, standing to let the other pass with a brittle courtesy that made me know it was finally over.

He had the kids' dog put down, Vicki would say at barbecues now, *without even telling them. The family dog. Andrew just had so many unresolved issues.* This would be later, after Vicki had counselling.

. . . . .

Wednesday afternoons I work through till six and drive out to the stadium for the match. The Westside Wranglers, middle of the ladder, and none of us tries too hard. Every guy in the team is my age, sick of jogging, nursing some minor nagging injury that requires liniment and strapping, and only three of us are still married. Sunday afternoons we train half-heartedly with lots of familiar banter and then on the weekends I don't have custody of the kids I drink stubbies with them in the social club while we watch the A-grade women's teams on the courts below us. The sounds seem to distort, hitting the high hangar ceiling – the whistles and shouts and squeaks of people's shoes as they pound up and down – sound bending like it's coming through water.

I watch people sometimes, wonder how they can walk around with the weight of what they know. Wonder if they feel like me, stumbling with lead shoes on the bottom of the ocean, swimming in a sea of the unsayable. It's a mistake we make, thinking it's words that tell us everything. It's sound that breaks glasses, cracks windows, sends cats up trees. Bats hear more than humans, understand more noise, let alone dogs. Maybe we're just not getting it, standing here listening for sensible speech, dying of loneliness and waiting for whatever it is. How do we know we're not calling and calling all the time, our throats so tight with it, it's too high to hear? At night I hear dogs barking, and think how much of their howling is outside my conscious range, so that I feel it like a vibration but mistake it for silence? Sitting in the club, turning my fourth and last stubbie on the Laminex, I want to phone my ex-wife. I want to say her name and then hold the receiver into air, let her listen to the roar of everything we can't bear to hear.

Can you hear it Vicki? I want to say. It's not words, it's nothing so coherent as words. It's all of us, hoarse with calling, straining in the darkness to hear something we recognise as our names.

. . . .

The Taxman's Mango

DAVID ASTLE

How can a careful man who works in taxation be happily married to an overblown, all-devouring wife? Deception keeps him going – the vision of a paradisal week with another woman. A sharply original story, imbued with a taxman's sense of profit and loss.

You and I know that Santa is a lie, and now Oscar knows. Oscar's five. It happened tonight. I was sneaking about his room, putting a gun in the stocking near his bed, when the boy reached out and touched me.

'You being Santa, Dad?'

It's one of those questions a parent dreads, along with 'What's that bull doing to the cow?' and 'Where do dead people go?' I told him the truth. I sat on his bed and told him deceit is a human constant. In those words. Oscar is precocious that way. At five he was using words like forgivable and transparency. I said, 'Sometimes lying is preferable. Furthermore, it's necessary.'

The gun Santa was giving him used raw potato for ammunition, unlike the one Oscar suddenly held to my head. I was powerless. I struck a deal. For Max's sake. Max slept in the parallel bed and was three. 'Don't tell your brother and I'll get you both a super-soaker.' Guns, you realise, are a very boy thing.

'Just one, Dad. Max doesn't need one.'

I held up my fingers in a peace sign. 'You need two for a war.'

. . . . .

Before we go on I must tell you two things: my wife is fat.

I work in tax. A third thing: I love my family very much.

When I say fat, I don't mean plump. Angela is huge. To borrow a phrase from popular speech, she has let herself go. At times the boys and I resemble stars to her planet, pilot fish to her whaleness. I won't go on – the metaphors are gross – but you get the picture. My darling is once, twice, three times a lady, which is why Christmas can be a stressful season. Imagine thinking of a gift that makes no reference to the mass of your loved one. I challenge you. It's next to impossible.

Like most big people, Angela is bashful about her condition. We'd love to blame the glands, a glucose deficiency or some technical term, but the bottom line is overeating. She nibbles ad nauseam. (Last week I found pistachio shells buried in the composter.) As much as I try to express my love for my wife, only food seems to give her the ultimate comfort. Or TV. And the two go hand in hand.

She wasn't always big. Heavy is a better word. Lately her spirit seems a basket of wet laundry she carries around the house, a weight to match the load on her bones – the mother load, you could say. When TV-watching frays into conversation she argues she's happy, but the keyword here is argue. Underneath is this teasing sense of freakness, the cruel, ironic torment of seeming 'less than'.

That's my impression. I don't know where she gets it from; Angela is adequate. I tell her when I can. She keeps the house on track, the boys; she knows the best groceries on Puckle Street, shops wisely, saves well. Her dolmades are state of the art. Yet all the while her voice on the phone is heavy, just like her mannerisms (that's right, heavy mannerisms), the way she wraps a towel around Max and rubs him dry like a carwash attendant. Italians call it *brio* –

that something she's lost, having replaced it with weight and a bright anxiety.

Tax is another human constant. The second oldest profession in the world. The Chinese had the abacus, the Incas the quipu, the Hindus their zero; man cannot exist without a subtraction system, though I prefer to call it evaluation.

I've been with tax longer that I've been with Angela. Say what you like, she married me with her eyes open. Far from sexy, tax is essential, life-giving, fundamental, the ground society stands on. Think of schools and hospitals and vaccine caravans – they all come from tax. That brand new seesaw in the park – tax. That patch across the pothole. The firetruck. Those library books. The four-legged frame that keeps your aunt from falling on her face. All tax.

Order is the other reason for tax. God cannot provide equilibrium. We all know life isn't fair, but tax is. The Lord giveth and taketh away, but never in equal measure. The Department keeps records. We take what is owed, and repay you manifold.

. . . . .

Max is crying. He can't figure out the potato side of things. Oscar is making the most of it, digging the muzzle into the spud and shooting his brother point blank. The pellets are harmless, soft wet plugs of potato that sprinkle the carpet and the tree. A white Christmas this year.

Angela waves her present – an envelope wrapped in stripy paper. A voucher, she guesses. 'Open it,' I say. She shakes her head. 'I like the suspense too much.'

The voucher part is right, though not for movies or sundaes or fantasy books – her drugs of choice – but a massage. A series of massages. Shiatsu. She opens the envelope and reads the small print. She looks puzzled, and who's to blame her.

I tell her the voucher is for her. 'But why?' she asks. In a perfect world. where x + x = 2X, I'd offer a mango by way of explanation.

. . . . .

Mangoes don't grow so well in Melbourne, for the same reason we don't get cockroaches down here. It boils down to latitude. The geography is important to the story, my mango story. The timing is also critical. November 1990, six months before Angela and I got married. No vows had been taken. By definition we were free agents, fiancees in the making but unbetrothed nonetheless.

I was working undercover near Bowen, the so-called Fruitbowl of Australia, as glamorous as taxwork can possibly get. I was part of a large-scale operation, a sting if you like, aimed at bringing the black economy of tropical fruit-picking into account. I was twenty-eight years old. My real name is Stuart Gascoigne but my alias in the field was Darren Lovell.

Like most Australians, I see tourism as something you do overseas – a package trip to Europe, a week at Phuket – but the mango farms of Merinda and Guthalungra were a major wake-up call. By a stroke of luck I'd landed in the Garden of Eden.

Work began at 4 am, Santa time, before the heat and flies. I slept in a dormitory with a dozen backpackers, shaving and dressing in a stupor, piling like POWs into a courtesy truck. Donabella farm ran the length of Edgecombe Bay. The mangoes hung like lanterns from the trees. We worked in pairs, one of us wielding pruning shears with long bamboo handles while the other walked alongside with a slack hessian tramp, catching the fruit as it fell. As a rule you traded roles at the end of each row, but Miriam was happy playing catcher for the duration. Have I mentioned Miriam? In most versions of the mango story her name is implicit.

. . . . .

My fingers struggle with the giftwrap. At last the paper gives way to reveal a blonde pine box. Cigars, I'm guessing, but the weight is wrong. On the lid, a mock coat of arms. I work the lid open. Angela chews her lip in anticipation.

Inside are eight silver baubles – for the tree, I think. I lift one out. It sits in my palm like a small grenade, and just as heavy. 'What are these?'

'Don't you remember?' she asks, disappointed. 'Our wedding day.'

. . . . .

To be fair to my wife I will describe myself, or let the clichés do the work: a rake, an egg, a bat. That's me in the imagery stakes – as skinny, as bald and as blind. If a hack cartoonist had to portray a taxation official without the use of captions, he'd probably resort to yours truly. I'm a bean-counting stereotype in full living colour. Standing at the kerb I am who you guessed I was, which is why the attentions of a young Greek girl, Angela Dominides, had an exaggerated effect.

We first met in Caulfield library. My PC had crashed at home. I was processing numbers for the Rebate Sector, earning brownie points with unpaid overtime, when my home system nosedived, and I went to the library to book an Apple Mac. But the machine was in use. By a girl. A simple thing, like fate, like anatomy. Angela was slimmer back then. Never slim – cuddly. Women in the personal ads rely on the word Rubenesque. She was lovely. Unhaunted. Her smile was like a gift the moment it lit her face.

We started dating in late 1989/1990, the hottest summer in Melbourne's meteorological history. Strings of forties from go to whoa. How we didn't melt and pour down a drain I'm hard pressed to tell you. Our love weathered a test of fire.

To the best of my knowledge I'm not a romantic. After so many years of misfitting, false starts, pornography, enforced chastity, alopecia, mathematics, I was probably kept from knowing the finer points of adoration. I lay awake beside her in those early nights – the heat and flattery making it impossible to sleep – counting her inhalations from one to a googol (not a figure the tax department is happy to live with), and reasoned we could be together as far as humans can theoretically go. Why not? What could stop us? Under my breath I counted kisses too. Back then I hated the idea of getting more affection than I gave. Love needed to be equal, or at worst lopsided in her favour. When Angela straddled my back, rubbing my shoulders and neck, I counted her kneads in clusters of ten, and ensured the number was raised to a random power when the pleasure was reversed.

Under such conditions we lasted past the winter, which is when the mango call came.

. . . . .

Miriam was English. She had a Druid rune tattooed on the inside of her thigh, which I guess is a self-condemning comment, but it is and isn't. Most of the pickers worked close to naked at Donabella farm. The rune itself – I first took it for an ampere symbol – was practically erased by her sunburn.

She daubed it in cream – mangoes and cream – but needed a second party to apply the 15+ to her shoulders. I was her designated pruner, a purblind spy with no hair to speak of, and she elected me. I was gobsmacked. Not by love so much, but the same sort of bloodrush that got Adam in trouble and that Eve played no small part in. A woman's attention can act like a drug, I've discovered. We had what you might call a holiday fling, excepting I was indentured to the Australian Taxation Department and she was picking mangoes without a valid permit. The moral ground got swampy when I phoned Angela on the second week to learn that her father had died.

I put the phone down. I panicked. I told Miriam to run. I said my name wasn't Darren and the farm was a trap. She panicked for different reasons. She took me for schizo, which was charming in a way, and boarded a coach for Townsville. I flew to Brisbane, staying the night with a senior colleague who helped me debrief the whole affair.

My exodus was a blur. I'll never forget the pucker on Miriam's forehead when I told her about Operation Guava, or sitting in the back of a Brisbane cab and realising I'd left my wallet eleven hundred and fifty kilometres north, locked away in the hostel's safe. Yes, the taxman was penniless. No cash, no cards, no ID – real or otherwise. Speeding through the streets of an unfamiliar city, I dug in my backpack to find the world's biggest mango. I was keeping it for Angela, or myself, I'm not too sure – a love-gift or a love-souvenir. Either way, I gave it to the taxi driver as legal tender. It got me as far as the CBD.

. . . . .

Oscar checks the crockpot for reindeer water. The boys had prepared for Santa's visit the previous evening by laying out a plateful of Anzacs and a stubby for the man himself. For three-year-old Max the evidence is overwhelming: biscuit crumbs, a drained bottle, lapped water. Santa Was Here. Oscar takes longer to find satisfaction; he's learning to speak in that collusive double-talk that parents develop in order to get by.

'Santa drinks the same beer as you, Dad,'

'One and the same,' I say.

'Lucky we had the right brand.'

'He's been here before, don't forget.'

The walk to the park is three blocks, far enough for Oscar and me to leave the others behind. 'Deceit comes in two forms,' I tell him, thinking as I say it, perhaps there's more. I've never counted them before.

'That time you killed the fish at Uncle Chris's place. Don't start, Oscar, I saw you. That trowel, you killed it. It doesn't matter. Fish die. We all do. God has set the taximeter on everyone. But lying made it worse, didn't it? For you, not the fish. It didn't concern the fish. It worried your mother – your lying eroded her trust in you. Can you see that?'

Oscar steps lightly to dodge the pavement's cracks. He lets my sermon wash over him. As I speak I wonder where self-deceit fits into the scheme of things (number three, four?), but even a bright spark like Oscar doesn't need the term to complicate the picture. Not today, at any rate. It's Christmas.

'Santa, on the other hand, is traditional. Everyone expects it of us. Mums and dads are in a lose-lose situation, when you think about it. Deceit is the only way out. It's forgivable, and fun. Isn't it fun?

'Put it this way, Oscar. Sure, Maxy would be heartbroken if he learnt the truth about the non-Santa situation. More importantly we have a bond now, you and I. Somehow he's twice the child for being excluded, and you're double the grown-up colluding with me. Can you see that? From now on you're in charge of guarding the truth, keeping it safe. Max relies on you to protect him in the same way I look after Mum. Keeping their interests at heart. We have no choice. Not if we love them, and we do.'

The park is a reason we moved to Moonee Ponds. That and Angela's desire to be closer to her mother. The beauty of the park is its blankness, allowing the visitor to imagine himself elsewhere. The play equipment is clustered in a circle of tanbark: monkey bars, slide, a tiny biplane on springs. Armed with potato guns, the boys make a beeline for the wooden fort.

Angela kneels and opens the box. The silver balls inside catch the sunlight, which plays in a watery pattern on her face. On some days her prettiness is preserved, like the glimpsing of a saint, or a memory, and I thank the day I asked her to marry me.

. . . . .

Mr Dominides, the dead man, was the traditionalist of the family. Priscilla, Angela's mum, wasn't fussed one way or the other. Greek Orthodox, Aussie Orthodox: as long as her daughter was happy. We settled on marrying in a summerhouse in St Kilda gardens, a summerhouse in winter, June 1991, the eve of a new financial year.

The beech trees were bare. The mulch on pathways acted as carpet. Angela was late; her limousine couldn't find a parking spot. I waited with the celebrant in the summerhouse, watching some Italian men play bocce on the grass below. At least they yelled like Italians, urging on their throws with tiny European flutters of their hands. Soon the whole gazebo resembled a stadium, my family-to-be turning to watch the players throwing the silver balls across the lawn. We started barracking. We developed factions and encouraged one man over another. Few of us in the wedding party understood the rules, but each of us could recognise a neck-and-neck contest.

Later, saying 'I do' and 'I will', sliding a ring over Angela's wrong finger and the laughter breaking the ritual's tension, it occurred to me that bocce, with all its inbuilt mystery, was the equal of marriage. I knew the rules and strategy of neither. At the reception, drinking too much in the back room of a Greek restaurant, standing like Jack-and-Jill-in-the-boxes for one toast after the next, I vowed to learn the basics at least.

. . . . .

Deceit is a human constant. The phrase came care of Allan da Costa, the Executive manager of the Melbourne Tax Office. Every month he delivers a pep talk to the staff, examining turnover rates, proportion of rebate percentages, successful hits. Morale is sky-high in the department at present. We're earning our money big-time, hauling in some serious fish without letting your standard tiddlers off the hook. These days I'm 2IC of Fiduciary and moving up.

'Never take anything at face value,' says da Costa, for the benefit of the newcomers. 'No matter how dense the paper trail, chase it down. Be convinced by the claim, not persuaded. Cross-check expenditure with transaction data. *Homo sapiens* is a slippery animal. If he sniffs the smallest loophole, he'll suck in his lungs and will himself through.'

. . . . .

I'm no Casanova. A week of sex in Far North Queensland had me jumping out of my skin, despite the *gravitas* the funeral called for. Even in her grief, Angela was perceptive. She knew my buoyancy amounted to betrayal of some sort, my spirit out of sync with her mourning, but opted not to press for details. We buried her father. We ate a cake called *psarakos* that tasted like chalk. Angela accompanied her mum and older brother walking around in a circle of relatives, sobbing, hugging, shaking hands, while I held court with a bunch of tailored children.

'Where does he go?' asked one of the kids.

'Who?'

'Uncle Taso. Now that he'd dead.'

I shrugged. My knack for handling earth-shattering questions had yet to develop. For handling Angela's questions too. A week past the funeral, she wanted to know the history of the smirk that persisted on my face like a belated birthmark. Mentally I tossed up the repercussions, bearing in mind we were fated to wed, the proposal yet to be formulated – imminent de factos, you could say, yet unwed all the same – and I told her, by way of telling her something, that Bowen is the Fruitbowl of Australia. A fob-off in other words. A phrase to fill in the blank on the form.

. . . . .

Chris was drunk. Angela's brother, happily drunk – all of us were that night. He wove across to our table and, being married himself, said it was customary for the bride and groom to leave the reception first.

Angela was a furnace of wonderful feelings. You couldn't hope to stop her. 'Why? We don' wanna leave. Hey Stu, you wanna leave?'

'No,' I laughed, though I wasn't sure.

Angela stood. She held her brother like a lover. 'Besides,' she said, 'the bridal couple is meant to do a *kalamatianos*, and nobody's done nothing yet.'

That night her will was our command. Tables were dragged and squeaky Greek music erupted from a speaker. I can still see my father, a sober man under normal circumstances, high-kicking like a cabaret girl, whooping and wheezing in tandem with Priscilla. Plates were smashed. Cups, bottles. By the time we left the restaurant – the very last people to go – the room resembled a recycling depot.

And that's when the realisation hit us. Wedding dresses don't have pockets, and my wallet was entrusted with Mark, our best man, who'd vanished after dessert with the lighting assistant. We were done up to the nines, and skint. Light rain was falling. Our honeymoon suite was fourteen kilometres across town and nobody knew us from Adam and Eve.

. . . . .

The rules to bocce are printed on the lid's underside – in Latin and French, and Portuguese. No language we know. Angela confesses she bought the box from a man at Preston Markets.

'Shouldn't stop us from playing,' I say.

'I felt nervous buying it. Remember, you were going to learn the game ages ago, but you haven't made any moves till now.'

'A Tournament of Champions should fix that.'

I pick out the small white ball we'd come to call the jack and toss it along the grass. Max and Oscar stand frozen on top of the fort, just like a wedding couple ten years before, watching the rituals of an undrafted game between Santa and Santa's helper. Angela treads an invisible line. She throws a silver ball in the jack's direction. The natural bias of the ground causes her shot to kink on target.

Between frames she says, 'I kept a receipt in case the set is flawed or something.'

'How would we know?' I laugh. She leads the tournament 3-1. If I didn't know Angela better I'd suspect her of practising the game on the sly. I pat her shoulder – she's warm with effort. 'Always good policy to keep a receipt.'

. . . . .

If my time with Miriam has a receipt, it is a mango. No particular mango of course, though the larger and riper the fruit, the more effectively it serves as documentation. I see a mango and remember the story, sometimes recounting a version of it – my days as Darren Lovell, Superspy in Paradise. The week feels like yesterday. The girl, Miriam, is submerged in the telling, though she occupies every frame. Angela can see her but doesn't know her name.

In a perfect world I want the shiatsu voucher to be the equivalent for Angela, a sensory token that balances the mango on our ledger, though I realise the gesture is vain from the start. Vain in both senses. My wife will be touched, and that is all, her enormity pampered as opposed to healed.

Assuming there's healing to be done. Who knows? I'm a stranger to approximation, and I cannot speak for Angela. She knows herself best. Inside her skin my wife could well be happy, happier than me, making my bids for readjustments an exercise in time-wasting, and there's no end to that. Despite my years in equity I find myself on strange turf, faced with things like metaphors and intuition, aiming to balance a book nobody can hold or see.

Generosity could be the answer, the act of giving her ground to compensate for my own indulgences. A quid for her quo. A parody of parity. Or maybe Angela will start to blossom – old Angela, the new Angela – when next I walk into the grocery on Puckle and see a mango as precisely that: a mango. The reflex pleasure of seeing what lies in front of you and forgetting about the unaccountable.

. . . . .

Angela tapped on the restaurant door, using her Greek to sweet-talk a favour. Money, I assumed, but the maître d' appeared with a leftover present from our slagheap of gifts. We unwrapped it in the street. A manual orange-juicer from my brother, stainless steel and vaguely medieval. The cab driver, when offered the device, refused the fare on the grounds of romance. He drove us with honour like a chauffeur through the streets of Richmond, juicer or no juicer, allowing us to pash in the back seat in silence. Angela tasted of wine; the cab smelt of pine trees. Looking up, I saw the numbers static on the taximeter, a string of stubborn zeroes recording a permanent moment in time. Our limo rushed through the rain-bright streets while the world of finance – the universe itself – was banished from the equation. From the outset, from our first nuptial snog, our marriage felt an entity refusing to elapse. Budge. Depreciate.

. . . .

Dreams as a Form of Travel

SARI WAWN

The family in this story have the appearance of normality, but strange things are occurring underneath. Nature seems to be laying siege to them. While Jim and the children do their best to go about their business, Pen, the mother, is beset by dreams of islands and distant places. More a teasing fable than a straightforwardly realistic story.

Drifting

One perfect summer's day, Pen was floating around the pool with her head resting on one end of a blow-up rubber boat and her feet dangling over the other. Her husband Jim had gone to the cricket, and her children Sam and Megan had gone to see a *Monty Python* movie. She had her book propped on her midriff and she intended to spend the afternoon reading *The Four-Gated City*, the fifth and final novel in Doris Lessing's 'Children of Violence' sequence. Pen drew strength from the way Martha Quest, Lessing's alter ego, tackled domestic life and politics. According to the blurb on the back cover, 'Gradually the novel becomes prophetic ... moves unobtrusively into the future ... into another dimension ... '

Soon she began to doze off, and little by little the sides of the pool receded, until they disappeared altogether. Next, the waves of freeway traffic faded and died on some distant shore, and she was cast adrift in her very own wilderness. Her craft, 'not' the package warned, 'to be used in the open sea or as a life saving device', transported her out into a vast ocean. Like an Inuit hunter waiting day after day in his kayak for a seal to emerge from the water, becalmed and suspended between water and sky, Pen experienced one of those rare unsustainable moments, when everything, even paying off the mortgage, seemed possible. Something like this had happened to her once before, on her honeymoon, when Jim had taken her to a surf beach. She was a country girl, unused to the turbulence of the sea, so after being dumped by several waves, she had swum out into the calmer water beyond the breakers, and momentarily beyond her fear of sharks or anything else.

It must have been late afternoon before the house, like some abandoned wreck on a remote island, appeared on her horizon and brought her back to reality. They would all be home soon and wanting dinner. Yet again her reading would have to wait.

Backyard dreaming
Pen and Jim had recently found a Cal Bung in need of renovation in one of Melbourne's leafier suburbs. They thought that it had potential and that they could do something with the garden. They were not earning much at the time but that was what you were supposed to do when you had kids. Move to the suburbs. Set up house. Be a family. Grow plants. Acquire pets. In the post-nuclear age no one could save the world, but they could return to a simpler life. Pen and Jim intended to tread lightly on the planet.

They didn't want a dog, because it would tie them down too much, so they held a family conference and decided on rabbits. Jim built a hutch and Fluffy and Sneaky were moved in. The first massacre was carried out by a neighbouring red setter soon after. Next Pen took the kids to the pet shop to buy some guinea pigs, and a book on their care. Except for the consternation caused by the picture on the back page of Peruvian women selling cavies at a roadside stall for food, Gino and Geraldine were a qualified success, until another dog attack. The aviary with painted quail and budgies was also a good idea, for quite a while.

Ancient wisdom

Alex and Maxine, the axolotls, or Mexican Walking Fish, lived in a square glass tank under the magnolia tree and were trouble free. Although they were supposed to be fish, they didn't swim much. They looked as though they were more suited to life on land than in water. They had a long fin running down their spine, but like dragons or lizards they had legs as well, and ferny gills, like some kind of plant. With their grim heads thrust forward, they spent their days standing on the bottom of their tank looking as if they knew that some catastrophe was about to happen. They liked to feed on live goldfish, but were happy enough to eat chunks of raw meat. If they hadn't been so weird they would have been easy to neglect.

When Sam looked up his encyclopedia for his Nature Study project he found out that they were reputed to survive fire and to weep tears of blood. There were stories around too that if they escaped, they could fend for themselves on the streets, and grow to the size of an average dog. Apparently in Mexico City they too were considered to be food, but they were obviously not as defenceless as guinea pigs. Pen worried that keeping them might be seen as anti-social, like flushing crocodiles into the sewers, or abandoning kittens when they turned into cats.

Natural forces

Each night, after eating the flower buds on the magnolia tree, possums rioted in the ceilings of the house. Rats scurrying about under the floorboards upset the cat. One morning the man next door saw a fox making its way to the chook pen a few houses down. The day heavy rain flooded the aviary and drowned all the quail, Megan found a tortoise in the swampy patch in the lower back corner of the yard. As if by some implicit agreement struck between the forces of nature and urbanisation, rainwater continued to follow its customary path along the line of their back fence and down the hill into the concrete drain that now replaced the original creek. Put another way, water finds its own level. Another day there was the snake coiled around the base of the birdbath.

. . . . .

The next thing they did was to put in the pool. Jim had taken on extra work to pay for it. During the long Christmas break and well into the autumn, like otters or seals, the children and their friends spent their days playing in the water and basking in the sun. Pen marvelled that children of hers could be so at home in the water. She and Jim agreed that seeing the kids have so much fun made it all worthwhile. If everyone else was happy, well, she must be too.

Undercurrents
The night Jim brought home a kilo of bacon from one of the old painters and dockers pubs in South Melbourne, he'd been having a drink with Al, who was just back from New Guinea. 'Now he's going to build a raft and float it to Tierra del Fuego. He's got hold of some old maps … and I've been thinking, we should travel too. You could teach. I'd get work building. We'd save money,' he said. 'While the kids are young, they'd love it.'

Pen knew that Sam, who was just thirteen, would love the idea, but Megan would miss her friends. She would be fifteen soon, and was losing interest in family ventures. And Jim always had schemes. Lately he had been thinking seriously about taking up landscape gardening. Before that it had been building marinas with his mate Dennis. Before that there'd been abalone fishing and excursions for Japanese tourists.

Jim's dreams were not the heart of their troubles. Pen didn't know yet exactly what, or who, was and wondered whether or not she wanted to know. She knew better than to ask questions, and she knew by now the futility of trying to sort things out with him. He had a way of making confrontations evaporate. 'Mim rang and invited us to go to Sydney for Easter' she said instead. 'I told her we'd think about it.'

'Sure. Why not?'

Jim poured them each a drink, and went in to watch television. He had been trying to persuade Megan to watch something else beside soap operas. Although Pen thought Jim was right about this, she could understand Megan's point of view. Pen no longer watched the news because all the reports of famines and floods filled her with helpless despair and she was embarrassed by her western affluence.

Prophecy
They didn't go to Sydney. Instead they settled back into the routine of the year, of school and work. 'Today in our Earthwatch elective' Sam told Pen 'we learnt how the earth's getting hotter.' He had borrowed the *Whole Earth Catalogue* from the library, and showed her a page with a series of cartoons of a beach being eroded by rising seas and a lighthouse toppling into the waves. 'When the lighthouse has been washed away' he said, 'the sea will drown all the suburbs near the beaches, and then it'll come all the way up to our

front fence. Instead of being on a hill, we'll be marooned on an island. People will go to work by submarine and there will be fish swimming past their office windows. Even if we build a sea wall along the front fence, the waves will take all the sand away from underneath it. When the sand's all gone, the house will fall over. The sea always wins … is there anything I can eat before I go to Dave's? We have to do a project together. His mum says that we can sleep in their backyard tonight, in a tent. We're going to build a biodome.'

He was out the door before she had time to ask him what to do about the margarine container marked Wild Bees she had discovered hibernating in the refrigerator, or the old beach bucket of bones soaking in White King in her laundry. Pen had also wanted to tell him how she had stayed with her grandparents once while her mother and father had gone to look at a farm on an island. It was four hours by road south of the city, and then another half-hour across a lake by boat. 'Living there would have been ghastly,' her mother had declared. 'We would have had to make our own bread.' That had been her last word on it.

Pen never told anyone that while her family stayed on in the city, she had often dreamt about the island. She would be marooned there all alone, and build a tree house. On sunny mornings she would ride her Arab pony along a beach of pure silver sand.

Over time her island became smaller and smaller until it almost disappeared, but now and again she still caught herself making lists of what she would need to take with her when she finally set sail. Pen didn't want to see her kids stranded by their dreams the way she had been, but she did want them to dream.

· · · · ·

During the winter months the whole family went into hibernation. The pool turned green with algae and a pair of ducks landed on it. Sam suggested to Pen that they use the pool for aquaculture, but the ducks didn't stay, they flew away.

When spring arrived Sam and Megan joined the local tribe of young nomads. They all travelled around the neighbourhood as one entity. They kept on going to school, but at weekends they slept away the daylight hours and then went out at night. Pen had led an isolated childhood, and assumed that this was what modern adolescents were supposed to do. She saw their independence and freedom as positive aspects of suburban life.

They were busy, they said, because they had formed an anti-nuclear party, and they were campaigning to make the whole of the city a nuclear-free zone. What they had all actually done was organise fake ID cards for themselves so they could go out drinking in pubs. Pen knew that it would not be long before they would be leaving for good.

Boat people
With Sam and Megan out so much, and Jim at last going to lectures on landscape gardening, Pen got back to reading again. She tried to read Simone de Beauvoir and others from the canon of women's literature, but they raised too many issues too close to home. She decided to look for something that took her right away from her daily life.

The librarian suggested Dee Brown's *Bury my Heart at Wounded Knee*, the tragic epic about the removal of Native American people from their tribal lands. She found it compelling, so she immersed herself in the study of their lives and their culture:

Before the god Sotuknang, she read, sent down the rains to destroy the Third World, he asked Spider Woman to help him save 'the people with songs in their hearts'. When they came to her, she cut down some hollow reeds and put the people inside them with some water and some cornmeal. Then Sotuknang made the rains begin.

Eventually the rain stopped. The people floated for some time, until they found the Place of Emergence into the Fourth World. As they came out, Sotuknang said to them: 'This world is not easy, like the previous ones. It has height and depth, heat and cold, beauty and barrenness. As you follow your star, what you choose will determine whether this time you will carry out the Plan of Creation or whether this world too must in time be destroyed ...'

Not so far-fetched thought Pen ... the rising sea ... the flood ... it's part of the Plan ... follow the star ... escape ... survive. The body drifts while the soul travels.

She dreamt that she was lost in a dark forest with the water rising all around her. She had climbed to the top of a tree, and couldn't get down. It was one of her recurring dreams. In the morning she could never remember how, but she had found her way home.

A change in the weather
In his lectures Jim studied gardens for the future, when watering would become taboo. People would not even have lawns because there wouldn't be enough water. There'd be water he said, but people would have to buy it, and it would be expensive.

Pen would be very happy to get rid of the lawn and the pool. She wanted to do something Japanese instead, with rocks and pebbles, and perhaps just a small fishpond.

She preferred the contemplative qualities of water to the turbulent energies of oceans. The garden could be a shared project and it would be much less risky than having another baby. She only thought about that when she was really desperate.

Ritual

Al finished the raft. He had to leave while the weather was good, so Jim organised a party. For Jim these days, life seemed to be one long party. When Pen asked how many would be coming, he said it was always hard to say with Al. Not many ... probably just a few ... It depended.

Jim cleaned up the pool, and early one Sunday morning, he put a lamb on a spit. All day the lamb turned over and over above a slow fire. The pungent smoke of burning flesh wafted out into the street, and people Pen assumed were guests arrived laden with alarming numbers of bottles. She thought she recognised the town planner who'd told them about the creek running along the back fence, the landscape gardening lecturer, and a couple of Jim's mates who'd been around for dinner when they'd been at a loose end. Whoever they were, and however they'd got there, they were clearly expecting what Al and Jim called a party.

The alcohol took effect long before the lamb was ready, and the social exchanges slipped into the usual series of drunken shorthand and a few fumbled gropes and passes. Everybody wept over Al in case it were the last time they would ever see him. Jim got distracted by a girl with long hair and a mini skirt, and didn't get around to carving up the beast. As people got hungry, they hacked off greasy chunks for themselves, and gnawed their way through them. Pen needn't have even bothered about the salads or dips.

Pen was resigned for Jim's next predictable move. He staggered and nearly lost his balance as he removed his boxer shorts. One by one the guests followed his example, until Pen was the only one left clothed. They laughed at her and invited her in.

As they dived and wallowed, Pen wondered if it was only whales that sometimes beached themselves. Then she remembered how much she missed the ducks, but what really pissed her off was Jim's supreme confidence in his sexual prowess. She wondered what it was about the over-nourished uninhibited human male that she just could not appreciate. It might be like acquiring a taste for truffles or blachan, or enjoying the squish of walking into a muddy dam. She willed the axolotls to climb into the pool and attack their extremities, and then she turned and went into the house. In the morning, she would be the only one who remembered any of this.

Ghost
Pen was standing on a beach with a wall of translucent green water towering over her; 'A wave travels like a ghost through the body of the sea', the *Earth Catalogue* had said, 'travelling across the ocean's surface. It is not water itself racing from place to place: the energy it carries existed before the wave and lives on after its crashing death.' Just before dawn, when the wave was about to break over her, she woke up and heard rain on the roof. Jim was lying here beside her, fast asleep.

Wreckage
Pen got up, and went to the back door to survey the aftermath of the party. The soggy yard was littered with empty bottles and glasses, greasy plates, disintegrating cigarette

butts, and shoes. Discarded clothing hung in the magnolia. The remains of the lamb had fallen off the spit on to the coals and lay there like some drought-ravaged animal that had expired at the edge of a water hole. Pen heard a scuffle, and then saw, or thought she saw a pair of large axolotls tearing at the lamb carcase. Overhead seagulls from the local tip were gathering.

Pen wondered how early she could ring Mim and say she would love to come to Sydney, soon. She would not even wait for the man with the shocking hair transplant and the Rottweiler who was coming to install the new pool pump that afternoon. Sam was leaving in a day or two to go north to monitor turtles during the hatching season. She would ask Megan if she would like to come with her. Jim could go with Al, or start the escort agency he had mentioned.

From Sydney Pen would go inland to Alice Springs, or Longreach, or anywhere a long way from the sea. She would find a rock to sit on, where she could wait until the water receded. Then she would follow her star.

. . . .

MEMORIES

My Father's Axe

TIM WINTON

Someone has stolen the axe that his father once wielded with such power and grace. Now that it's gone, the son is invaded by terrifying dreams. Is this what he must endure to become a man and father himself? Like its subject, this is a tale that cuts deep.

1

Just now I discovered the axe gone. I look everywhere inside and outside the house, front and back, but it is gone. It has been on my front verandah since the new truckload of wood arrived and was dumped so intelligently over my front lawn. Jamie says he doesn't know where the axe is and I believe him; he won't chop wood any more. Elaine hasn't seen it; it's men's business, she says. No, it's not anywhere. But who would steal an axe in this neighbourhood, this street where I grew up and have lived much of my life? No one steals on this street. Not an axe.

It is my father's axe.

I used to watch him chop with it when we drove the old Morris and the trailer outside the town limits to gather wood. He would tie a thick, short bar of wood to the end of forty feet of rope and swing it about his head like a lasso and the sound it made was the whoop! of the headmaster's cane you heard when you walked past his office. My father sent the piece of wood high into the crown of a dead sheoak and when it snarled in the stark, grey limbs he would wrap the rope around his waist and then around his big freckled arms, and he would pass me his grey hat with bound hands and tell me to stand right back near the Morris with my mother who poured tea from a Thermos flask. And he pulled. I heard his body grunt and saw his red arms whiten, and the tree's crown quivered and rocked and he added to the motion, tugging, jerking, gasping until the whole bush cracked open and birds burst from all the trees around and the dead, grey crown of the sheoak teetered and toppled to the earth, chased by a shower of twigs and bark. My mother and I cheered and my father ambled over, arms glistening, to drink the tea that tasted faintly of coffee and the rubber seal of the Thermos. Rested, he would then dismember the brittle tree with graceful swings of his axe and later I would saw with him on the bowman saw and have my knees showered with white, pulpy dust.

He could swing an axe, my father.

And that axe is gone.

He taught me how to split wood though I could never do it like him, those long, rhythmic, semicircular movements like a ballet dancer's warm-up; I'm a left-hander, a mollydooker he called me, and I chop in short, jabby strokes which do the job but are somehow less graceful.

When my father began to leave us for long periods for his work – he sold things – he left me with the responsibility of fuelling the home. It gave me pride to know that our hot water, my mother's cooking, the living room fire depended upon me, and my mother called me the man of the house, which frightened me a little. Short, winter afternoons I spent up the back splitting pine for kindling, long, fragrant spines with neat grain, and I opened up the heads of mill-ends and sawn blocks of sheoak my father brought home. Sometimes in the trance of movement and exertion I imagined the blocks of wood as teachers' heads. It was pleasurable work when the wood was dry and the grain good and when I kept the old Kelly axe sharp. I learnt to swing single-handed, to fit wedges into stubborn grain, to negotiate knots with resolve, and the chopping warmed me as I stripped to my singlet and worked until I was ankle-deep in split, open wood and my breath steamed out in front of me with each righteous grunt.

Once, a mouse half caught itself in a trap in the laundry beneath the big stone trough and my mother asked me to kill it, to put it out of its misery, she said. Obediently, I carried the threshing mouse in the trap at arm's length right up to the back of the yard. How to kill a mouse? Wring its neck? Too small. Drown it? In what? I put it on the burred block and hit it with the flat of the axe. It made no noise but it left a speck of red on my knee.

Another time my father, leaving again for a long trip, began softly to weep on our front step. My mother did not see because she was inside finding him some fruit. I saw my father ball his handkerchief up and bite on it to muffle his sobs and I left him there and ran through the house and up to the woodpile where I shattered great blocks of sheoak until it was dark and my arms gave out. In the dark I stacked wood into the buckled shed and listened to my mother calling.

I broke the handle of that axe once, on a camping trip; it was good hickory and I was afraid to tell him. I always broke my father's tools, blunted his chisels, bent his nails. I have never been a handyman like my father. He made things and repaired things and I watched but did not see the need to learn because I knew my father would always be. If I needed something built, something done, there was my father and he protected me.

When I was eight or nine he took my mother and me to a beach shack at a rivermouth up north. The shack was infested with rats and I lay awake at nights listening to them until dawn when my father came and roused me and we went down to haul the craypots. The onshore reefs at low tide were bare, clicking and bubbling in the early sun, and octopuses gangled across exposed rocks, lolloping from hole to hole. We caught them for bait; my father caught them and I carried them in the bucket with the tight lid and looked at my face in the still tidal pools that bristled with kelp. But it was not so peaceful at high tide when the swells burst on the upper lip of the reef and cascaded walls of foam that rushed in upon us and rocked us with their force. The water reached my waist though it was only knee-deep for my father. He taught me to brace myself side-on to the waves and find footholds in the reef and I hugged his leg and felt his immovable stance and moulded myself to him. At the edge of the reef I coiled the rope that he hauled up and held the hessian bag as he opened the heavy, timber-slatted pots; he dropped the crays in and I heard their tweaking cries and felt them grovelling against my legs.

During the day my mother read *They're a Weird Mob* and ate raisins and cold crayfish dipped in red vinegar. We played Scrabble and it did not bother me that my father lost.

Lost his axe. Who could have stolen such a worthless thing? The handle is split and taped and the head bears the scars of years; why even look at it?

One night on that holiday a rat set off a trap on the rafter above my bed. My father used to tie the traps to the rafters to prevent the rats from carrying them off. It went off in the middle of the night with a snap like a small firecracker and in the dark I sensed something moving above me and something warm touched my forehead. I lay still and did not scream because I knew my father would come. Perhaps I did scream in the end, I don't know. But he came, and he lit the

Tilley lamp and chuckled and, yes, that was when I screamed. The rat, suspended by six feet of cord, swung in an arc across my bed with the long, hairy whip of tail trailing a foot above my nose. The body still flexed and struggled. My father took it down and went outside with its silhouette in the lamplight in front of him. My mother screamed; there was a drop of blood on my forehead. It was just like *The Pit and the Pendulum*, I said. We had recently seen the film and she had found the book in the library and read it to me for a week at bedtime. Yes, she said with a grim smile, wiping my forehead, and I had nightmares about that long, hairy blade above my throat and saw it snatched away by my father's red arms. In the morning I saw outside that the axe head was dull with blood. After that I often had dreams in which my father rescued me. One was a dream about a burning house – our house, the one I still live in with Elaine and Jamie – and I was trapped inside, hair and bedclothes afire and my father splintered the door with an axe blow and fought his way in and carried me out in those red arms.

My father. He said little. He never won at Scrabble, so it seems he never even stored words up for himself. We never spoke much. It was my mother and I who carried on the long conversations; she knew odd facts, quiz shows on television were her texts. I told her my problems. But with my father I just stood, and we watched each other. Sometimes he looked at me with disappointment, and other times I looked at him the same way.

. . . . .

He hammered big nails in straight and kissed me goodnight and goodbye and hello until I was fourteen and learnt to be ashamed of it and evade it.

When his back stiffened with age he chopped wood less and I wielded the axe more. He sat by the woodpile and sometimes stacked, though mostly he just sat with a thoughtful look on his face. As I grew older my time contracted around me like a shrinking shirt and I chopped wood hurriedly, often finishing before the old man had a chance to come out and sit down.

Then I met Elaine and we married and I left home. For years I went back once a week to chop wood for the old man while Elaine and my mother sat at the Laminex table in the kitchen listening to the tick of the stove. I tried to get my parents interested in electric heating and cooking like most people in the city, but my father did not care for it. He was stubborn and so I continued to split wood for him once a week while he became a frail, old man and his arms lost their ruddiness and went pasty and the flesh lost its grip upon the bones of his forearms. He looked at me in disappointment every week like an old man will, but I came over on Sundays, even when we had Jamie to look after, so he didn't have cause to be that way.

Jamie got old enough to use an axe and I taught him how. He was keen at first, though careless, and he blunted the edge quite often which angered me. I got him to chop wood for his grandfather and dropped him there on Sunday afternoons.

I had a telephone installed in their house, though they complained about the colour, and I spoke to my mother sometimes on the phone, just to please her. My father never spoke on the phone. Still doesn't.

Then my mother had her stroke and Jamie began demanding to be paid for woodchopping and Elaine went twice a week to cook and clean for them and I decided on the Home. My mother and father moved out and we moved in and sold our own house. I thought about getting the place converted to electricity but the Home was expensive and Elaine came to enjoy cooking on the old combustion stove and it was worth paying Jamie a little to chop wood. Until recently. Now he won't even do it for money. He is lazier than me.

Still, it was only an old axe.

2

Elaine sleeps softly beside me. Her big wide buttocks warm against my legs. The house is quiet; it was always quiet, even when my parents and I lived here. No one ever raised their voice at me in this house, except now my wife and son.

It is hard to sleep, hard, so difficult. Black moves about me and in me and is on me, so black. Fresh, bittersweet, the smell of split wood: hard, splintery jarrah, clean, moist sheoak, hard, fibrous white gum, the shick! of sundering pine.

All my muscles sing, a chorus of effort, as I chop quickly, throwing chunks aside, wiping flecks and chips from my chin. Sweat sheets across my eyes and I chop harder, opening big round sawn blocks of sheoak like pies in neat wedged sections. Harder. And my feet begin to lift as I swing the axe high over my shoulder. I strike it home and regain equilibrium. As I swing again my feet lift further and I feel as though I might float up, borne away by the axe above my head, as though it is a helium balloon. No, I don't want to lift up! I drag on the hickory handle, downwards, and I win and drag harder and it gains momentum and begins a slow-motion arc of descent towards the porous surface of the wood and then, halfway down, the axe-head shears off the end of the handle so slowly, so painfully slow that I could take a hold of it four or five times to stop it. In a slow, tumbling trajectory it sails across the woodheap and unseats my father's head from his shoulders and travels on out of sight as my father's head rolls onto the heap, eyes towards me, transfixed at the moment of scission in a squint of disappointment.

I feel a warm dob on my forehead; I do not scream, have never needed to.

The sheets are wet and the light is on and Elaine has me by the shoulder and her left breast points down at my glistening chest.

'What's the matter?' she says, wiping my brow with the back of her hand. 'You were yelling.'

'A dream,' I croak.

3

Morning sun slants across the pickets at me as I fossick about in the long grass beside the shed finding the skeleton of a wren but nothing else. I shuffle around the shed, picking through the chips and splinters and slivers of wood around the chopping block, see the deep welts in the block where the axe has been, but no axe. In the front yard, as neighbours pass, I scrabble in the pile of new wood, digging into its heart, tossing pieces aside until there is nothing but yellowing grass and a few impassive slaters. Out in the backyard again I amble about shaking my head and putting my hands in my pockets and taking them out again. Elaine is at work. Jamie at school. I have rung the office and told them I won't be in. All morning I mope in the yard, waiting for something to happen, absurdly, expecting the axe to show like a prodigal son. Nothing.

Going inside at noon I notice a deep trench in the verandah post by the back door; it is deep and wide as a heavy axe-blow and I feel the inside of it with my fingers – only for a moment – before I hurry inside trying to recall its being there before. Surely.

I sit by the cold stove in the kitchen in the afternoon, quaking. Is someone trying to kill me? My God.

4

Again Elaine has turned her sumptuous buttocks against me and gone to sleep dissatisfied and I lie awake with my shame and the dark around me.

Some nights as a child I crept into my parents' room and wormed my way into the bed between them and slept soundly, protected from the dark by their warm contact.

Now, I press myself against Elaine's sleeping form and cannot sleep with the knowledge that my back is exposed.

After an hour I get up and prowl about the house, investigating each room with quick flicks of light switches and satisfied grunts when everything seems to be in order. Here, the room where my mother read, here, Jamie's room where I slept as a boy, here, where my father drank his hot, milkless tea in the mornings.

I can think of nothing I've done to offend the neighbours – I'm not a dog baiter or anything – though some of them grumbled about my putting my parents into the Home, as though it was any of their business.

I keep thinking of axe murders, things I've read in the papers, horrible things.

In the living room I take out the old Scrabble box and sit with it on my knee for a while. Perhaps I'll play a game with myself …

5

This morning when I woke in the big chair in the living room I saw the floor littered with Scrabble tiles like broken, yellowing teeth. Straightening my stiff back I recalled the dream. I dreamt that I saw my body dissected, raggedly sectioned up and battered and crusted black with blood. The axe, the old axe with the taped hickory handle, was embedded in the trunk where once my legs had joined, right through the pelvis. My severed limbs lay about, pink, black, distorted, like stockings full of sand. My head, to one side, faced the black ceiling, teeth bared, eyes firmly shut. Horrible, but even so, peaceful enough, like a photograph. And then a boy came out of the black – it was Jamie – and picked up my head and held it like a bowling ball. Then there was light and my son opened the door and went outside into the searing suddenness of light. He walked out into the backyard and up to the chopping block in which an axe – *the* axe – was poised. I felt nothing when he split my head in two. It was a poor stroke, but effective enough. Then with half in either hand – by the hair – he slowly walked around the front of the house and then out to the road verge and began skidding the half-orbs into the paths of oncoming cars. I used to do that as a boy; skidding half pig-melons under car wheels until nothing was left but a greenish, wet pulp. Pieces of my head ricocheted from chassis to bitumen, tyre to tyre, until there was only pulp and an angry sounding of car horns.

That does it; I'm going down to the local hardware store to buy another axe. It's high time. I have thought of going to the police but it's too ludicrous; I have nothing to tell: someone has stolen my axe that used to be my father's. A new axe is what I need.

It takes a long time in the Saturday morning rush at the hardware and the axes are so expensive and many are shoddy and the sales boy who pretends to be a professional axeman tires me with his patter. Eventually I buy a Kelly; it costs me forty dollars and it bears a resemblance to my father's. Carrying it home I have the feeling that I'm holding a stage property, not a tool; there are no signs of work on it and the head is so clean and smooth and shiny it doesn't seem intended for chopping.

As I open the front gate, axe over my shoulder, my wife is waiting on the verandah with tears on her face.

'The Home called,' she says. 'It's your father…'

6

The day after the funeral I am sitting out on the front verandah in the faint yellow sun. My mother will die soon; her life's work is over and she has no reason to continue in her sluggish, crippled frame. It will not be long before her funeral, I think to myself, not long. A tall sunflower sheds its hard, black seeds near me, shaken by the weight of a bird I can't see but sense. The gate squeals on its hinges and at the end of the path stand a man and a boy.

'Yes?' I ask.

The man prompts the boy forward and I see the lad has something in a hessian bag in his arms that he is offering me. Stepping off the verandah I take it, not heeding the man's apologies and the stutterings of his son. I open the bag and see the hickory handle with its gummy black tape and nicks and burrs and I groan aloud.

'He's sorry he took it,' the man says, 'aren't you, Alan? He –'

'Wait,' I say, turning, bounding back up the verandah,

through the house, out onto the back verandah where Elaine and Jamie sit talking. They look startled but I have no time to explain. I grab the shiny, new axe which is yet to be used, and race back through the house with it. Elaine calls out to me, fright in her voice.

In the front yard, the father and son still wait uneasily and they look at me with apprehension as I run towards them with the axe.

'What —' the man tries to shield his son whose mouth begins to open as I come closer.

I hold the axe out before me, my body tingling, and I hold it horizontal with the handle against the boy's heaving chest.

'Here,' I say, 'This is yours.'

. . . .

A Kind of Peace

MARSHALL BROWNE

Something has been quietly corroding Julia's peace of mind, and when she returns to the town where she grew up, for her aunt's funeral, it floats to the surface. Can she face it, this long-ago childhood tragedy? Can she finally consign it to the depths? The drowning at the centre of this story is all the more compelling because it is never fully spelt out.

Through a parched and eerily empty landscape Julia drove north, travelling unconfidently to the funeral of the woman who'd brought her up. On the horizon, the dead-straight road shimmered, crazily. Like her nerves. Not much fun, Julia, she murmured.

Her aunt's death wasn't the predominant matter in her mind, and she felt guilty about that. Carl, the avid user of hackneyed proverbs, might've quipped: 'Killing two birds with one stone, Julia?' But then Carl knew nothing of the dream which had begun two months ago.

It was an incandescent noon, eye-aching, even behind sunglasses. She steered around the long arc of an embankment, her eyes riding the curve to where the old bridge on the state border waited. What a survivor! It looked blown up, carelessly re-assembled in a spindly construct of bone-dry timbers. A grey ghost, even in her childhood. Cautiously, Julia drove across it, remembering fatal accidents. Under the car-wheels, rough-hewn planks thundered and heaved like muscles. Thundering and heaving in her memory. And below slid the river, slime-green as a tortoise's back.

The bridge didn't augur well for the town, but the town had seen a modest revival. Hotel's cast-iron balconies were gone, the facades re-born in glitzy ceramic. Street clean, shops neat. But *The Sentinel* building still looked like something on a Hollywood wild west film lot. Smack-bang on its patch of tough buffalo grass sat the stone memorial to the 1914–18 fallen. 'Remember me,' each name on its marble tablet had whispered in Julia's teenage mind.

R.I.P., she thought now.

Sweeping her eyes from side to side, she drove on.

The hearse and twenty or so cars were parked at the church. From its steeple, the single bronze bell winked at the river. Carl will be here, she thought.

The service was brief. The old lady had outlived her contemporaries. Present were nieces, nephews, a few grown children of her dead friends. The pastor spoke of her country-woman's life. Julia brushed at a tear, Aunt had been brought up to expect the worst, and had brought them up the same. A rough kind of talisman for a life's journey. Carl had wasted no time in shedding it. Like a snakeskin, she thought.

'Rest in peace,' the pastor intoned. She and Carl sat together, afterwards stood together.

Relentless sun, relentless flies. 'A stinker,' Aunt would've said.

'See you back at the house?' Julia said to Carl. He nodded. He was going to the cemetery with the men.

Julia drove out along the river road. She thought: It's falling down. The house looked adrift on a swell of spear-grass. The verandah's roof sagged, the roof-iron was rusted, weatherboards split and sun-seared. A few cars had arrived. From the homestead track, a sand-soft plume of dust rose to smear a ceramic sky as blue as Aunt's best dinner plates.

I wish I could leave *now*.

But she had to go down to that place at the river; and she needed to talk to Carl.

Beginning in this house, all her life Julia had had vivid dreams. Dreams that frightened, mystified, pleased her in a rough-handed equality. But the dream on the night of her fiftieth birthday two months ago, and nights since, was something else. How could you describe it? A force, a call to action? Yet with a soft, back-slipping quality – a sly elusiveness – redolent of the river of her childhood, of its muddy banks, of a shy child being pushed into a group by a guiding hand.

To remember something? The pressure had built up, and she couldn't cope with pressure.

It repeated the same scene: she and Carl, five-year-olds, down by the river acting their parts – squabbling, pushing, competing, each vying to float the miniature paddle-steamer. Above them on the bank, the small white figure watching. 'Go 'way,' Carl said. 'Take a powder.'

She awoke, heart thudding, and the dream dissipated.

Then Aunt had died.

She parked the car and stared at the house. 'Relax. Feel the stillness. That's all you have to do.' The video from her Transcendental Meditation class was running in her mind. She breathed deeply.

Aunt kept the house dark in summer. Dark meant cool, and airless. You were blind as a bat when you went outside, or came in. If there was a breeze on summer evenings the windows were opened and the curtains billowed out in the kerosene lamp-light. Exotic dancers. Stuff like that ... easy to remember.

Now, the blurry women with smudged figures passed through the rooms with trays of tea, sandwiches, beer, speaking sparingly, quietly. A few stood yarning in corners; most were still coming from the cemetery.

Julia drifted through the rooms. Five years since she'd last visited. She'd written from her messed-up life, too ashamed to come. Same furniture, same positions. These rooms at the heart of the house were cherished; rooms on the periphery were closed up. She opened doors.

The country had taken the garden first. If you had known it and remembered, you could find traces of the terraces, the formal rose garden, the gravel paths. Residual lineaments of beauty – as on Aunt's face. A few ornamental trees survived. Gnarled markers.

'Julia has a fertile imagination,' Aunt said. 'And she's such a kind and considerate child.'

She stepped out of a side door. Instantly blind. Behind her, a restrained laugh. Ahead, down the slope and across the vanished garden ran the iron water-pipe. Their path to the river. She couldn't see the river, only the tree line in a slack-bellied loop. Grasshoppers shrilled at full volume. Her nerves quivered, the head-splitting sound terminated in a deadly pause, resumed in a different pitch. She stepped off creaking boards into rustling grass.

The path was gone but she followed the pipeline. The dry grass scratched at her legs. The sun burned through her silk dress. A brown snake slid away into the grass; she stopped and watched it go, plotting its line of departure. 'Like a good girl.'

The gully, looking smaller, was still there. Dense with dried thistles. Insistent whisperers. She walked along the top of its eroded bank, looked ahead and saw the river. Sleek. Shiny. The million gleams hurt her eyes; sunglasses were in the car. She went on down, head aching.

Off to her right, giant river gums guarded stagnant lagoons. Ibis waded in slow motion, frogs croaked, fat purple leeches ... waited. The smell of decaying matter oozed on the meanest of hot breezes. She had it all. A no-go place.

Here. Below. The small beach, a minuscule crescent of floodplain sand pierced by tree roots overshadowed by the giant rock. She lowered herself down into the crunching coolness. Into her childhood.

Carl had the paddle-steamer, holding it in his hand, ploughing it across the gentle eddies of the backwater. She looked up, almost vertically, to the bank. The small white figure stared down at them. She blinked to see it better. It watched them, finger in mouth. Voices were a short way along the river. It was absorbed in what they were doing. Carl looked up, and lifted the steamer out of the water. 'Go 'way,' he said. They ignored it. But it stayed, a silent presence taking part in their game. 'Take a powder!' Carl threatened, using Uncle Max's expression.

The outer limits of the dream. Suddenly, like a tunnel opening through morning river-mist: *She crawled up through the tree roots and lifted the child under the arms, hardly more weight than a doll, and slithered down to the beach*. It had flashed to her with the points of light from the water. Her heart beat quickly.

Nothing more. Her voice startled her: 'Memory or dream?' The words echoed over the water.

They'd go to the river, slipping away from Aunt absorbed in her gardening, reluctantly returning to her distant calls. Coming and going their secret way. But the child in white?

Concentrate, Julia. Go back to the beginning. She stood stock-still, the sucking of the water in her head. Lips compressed, hands on hips, she drove her mind back to the child in white.

'Not the way' – the master's voice. Gradually, she let it go, as if fingers were being released from her own. She'd read books about memory – 'study it up, Julia' – they were as nebulous as this wandering, time-haunted river.

Mid-stream, a fish jumped as one had forty-five years ago.

'I've been down to the river,' Julia said.

'You look washed out.' Carl was smiling.

'Do you remember our days of going down there?' she asked.

He looked at her, curiously. 'I remember.'

But he wasn't remembering. Not the right time; not *the* time.

'The redfin would come on the bite at dusk. Among the snags.'

'*Earlier* than that.'

'Earlier?' He looked again at her face in the gloom.

One of the books had quoted Shakespeare: 'Call back yesterday, bid time return.' Easier said than done. And with tricky possibilities. Leastways, for a mind like hers.

Julia held a cup of tea. 'A wonderful lady,' the woman said, moving on. The house had become crowded with such figures. Some had up-ended small tables and chairs and were peering at them.

'How far can you remember back, Carl?'

'That's hard. Prompt me.'

She was cautious. 'The boat trip to the island with the wild pony.'

'Can't say I do.'

'No. I thought not.'

'You detect some deficiency there, Julia? I'm in computers. I know about electronic memories. That's enough to keep me busy.' He laughed, slipped her a look.

Poor old Julia, doing some back-tracking, pushing up dead-ends.

Watching his face, she stared back. The smug bastard.

Making peace, he said, 'Aunt's tagged everything. There's a master list on her desk. Want to see what you've scored?'

He peered at the list. Our old bedroom, he said. They walked through the house. Every stick of furniture, every vase, had small neatly printed adhesive labels attached.

The two beds were together. On his were a stack of books, and a cricket bat. He took up the bat. 'What do you know? I spent hours brushing turpentine into the blade.' He'd never used it in a match; it'd been too good.

She looked at her own stack of books, the china dolls laid out in a row.

There was a silver bangle. She stared at it.

'What's this?' he said.

She turned. He was holding a miniature paddle-steamer. 'I don't remember this? Do you?'

She turned away, the silver bangle in her fingers. It had been cleaned. The intricate, etched chasing around it was old-fashioned and beautiful. A baptismal thing.

Out of her mind's stream, like that fish jumping: a tiny, white wrist and the bangle slipping off ...

Carl was half-talking to himself. Julia stared at the gleaming circle in her hands. *The space in the skirting board, behind the chest of drawers.* It had been there, had been forgotten there. But how had it got there? She waited for more, but in vain.

'That's pretty,' Carl said.

Julia stayed the night at the motel. The air-conditioner purring away lulled her to sleep and there was no dream. She'd left the house before dusk, declined a cousin's dinner invitation, and eaten alone, thinking over the day.

Overnight, the bangle rested on the dressing-table.

What comes next? When she dreamed that dream again, would it have her lifting the tiny white figure down the bank? Would the bangle be in it now? On that tiny, white wrist, slipping off?

Washed out, Carl had said.

In the hard morning light, in the mirror, she looked at herself. The day had begun its inexorable grind into heat but in the room she felt as cold as ice.

You're sick, Julia. A sick woman, with a beat-up mind and a memory as rotten as a white-anted floorboard. Was *this* the seam of poison in her mind, finally working its way to the surface?

She drove to the *Sentinel*. Nothing moved in the street, or in her mind, except the suspicion, seeping like a slow-bleed into a cloth. She wondered if she had the strength to do this.

A curious look, and the young woman brought her the bound book for the 1930s year. She sat down and began to turn the yellowed pages. An hour passed, and she asked for the year following. The history of the town passed before her eyes. Births and deaths, droughts and good seasons, agricultural shows, balls and fetes. Another war had come and gone.

She turned pages steadily, scanned carefully. Her eyes moved, her hand moved. The black headline in old-fashioned print shot up at her:

Thirty-month Girl Missing in River
Feared Drowned

. . . . .

Her eyes consumed the helter-skelter lines. Missed after five minutes by her picnicking family ... several boats searched the river … fifty men tramped the banks until dark, continued at dawn. Briefer reports the next week, and the next: the child's body not found.

Julia sat in her car for a long time staring across the street; staring into her mind like a hawk riding the air currents, watching the wrinkled terrain for tell-tale movement.

Nothing more. Nothing more than the dream had presented, the river had flashed to her, the placing of the silver bangle on her bed and the newspaper file had yielded.

Had Aunt, heartsick, watching over them all those years ago, also had a dream, been impelled at the last to break her silence?

Unconsciously, Julia started the car and drove up the main street. The bridge looked even more decrepit. She thought: an accident waiting to happen. She turned on to it. The sun flooded into her eyes. Something small and white moved in the blinding haze. Her heart froze, she braked hard. The car swerved, hit the left-hand rail with a bang, and skidded back to the centre. 'Take it easy,' the master said.

She drove on across the bridge. Her hands were locked on the steering-wheel. The old planks were heaving and shuddering, intoning a complaining goodbye. She drove south. Carl would be driving north with his deadly amiability, back to his computer software, his $200,000 package. And she, back to the real world of two failed marriages, a nervous breakdown, therapy, meditation.

Yet now, perhaps, a kind of peace.

She had stopped on the bridge, not to inspect the damage but to drop the silver circle, down, down, perfect and glittering, to the sliding water, and down into her mind, 'the treasury and guardian of all things'.

. . . .

Word from Stan

BILL COLLOPY

Old Albie likes to sit on his front verandah, staring out at the street for the postman, a neighbour, anybody. But the real visitors are his memories. As the present recedes, what's behind it creeps closer: his war, his dead wife, his lost son. Collopy deftly interweaves them into a single, fading consciousness.

A shot cracks his house. It's the metal roof, expanding in day heat. He should be used to it by now. But he's dropped his cup of tea. Finding a cloth to mop up the spill Albie gathers shards of bone china, Geraldine's last uncracked one. He doesn't have the strength to swear. Instead he strolls out to stand by his gate. Men from the Shire have planted new trees in mounds along the footpath. Sun is cooking his scalp. He retreats to verandah shade where he sits and fidgets, rubbing the remaining thatch on his head. In a cane chair so parched that it peels he is tapping toes.

'Morning, Albie,' calls a young woman wheeling her pram past.

He forgets her name, watching legs and an infant in blue wrap, whose name is ... can't remember. His recall of older events is in fine shape. The further back he goes, the clearer it becomes. There is a stamp of feet, with scraping voices and a sergeant's face. Albie studies skin-leather contours like a map while standing on parade. Though sun presses his head into his shoulders he can still do a roll call of nicknames for each enlisted man in his company, including the non-coms. He counts as they march up a gangway, to ship out for the Middle East.

Albie is lying in a field hospital. Shrapnel throbs in his thigh, a wound infected during his escape. He blinks away sand stinging as the desert wind rears up. Simoom, they call this one. Such odd names they have for things like wind and rain. He runs. Shellfire. Mortars. In a village he shoots a soldier. But it's an old man, last line of resistance, pouring petrol into a well. With a final choke the old man curses. Albie hears sobbing, then finds the girl. She's been left behind, forgotten, not grieving for the dead old man, and maybe even grateful. There are marks on her legs and shoulders. She's fifteen years old, perhaps sixteen. They are mere miles from the fighting. There is no food or water. He tastes her love in mended sheets. Her skin is without blemish, aromatic as spice. He knows that rescue is no longer possible. German tanks close in, ripping the sands, a steel simoom. But he wakes in another bed. His limbs have been bathed and bandaged. A nurse swabs him. Faint details print the retina, from a rout, his salvation. Then papers intrude. Already he's being demobbed with other diggers, stretchered home entire, without even a smoker's cough, while mates remain under Egypt sand. He wonders what happened to that girl.

Seas churn his stomach. Parched, despite gallons of drinking water, Albie is twisting in his bunk. The ocean pitches nightmares of mustard gas and trench mud: his father's war. Albie has been fighting Rommel in terrain stripped of leafy cover and civilians – like a crusader of old – with a little help from Kiwis and Poms. He returns home without injury, to spend weeks with family. Then the army sends him to New Guinea.

On a verandah his tongue clicks the soft palate. The pram lass is chatting to some neighbour. A passing car drowns her words. She's not much older than that Arab girl who may have carried his child. Warm work this –

sitting and waiting. Albie's mouth rasps. A killing sun. And such dust …

No volume of beer or ice water slakes the Cairo thirst. Their sepia faces are shaded by slouch hats. Once home they separate into civilian lines. Albie remains under hat shade, unwilling to come out, to admit to Geraldine how things really are. He keeps back the buggery and blood, and a danger-relish of love. Too much remorse. He never describes the game of football they make with a German helmet, its German head still inside. Nor does he relate the sport of tormenting prisoners, other men's sons. He's supposed to swear faith – for monarch and country – each year as Remembrance Day comes around. Albie knows the drill, shutting down his feelings. He does the soldier squint, speaking verse. Those that are left grow old. But he cannot forget. Acids of anger scratch his insides.

The pram girl departs. He catches a glimpse of her legs, with a gurgle or two from the child, some little boy with grandparents and a home.

Staring at foothills so far off they seem indigo, Albie photographs Geraldine in her white-banded hat, honey-mooning in the Blue Mountains. Not a great beauty, she has that smile, and infinite tolerance. Never a cross word between them can he recall, other than a spat about naming their baby. Albie prefers Peter, his father's name, but Geraldine gets her way. The child is christened Stanley, after her brother killed in Singapore. At the Baptism her Dad recites a poem, composed by the hero – namesake and eternal youth. The sight of baby Stanley moves old Jack to tears. His soldier son is said to have written poetry but the verses never reached paper. All Stanley's words might die but for a pair of surviving POWs who rescue one poem, memorising it before Stanley's execution. A grand fellow, they tell old Jack. A top bloke, our Stanley. Geraldine learns the poem by heart.

On his verandah Albie curses, unable to recall more than one phrase.

In a compass of our mind, the sum we leave behind ...

Words forgotten cut him adrift. He notices the girl with the pram but loses his labels, detached from people: from Geraldine, from Stan.

Gold-curled, the baby is – some say – the image of that late uncle. Geraldine's old Dad reckons Heaven has sent them an angel, for the one God has taken home. Stanley. Little Stan the man.

Albie shivers, despite morning heat, as if vandals are digging up his grave. He can feel fire again, sniff its smoke. Stanley is waking them, running down the corridor screaming.

'Everyone get out ...'

Albie and Geraldine scramble outside in pyjamas. In moments the flames are licking their house. Little Stanley becomes a hero, courtesy of the local paper. School and Shire officials make such fuss. Albie tells everyone the fire is an accident. Seven years old, cherub-eyed, Stanley is a photogenic boy whose parents have lost heirlooms and photos and medals. The congregation takes up a collection.

Albie pats his pockets, searching for... he can't recall. The TV remote perhaps. Or he may have forgotten to turn off the gas. He's given up wearing a watch. Often he forgets about meals. Not only does he struggle to fix names to townsfolk he can't think what to call those flowers around the war memorial, or that pipe tune at the dawn service. He does know the names of dead cricketers and discontinued brands of cigarette. His face darkens, as though biting on rage.

'Bloody thing ...'

He can't retrieve lines from a simple little poem.

Craning towards his street, Albie continues to watch for the postman. Tom is due to cycle past any time now, hat angled to the sun ... Or is it Tim ... ? Heat presses on the verandah shade, trickling sweat from scalp to singlet. Thirsty work, this waiting. A few years ago Albie would be down at the Lord Liverpool by this hour. But a Vietnamese doctor has warned him off booze. And smokes. No Geraldine any more, no fags and no beer. There's not much for a bloke to look forward to each morning, unless the postie stops for a chat.

'Mate, people don't write letters any more, except for banks ...'

Albie writes to Geraldine at the base hospital during her training. He reads her replies during lunch behind the shop: a busy boy, leaving school to help his father run the grocery, though he lacks a future there, intending to quit town and try his luck in the big smoke. Instead he takes a shine to Geraldine, younger sister of a classmate. The brother surprises everyone by signing up. Stanley fibs his age and off he goes, later becoming an officer with the 2/11 field regiment. He writes to tell his sister how exciting it is, what a privilege to serve. Stanley's whereabouts remain secret, sections of the page blacked out. He knows it will happen, yet still he writes.

Albie volunteers too, against Geraldine's wishes. He says he'll be all right. His parents are so proud and so worried. All the young men go. Four summers later Albie returns, though another son and many school-friends do not. His eldest brother comes back from Kokoda in a wheelchair. The Japanese kill Stanley, decapitating him with a sword.

The whole town assembles for a memorial service. Geraldine shows Albie one last letter from her brother, which talks of new manoeuvres, without poetry.

An old man shakes, angry enough to rip newspaper. He often does that, getting it delivered then shredding the pages with his hands. He can no longer read close print.

'Damn bloody thing ...'

He obtains a position with the Shire pay office, a quiet desk job. The Middle East has been bad but the New Guinea jungle is worse. Leaf and branch drip with waiting death. Once home he loses the wish to run off and seek glory. He asks Geraldine to marry him, takes up accounts work, becoming the Shire paymaster. Upon retirement Albie has made it to town clerk, a post of respect. But by then he's lost Geraldine and his son.

Returning from an errand the pram girl passes by, sturdy looking, with tanned arms and legs. She waves. Despite straining he can't find her name. He does remember her grandfather, a sapper who lost an eye in North Africa. In the heat shimmer Albie spies a trellis where tomatoes peep from a neighbour's fence. His own crops fail. Crows get in first. He has read a few novels but his eyesight begins to fail. He adopts a cat that sleeps on his bed, a patch of warmth at night. He holds conversations with Puss about the desert, describing its barrenness and forbidden fruit. The animal is wretched, almost deaf. One night she gets skittled by a touring coach.

On his verandah Albie likes to sit until dusk, drifting inside to warm up soup, maybe thumb TV channels and stare at blurred homemaker shows. He refuses to watch hospital drama, having seen too many surgical wards during Geraldine's radiation treatment. Hiding under a scarf she loses hair and strength, disintegrating piece by piece. He accompanies her to a big city hospital, reading doctors' pamphlets in language he can't follow. Whenever she's feeling well enough Geraldine insists on attending Mass, to sing hymns, to take Holy Communion. Albie can remember his mother in a black mantilla, with the words in Latin as scrubbed altar boys bear the Blessed Sacrament, eyes down, innocent as little Stanley.

In New Guinea a young man finds the Devil at work. What Albie and other diggers must do is not recorded on the newsreels. They blow up bodies. They sever torsos. He finds prayer increasingly difficult. Arriving home, draped in hero colours, he becomes a married man, with a child. His boy grows up and moves away. Then his wife gets sick, fighting a war. Cancer eats her. As clear as last week Albie can remember sudden emptiness, a moment when he finally gave up on God, witnessing Geraldine die by inches and then yards. She lingers in remission before the seams split open. Life ebbs without dignity. Albie cannot continue to believe in mercy.

She has been buried some years when Stan finally writes. Only just heard about his mother. So very sorry. A letter from Thailand, where he is detained on a minor possession charge. Can his Dad send money for a lawyer? Stan promises to write again, maybe phone. Months pass. At last Albie does get a long-distance call, from some stranger, accent-thick, saying that Stan wants his old man to know before it appears in the papers.

Albie insists on going. He writes to ambassadors, aid agencies, even the RSL. Words are air. People warn that he'll get no special treatment. He staggers from one interview to the next. Memory flickers like a TV remote: rooms of light dazzling and smudged faces. He bumps into reporters, a footsore digger walking Asian streets and wishing for an ounce of Geraldine's strength. Men in suits fob him off with documents, preventing him from seeing his boy, allowing him to read only the one letter, thanks to a sympathetic prison officer, though he's not allowed keep it and cannot lay eyes on the author.

Friends have all dried up, writes Stan. *There's only my old Dad left ...*

The jungle veteran sees himself on video replay, a white-haired fool tripping on camera cable, microphones in his face, embarrassing officials and countrymen.

Stan writes.

On my way home, Dad ...

His boy is joining him on their old verandah. Down the main street Stan swaggers, hair swishing in a breeze, cricket bat under his arm. He breaks town girls' hearts all over again. He and Albie are sitting side by side; talking about this or that scrape the lad has been in, sharing a cold beer and laughing fit to burst.

Whack ... !

The roof again. Albie's street is empty: no pretty girl or pram or postmen. He listens for one human voice, even a motor. Perhaps his hearing too is finally packing up. Then he catches the school bell and has no need to see children swarming their playground. He listens to a vehicle passing and can imagine the nod from a young constable at its wheel. Not Albie's first experience with the law.

Seventeen years old, Stan is stealing from Geraldine's handbag when his father catches him. Albie stares into eyes no longer angelic but rimmed red. The boy's skin is chalky, chest and cheeks hollow. His parents have been praying it will stop. But enough is enough. Albie throws the boy out. He can get himself a job, ungrateful wretch. Geraldine is angry, yet wanting to forgive. She prays for Stan. At twenty-one he returns, on parole. Valuables soon start to go missing. Albie has given their son every chance. No more. He kicks Stan out, for good this time. Geraldine writes to every last known address, for years. Not a word.

Snap … !

Like a firing squad, that one. Albie can almost feel the metal breaking: a gun salute of his roof. After all these years he should be used to it. But today feels strange. Odours taste fresh: each sound, each memory. He hasn't thought about that Arab girl in years, wondering whether he has sired a half-and-half child in a foreign land. He sniffs ripe tomatoes from vines next door. He can feel every creak and rustle, as if brand new. Windows on the house opposite blink behind great glasses. A pink door speaks. Weatherboards stretch arms.

Piece by piece Albie is re-assembling that first home: a bungalow with shutters, a lemon tree, a terrier, Geraldine – and the beautiful baby. A doctor is explaining that Stanley can have no brothers or sisters – some problem of blood grouping. Albie cherishes that boy as if his own life does not matter.

Squeaking of wheels. Finally. Leaning forward he feels confident this must be the postman coming into view, stop-start cruising from house to house. A man calls across the bitumen, no doubt sweating under a hat.

'How are we today, Albie? Another warm one …'

With a push of legs the postman cycles on, armpits probably wet, not needing to cross the street today.

Albie rises, with a back and neck stiff. He shuffles down

the path then strains his gaze beyond the fence: no sign of legs or postie or schoolchildren. Empty as a ghost town. He trundles inside to put on the kettle.

At a table sits a man with no envelope in his hands, fingering grain in the timber. He turns pages in his mind, tracing for the thousandth time a letter from a Bangkok cell. A thin figure pores over paper, writing appeal letters that authorities will not forward. He rests his head on a table, smelling wood.

. . . .

DISUNITIES

A Mixed Marriage

LILY BRETT

Lola, mundanely married, discovers love and leaves her husband, to the horror of her parents. Brett plays out a familiar story against the rituals of Melbourne Jewishness, writing with a simplicity that gives the narrative the seeming inevitability of a folktale.

From the day that Lola fell in love with another man, her husband smelt bad. The smell was like stale, sweet cheese. It came from his body and hovered in a thick net around the bed. It made Lola feel bilious.

She began sleeping with the window open. For thirty-five years she had lived with deadlocks, combination locks and iron bolts; her home security system was updated annually. Now, her fear of rapists, burglars and murderers paled next to the horror of the smell.

It came from his ears, his feet, his hands and his neck. She could smell it in the bathroom when he showered. In the kitchen, it crept across the breakfast table. It soaked into her coffee and filtered itself through her grapefruit juice.

Was Rodney suspicious? Was this his body's reaction? Like a skunk putting out a stink when it feels in danger?

But Rodney didn't know that she was in love with anyone but him. She had been devotedly faithful to him for thirteen years. More than that, they were the ideal couple. Lola loved the image of herself, a dark, wild-haired, large-eyed Jewess, standing next to the tall, pale son of the city's establishment.

The smell lodged itself in Lola's throat. She was unable to eat. She got up and called to her children through the intercom system. 'Kids, we have to leave in five minutes or you'll be late for school.' Lola had never been late for anything. In all her years of psychotherapy, she had not missed one minute of one session. Lola liked to deliver her children to their schools an hour early. This allowed time for possible delays due to heavy traffic, a flat tyre, a mechanical failure or other emergencies. Lola felt that she would be able to tackle any emergency clear-headedly, secure in the knowledge that she would still be on time.

. . . . .

The night before Lola's first day at school, her mother had sat her down for a talk. The family had been in Australia for three years. Mr and Mrs Bensky worked behind sewing machines in a factory during the day, and behind sewing machines at home at night. 'Lolala, my Lolala,' Mrs Bensky said. 'You will be in a school now with Australian children. I want you always to remember that a Jewish boy will make you the best husband. Australian boys, they learn from their fathers to drink beer and to smack their wives. My Lolala, what do you know what it is to be smacked? To be treated worse than a dog?'

Lola couldn't imagine anyone smacking the beautiful Mrs Bensky. She knew that the Nazis had. They had tattooed a number on Mrs Bensky's slender strong arm. Lola told anyone who asked that this number was their new phone number.

'Lolala, look at Mrs Stein's daughter. She married someone who is not Jewish. A nice man he seemed. An accountant. Look at her Lolala. Three children, no money, dirty everything. He is in the pub every day straight after work, then he comes home and gives her a nice klup on the head. That's what will happen to you, Lolala, if you marry an Australian.'

Lola wasn't surprised at this prospect of violence. Lola

knew that she didn't yet know half of how frightening the world was. She did know that there was danger everywhere, and that life was a series of narrow escapes. By the time she was thirteen she had a highly evolved, complex system of warding off evil. She had to touch all the doorknobs and cupboard handles in her bedroom ten times each in the correct order, from left to right, before going to bed. Then she could sleep.

On Sunday nights the world looked better to Lola. In the afternoon Mrs Bensky would bake a sponge cake. It always came out with a soft crown covering, like lightly spun velvet. Next she laid out the bowls. A bowl of dark, shiny chocolates, a bowl of delicately sprigged branches of muscatel raisins scattered with almonds, a bowl of black, fat prunes, and a bowl of fruit-flavoured boiled lollies.

Then she prepared supper. It was always the same. Grated egg and spring onion salad, schmalz herring, smoked mackerel, chopped liver, dill pickles, radish flowers, sliced tomatoes, some rye bread and some matzoh. After that, she unfolded four card tables and chairs and arranged them in the small lounge room. At four o'clock Mr and Mrs Bensky had a nap for an hour. By eight o'clock the air was scented with heady perfume and cigarettes. Mrs Ganz's long, polished nails sparkled as she dealt the cards. Lola loved Mrs Ganz's husky voice and the way that her breasts moved with her breath.

Mr Ganz argued with Mr Berman: 'Chaim, you are an idiot! You walk with your eyes shut. You will be finished if you go into partnership with such an idiot like Felek Ganzgarten. You mustn't do it.'

'Gentlemen, gentlemen,' Mr Bensky admonished them in his most formal English.

Mrs Small sang in a low voice as he played. 'Motl, Motl vos vat sein mit dir, der Rabbi sogt du kanst nisht lernen,' she sang – 'Morris, Morris what is going to become of you, the Rabbi says you are not learning.'

And Mr Small, as usual, slipped Lola a couple of very expensive, large, chocolate-covered liqueur prunes. Mr Zelman whistled an old Polish lullaby as he smoothly swept his winnings over to his corner.

Sometimes the hum of the room was low and calm, and other times the atmosphere was feverish. Moves were disputed, news was dispensed, rumours were scotched or debated, advice was given and taken, and money was won and lost.

Mrs Bensky never played cards. She made cups of black lemon tea, refilled the glasses of soda water, emptied the ashtrays and served the supper.

. . . . .

Driving the children to school, Lola remembered Rodney, twenty three years old, his speech almost a stutter that was expelled in short bursts. He had looked much happier when he was not speaking. And Lola was then free to imagine his thoughts.

One day, Rodney told her that he was never going to marry. He said that he would be too worried that his wife would leave him. This revelation was at odds with Lola's understanding of Rodney. She saw him as independent, self-contained and peaceful. The thought of not being the one who had to worry about being left appealed to Lola. Six weeks later they were married.

Lola and Rodney became good friends. They laughed together. They blossomed as parents and were bound together by a fierce pride in their two beautiful and clever children.

For the first few years of the marriage, Lola was captivated and wholly satisfied by Rodney's blondness. She would lie awake next to him for hours, looking at the golden hairs on his arms.

. . . . .

Lola dropped the children off and parked the car in the supermarket car park. She walked to a taxi rank and caught a taxi to Garth's apartment.

In the taxi, the lies, the deception and the tension of the last month visited Lola briefly, but her happiness crept up and covered her.

Garth was waiting for her. His smile looked as though it might lift him off the ground. He trembled as he held her. He had prepared coffee. She watched him pour the coffee.

The first time they made love, Lola had felt like a virgin. She and Rodney had shuffled in and out of sex comfortably, companionably. Now she ached. She had forgotten what it was like to ache for a man. It felt like a violin screaming between her legs.

That evening at dinner, Rodney said, 'I think Garth Walker is in love with you.'

'What?' she said.

'I've seen the way he looks at you,' Rodney answered. 'He doesn't take his eyes off you. He talks to the kids and he looks at you. He talks to me and he looks at you.'

'Don't be silly,' said Lola. She felt bilious.

'It's infatuation,' said Lola's closest friend, Margaret-Anne. 'It wears off. After a few years you and Garth will be like you and Rodney. It's not worth the bother.'

Lola fantasised about finding another wife for Rodney.

She would find someone intelligent, well-read and with a good sense of humour, and they could all be friends. They could buy a small block of flats and create two large apartments. They could eat together. They could share holidays. And the children wouldn't miss out. The prospect of this happy communal life made Lola feel exhausted.

. . . . .

Lola knew it wasn't going to be easy to tell Mrs Bensky that she was going to leave Rodney.

'So, Hitler didn't kill me, now you are going to do it for him!' screamed Mrs Bensky.

Mr Bensky said: 'I lived through the labour camp to hear this news? I wish I would have died.'

Mrs Bensky rang Rodney to tell him that she would do his laundry. She said she didn't want Rodney to suffer the humiliation of having his clothes washed by a wife who was in love with someone else.

Lola had not had such an effect on her parents since the day she told them that she was going to marry Rodney.

'Lolala, Lolala, how can you do this to us?' Mrs Bensky had wailed. 'What will our friends say? They will say that we didn't bring you up properly. They will say that we should have sent you to Mount Scopus, not to an Australian school. Lola, get me some Stemetil. I feel sick.'

Now, Mr and Mrs Bensky were hysterical. 'Lola, you and Rodney were our big hope, our example of how a mixed marriage can work. Everyone says what a wonderful man Rodney is and what a wonderful couple you are. Lolala, wake up!' Mrs Bensky screamed.

For most of her adult life Lola had had trouble waking up. She used to daydream while she was cleaning, while she was driving, while she was reading or watching television, and while people spoke to her. She would nod from time to time, and on the whole no-one noticed.

She had a whole set of fantasies she could slip into. When Mrs Bensky delivered her regular lectures about losing weight, Lola would plug herself into the dream in which she had just completed her fifth best-selling novel. A novel that had made millions of readers weep. A novel that had earned Lola hundreds of thousands of dollars. A novel that had caused passionate debate in dining rooms in Paris, London and New York. Last week, when Mrs Bensky finished her speech, Lola was being interviewed by Johnny Carson on the *Tonight Show*.

. . . . .

When she was with Garth, Lola was wide awake. So awake she could feel every part of her body. She could feel her nervous heart. She could feel her knees. She felt as though she could inhale the earth and touch the stars.

Garth taught her about art. He played her music. Mahler, Satie, Berg, Poulenc, Glass, Stravinsky. He read her poetry. Poems by Akhmatova, Tsvetayeva, Brodsky, William Carlos Williams. Poems by Anne Sexton. And he never stopped looking at her. He looked at her as they walked. He looked at her when they talked. He looked at her while they ate. He looked at her as they made love. And he painted her. He painted her happy and he painted her sad. He painted her pained and he painted her exuberant. He painted her as a madonna and he painted her as a warrior queen, a Boadicea streaking across the canvas. Hundreds of portraits of her were stacked around the walls of his studio.

. . . . .

Mr and Mrs Bensky had observed every detail of Lola's life. What she ate, how often she changed her underwear, who she spoke to in the school ground. Mrs Bensky would watch Lola every lunchtime, after she had delivered her daily hot lunch. Later on, Mrs Bensky kept a record of Lola's menstrual cycle on a chart inside the pantry cupboard. And the intercom system that connected all the rooms in the house was always switched on.

Everything was a potential catastrophe. A sneeze indicated pneumonia, a cough was a sign of asthma, a stomach ache pointed towards kidney and liver trouble. An unexpected knock at the door would leave Mrs Bensky breathless, and if Lola was ever late home from school, Mrs Bensky prepared herself for the worst.

Lola, who still complained that nothing she did escaped her parents' scrutiny, became an observant parent herself. Lola adored her son Julian. For the first year and a half of his life she recorded his every bowel movement. She drew up a chart and headed the columns Time, Size, Consistency and Colour. Another chart recorded every mouthful of food baby Julian swallowed. This was headed Food, Description and Amount, Time, and Attitude.

By the time her daughter, Paradise, was born, Lola was not so intense about being a parent. She allowed Paradise to pat stray dogs and to eat her food from the kitchen floor. Paradise spent hours smudging her meals into the brown quarry tiles under the table before scraping the food into her mouth.

Lola worried about the consequences of allowing Paradise to eat off the floor, but she consoled herself with the thought that at least Paradise was a good eater. Julian was such a fussy eater that Lola had had to pretend that everything she fed him was chicken. Most of Julian's chicken chocolate custard or chicken fruit salad or chicken chops went into Lola.

Mr and Mrs Bensky spent the Saturday afternoons of most summers at St Kilda Beach. The whole gang would go. Mrs Bensky always brought cold boiled eggs and rye bread, and Mrs Ganz made her special carrot and pineapple salad. The Zelmans brought ham and Mr Pekelman brought long cucumbers from his garden.

They sat under the ti-trees on the foreshore, on thick, soft rugs, and ate and drank and talked. The Italian man who sold peanuts was always happy to see them. They bought twelve large bags. Enough peanuts to last until dinner.

Every now and then, someone would go for a dip in the water. Most of the gang couldn't swim. Mrs Bensky was the only good swimmer. She would stride into the water in her gold lamé bikini, or her silver and purple polka-dotted pair, or the green pair covered in latex leaves.

As a child, Lola used to wear lumpy, frilly bathers. They had a gathered yoke and a full skirt, which Mrs Bensky said disguised Lola's hips and thighs.

Now, Lola would soon be able to wear her first pair of bikinis. The weight was dropping off her. Every day she was thinner. Garth satisfied all her appetites and she no longer felt hungry.

. . . . .

At five o'clock, Lola started getting ready to go home. Garth phoned for a taxi and then came and sat down next to her. 'Lola, I love you. I'll always love you. There'll never be anything in my life more important than loving you. I feel as though I was born to be with you.'

The next day, Lola told Rodney that she was moving

out with the children. All he said was, 'Have you slept with him?'

'No,' she lied.

Garth, with his dark hair and large, heavy-lidded eyes, looked Jewish. Lola hoped that the Benskys would see this as progress.

. . . .

From *Lily Brett: Collected Stories*, UQP, 1999

The Milk

JESSICA ANDERSON

Marjorie, late in life, decides to leave her husband Bruce and set up on her own as an illustrator in a cramped flat. Anderson's story flickers with subtle insights into what Marjorie's determination to be independent entails.

When Marjorie's son Emlyn returned to Sydney from Europe, he demanded to see the little flat she had rented but had not yet moved into. She divined his opinion from the way his feet came together in such an abrupt stop on the threshold. 'See the nice broad window sill,' she said, going briefly to sit on it. 'And I shan't be here for ever, you know.'

He was in the tiny kitchen. 'It's not secure,' he shouted.

'What?' She stood beside him. 'What isn't?'

'That.'

'A servery. Oh, good. I didn't notice that.' She opened it with one finger. It was certainly dirty. 'It's for the milk,' she said.

'They put kids through those.'

'Not in these parts, surely. There can't be much to steal.'

'Everyone has a television.'

'I haven't.' She shut the servery. 'It's only for a while,' she coaxed. 'Only till the divorce.'

. . . . .

Although it was one of Marjorie's rules never to do anything drastic in the January heat, it was in January that she had managed at last to convince her husband that she was serious about leaving him.

'No contentious matters at dinner' was another of her principles, but no principle could stand against the momentum gathered, and it was at the dinner table that she achieved that communication.

Bruce rose abruptly. The look on his face was murderous, as was the one brief and thickened sentence he spoke. Even in the immobility of her astonishment, she did not believe he would actually murder her, but did realise that such venom not only made impossible the amicable kind of divorce she had just proposed, but made it impossible for her even to stay in the same house. She packed two suitcases and went to a private hotel suggested in a hurry by her friend Carla. She went by taxi because, while she was packing, Bruce took her car keys.

The hotel, on the northern shores of the harbour, was a place of somnolent residents and saggy beds. 'Well,' said Carla, in Marjorie's room there, 'you did say somewhere cheap.'

Marjorie noticed that Carla avoided looking at her face. 'Poor old Brucie,' said Carla.

This was in 1976. The divorce laws had been reformed the year before, sweeping away grounds such as adultery, cruelty, and desertion, and putting in their place only breakdown of marriage. Carla said, 'He can't believe you can leave him, and not be legally punished.'

'Nonsense. He reads the newspapers.'

'But he can't take it in. It doesn't seem natural.'

'Oh,' said Marjorie, 'I dream about him.'

'He says it must be your change of life.'

'It probably is.'

'Well, Marj, in that case,' said Carla.

'Why shouldn't it be?' said Marjorie. 'Why shouldn't

change of life be like adolescence? The two great changes. So? The two great chances.'

'Chances of what?'

'Exaltation. Remember?'

'Not really.'

'And suddenly seeing the truth. And knowing just how to do things.'

'Oh my,' said Carla. 'Perhaps now you'll be able to draw feet.'

Carla and Marjorie had been at art school together. Carla had become a commercial designer and had continued in it in spite of marriage and children. Marjorie, an illustrator specialising in botany, had dropped that, and all of her training, until the sixties, when, under the influence of a group of local women, she had begun to sculpt in the garage. But, abstract and incisive though her pieces were in conception, all turned out to have a trivial and fiddled-with look. Nor did persistence bring improvement. 'It's the surfaces,' she said. 'Like badly iced cakes.'

But when she returned to small-scale drawing, she found a new enjoyment in her materials, and an excitement in each day's first contact of pen or chalk with paper. She also discovered in herself a reluctance to say anything to anyone about these pleasures. Her stylish and accurate pen drawings soon began to earn her money, but even though the unsparing truth of her instinct told her she would leave Bruce, she did not face that truth to the point of providing for it, and remained lax in commission and shy about naming her price. All her drawings were of plants or objects, although she could usually manage a figure hovering behind the cooking ingredients, or a distant child in the garden. 'With its little feet behind the herbaceous border,' Carla would say. It was often Carla who commissioned these drawings. Now, in the hotel, Carla said, 'It makes it harder to find work for you.'

'I've a book of West Australian wild flowers to do. All from photographs. Easy.'

'Then for God's sake, get it in on time, and see that you get decent money. Have you got a lawyer?'

'Of course not. I always thought Bruce and I would talk, you see, discuss –'

'Oh, Marj, get one, get one.'

'Legally, I am sure I am –'

'Within your rights. Yes, but the law's a new one. Not many precedents. Martin, of course, won't – well, he can't can he?'

Carla's husband, Martin, was a lawyer. 'Of course he can't,' said Marjorie. 'Do you think I expected it?'

'Not really.'

'Does he recommend anyone?'

'No.'

'I see.'

'Sorry.'

'So I'm to be put in solitary.'

'Marj, give people time to get used to it.'

'I can't work here. I'll have to get a flat. Look, there isn't even room for a table. Carla, am I imagining it, or are you really trying not to look at my face?'

Carla laughed, abashed, and picked up her bag. 'It's just that I'm sorry for Brucie.'

But she still did not look at Marjorie's face, kissing her goodbye instead.

. . . . .

All the flats Marjorie saw in the territory familiar to her, the north and east, were too dear. It was Bruce's edict that they should communicate only through lawyers. Marjorie went to see her lawyer, who was named Gwen.

'Look, since I'm not claiming maintenance, or even my full legal share of our property, don't you think Bruce should allow me something to go on with? I've got a thousand or so in my own account, but the rest of it is all muddled up with his. I'm earning, but I must rent a flat, you see, working space. And here is a list of the things I need from the house. Basic, as you see. Bed, table, etcetera. But will you ask about the money?'

Gwen, like Carla, did not look at Marjorie's face, though for a different reason. A big peachy Rubens beauty, she set herself up to be looked at rather than herself do any surveying. She swung aside her waist-length hair and directed at her bookshelves the sweet pensive smile often seen on television, where she spoke on women's affairs. Her voice was very soft.

'I'm afraid he still insists that because you're the one who left, you're not entitled to a cent. Of course under the new act he's wrong, but I'm afraid it does mean that unless you're prepared to put out a good bit of money, you're going to have to wait till the case comes to court.'

'Which will be?'

As she watched Gwen shrug, Marjorie in her imagination cut her hair to shoulder length and removed some of her eye-shadow. She never made these fast and absent-minded rearrangements in the appearance of her friends; they simply seemed to take place of their own accord in suspenseful or awkward moments with people hardly known. 'Will it be,' she asked, 'say, three months?'

'More like six,' said Gwen.

'Then he's just being *mean*,' cried Marjorie, like a child.

'We so often express our injuries through property,' murmured philosophical Gwen.

'What about that list, then? Can Trevor persuade him to let me have those things?'

Trevor was Bruce's lawyer. 'Oh, I expect he can, yes. I'll ring him now.' Gwen put a hand on the phone and gave her delicious smile. 'Leave a hundred with Isolde on the way out, will you?'

. . . . .

Marjorie went south to Newtown, where she found a small flat – one room, kitchenette and bath – with good light, in a big old block set among patched-up terrace houses, small shops, and light industry. Her son Emlyn and his wife Fiona returned from Europe two days before she was to move in. They had heard nothing of the separation. Fiona was agog but amused. 'It gave him a bit of a shock, I bet.' But sweat had broken out under Emlyn's eyes. 'Shut up, Fee. Mum, tell us what we can do to help.'

By now Marjorie was used to people who avoided looking at her face. She understood that Emlyn's modernity was in conflict with his grief and disapproval. All the same, she was pleased to see his censure deflected to Fiona, who only hugged him and said, 'Shut up yourself. Yes, Marj, what can we do?'

'I want to look at this flat you've taken,' said Emlyn, pushing Fiona away. 'Wouldn't you know this would happen when we're overdrawn on our Bankcard?'

'Don't worry. I've two books to do. You can look at the flat tomorrow.' Marjorie smiled at Fiona. 'And on Thursday, if you like, and of course if you can get time off, you two could help me to move. I've got this sore shoulder. Here, at the back.'

'Get it looked at,' said Emlyn with ferocity.

'It was the suitcases. I will go. If you like, you two could go with the carrier to pick up the things Bruce – your father – oh, what shall I call him? – anyway, the things he is letting me have for the flat.'

'You won't fit much in one room,' said Emlyn.

'I adore Newtown,' said Fiona.

'Fee got that dress from Valentino,' said Emlyn.

. . . . .

Marjorie laughed when she saw how Bruce had interpreted her list. A weathered outdoor table with its two slatted chairs, a folding bed, a pale-blue chest of drawers from Emlyn's childhood, a bagful of worn linen and blankets, a box of pots and pans without lids, and her worktable, stool, and the old tea trolley on which she kept her materials. She laughed out of the strained amusement she was finding it more and more easy to summon, and because his meanness relieved her guilt, and because she did not want to further inflame Emlyn, but to co-operate with Fiona in keeping it light and funny.

'Love that window sill,' said Fiona. 'Wow.' She sat on it. 'I want it.'

'Well, mum, if that's really all?'

'Thank you, dears.'

'Come on, Fee. I'm late as hell.'

'See you soon then, Marjie.'

In the doorway Emlyn stopped, as he had done the day before, and morosely surveyed the room. Fiona could be heard running down the stairs. Unzipping the bag she had marked FIRST THINGS, Marjorie hardened herself against her son. She was tired. Her shoulder hurt. There would be cockroaches. Emlyn had himself divorced his first wife (under the old laws) in order to marry Fiona.

'I wish you would let me nail up that bloody servery.'

'I don't know how long they let you park down there, Emlyn.'

As soon as he had gone, Marjorie abandoned the bag and went to the window. As she had hoped, the sill was wide enough, and broad enough, to contain her sitting figure. She sat resting in the embrasure, her legs along the seat, her back against the wall, her face turned to the window.

No tree broke her view of the street, which on this late afternoon was fairly busy with traffic and pedestrians. After a while she noticed that most of the people were burdened. Shabby young mothers bore heavy, sleeping babies. Women were weighted down on both sides with plastic sacks of provisions. Men carried bulging airline bags and packs of beer. Those waiting on the bus seat had bags and cartons on their laps or at their feet. Only the boys and those children not tethered by an adult hand were free. A group of boys, Aboriginal and white, came running. Knocking into each other, yelling, guffawing, inventing dangers, they brought a neat Chinese for a moment to the door of his grocery shop.

When travelling in Europe, Marjorie had looked down from hotel windows on traffic and human activity, but in Sydney she had lived all of her life from infancy in quiet neutral streets, where the neat squat houses were separated by splendid trees, and where almost the only pedestrians were school children. She had nursed a longing for the sea, and after the friendly divorce she had planned from Bruce, she had intended to find a small cottage near the beach where she had spent holidays as a child. She looked down on the street with an alertness that asked for no explanations, as if she were living only with her eyes. The café next to the grocery came alight through its netted shopfront. Lights came on in the terrace houses and revealed people cooking in corners of bedrooms. In the flats a television roared and was cut down. A phone rang; water throttled in a pipe. When heavy steps ascended the stairs outside her door, she was amused to be able to match them with the visible gait of a man she had just seen crossing the street. She got up and went to the peephole in the door.

She had never looked through a peephole before. The man had disappeared, but the distorted perspectives were mesmeric, and kept her there. The corridor looked so long, almost noble, but threatening too, the towering doors curving inward at their height. She told herself that one of those doors must open and admit a figure to her view, and under the alertness of this expectation, the scene grew more and more eerie. It was only a game, but when she withdrew her eye, having seen no figure, she was touched with solemnity.

She turned on the small battery radio Emlyn had left her, seized the bag marked FIRST THINGS, and took from it cleaning gear, a spray can of insecticide, and two rolls of Marimekko paper. She quickly washed the kitchen shelves, the drawers, and the servery, then lined them all with the paper. She refused to care that the chastity of the paper, its gloss and small vivid geometric daisies, made so sad the scarred and discoloured paint. In the room she took from among her work things a piece of card and a felt pen.

. . . . .

MILKMAN – When you see the servery door open,
it means I want milk
Bottles only please. I don't take milk in cartons.   M.T.

She folded the card and set it like a neat tent on the paper. Beside it she put the clean milk bottle she had remembered to bring, and beside that, the exact money. She pushed open the outer door of the servery, and shut the inner one.

She held her breath as she rapidly sprayed insecticide behind the stove and refrigerator and along the skirting boards. On an explosion of breath she staggered out of the kitchen, kicking the door shut behind her so that the poison could lose its first stench while she ate and slept.

Carla had brought to the hotel that morning a little wicker hamper. As Marjorie examined its contents she compared herself to Carla. She would have remembered the wineglass, but forgotten the bottle opener.

She ate and drank in the window embrasure. The wine eased the pain in her shoulder, but relaxed her strained alertness and returned her burden to her. As bad, precisely as bad, as going back to Bruce, was the burden of her guilt. She longed above everything (everything but that) to be forgiven. She jumped up and stood boldly, with one knee on the sill, and finished the wine. She became drunk enough to be quite pleased with the improvisation of the folding bed, and to be comforted by the semblance of a cubby house given by the dim shapes around her of her unpacked, mismatched things.

. . . . .

In her dream, Bruce is hurrying to meet her, as he had done that time at the airport. He almost runs, shouldering his way through the crowd, his face congested with the familiar sizzle before his laughter would break. But in her dream, she was appalled by his joy, as she was at the airport, having brought herself on the long journey to her irrevocable decision. In her dream, indeed, she is not at the airport, but is in the folding bed in the Newtown flat, and Bruce is advancing, one hand extended, across the floor. She sees behind his laughing face the floral curtains she had drawn against the streetlights. She sees her work-table and trolley. She is amazed to be forgiven; the bliss of his forgiveness makes her gasp. She reaches for his hand and sees not the laughing face, but the malevolent face that had looked down on hers as he rose from the dining table. His extended hand would kill her. It presses on the bone between her breasts. She rolls off the bed to escape, and as she scrambles, sobbing, to her feet, she hears a loud crash, and a door slamming. She fumbles along the wall and finds the light switch. The room is exactly as it was when she went to sleep. The crashing is no longer loud; she recognises it as the jiggling of milk bottles in a carrying crate. Her search for the light switch has brought her to the door. She rolls against it and puts her eye to the peephole. Far down the long and stately corridor she sees a dark little gnarled figure running weighted on one side with his milk and disappearing round a corner.

The suffocation in her chest becomes a searing pain. She considers a heart attack, but cannot believe in it. When the pain grips her entrails and forces her to a bowed position, she remembers the wine so quickly drunk. 'Fool!' she sobs. 'Fool!' But she is able to be amused by her ignominious cramped run into the kitchen. Milk will help. Even to envision the calm white bottle on the clean paper is a solace. She opens the servery. Her card stands there, and there, on the Marimekko paper, is her money, and there stands her empty bottle. The milkman has been, and has rejected her request. She drinks water, glass after glass. The pain leaves her belly, but spreads across her chest again, and goes on and on, attended by the old steady pain in the back of her left shoulder.

. . . . .

It seemed to help Doctor Furmann's powers of diagnosis if, as he tapped, as he listened, as he pressed fingers beneath her rib cage, he looked into the distance. But when she was dressed again, and sitting opposite him at his desk, he did look fully and very attentively at her face. He was a ferret-faced young man with notably intelligent eyes.

'I think you have a stomach ulcer.'

'Is that all?' said Marjorie.

'All? Ulcers are no joke.'

'No, but the worst pain last night was across my chest, and the pain I've had for weeks is behind my shoulder, so naturally, you know,' said Marjorie, with her shrugging, 'I thought, heart.'

'Would you prefer that?'

'I don't care one way or the other.'

'You're divorcing, did you say?'

'Yes, I did say that.'

Marjorie guessed by the sympathy in his eyes that he thought her the abandoned one. She would have liked the luxury of allowing him to think so, without the discomfort of deception. She said coldly, 'I left my husband.'

The sympathy remained. His splendid dark eyes reminded her of Emlyn's. His hairline was so uneven that in this pause she began to straighten it by electrolysis. 'It seems to me,' he said at last, 'that at your age, it doesn't matter who leaves who, not so far as my work is concerned. I want you to have an X-ray.'

'What will it cost?'

'Don't you belong to a fund?'

'My husband did all that.'

'You're still legally his wife.'

'Please give me a referral.' Marjorie knew she would pay for it herself. 'I'll go to a hospital.'

'You'll wait longer.'

'Never mind. I can take something, I suppose, in the meantime.

He gave slow instructions as he wrote the referral and two prescriptions. 'No alcohol. And you don't smoke, so that's okay. No coffee. No aspirin. Not much tea. Eat little and often. If not solids, milk.' He handed her the flimsy sheets. 'If you find milk helps.'

'Milk!' Marjorie laughed, then lifted the top prescription and said sternly, 'Tranquillisers?'

'Don't indulge your opinions at the expense of your health.'

'But I told you, I must work.'

'Then take one when you stop work, and another at night. That pain in your shoulder, by the way, it's my guess that's referred pain.'

. . . . .

Coming home one day with her plastic sacks of provisions, Marjorie encountered the woman who lived in the next-door flat. Marjorie would have been diffident about knocking on this neighbour's door, but when she saw her in the mundane and undistorted corridor, she was bold enough to accost her.

'I wonder if you could tell me what I must do to get milk delivered.'

'Easy,' said the woman. 'Leave your money out. No money, no milk.'

'But that's what I do.'

'And I always leave the servery door open.'

'I do that, too.'

'Well, I get milk, no trouble. Except when I forget to leave the money out. Then I get a carton across at Wong's. It's no trouble to slip across to Wong's.

'That's what I've been doing. But I liked bottled milk. Besides, I just don't understand it.'

'Well, it's no good telling you to ask him. He comes at three-thirty. Why don't you ring the company?'

Marjorie rang the company from the smelly public phone booth on the corner. Her name and address were taken, and delivery promised, but the next morning, and the next, when she went to the kitchen and opened the little door, she saw only her note, her money, and her empty bottle. She knew her disappointment was ridiculous, but it was unconquerable; it gave a lagging start to her days. She went again to the booth on the corner, but vandals had been there, and the receiver lay smashed on the floor. She hoped it had not been done by the group of boys she had come to like and watch for. She walked to the post office and found an undamaged phone. The company passed her from person to person, and while waiting for someone named Miss Vinson, she was cut off. After that, she would open the servery door merely to exercise her cynicism, and would smile as she banged it shut.

Emlyn was furious with her for having no phone of her own.

'Mum, even professionally –'

'Emlyn, if you would listen –'

'Even professionally, it's crazy. Fee and I are financial again. We'll shout you a phone.'

'Emlyn, I've been trying to tell you, I've paid for my phone. I asked Harrap for an advance on the cookbook. They didn't mind a bit. It was amazing. Now I'm waiting on Telecom to connect me.'

'God! What a service! How long are you supposed to wait?'

She hoped that Emlyn was expressing his affection through this indignation, since at present he was inhibited in expressing it in any other way. She did notice also that he had begun to look at her face, though as often as not his glance would slip quickly to her collar.

'And what about this milk Fee tells me is so important to you? Cartons are okay. We get cartons.'

'It's just that I wanted to get up in the morning, and open the servery door, and see it there.' She made the shape of it with her hands. 'And reach out, like that, and take it in. But you're right. Cartons are okay.'

Emlyn went to the servery and opened it. He picked up her note. 'What's he like?'

'I've seen him only once. He comes before dawn. I don't wake out of my drugged sleep. In the distance he was little and dark, not young. Don't worry about it.'

'I guess he doesn't read English.'

'That's not it. He wouldn't need to.'

'No. The bottle, the money. That says it.'

'Right. So.' She took the note, tore it up, then padded in her bare feet to throw the scraps into the carton of waste paper beside her worktable. She hoisted herself on to her stool and spread her hands. 'Look at all the work I've been given.'

'Mum, I had a go at talking to dad. Useless.'

'I don't want to know about it.'

'Yes, but look here, mum, this –,' Emlyn slanted his head to indicate the room '– this just isn't a fair go. You need better legal advice than you're getting from that Mae West character. If ethics mean you're stuck with her, which is bloody nonsense in my opinion, instruct her to engage a barrister. Carla's husband would recommend someone. Or I'll find someone.'

'My dear –'

'Don't talk to me about money. Don't insult me.'

'My dear, I am here in this room, and I wish to stay here, working every day, until the case is heard. I have set myself on a course. Don't divert me. Don't upset my balance. I mustn't fall off my rope.'

He was looking her full in the face, but as if it were the face of a stranger. After a while he said absent-mindedly, 'Right.' Then he said, 'When do you get those X-rays done?'

'They'll let me know.'

'You look well,' he said in the same tone. 'Fee was saying you're looking really good.'

'I feel fine.' Now that Emlyn had dropped his ferocity, she seemed to have picked it up. 'I don't believe there's anything wrong with me at all. And I don't need help. And I don't need to know anything about your father.'

'I get it,' he said. 'And anyway, look here, dad's okay.'

. . . . .

His sympathy had brought her to the point of telling him how intensely she was enjoying her work, but she drew back out of the superstitious fear that to reveal it was to risk losing it. She did not overvalue her work. She knew its first importance was that it earned her money, but she was surprised and grateful that in her present circumstances it could so deeply engross her, could give her such a sense of urgency. Every day in the humid heat of January, February, and early

March, she rose and folded up her bed, ate her breakfast and bathed, then put on one of her loose dark batik dresses and went to her worktable. She pinned her hair high on her head to free the nape of her neck; she wore no pants nor bra, no shoes. The dress itself was a concession to her visibility from the street. Curtains or blinds reduced the light, and she had besides become accustomed to making quick little sketches of the people in the street, and dropping them, done or half-done, beside her worktable, where they lay gathering grit and dust. When she had to go out for food, she put on pants and the rubber thongs she had bought at Woolworths. She wore these same clothes to the hospital, where she was given a barium meal and X-rayed. She had to wait four hours, which slackened her sense of urgency and made her feel restless and tense. The urgency was exciting and exhilarating except during enforced waits or when she had to go to the city to collect or deliver work. She hated these occasions because she felt obliged to wear full underclothes, a dress of a more formal sort, panty hose and shoes, even make-up. To dress like this she felt as a serious and even dangerous intrusion, and she would arrive back at her flat in a state of anxiety or even of slight hysteria, and would violently pull the hated clothes off her sweating body. She wished she could afford couriers. If it were Carla who had given her one of these jobs, Marjorie would beg her to bring it herself. Carla riffled among the drawings on the floor, casting some aside and picking out a few at which she cocked her head and lifted one corner of her mouth. 'It's no miracle that you can draw feet,' she said one day. 'It's just this.' She tapped the drawing she held. 'Practice, practice, practice.'

'I can draw feet because I need the money.'

Carla appreciated the humorous hardness of this. Marjorie

wondered if Carla believed it to be entirely true. Carla wisely nodded, in any case, as she returned the drawings to the dusty pile.

The glass of milk Marjorie kept on the window sill she covered with an envelope. Dust and grit gathered also in the servery, on the coins, the bottle, and the Marimekko paper. Although Emlyn had been assured by the milk company that there was no possible obstacle to Marjorie getting her milk, the servery continued to present, on each morning's sardonic inspection, the same picture as before. She pretended to Emlyn that his complaint had been effective; she did not want him to go on a crusade about a bottle of milk a day. He had already been on a crusade about her telephone, and whether or not as a result, it was now connected.

Once, in the early afternoon, hearing faintly the clink of coins, she slipped quickly from her stool and ran into the kitchen. The money had gone. Feet in thongs were slapping down the stairs. She heard the laughter of the boys, and yelled down the staircase after them that they were devils, as she had heard Mr Wong and the people in the street do. She did not replace the money, but in bed that night found the omission gave her a superstitious uneasiness, and impatiently she got up and put the three coins in the servery. The rolled newspaper she carried in the other hand was for killing cockroaches; she never went into the kitchen at night without it; another superstition she had developed was that insecticide would kill her as well.

. . . . .

The radiologist reported that Marjorie had a large ulcer crater on the posterior wall of the upper third of her stomach. As Marjorie read this, she heard Doctor Furmann remark, in a pleased and enthusiastic voice, that he had been quite right about that shoulder pain.

'Referred pain. Come here, and I'll show you the crater on your X-rays.'

'I can't stop work to have an operation,' Marjorie warned him swiftly.

'I don't suggest it. Now, that silvery area is your stomach. Now, see that dark intrusion? I'm tracing it, see? That's it.'

'And that is my monumental backbone. And those wavy things, which I must say are quite pretty, are my intestines.'

'If I may have your attention.'

'Perhaps I could wear myself inside out. Well, all right. It's awful. It's huge. It looks like the Gulf of Carpentaria.'

'Yes, it does. It's deep, all right. That one hasn't grown overnight. Well, it's our job to close it up. On each X-ray you will see it get smaller.'

She asked with horror, 'How often must I have these X-rays?'

'Every month.'

'And how many months will it take to cure?'

'That's partly up to you.'

'Give me some idea.'

'No less than three.'

'Which I suppose,' she said bitterly, 'means six.'

'Sit down,' he said, 'sit down. There's a drug recently developed. Cimetidine. Perhaps it's for the lucky future. I don't prescribe it yet. It's still at the trial and error stage.'

'Like the divorce laws.'

'I know it's no use telling you not to worry.'

'I thought not worrying was exactly what I had been doing.'

'I know it's hard.'

'I've been feeling so well,' she said angrily.

'Fine. You've responded to treatment. So now we're sure of our ground, we'll give you something stronger.' Again his voice went on as he wrote. 'These may have the side-effect of raising your blood pressure, but we'll keep a weekly check on that.'

'Weekly!'

'Yes, and give you something for it if the need arises. It's a matter of maintaining a balance.'

'Oh, I see. A balance.'

. . . . .

All the next day Marjorie lay on the bed in her nightgown, stubbornly reading out-of-date magazines. She read about Patty Hearst and Princess Caroline of Monaco and how to stretch your budget. Carla rang. Emlyn rang. 'Mind your own business,' she wanted to say. But their solicitude was her own fault, for having told them anything at all. So she said it was only a small ulcer, nothing really, easily fixed. She ignored a knock on the door, but when she got up in the evening, and saw the agent's card under the door, she remembered it was rent day. There was hardly any food in the kitchen. She got dressed and went over to Wong's.

'And your milk?'

'Yes, please, Mr Wong.'

Just before dawn on the following day, she dreamed again of Bruce. He stood at the dinner table, looking down at her. 'From now on,' he said, 'every mouthful you eat will poison you.' It was near enough to what he had actually said to make her rise and spend the remaining hour till daylight hunched in a shawl on her worktable stool, looking out of the window at the street cleaners, the garbage collectors, and the derelict men and bag women freshly routed from their cubbies. But just as she did not remember what she had read about Patty Hearst or Princess Caroline, so she did not now absorb what she looked at.

She was too tired to work that day. In the evening Emlyn and Fiona came and presented her with water biscuits, creamy cheeses, and a book on herbal medicine. They were still there when Carla came with her husband Martin. Carla bore the food of childhood, a milky rice pudding in a homely earthenware dish. Marjorie had to open the folding bed so that they could all sit down. She noticed that now everyone could look easily at her face, except Martin, and even he was able to address her in a natural tone of voice. The next day, via Carla, he suggested the name of a barrister Marjorie might instruct Gwen to engage. Marjorie refused. Though she had returned doggedly to her work, she could not afford to add this factor to all the others to which she must now adapt her balance. At the end of the week, when Doctor Furmann prescribed tablets for her raised blood pressure, she accepted the instruction passively and in silence, and as passively took the tablets at the ordered times.

She had lost her sense of urgency. She did her work faithfully, but without her former delight. One day, warmly complimented on it, she was startled, and took the piece back and looked at it again, and saw that, yes, it was better than she had done in her exalted state. She sighed with incomprehension.

Perhaps because the cool days had come, she no longer found it hateful to dress to go to the city. She did not dream of Bruce again, but although she increased her dose of tranquillisers, her sleep was often broken. When she heard the milkman's bottles jangling away down the corridor, she assumed that what had brought her awake was his banging her servery door. In the morning it was always shut, and she would viciously slam the inner door she continued to open for her inspection. Then one night, as she was about to go into the kitchen for water, she heard him stop outside her servery. It was not a full second before he banged the door and jangled away. She threw down her rolled newspaper, seized the money and the bottle, and ran in her bare feet down the corridor after him.

She caught up with him while he was scooping money from a servery. She stood with arms extended, proffering the money in one hand, the bottle in the other.

'What about me? Flat forty-one?'

He put two bottles into the nearby servery and shut the door. 'Good,' he said. He took the money and the bottle, gave her a full bottle, and picked up his crate.

'Wait! Why don't you deliver it?'

He was certainly Italian: small, lumpy though thin, with black mordant eyes and a look of disgust on his simian mouth. She had seen his counterpart among his comely people, and concluding him to be a relict, almost bred out by prosperity, she had been surprised that he had so often crossed her path. He had cheated her in five Italian cities, and in those same cities had directed her lost footsteps with kindness and even gallantry if she were quick to understand, and with testiness and contempt if she were not. In Sydney he had spared some of his time and authority to help her to buy unfamiliar food, and last year, when she had bent to the driver's seat of his taxi and offered a fifty dollar note he could not change, he had all but screamed his anger and abuse. She was in awe of his inheritance, the implant of poverty and unnatural labour. She said (for his English had been no better than her Italian), 'Everyone else,' and pointed to the row of doors, 'but not me,' and pointed to the door at the far end. 'Why not?'

He scowled as he put down his crate and took money from his bag. 'You do this.' He extended his hand, the money on his palm. 'I give milk.'

'That's what I *do!*'

But he had picked up his crate and was moving away, and when she called again for him to wait, he responded with what sounded like a curse, and gave a backward flip of his free hand. In none of his manifestations had he been patient. Herself cursing under her breath, she ran after him, but he had turned the corner, and when she reached it his only visible part was the small head bobbing down a narrow service stairway she had never seen before.

Without gratification she put the bottle of milk in the refrigerator. She knew he did not expect her to run after him in her nightgown every time she wanted milk. He meant her simply to pay him. Her end of the corridor was dimly lit. She put another three coins on the paper, then went out into the corridor and opened the servery door. The money was clearly visible in the light from her kitchen. But usually, the kitchen was dark, the inner servery door shut. She went back, shut the inner servery door and turned off the light. And this time, she saw that it was difficult (though not impossible) to distinguish the coins from the small geometric daisies on the Marimekko paper.

In the morning she went out and bought sandpaper and a tin of white enamel. She sanded down the old cream paint and put fresh white paint on all planes of the servery except the base. For the base, she folded a sheet of layout paper to the right size. In the evening, after her work was done, she polished three coins and washed and dried a milk bottle. A soft laugh broke from her as she did this, and again as she slowly and ceremoniously set down the three coins. She did not know if he had failed to leave her milk because, in days filled with the same desperate impetus as hers had been, he had not bothered to give the second glance that would have distinguished the coins, or whether it angered him that he found them hard to see, and he was forcing her to show them as clearly as he had done when he had displayed them on his extended palm. She thought the latter more likely, but did not care, such was her certainty that the milk would be there in the morning.

Yet she could not have been so certain, because, in the morning, when she opened the door and saw it standing there in its simplicity, amazement preceded her delight, and amazement was in her smile as she reached out with both hands and brought it in. During the day she had only to think of the sight of it, standing there, for the sensation of smiling to spread through her whole body.

She did not continue to polish the coins, but took care to set aside for that use the cleanest ones in her purse. During her next restless night, when her wakeful period included half-past three, and she heard the milkman's fast padded steps, and the jangling of his crate, she listened intently enough to hear him take the coins and set down the milk. He did not slam the servery door. He closed it gently. She told nobody of the incident. Each night, she changed the white paper, and took pleasure in setting down the three coins in their invariable pattern.

. . . . .

She was disappointed when she studied her second X-rays with Doctor Furmann.

'What?' he said. 'Did you expect a miracle?'

'Yes,' she said.

'I thought you would be pleased. It's so much reduced.'

'Oh, it is,' she said, to appease him. 'Now it's like Spencer's Gulf.'

'You mean Spencer Gulf.'

'Your geography is as good as your treatment.'

'Next time it will be like Port Phillip Bay. Roll up that sleeve, please.'

In the winter, the sunless flat was cold all day. She bought a small radiator, but its heat made her lethargic, so after her morning shower she walked into fur-lined boots and swaddled herself in layers of clothes before she started work. She picked up her sketches from the floor, dusted them, and put them into different coloured folders in order of preference. Each time she added new ones, she found that her order of preference had changed. Though her divorce was not yet listed, she began to think of a garden, the smell of basil and geraniums, and the feel of a warm stone path under her feet. But when she studied advertisements for cottages at that northern beach, she felt less certain about wanting to live there.

Carla, when she came to the flat, would often, as she was about to leave, fall into the kind of silence that made Marjorie suspect her of hanging about to find a chance to say something about Bruce. 'I hope you don't think I'm going to put myself into reverse at this stage,' said Marjorie on one of these occasions. 'I mean, about the divorce.'

'No, I don't expect you can,' said Carla.

'It's no help to talk about it.'

'It was you who mentioned it.'

'It was you who so clearly wanted to. Tell me something.

I can't get my money from Manzell and Rogers. I've sent my account twice. Do you know anything about them?'

Her divorce was listed the day after she had her third X-rays. These showed the ulcer crater reduced to the proportionate size, if not the shape, of Port Phillip Bay. 'Don't be over-confident,' warned Doctor Furmann. 'Don't relax your care. When is your divorce?'

'In three weeks.'

'Just what part stress plays is not known for certain.'

The day after this, Marjorie put some documents in an envelope, put money in her purse for Isolde, and went to the city to see Gwen. Early for her appointment, she decided to go to Nock and Kirby's to buy paint for the outdoor table and slatted chairs. It was a quarter to two; the counter was crowded, and while she was waiting her turn she saw Bruce standing on the downward escalator. He wore an unfamiliar tie, held his attache case in one hand, a walking stick in the other, and was carefully regarding his own feet. When he reached the floor, he stepped on to it with a slightly fumbled and panicky step, then with one hip swinging wide, limped quickly away towards the George Street entrance.

Marjorie abandoned the paint and hurried distractedly out of the York Street entrance. She took four antacid tablets on her way to see Gwen, who was magnificent that day in magenta and purple. When Marjorie got home she rang Emlyn.

'Emlyn, I saw your father in Nock and Kirby's.'

'Did you?'

'Has he had an accident?'

'No, mum, he hasn't.'

'Then why is he lame?'

'Mum, we all saw your point when you said you didn't want to hear anything about him.'

'Yes, but now I've seen him, it's better if I do hear something.'

'Well, you remember his arthritis?'

'But it was nothing. He called them twinges.'

'It's something now.'

'Twinges. But I do recall,' she said, since Emlyn was silent, 'that most of the twinges were in one hip.'

'Right, that's where he copped it.'

'Will he always be lame?'

'I don't know. There are things they can do. He's going to a specialist. A top man. And anyway, mum, even if he is always lame, he's not the kind of guy who can't handle it.'

'No,' said Marjorie, 'he's not.'

But as she put down the phone she thought of how characteristic it was of them each that she should take the wound in the soft tissue, while he should take it in the bone. She sat with her hands folded, wondering if it was only bad luck that she had not found, at the right time, the right, miraculous seeming, gesture of conciliation; but after a while she jumped up and turned her mind to other things, knowing she could not afford to enter that labyrinth. She had collected her mail on the way upstairs, and was pleased to see that Manzell and Rogers had paid her at last.

. . . .

Rocks

MILES HITCHCOCK

This story drops you straight into the dark, deafening blare of rock and roll. As Bazz, the lead singer puts it: 'Try sitting around in pubs for five hours a day and not getting fucked up'. 'Rocks' has the raw energy of the milieu it's describing – a smoky, sweaty world where rage and riot rule.

Music is magic. Try it: scream any line of poetry or everyday phrase over a hundred decibels of heavy power-chords and no shit – it turns from something dumb into a chant of truth, a love-note, a knife in the throat.

Rock is sonic graffiti. It punctuates an attitude, a performance, a whole belief system. Rock music raises spirits – spirits of your imagination, even the spirits of the age. Right now, across the world's cities, bars and bedrooms, people are plugging in, tuning up and finding the perfect escape in three chords and a bridging melody. It's the high art of the highway, the Teleos of the takeaway, the Budoh of the public bar, and at five bucks at the door, these are glorious times.

Jason backs the car up behind the pub. 'We're last to soundcheck again,' he notes, and I laugh. I bang on the heavy black doors, and some long tangled hair opens up – 'Hey Bazz'.

'Hey.' Jonah unlocks his hatchback and we grab cases. It's almost pitch black inside. A weak bulb hangs over red dots on the fold-back desk. A lightie on a ladder twists cans, cables in mouth. Toby is doof-doofing his drum check in a Garbage t-shirt. I wave an arm at Rick behind the desk. He shouts 'Bazza!' and we start heaving gear.

Soon I'll be screaming my lungs out, and the crowd'll be surging and surfing at my feet, connecting to something bigger and louder, bouncing in rhythm to our wider world.

It'll be the most important 45 minutes of our week. The guitar, the effects pedal and the microphone are the everyday, scruffy-ass kid's conduit to Beauty and Truth. The song has become scripture, and fame has become a religion.

'Kit!' Toby falls into a simple motown. Al kicks in with a discordant scale and Jason and I are soon fucking it up with tempo changes and just to prove my point I start howling my bowdlerised Dylan T: *'Am I stuck on the hot and rocking street spinning to stare at an old year? Because the pleasure-bird whistles over the hot wires shall the blind horse sing sweeter?'* With Rick scampering onstage to change mics and leads and shift stands until he lifts both thumbs up and heads for the front bar.

It's the long five hour wait to show-time, and generally there's nothing else to do but sink piss. I'm told we're legendary for getting wild and fucked up on stage – some blurry sick shit HAS happened I believe, mainly involving my big mouth – but I maintain it's not a bad attitude as much as the working conditions. Try sitting round pubs for five hours a day and NOT getting fucked up, especially when some punter sees the chance to share his speed with a local rock singer, or the barmaid keeps automatically refilling your middy because one day you asked her name.

So it's after soundcheck and Toby's trying to spin all his marketing and promotions shit. 'Guys,' Toby's saying, 'we've gotta get the CD *out*. The demo tape's fine but CDs and national press are all A and R guys bother with now. Even just something quick to send out to you know companies and journos. Sell at gigs.'

Despite what you read rock'n'roll is not full of artistically-inspired people, refining their creative vision. It's an amateur talent quest of mimics, babblers and stoners, orators and prima donnas. It's driven totally by the power of personality. Yet Toby seems to me a new category: upwardly mobile spin-doctor, middle class fame junkie. I clear my throat and signal for another.

'Selling at gigs is good,' Alan adds. 'We gotta have that. On a big night, man, we'd clean up.' Alan and Jason are nodding and agreeing to this shit.

'Whaddya reckon Bazz,' Toby asks, serious and demanding.

'Aw, yeah, uh, I dunno … I dunno,' I dunno how to deal with this now, and stare at the roof. 'Er, when?' I finally manage.

Toby grins his little I'm-gonna-impress-ya smirk. 'Well, that's what I'm getting round to. Whaddya think of this: Blur.'

He looks in our eyes one by one, waiting for something.

'Yeah?' Jason asks. 'You want us to burst into Song Number fucken Two?'

'No arsehole. The support man, the support!' Toby squeals. 'We got offered the fucken Blur support man!' He holds out his arms like he's gonna hug us.

'Shit yeah!' Alan punches the air.

'No shit?' Jason shakes his head. 'That's majorly cool!'

Afterglow drinks are bought. Afternoon drunks are looking around. I gotta admit that's pretty hot news. Even though I hate Blur.

'And.. *it's at the fucken concert hall man!*'

'Woo hooo!! Woo hoo!' Jonah yelps. I'm grinning and slapping shoulders and also saying 'Seriously hot, wow,' and seeing us on that big stage.

'Bazz mate!' Toby punches my arm, and I'm feeling a bit light-headed. 'You ready for this?'

'Good news guys?' Kate the barmaid walks past and we tell her. 'Cool one guys! You deserve it.' She pulls more middies.

'Now guys guys,' Toby tosses his beer back and puts his Blundstone up on the slops rail. 'At the concert hall you get the older alternative crowd, *and* the fuckin' teenyboppers. This is our chance at major crossover. We gotta have a CD out when we walk onto that stage! Launch it the week after the gig. Toss CDs at the crowd. Cover the floor in flyers. Picture it. It'll be farken huge.'

I straighten up my leather jacket. 'And somewhere in there we're gonna play the songs?'

'Of course,' Toby pauses, hooks his hair behind his ears.

'It's pencilled in!' Jason guffaws.

'We'll blow them out the fucking door.' Toby interjects. 'We always do.'

'Oh. So someone's girlfriend's on the door...?' I turn back to my middy on the bar, scope the old cunts scoping their ponies. Light a ciggie. I sense the other guys shrug at each other and keep going: '... yeah man it's a huge break...' 'OK lets burn some CDs.' 'Blah blah' and Toby's sucking on fags and nodding and blowing smoke until he cracks: 'Fuck, Bazz, what's ya big problem? We get a great gig and all you do is go sour like ya couldn't give a fuck! Jesus lighten up.'

I pause, consider, blow smoke. Those everyday lines, these crescendoes and beats, have to be done right. That's what I keep telling these guys. 'It's not,' I say slowly, 'that I couldn't give a fuck, it's that *you* don't give a fuck.'

Toby sees a monster. I see Jason smirk – he of course knows this shit's been coming.

'O right,' Toby slit eyed, '*I* don't give a fuck. I bust my guts so you can march out on stage and be Mister-Fuck-You-I'm-Gonna-Be-a-Rock-God, and that's *my* crap attitude. Riiiight...'

Kate the barmaid checks us out from the taps, looks back down.

'Shit! *I* don't wanna be a rock god man! Do you? Cos I don't. You miss the point as per fucking usual. I play *music*. We *perform* songs. We get up on stage and it's us and the songs, and the meaning and the power and the... spirit of the songs. Coming out of our hands. That's what its about, man. Live fucking rock and roll. Something *you* don't know shit about!'

He stares. He blinks. He starts. 'I've played every stage in this city fifty fucking times. I've sweated, slept and spewed *up* on those stages, and you say I don't know shit about rock'n'roll?'

The roar of the bar. Kate pauses midpour. The two speed dealers stop playing pool and look across.

'Yeah, cos you wanna throw our CDs away. Our music is *not* something to toss at teenyboppers or give away to some company prick. What I care about is recording and playing the songs, properly man, *as* they are, the *best* they can be, and it's *not* disposable, not to me anyway. But for you a record's just another flyer on the floor!' I taunt. 'Isn't it, Tobes?'

A bunch of pony-tail guys look around, tuning into the aggro. Pretty much the whole front bar is quiet. I must really be giving him the eyeball. Jason's head is darting back and forth between Toby and me, blonde dreads flying, enjoying the trouble, revelling in truths bursting out from all directions and exploding.

'Come on guys, where'd all the smiley faces go?' asks Kate, gripping the bar, elbows up, twitches in her face.

'You sure have a diplomatic way of expressing your opinion, Bazz,' Toby says in a low voice, and strides from the bar.

. . . . .

The support band cranks up as I'm sitting at the door, wrist-stamping the punters flocking in. Every time the door swings open there's a blare of feedback, shouts and cymbal crashes, then it closes on a heavy subsonic thud. The thing that shits me is that I agree *completely* with Bazz about the music, but he thrives on feeling creatively superior to everyone. He's the star of his own never-ending road documentary. Another blare lets in another five bucks.

'Hey ya piece of poo, why so glum?'

It's Lucy, jumping on my knee. She's looking good: purple eyeliner, glossy red lips, that sequin bodyhugger. 'Hey, doll,' I say, 'didn't see ya come in.'

'Surprise. And you didn't call me either.'

'Oh yeah! Big fucken rush today, as usual.' I give her a squeeze, slip my hand along her orange tights.

'Hey!' She slaps and grabs my hand. 'It's the fucken *line* moron! Don't!'

How I met Luce: a superhot one-night stand that never sat down. We just smiled at each other in a club, and SLURP like horn magnets just started pashing without (1) being on E or (2) getting past 'hi'. One hour later we were fucking across the doorstop of my house. She stinks of moselle. I cuff her face.

'Eerrghh! So why the jaded-muso look?' She grabs my cheeks. Truth is being the drummer I don't have much say over the music. As the singer-songwriter, Barry has it. He pulls the crowd, so I get the venue. He should understand that. Yet he sits at the bar, scowling over his thirteenth middy, while the punters pour in, and he calls it all promotional bullshit.

'Nothing. Bazz's just being a shit again.'

'What's new-hoo!' She sings, looking at everyone, swaying on my knee.

'You're pissed,' I tell her.

'Girls've been having fun! Hey! Morons!' she screams out, 'the singer's a FUCKING *SHIT!*'

I grab her mouth – 'Luce fucken HELL,' and we topple off my stool and wrestle – 'You guys!' shouts the door bitch, holding the table – I pull Luce's ear, she thumps me – 'Bastard!' – we knock into people opening the door. Luce tugs her dress down, grins lopsidedly. 'Buy me a drink for that, cunt!' And pushes me through the door. She screams, 'Debster where are you!' and I drag her into the loud dark blare. Buzz and I are both cool. There'll be a compromise somewhere.

'Damn Damn!' The bar always cashes my paycheque and I'm standing there with three drinks in front of me and two bucks change on the bar. The girl behind the bar is shrugging, 'well until it turns up mate you gotta pay for the drinks. Sorry.' I stalk up to Luce and Deb. 'Got any dough? I've lost my fucking paycheque.'

'What?' They squeal. Blue and white spotlights in their hair as I shout into their tiny cupped earholes.

'Aw no!' They scream, and we go through it and get the drinks and I start to realise.

I spill my middy on Luce and run for the back door.

On stage 40 mins. Ten minutes there, in out, no worries.

Traffic on Lake Street is a Friday night crawl. Motors rev, music thumps, drunken diners weave between restaurants. The buildings look like movie props with all the globes and neon. There isn't going to be a parking spot so I follow the bumpers, pull up on the sidewalk and run in.

The floor is packed with office leftovers and bar crawlers, talking smoking swearing, and I fight to the bar where Luce and I sat this arvo. I kick chip and smoke packets between barstool legs and when the barman comes I have to shout several times 'Has anyone given you/handed in a cheque mate?' And he goes out and comes back and shakes his head and I scowl and swear and prowl round the bar and crouch down and THERE IT IS pinned under a barstool. There's a big fat bastard on the stool and I tap his stretched shirt and a sullen red face looks at me for a while and says, 'Yeah what?'

'Ah, scuse I dropped something under your stool and could-ja, you know …'

He's looking down. 'Yer nose ring is it mate?' His mate snorts first, shoulders hunching at the bar.

'Nah, it's my fucken *dick*,' I pronounce.

He stops grinning, his nostrils flare. 'Yer trying to get smart with me fellah?'

'Nah, not really.' I say. 'I just want my cheque.'

He scowls. 'Ya what?'

'My paycheque. It got stuck …'

'How the fuck did it get there?'

'Well, it was attached to my nose ring when I was sucking beer off the floor earlier…' I stop, he glares, we realise this is stupid piss-talk.

'Jesus, you look like ya need the help,' He staggers off the chair, and shouts back, 'Jeff the dork lost his paycheque on the floor!' I kneel in the grime, grab it, wet with beer, check it's actually mine, kiss it, split, find pedestrians squeezing around the fenders, a cop shining a torch through the window of my car. No problemo. I unlock the door.

'What. Do you think. You're? Doing?'

'I'm er playing here tonight. Dropping off ... musical equipment. Officer. I'll move right now.'

'Wait there.' The cop saunters to the bouncer at the door. I get in, kick it over. Cop saunters back.

'Turn off the engine mate. Step out of the car.' I sigh and get out. 'There's no live music at this venue tonight, so you just bullshitted me.'

'Nah, I'm not playing *later*, I mean I'm picking gear up from earlier for another gig I'm going to now.'

'You're so busy you can park on the sidewalk?' he asks.

'I always, I mean, I had ta, like it was just for a coupla minutes, my *full* apology officer, I wasn't meaning to flout the law. I'll gladly accept a fine.'

'I decide whether you accept a fine or not, mate.' He grimly does the saunter-round-the-car routine, as if it's just been dragged from a lake. He gets back, flicks a tiny pad. 'Name.'

'Peter Porter.' My magazine nom-de-plume. 'Address.' He pencils them down. 'Now get outa here before I decide.'

He walks and I turn straight into a skinhead snarling beside my door, a fat forefinger poised on my breastbone. 'You've gotta fucked attitude, mate.' He's wearing black leather and docs.

'Who the fuck are you?' I retort. He snarls and jabs his finger again. He's a hyped-up speedfreak. I knock his hand away and reach for the door. 'Right!' He slams me back into the car, and holds a blue police ID in front of my face. 'That's who I am! And you just showed me a *very* fucked attitude!'

'Shit, I, I'm sorry.' I squeal, panicked. He keeps holding my neck against the car. People are hurrying on.

'What? I can't hear you!'

'SORRY, officer!' I shout. He pulls me off the car and shoves me up the street to where the first cop is turning back, raising his eyes skywards. 'Check him out again.'

'I was leaving OK?' My hair's stuck across my face. I brush it away. 'I gotta get to a gig ...'

'Ah. A right rock'n'roller arncha mate! Got any smack onya?' He thrusts his hand through my pockets, grips my arm behind my back, chucks me up on the car again. People stop hurrying and gather round.

'The name doesn't register,' the other cop is back with a walkie talkie. 'Is your real name Tobias Hendricks?' he asks.

I wince. How do they know that?

. . . . .

I've just plugged in when Toby's girlfriend runs a-flurry thru the black curtains. 'Isn't he back yet?' she asks, staring around. I look over my shoulder at the kit and its empty.

'Wasn't he here before?' I ask, feeling the first lick of the trip Rick just gave me.

'He took off about an hour ago.'

'Took off? Where?' Be just like him to crack the shits about earlier.

'I dunno. Lost his paycheque'n ran off.'

I wander back onstage. Spotlights flare nauseous, my gut sweats and the house music – a Tom Waits' growl – swirls around. 'Hey! Where's Toby?' I ask the mic, get whistles from the crowd, movement to stagefront.

I unstrap, and walk offstage. Shouts and fizzog.

'Whatsup?' Alan asks over my shoulder.

'Toby's pissed off.' The other guys unplug. We stand backstage, gulping stubbies. Wildeyed Lucy: 'Sheeet! What'll we do guys?' The other girlfriends burst in. 'Where is he?' 'The cunt,' everyone says. Pearl Jam comes on front of house. More boos. Rick appears.

'Has somebody ... exploded?' He grins.

'Let's go on anyway.'

This is the beauty of it – the beauty of shit happens. The beauty of dirty hair and shouting mask: nature caught in the raw. Our music is like a spray of blood, a red-hot jet that electrifies, terrifies, deafens. The racket that slams into the room is belted from a deep demanding piece of gut. There is anger in it. Where is this anger from?

A lightning ball of steel wool – Alan's guitar – scours the stage.

'*Stuck on the rocking street! The blind horse sings sweeter!*' I'm shrieking.

The crowd's in the mosh-pit spraying beer foam and heckles. Al works his pedals. Jason plays lead bass. It's like a giant banshee banquet. It's not art, its just frustration: a sonic way of quitting – *everything*, the band, the gig, the day-job – and we all just follow. This is what people want to see: the *real thing*, the mystical flower alive on stage, in the hands of a bunch of drunks. People want to see something being born, and something die.

Jason throws his guitar headlong into the crowd. It nose-dives, cranes someone on the back. Tempers fly: he's pulled off stage and there's punching, twisted shirts. There's a terrible thunder-feed from his amp. It suddenly seems the stage is a ship of madmen passing through a storm.

Like waves crashing together they split apart. Somehow Jason grabs his guitar back and swings it at arm's length, separating the wild crowd. He hooks it back on and crushes them with a cliff-wall of sound.

'Driving to work we are fighting!' I shout. *'Switching on TV is an act of war!'*

This is now an arena of accidents, a world of disappearing limits. Actions slide out of sight, far out, into brilliance, oblivion, depravity. Disgust is advertised. *'Malls are plunder from starving families!'* Mistakes magnify into crimes.

But it suddenly changes. The crowd's heckles dim like the coughs of a first night audience. The stage suddenly seems lonely – a place where actors sleep, swap wigs and lines. I wander back. Motes glow in the cross-lights. Cars and houses are floating in the beams. A bin is full of rotten food, there's a broken toilet seat speckled with stardust. I drag them into the spotlight.

People shout from the floor. Alan climbs a mast shouting. Jason crawls back on deck. There's sand in my droopy hair, fish-heads at my feet, the sun sparkle of guitar in my eyes. I try to remember the words but they are circling like gulls before me, then they start to dance into the nonsense world.

Bazz just stares, leaning on the mic-stand, looking at the pallid faces swaying. Sharp teeth yell, fins and three-fingered hands wave, the front of stage is shoving at him like a beast.

'Tobeee!'

The bin tips. Click-click BOOM! The stage slams into Barry's head. Power-chords blare. Trash spills. Sideways he opens up: *'We walk the streets! Watch cars slam people run from the buy and sell!'*

Bazz springs upright into rock and roll heaven. The band leaps into the air. Thunder and lightning, transistor harmonics, the toilet seat swings hoola hoop round his head and his lungs are a gift from Thor.

. . . .

Home

LARISSA BEHRENDT

Garibooli, a young Aboriginal girl, is taken from her people and put to work in the mansion of the Howard family. Domestic servitude is exploitation enough, but worse follows. The plainness of Behrendt's style conceals the artfulness of the telling.

'You are a lucky girl, Elizabeth. You have been given a chance, a chance for a better life.' The train clicked on. Mrs Carlyle stared out the window again for a moment before returning to stare at the teenaged girl whose head was bent down towards her shiny new shoes.

'*Look* at me when I speak to you, Elizabeth.' Garibooli lifted her face and looked across into the blue eyes. She had been taught to look away when an older person addressed her. But then, she realised, Mrs Carlyle was not Eualeyai or Kamillaroi so it must be different for her. She looked at Mrs Carlyle's sky-coloured eyes, noticed the wrinkles that danced around her tightly wound mouth and the thin layer of powder that clung to her skin.

'You must do *exactly* as you are told in the house and do *everything* that the housekeeper tells you. *Without* complaint. And as best you can. The Howards are very kind to let you stay with them and earn your keep so you *must* do everything you're asked. Do you *understand*? And from now on, your name is *Elizabeth*, and Elizabeth *only*.'

Elizabeth – once Garibooli, now Elizabeth, and Elizabeth only – nodded, too fearful to ask the one question, the only question, that mattered to her: when was she going home?

. . . . .

It was mid-morning when Elizabeth arrived in the country town whose trees were bursting with pink and white blossoms. The name was written on the station building, in big black letters: PARKES.

They were met by a warm-looking, fleshy young woman in a brown felt hat. Elizabeth felt a surge of relief at the sight of the butter-coloured woman, a contrast to the steeliness of Mrs Carlyle. This was Miss Grainger, the housekeeper.

Mrs Carlyle peered sternly into the young girl's face, 'Remember what we spoke about on the train, about you *behaving* and doing your best. Miss Grainger will look after you but you must be obedient and *respectful* to both Miss Grainger and Mrs Howard. Do you *understand*, Elizabeth?'

Elizabeth nodded, even though there was very little she understood about why she was here, sent so far away, to be with Miss Grainger in the home of Mr and Mrs Howard.

The house, with its white Federation accents, was dark against the morning sky as it shielded the rising sun. Massive and ornate, even in shadow it looked mythical. Elizabeth and Miss Grainger entered through the back door and Elizabeth was shown to her room, just off from the kitchen. 'You will sleep in here.' Miss Grainger pointed to a thin mattress on a wooden bed frame with a blanket on the end. 'We'll make some curtains and things and fix this little nook up, and it'll look much more homey then.'

Elizabeth didn't quite know what Miss Grainger was talking about but recognised kindness, somewhere in her soft, chubby flesh and her subtle scent of lilac and flour. Elizabeth's 'Thank you, Miss Grainger' was for the tone in her voice and the tenderness in her eyes.

Miss Grainger showed Elizabeth the clothes hanging in the closet — two black dresses, two white aprons, two white caps, and a calico nightdress – then left her to settle in.

Elizabeth had cried so much she did not think she could cry again. She lay on the bed and tried to get comfortable. She looked at the sloping ceiling and thought about everything that had just happened to her. It was only two nights since she listened to old Kooradgie's stories and looked up at Mea-Mei, her head in her mother's lap. She closed her eyes and tears slid down her face. She imagined the world as it looked from up in her tree and saw the figure of her baina tending the campfire. She heard her brother calling her name. She saw his face, getting smaller and smaller as she was carried faster and faster, further and further away. Then she saw Euroke's face again, this time larger. It was still distorted, but with laughter as she tickled him, teasing him that he would be eaten by a big fish.

. . . . .

*My name is Garibooli. Whisper it.
Whisper it over and over again.*

. . . . .

The inside of the Howard's house on Hill Street fascinated Elizabeth with its polished wood, sparkling glass and gas lights. It offered a thousand curiosities in the shiny silverware and crystal that danced in the light and in the fine china plates that seemed to be the same white colour as Mrs Howard's skin. The dining room was a mysterious place with heavily embroidered chairs, garland patterned rugs and a long teak table. Heavy gold-framed pictures of stern men with whiskers and women in stiff, starched garments hung on the wall. Light refracted off every shiny surface. What Elizabeth loved most was the dark wood dining-room table's centrepiece: its silver vine with silver leaves holding real flowers and candles. When the flickering candles were lit, the glass and gold in the room would radiate and she would be hypnotised, her eyes darting to catch every escaping sparkle.

Miss Grainger, plump and neat, her golden hair tied back into her cap, ensured that most of Elizabeth's time in the kitchen was spent usefully and efficiently. Her work was to be that of a kitchen maid, Miss Grainger told her, but she would also do some duties of a house maid, such as sweeping the rugs, washing the linen and the interminable dusting.

Elizabeth's day was more than thirteen long hours of hard work from six in the morning until ten at night, with a half hour for dinner and an hour and a half in the afternoon. This was supposed to be free time, but instead Elizabeth seemed to be required to do needlework. There was a hierarchy of servants: Miss Grainger, as the housekeeper, was on the top, Elizabeth was on the bottom. Other girls from the town were employed in the Howard house, but only Elizabeth and Miss Grainger lived there. Elizabeth often found herself on the receiving end of the teasing of the casual staff, to be saved only when Miss Grainger overheard and intervened. Keeping Elizabeth in her place was a privilege jealously maintained by the housekeeper.

Her first duty of the morning was to clean out the large stove before the cook arrived. She couldn't tend to the ashes without thinking of the fires of the camps. She would be reminded, as she brushed the hearth and arranged freshly cut wood, of the way her mother would stroke her hair, the strength of her father's hands, the way Euroke would lead the younger boys off to fish, her aunt's soft singing and Kooradgie's stories. She would think of these glimpses of the life she wanted to return to before turning her mind to the rigorous schedule of the life she now had.

Elizabeth was shown how to scrub, wash, iron, sew and cook. She would bake bread, make butter and light the copper to wash the clothes. With her skin raw and red, she would scrub with soap she had made until the dirt was lifted from fabric and then she would boil the linen and garments again. She preferred the ironing where, on the cold mornings, she could be close to the heat of the stove. Miss Grainger once told her that making the material for a shirt takes thirty minutes but requires about twelve hours of washing, starching and ironing throughout the years of its use. Although she burnt herself several times at the beginning – once so badly that the cast iron's triangular scar remained – Elizabeth became adept at laundering. She observed closely and learned quickly.

If Miss Grainger told her the proper way to iron a shirt or instructed her to make the tea a certain way, she would do her best to make sure that she did what she was told. It was a reward to her when Miss Grainger would study what she had done and would announce, 'Yes, that's right. Good.'

Miss Grainger would dispense sixpence a week pocket money on Fridays, except for the times when Elizabeth broke a dish or damaged her uniform. Elizabeth lived in secret hope that Miss Grainger might show her some affection and that if she were good, if she did as she were told, she would get to see her parents and her brother again. Obedience and respect, instructed Miss Grainger, were important qualities in domestic servants. Elizabeth was instructed to model herself after Christ, the Suffering Servant, and sacrifice her own interests without complaint for those of Mr and Mrs Howard. The lessons from the Bible would remind her of the Reverend who lived near Dungalear Station. The memories of those sermons and the way the children would giggle at the Reverend when his back was turned, brought back memories of the home that she had left behind, of the place where the rivers met.

・・・・・

Running day and night. Never stopping to catch my breath.
But without the wind in my face.
Without the grass against my legs.
Without the soil under my feet.
Without the pleasure to move free.

・・・・・

Elizabeth slowly became accustomed to the world of the Howards' house; she came to know its rhythm and pace, its rules and routines. She was not allowed to enter the house through the front door and she was not allowed to speak to the tradesmen who came to do work at the house. When Peter, the boy who delivered the mail, came he would try to make jokes with Elizabeth to make her grin. 'There's a lot of letters here for you,' he would wink. 'You must be real popular.' He would smile at her and his face, with its crooked nose, would transform and seem almost handsome. Elizabeth couldn't keep from giggling.

'Watch him,' Miss Grainger would caution. 'He's a Catholic,' she would add, as if that were enough said. Despite this stern warning, Elizabeth was always happy when it was she who received the mail.

Miss Grainger was Elizabeth's only ally. It was only when Miss Grainger's own frustrations ran high that she would scold and smack Elizabeth, though remorse and generosity with pocket money followed any cross outburst. Elizabeth came to notice that Miss Grainger's mood swings usually occurred when Mrs Howard was at her worst; it was then that Miss Grainger would withdraw her kind words into a sullenness that would not lift easily.

Elizabeth also learnt to avoid Mrs Howard, who was always uncivil towards her with a briskness that shook her youthful sensitivities. Just as Miss Grainger's comments about how good her work was felt like a pat on the head, Mrs Howard's indifference made her feel scolded. When cleaning or dusting in a room that Mrs Howard was in, Elizabeth would fuss and work harder in the hope of being noticed. This only seemed to irritate Mrs Howard more. She would respond with a frustrated, 'Come back and do that later.'

The girl noticed that Mrs Howard was bitingly curt if her husband had just left, had just arrived or was about to leave. Elizabeth had been curious yet frightened of Mrs Howard from their first meeting but she was also intrigued by the fine bone features and luminous skin with soft trails of veins, like a fragile flower petal. She was fascinated by the silky flowing floral cloth that hung softly over Mrs Howard's twig-like-figure. Elizabeth had been surprised that Mrs Howard was not much older that Miss Grainger; she seemed to be made from a totally different material. For Elizabeth, it was easy to work out; everyone at home was descended from different animals. Elizabeth was a *dinewan**, and so was her mother. But her father was Biggibilla, echidna. Elizabeth thought, even though she was white, that Miss Grainger was like a rabbit and Mr Howard was like a fox and Peter was like a camp dog and Mrs Carlyle had been like a sheep. Mrs

*dinewan = emu

Howard didn't seem to be made from anything. It was as though she had come from thin air.

But it was Mr Howard's presence that filled Elizabeth with an anxious anticipation. He was tall and muscular, with tawny features and eyes a colour Elizabeth had never seen before, the stagnant green of slow-moving water. They would sweep past her, sparingly acknowledging her – she could have been painted into the fine patterned wallpaper. Like Miss Grainger, her eyes would follow his figure as he moved past, though Miss Grainger's stare lingered.

· · · · ·

Elizabeth had little chance to explore the town, except when doing errands for Miss Grainger. At those times, she enjoyed the walk amongst the banks, stock companies, and hotels housed in wattle and daub with corrugated-iron roofs and plaster surfaces ruled to give the impression of masonry or bricks.

She was, on occasion, sent to the Chinaman's store for forgotten or newly needed provisions. She felt trepidation when face to face with the Chinese shopkeeper. His abrupt speech sounded like a barked order.

Elizabeth would not have been nearly as brave had the shop owner's daughter not been there. Behind the crowded rows of food, the large canvas bags of flour, the large crates of oils and the tins of tea leaves, the girls would talk timidly.

'You're new here,' the Chinese girl said to her on Elizabeth's first unaccompanied trip to the store.

'Yes. I'm at the Howard's house. I work there.'

'It is so big.' The Chinese girl said, her eyes widening, 'What is it like inside?'

'Well, there are lots of glass and shiny things. A big chandelier and the biggest table decoration you ever saw.'

'You're lucky to live there.'

'Well, the part I live in is like one of those crates over there. And all those fancy lights and ornaments, they just make for more dusting.'

The girls' giggles quickly escalated into laughter.

The Chinese girl had two names, Elizabeth would learn. She was 'Helen Chan' for white people but was born 'Chan Xiao-ying'. Helen's secret name was like music. Xiao-ying, like a soft breath, was much more captivating than Helen, just as 'Garibooli' was to 'Elizabeth'. The language Xiao-ying spoke with her father was Cantonese. When he used the language he knew best, his voice softened and he would appear a calmer man than the one who spoke English.

The physical differences between Xiao-ying's family and her own fascinated Elizabeth. They were as unlike Mrs Carlyle, Mrs Howard and Miss Grainger as her own mother and aunts were. One time, screened behind the shop's crowded stock, Elizabeth had touched Xiao-ying's eyes; their shape captivated her, the skin around them pulling them tight, making them the shape of gum leaves. In response, Xiao-ying felt Elizabeth's skin, rubbing it softly, giving her forearm a tentative caress. Their differences, under their fingertips, were tangible.

'Where do you come from?' Xiao-ying had asked her.

'My family lives far away from here in a place where the rivers meet,' Elizabeth explained as clearly as she herself could understand it.

'Did they not want you?' Xiao-ying asked, her voice low and her eyes cast to the ground.

'They made me leave,' Elizabeth answered, realising as she spoke that she had not made it clear who 'they' were.

The young Cantonese girl's fingers fumbled to unclasp

a small brooch. She placed it on Elizabeth's calloused palm and wrapped Elizabeth's fingers around the small gift. It was all she could think to give a girl whom no one wanted, a girl who caused a flood of feeling inside her, which Xiao-ying hoped could be relieved through this tiny gesture.

Elizabeth studied the carvings in the deep green jewellery that looked like a flower shedding its petals. She felt the coolness of the stone on her fingertips.

'I've never had anything so pretty before. It's even more beautiful than the things that Mrs Howard has.'

Elizabeth was awash with guilt for not having explained herself properly but she did not know how to correct the misleading impression she had given, especially after her new friend had shown her the tenderness that she had not been able to elicit from Miss Grainger. She didn't know how to explain that her family – although they loved her – had not been able to stop her from being taken away, and had not come for her, at least not yet.

. . . . .

My name is Garibooli. Whisper it.
Whisper it over and over again.

. . . . .

Elizabeth would sit on the back porch in the dark of the late evening and look at the stars. Other nights she would walk out into the endless back garden and lie on the cool grass, her body pressed against the earth, the blanket of sky above her. The stars were scattered in the same patterns as they were where she came from so, she reasoned to herself, she could not be that far away from her family and the camp. The moon hung above her, an incomplete question mark: the

Mea-Mei, the seven sisters, twinkling down over her. She could hear Kooradgie, the old storyteller, his voice rising out of the sounds of the evening.

. . . . .

Wurrannah had returned to the camp and was hungry. He asked his mother for some food but she did not have any. He asked other members of his clan for something to eat, but they had nothing either. Wurrannah was angry and left the camp saying, 'I will leave and live with others since my own family is starving me.' So he gathered up his weapons and walked off into new country. Wurrannah travelled a long way until he found a camp. Seven girls were there. They offered him food and invited him to stay and sleep in their camp for the night. They explained that they were sisters from the Mea-Mei clan. Their land was a long way away but they had decided to come and look at this new land.

Wurrannah woke the next morning, thanked the sisters for their kindness and pretended to walk off on his travels. Instead, he hid near the camp and watched. Wurrannah had become lonely and decided that he would steal a wife. So he watched the sisters and followed them as they set out with their yam sticks. He watched as the sisters unearthed the ants and enjoyed their feast.

While the sisters were eating, Wurrannah crept up to where the women had left their yam sticks and stole two. After lunch, when the sisters decided to return to their camp, two sisters discovered that their yam sticks were not where they had left them. The other sisters returned to the camp, believing it would not be long until the two found their sticks and would join them. The two sisters searched everywhere. While they were looking through the grass, Wurrannah stuck the two yam sticks in the ground and hid again. When the sisters saw their sticks, they ran towards them and tried to pull them from the ground, where they were firmly wedged. Wurrannah sprang from his hiding spot and grabbed both girls firmly around their waists. They struggled and screamed but their sisters were too far away to hear them. Wurrannah kept holding them tightly.

When the two sisters had calmed down, Wurrannah told them that they were not to be afraid. He was lonely and wanted wives. If they came quietly with him and did as they were told, he promised to look after them and be good to them. Seeing that they could not escape him, the sisters agreed and followed but they warned Wurrannah that their tribe would come to rescue them. Wurrannah travelled quickly to avoid being caught.

As the weeks passed, the two Mea-Mei women seemed to settle into their life with Wurrannah. When they were alone they talked of their sisters and wondered whether their sisters had begun to look for them, knowing that they would be rescued.

One day, Wurrannah ordered them to go and get bark from some trees so his fire could burn quicker. They refused, telling him that if they did he would never see them again.

Wurrannah became angry. He said to them, 'Go and get the bark!'

'But we must not cut bark. If we do, you will never see us again.'

'Your talking is not making my fire burn. If you run away, I will catch you and I will beat you.'

The two sisters obeyed. Each went to a different tree and as they made the first cut into the bark, each felt her tree getting bigger and bigger, lifting them off the ground. They clung tight as the trees, growing bigger and bigger, lifted them up towards the sky.

Wurrannah could not hear the chopping of wood so he went

to see what his wives were doing. As he came closer, he saw that the trees were growing larger and larger. He saw his wives, high up in the air, clinging to the trunks. He called to them to come down but they did not answer him. The trees grew so large that they touched the sky, taking the girls further and further away. As they reached the sky, their five sisters, who had been searching in the sky for them, called out, telling them not to be afraid. The five sisters in the sky stretched their hands out to Wurrannah's two wives and drew them up to live with them in the sky forever.

· · · · ·

Elizabeth took comfort from the story of rescue. Looking at the familiar patterns and recalling these stories made her feel as though she was lying only a few feet from her home, as if she could look across and see the fire and the shadows of her family through the trees at the end of the Howards' yard. Maybe, she thought, the train journey took less time than she had imagined. She had been so afraid, everything was unfamiliar, perhaps it felt longer than it was. A journey always seems longer the first time it is taken, she thought. After all, walking to the store always seemed to take more time than it took to walk back. So maybe, she hoped, she was closer to Euroke, Guni, Baina and Kooradgie and all her family than she had thought. Her family, still Eualeyai. Unlike her, with an altered name. She thought of them as solid and unchanging.

· · · · ·

> *My name is Garibooli. Whisper it.*
> *Whisper it over and over again.*

· · · · ·

Sometimes, after the work was finished, late at night, with limbs numb from tiredness, Elizabeth would spend time with Miss Grainger. With this feeling of ambient afterglow, Elizabeth felt bravest and the older woman felt affection for the child, more, she reflected, than she ever thought it possible to feel for a little darkie.

Frances Grainger had been of the opinion that the Aborigines were too primitive to be able to adjust to life in the civilised world. She could remember her father's comments that they were all dying out. Mr Howard had explained that the best that could be done was to rescue the children and try to train them. Reflecting on the way in which Elizabeth always tried so hard to do her chores exactly the way she was told, Frances had to concede that on this matter, as with all else, Edward Howard had been right. When the young girl seemed to yearn for her family and her home, Frances would reassure her that what was being done was for her own good and that she ought to adjust to it as best she could.

'I wish I knew when I was going home,' Elizabeth would say, as the two sat together on the stone back step.

'You can't always get what you wish for. Sometimes home just doesn't exist anymore.' Miss Grainger would offer these observations with such measured sadness that Elizabeth knew that there was sorrow as deep as her own within the woman whose gaze seemed to stare inward rather than out towards the stars.

Elizabeth reflected quietly as she looked out into the darkness. She felt that wherever her mother was, wherever Euroke was, wherever her father was, wherever her tree and her camp was, there was home.

. . . . .

I am running through the grass.
Running further through the grass.
I can feel it whip against my legs.
I can feel the hot sandy soil beneath my feet.

. . . . .

These rare, quiet moments with Miss Grainger came closest to breaking Elizabeth's loneliness, but any intimacy built up in the late evenings had dissipated by morning when an air of friendly formality would fall between the two once more.

Elizabeth observed the way the adults around her behaved towards each other. Because she was not considered very important in the scheme of things, she was often assumed to be too stupid to see what was really going on. But, she thought, I am smarter than Mrs Howard who does not seem aware of how much Miss Grainger dislikes her. Elizabeth also noticed the way Miss Grainger would repeat everything Mr Howard said, magnifying its insight each time she repeated it. And she saw how, when he was at home, Miss Grainger would make an extra effort with her hair, long and like strings of honey, the prettiest thing about her.

. . . . .

At the end of the day, with the dinner dishes washed and dried, the ironing done, the darning completed, Elizabeth could fall asleep. Her last thoughts were always of Euroke.

. . . . .

He will come and rescue me.
He will come and rescue me.

. . . . .

When the heart of winter came, Elizabeth found herself overcome by exhaustion. Tired when she awoke, her eyes struggled to open. Throughout the day, her bones would ache until eventually, late in the night, she fell back into bed, limp and lifeless until, not quite refreshed, she had to rise. She was a sturdy girl and had been used to her share of the work in the camp. Now in the Howards' house, the drudgery and loneliness of a kitchen maid's life and the winter chill highlighted her despair of ever returning home.

All she had was the odd lost word from a distracted Miss Grainger, the sly glances from the men who delivered groceries and wood to the back door, the shy smiles when Peter delivered the mail and the occasional longed-for talks with Xiao-ying.

. . . . .

At night I lie and think about running through the grass.
I am so tired that I only have to imagine that I am running,
and sleep finds me.
I run and run towards my dreams, towards my home.

. . . . .

'Come here,' Mr Howard one day said to her in the kitchen, a place where Elizabeth had never seen him venture before. She obeyed, just as she had been taught to do. He was home more and had been less distant with her than when she first came to the house. Now that she had settled in, he would watch her as she walked past. He would ask her to come over and take his plate from him as he sat on his own at the big dining table and she would be forced to brush against him. These encounters, brief and innocent, made her feel nervous but also secretly pleased that Mr Howard was paying attention to her. Once she came upon him in his study when she was dusting and he told her she was a good girl with pretty hair and he had stroked it as he told her she must look after it. He had asked how old she was and when she said that she was now almost sixteen, he had told her that it was a lovely age to be but she was very grown-up.

Elizabeth was pleased that he considered her to be as responsible as the others who worked in the house. Too often she was the lowest in the pecking order; everyone got to tell her what to do. It made her happy that someone would notice that she was clever too, especially if that someone was Mr Howard. Miss Grainger always chattered on about how important Mr Howard was, how he was a real gentleman, and she would go quiet as she floated off into her own thoughts. No one has ever noticed my hair before, Elizabeth would think to herself, and began to make an extra effort to make sure it was neat and pretty, just like Miss Grainger did.

Now in the kitchen with her, Mr Howard beckoned her and as she moved towards him, he leaned in to her and kissed her on the mouth. At first she liked it, the warm-wet touch of his lips, but as his hands moved and grabbed her sides she stood stiff, afraid. He brushed one hand across her breast, down her side, across the curve of her hip and squeezed her, feeling her under her clothes; his other hand held her hard. He was murmuring as though tasting something sweet and melting. Elizabeth was flushed with quivering relief when he stopped, the initial sensual pleasure now erased by her anxiety and the unfamiliarity of being so close to a man. Her whole body was alert with it.

He drew back, studied her lips and whispered, 'Of course, we can't be seen like this, can we?' He turned and exited the room.

Elizabeth stood motionless, her body inert, her mind racing with a flushing guilt. She had liked his touch at first; then she had hated it, that feeling against her skin, his taste and his force. She was fearful of his weight crushing against her, afraid of what he would do next. She felt ashamed of how she had felt both attraction and revulsion, both on her skin and in her body.

She ached to tell Miss Grainger, but she sensed that the older woman would be displeased. She was not even sure how to explain it, what to call it, which words to use. Nor was she sure what it meant. She couldn't even be sure, now that the pot was filling with washed and peeled potatoes, that anything had even really happened, whether Mr Howard had been there at all.

. . . . .

She slipped out after dinner and went to find Xiao-ying. As they lay in the grass in a paddock at the back of town, looking up at the sky, Elizabeth wanted to tell her friend about the strange encounter with Mr Howard. She felt a wariness about revealing it, even to her only friend.

'Do you ever think about boys?' she asked instead.

Xiao-ying laughed. 'Do you mean like to kiss and cuddle?'

Elizabeth smiled at Xiao-ying's amusement and nodded.

'Well, I don't think that my father would be very friendly to any boy who came to take me out for a walk or something like that. But,' she giggled, 'I do think that the boy who delivers the mail, Peter, is very handsome. And,' she paused with a cheeky grin, 'I think you do too.'

Elizabeth felt herself blush and this made Xiao-ying laugh even more. The laughter was contagious and Elizabeth lost herself in it. When their giggles subsided, Elizabeth said to her friend, 'Before I was brought here, my family was still trying to figure out who I should be married to. There was one man, but he was taken away by the gunjies for stealing a horse.'

'What's "gunjies"?'

Elizabeth smiled at her mistake, 'That's what we called the police back home, in our old language. Sometimes when I am talking I still forget to change some words.'

She paused at the thought of the way Miss Grainger would slap her hand when she didn't speak English properly. Then she looked over at Xiao-ying who was still staring at the stars. Elizabeth continued the conversation. 'My mother said they used to arrange marriages but all the old ways are hard to follow now and the white people do not like it. Will you marry someone who is Chinese?'

'I guess so. My parents haven't said but I think that's what they want me to do.'

'Do you find white people good looking or do you like Chinese boys better to look at?'

'I like both. I must like white boys because I think that Peter is very handsome.' As she made this last remark, Xiao-ying lapsed once more into fits of laughter. Elizabeth, despite her embarrassment that her secret was not so well kept, smiled.

The happiness of spending time with her friend, the teasing and shared wishes, made the encounter with Mr Howard seem far away.

· · · · ·

One morning, not long after the announcement that the war was over, Miss Grainger had come across Elizabeth hunched over and vomiting on the back verandah. She looked suspiciously at the young girl, noticing the emerging dark circles under her eyes and that her skin was unnaturally lighter. Upon witnessing the same the next morning, Miss Grainger became concerned. She left Elizabeth curled over on the back steps and went to see Mrs Howard in her morning room. 'Excuse me, ma'am,' she nervously started.

'Yes,' Mrs Howard replied, her eyes trained on her letter to emphasise her displeasure at being interrupted.

'I need to speak with you on a matter of some importance … and delicacy.'

Mrs Howard looked up, her expression already communicating deep disapproval.

Miss Grainger continued: 'I think the little darkie is … indisposed.'

'The little kitchen girl?'

Miss Grainger nodded, wondering what other 'little darkie' there could be.

'How did this happen?' asked Mrs Howard sharply.

Miss Grainger started to blush but was relieved when she realised that Mrs Howard (who was, after all, a married woman) hadn't really meant her to answer.

Mrs Howard sighed, 'Send for Dr Gilcrest.'

. . . .

An extract from the novel *Home* by Larissa Behrendt, UQP, 2004

ETHNICITIES

My Mother-in-Law in the Family Tree

PADDY O'REILLY

Ma and Papa, Dorothy's Asian parents-in-law, convert the garden into a vegetable plot and can't see the point of a nature strip. Ma's subservience to her son gets on his nerves – 'She's smothering me. She doesn't belong here.' But Ma desperately wants to stay. Cultural differences tellingly highlighted through character.

My husband's mother can't pronounce my name. She tries to say 'Dorothy' but the word comes out all mashed so she has taken to calling me 'Doh'. Her native tongue is harsh and guttural. The language is full of ughs from the back of the throat and chopped syllables. When she says 'Doh' it sounds like a command, like an expletive, like Homer Simpson venting his frustration. 'Doh,' she shouts. She always shouts, as if she is still in the village where she was born, calling out to her neighbour across the bamboo grove. 'Doh, I make sticky rice. Where pot?'

I look at my husband, a suave, urbane computer analyst, and I wonder that he has issued from his mother. At night he arrives home from work and his mother presents him with a drink or a snack and they speak their language in rapid barks but he is looking over the top of his short, squat mother's head to see me. I am just home from work too. It is my son, Sean, who runs to me. He is six years old and we are his whole world. His mother, his father, his grandparents. My husband is my mother-in-law's whole world. I watch her sometimes as she fusses around him and I am overawed by the amount of love she holds for him in her body, like muscle tissue, hard and fierce and tensile.

Here in this Melbourne suburb, the neighbours on our right have a Zen garden of polished white river-stones.

Tasteful granite statues of Buddhas and curved shapes like triple-mounded buttocks line the edge of the sea of stones. Weeds are dealt with swiftly. On the left side the neighbours nurture exotic succulents with flowers of orange and yellow that burst out one day then disappear overnight. Before my husband's parents came to live with us, our garden was the local disgrace. Fat untended hydrangeas and straggly geraniums had overrun the garden beds and patches of dirt and yellowed couch grass marred the lawn.

'So,' my neighbour, Narelle, said when I stood with her in the supermarket, the after-work shoppers flowing around us like we were stones in a river. 'So, how's it all going with your parents-in-law?'

'Oh it's fine,' I answered. 'My mother-in-law's always busy. And my father-in-law just potters about, you know. He's the strong silent type.'

My neighbour reached across me and picked a packet of instant porridge from the shelf.

'They're busy in the garden, then?'

'Yes, they love the vegetable garden. Where they come from, you know …'

'I see them sometimes, when I'm home. I only work part time, of course, because of the children.'

There was a pause and I wanted to bolt. Something was coming. I wanted to run home and feel Sean's chubby arms around my neck and smell the garlic and chilli my mother-in-law would be frying up in the big pan.

'Well then,' I said. 'I'd better …'

'I noticed your mother-in-law yesterday shimmying up a tree in your yard. Surely that can't be good at her age?'

There is a kind of nut that grows on a tree in our back yard that Ma, as Sean first named her and we all now call her, likes to grind and cook into food. The nuts are poisonous when they come down from the tree. They can only be eaten after a long process of boiling and leaching. Days later they arrive at the table in a thick brown spicy curry. The curry tastes nutty and bitter at once. It is an acquired taste and demands a level of courage. It took me months before I would even try it, and then months more before I let Sean have any. He loved it. 'Yum, poison nut curry,' he says. Once he climbed a chair and tried to reach into the bowl where the nuts were soaking. Ma slapped his hand away with a ferocity that relieved me. 'No touch,' she shouted. 'Sean no touch.'

My neighbour chose the right word for Ma's expeditions. Even though she is not strong, Ma shimmies like a dancer up the tree. She shimmies up with her skirt tucked into her underwear, wrinkled old legs gripping each side of the trunk as she reaches for the next handhold. If you look up you can see her squinting through the branches, then out over the suburb. The first time she climbed the tree she came back down and shouted, 'Doh, next door full of rock! I give her vegetable!'

My parents-in-law have grown vegetables from what was once grey dust. Papa hoes his way slowly down the lines of leafy greens and yellow and red chillies every Saturday morning with Sean trailing behind him, learning to talk their language almost as well as he speaks mine. Over two years I have watched from the back porch, sipping my tea with Ma squatting beside me grinding spices with a mortar and pestle, as the couch grass was tamed and the hydrangeas trimmed back and finally, when they thought I was not looking, uprooted and composted. Sometimes my husband stands behind me with his hand on my shoulder, watching as well. I hear him tssk.

'The neighbours are going to start up again,' he sighs as he watches Papa spread horseshit, found on one of our driving trips, across a newly ploughed bed. My husband has no idea about what the neighbours think, except for a few morsels I let slip. They complain to me whereas to him, the tall, handsome Asian stranger among them, they nod and wave, or bob in what seems like a half curtsey to demonstrate how tolerant they are.

Not so with Ma. When she shouts, 'Hello, Missus,' at them, they shout back.

'The rubbish bin goes THIS WAY,' Narelle says in a voice louder than you would expect her neat figure to produce. 'Or the truck CAN'T PICK IT UP.' She seethes at Ma's singing, at the square of dirt Papa dug into the nature strip.

'This is supposed to be LAWN!' she enunciates at him when he is on his knees, pulling weeds and coaxing green vegetables from the soil. 'LAWN.' He nods and smiles at her, pointing accusingly up and down the street where the nature strips stretch on in endless smooth green like rolls of upholstery material. He understands her – his English is much better than Ma's – and pretends he doesn't.

But when Narelle talks to me her words are soft and reasonable.

'They're lovely people, aren't they,' she says. 'How hard it must be for them here. We all try to help of course. Just small things, helping them with the bins and what not.'

My parents-in-law didn't come to our wedding. Instead they spent the money on our honeymoon, paying for us to travel to their country and stay in a five star hotel that they visited in their best uncomfortable clothes. On our first meeting, we sat in the coffee shop of the hotel, surrounded by brown and cream and tan upholstery. The silver coffee service squatted like a trophy on the table between us, obscuring my father-in-law's head from my view, and a waiter came by regularly to top up our coffee cups. Outside the hotel window I could see the heat shimmer, like a damp hot hand pressing against the window.

'My mother wants to know if you like the food here,' my husband translated for me. I told her through him that I enjoyed it very much.

'She wants to know if all Australian girls are as beautiful as you.'

I smiled at him. The waiter poured more coffee and we all watched the thin brown stream sluice into the china cup in front of my mother-in-law.

'What did she really say?' I asked.

My new husband laughed. 'No, really!' he protested.

I suspected his mother was making fun of me. I am not ugly, but I'm hardly a movie star. I frowned and he said, 'It's the kind of thing people say here. She's just trying to please you.'

'Oh,' I said.

He laughed again. 'Don't worry, you're family now. That won't last.'

My husband arrives home and Ma brings him slippers, as if we are living in a 1950s American sitcom. She massages his feet when we sit in front of the television at night, and she cuts his toenails. At first I found this disturbing, almost incestuous to watch. I wandered out to the kitchen, where Ma had arranged the pots on the stove for the next day's meal, then into the study, where Ma had tidied my papers and my husband's into neat piles, then back into the lounge room where Papa was polishing shoes on a carefully laid carpet of newspaper. 'Doh,' Ma would shout, 'Sean need food now.' Or 'Doh, where tea?' I gritted my teeth and slammed utensils around the kitchen and brought a tray back into the room. I secretly named her 'the poison nut'.

I did stupid things. I bought newspapers from her country to make her homesick. I made sausages and rich casseroles and other foods distasteful to her night after night until even Sean asked for a salad. I found myself trying to hoard Sean's affection. 'Where's Ma?' he asked me one day when we were on a shopping trip. I told him not to worry about it. 'I wish she was here,' he said. When we got home, he ran to her and hugged her and babbled on about the trip, and as I trembled with rage like a jealous child, I heard her say, 'That nice. You have nice time with Mum. That good.'

These days I sit in the front seat of the car next to Papa on our monthly drives, leaving Ma jammed happily between my husband and my son in the back seat, worrying at Papa about something in words I cannot understand. We coast up to the flat plains of the Western Highway and stop to wander through a display home, or to pick a weed by the roadside that we will later eat, or to marvel at a caravan park. For a long time Papa and Ma, still shy after their arrival, were uncomfortable in the spacious bedroom with ensuite we had put at their disposal. They discovered caravans on their first Western Highway trips, when my husband was teaching his father to drive.

'Doh,' Ma shouted at me when they got back one day. She always travelled with them during the driving lessons, issuing loud instructions to Papa from the back seat as he crept nervously along the left lane of the Highway at sixty kilometres an hour, the car rocking in the wind wake of speeding trucks. 'Doh,' she shouted. 'We like caravan. We sleep caravan here.' She stomped over to a corner of the back yard and pointed at the dirt. 'Here.' She kept looking at the ground. 'Better for you,' she said in a voice so soft it shamed me.

It took me months to dissuade her. She finally accepted the bedroom as her home when I bought a rocking chair and placed it near the window. She sits there now in the late afternoon and stares at the sky. I wonder if she is remembering or wishing. Or regretting.

It's not just the neighbours who complain. The irony is that now I have learned to live with my mother-in-law, my husband wants his parents to go home. 'She's smothering me,' he says. He tells me this in whispers at night after we have made love and lie wound around each other under the bedclothes. 'She doesn't belong here. She's too much.' I cannot imagine how much they sacrificed to send him here when he was sixteen. He went to boarding school, learned the manners of the privileged classes, gained the confidence of a boy who knows he will succeed simply because of the school he has come from. Even though he arrived speaking broken English and feeling like a refugee, he has cast all that aside and now he boasts about the business strategies he uses in meetings to throw millionaires off balance.

'She doesn't belong here,' he says each time he sees her shimmying up a tree or trying to haggle in the supermarket or rocking in her chair and staring at the sky, a different sky to the one she used to know. And now she is starting to show her age, he shakes his head more often. He takes her to the doctor and interprets for her, but he has no language for words like aorta or osteoporosis. His words are the words of a sixteen-year-old, where he left off speaking the language until his parents came over. I ask him what he is saying to her and he blushes, so I know he is lying. 'I've told her she should take it easy,' he says. But I wonder what he is really telling her.

Last week she said to me, 'I no want go home, Doh.'

'You're happy here?' I asked.

'My son here, my grandson. My village, gone. I no like city.'

Before they came to live with us in Australia they had been forced off their land by a clearing program and housed in a large block of flats in the capital. My father-in-law went to work in a factory producing tyres and my mother-in-law cleaned houses for wealthy people in a suburb an hour's bus trip away. Here, Ma doesn't believe she lives in a city. There are too many trees and lawns, the skyscrapers can't be seen from our backyard. She has made her own village of our street. She treats the supermarket like the market at home, where she picked up fruit and sniffed it loudly, shook melons to hear their ripeness, pushed her thumbs into cuts of meat. When she hangs at the top of the tree in our yard, surveying the gardens beyond, she is home. Perhaps this is not the home she loves the best, but it is her home now.

'I no want go back,' she repeats like a child. After a morning in the garden she sits in her rocking chair, swinging back and forth. She is thin now, her wrinkled face floppy with spare skin. Sean runs in when he comes home from school and flings himself onto her frail body and she holds him close then scolds him in her language. He just laughs. Then at six o'clock she gathers herself and comes downstairs to welcome home my husband. These days he frowns and tells her, or at least I think he tells her, to go back and lie down. But she wants to see him settled next to her husband in the lounge room, Sean at their feet.

'My son need me, Doh,' she shouts. 'You lazy girl. No good cook, no good clean. I make good house.'

The worst thing is that it's true. Slowly, over the last two years, I have let her take over the running of the house and we eat better than anyone I know. Still, when she makes remarks like this the old anger surges and I turn my face away, my cheeks reddening. She hits me affectionately in the arm. 'No, no, Doh. You good girl.' She shakes her head vigorously. 'I no mean bad feeling. You good girl, Doh.'

Last night, for the first time in months, I saw her up the tree. She only ever picks off a few nuts at a time, as if she is measuring out the life of the fruit. Sean came and stood beside me. 'Poison nut curry!' he said delightedly. I sent him back to his room while I kept watching. She has taught me to cook many dishes from her country but not this. She is the only one who knows how to draw the poison from the nut and make it palatable.

Her climb down was slow and arduous but she concentrated on each foothold and when she reached the bottom she patted the tree trunk and grunted. I stepped back behind the curtain of the lounge room. Maybe I am wrong, but I thought she would not like me to see the difficulty of the climb. I only kept watching because I am hoping for the return of the shimmy.

. . . .

The Hafli

EVA SALLIS

Abd al-Rahman, newly arrived in Australia from Iraq, is an uncertain guest at a boisterous Lebanese get-together. For the other guests, thoughts of their homeland involve no more than a bitter-sweet nostalgia, but for him it's the unbearable pain of loss. Sallis captures the vitality of an Arab culture determinedly maintained in a foreign land.

Abd al-Rahman arrived at the party with his lawyer Sahar in her sleek black BMW. He had stared out of the black comfort of the car, only half listening to her telling him that, although this was Australia, things were quaintly traditional, controlled by gossip and tyrannised by memory; that he would cause a stir just by arriving with her. The sunset lingered on the rooftops and glinted still in the blue shadows among trees. What a pointy city! Such an agitated architecture, eager and uncertain. So Western! Big windows, but shuttered or filmed over. From the car, the suburb seemed to slide by utterly soundless. It was clean and beautiful, the stuff of dreams. The red, green and silver roofs, each different. He wanted a roof like that.

He had seen few people. Sometimes a couple dressed in shorts, walking a dog on a lead. No children. None at all. What strange gardens, all out the front, empty except for roses, other flowers he didn't recognise, shapely trees and carpets of orange-lit grass. Public gardens, gestures, but with small fences. We are not afraid, these gardens said, but don't enter. They made him uneasy, and he realised that he didn't know what sort of people would live like this. Such dark, inward-looking houses, once you entered them.

'... Australians are the same, really.' Sahar said just then, and he was jolted.

Zein and Amin's house was a little Lebanon, something Zein told everyone the moment they entered.

'You've arrived! Ahl*aan*! Ahl*aan*!' she shrieked. 'Step ashore!'

Upstairs Christians and Druzes chatted over the railing, hurling the few French phrases they could dig up back and forth, looking down on the atrium in which East and West Beirut, Christian and Muslim, met and mingled. A gilt-edged photo of an ancient cedar hung on the keystone of the entrance arch, announcing unnecessarily to the Lebanese that Zein and Amin's house was their house, regardless of religion, and vaunting their origin to everyone else. Framed portraits of long-dead socialist patriots hung above doorways. Zein's little memento of the village of Zahle, a tiled fountain, tinkled at the centre of the atrium, lit up by fairy lights trailed around the concrete thighs and bosom of its rustic girl water-pourer. People milled and greeted, leaning back with arms outstretched at the sight of each relative or friend, and then sailing forward to land kisses on each cheek thrice, asking, *How are you, how is the family? In good health? Praise be to God. Me? Yes, in my best state!*

Ibtisam and Haifa, arms linked, greeted Abd al-Rahman warmly. But as he moved away their eyes followed him as they leant in close to each other, their lips moving.

Sam, Farhan and Amin chatted, standing unusually erect, shoulders squared, as they always did at parties. They liked to overhear their wives whisper, 'Pillars of the community!'

The long-time refugees were there, those who had lost Palestine, those who had lost Palestinians. Abd al-Rahman was the most recent refugee and the only Iraqi. 'Welcome to exile,'

Farhan said to him, nastily, and was haughty to the point of social disgrace. Sahar quickly steered Abd al-Rahman away.

'*Haram*, poor Farhan,' she murmured into his ear but without sympathy. 'Many people here are very Australian about the new refugees.'

'Le petit Lib*an!*' Zein sang at him from the other side, and grabbed Abd al-Rahman's arm with no restraint, tearing him from Sahar, jiggling and shimmying her huge body, to drag him off into Beirut.

He had never been to Beirut.

The *hafli* was soon in full swing. The younger generation shouted foul Arabic insults affectionately at each other, parodying their parents on a bad day. Marie and Rima flirted with Salah, trying to excite and shock their elders.

Munira and Rayya arrived late, carrying platters of *waraq al-inab* and *mutabbal, tabouli* and *manaqish al-zaater*. They sailed in like richly laden ships into harbour, the heady smells of fresh mint, burnt thyme, and the spiced chickpeas and eggplant filling the entrance and kitchen. The two friends shrieked their greetings to each cluster of friends and relatives they ploughed through, leaving twin plum and ruby-red slashes on the cheeks of the adolescents and children. Munira's youngest son slouched and shrugged in their wake, rolling eyes at his cousins.

There were almost no young men and women at the party. Just children, adolescents and their parents – the older exiles, emigrants and refugees, and those they still controlled. The middle generation, the young married and divorced couples, were missing; a silent hole in the hearts of their parents and secret role models for their younger brothers and sisters.

. . . . .

There was something completely familiar about it all, and that made it more disorienting. Abd al-Rahman could not relax. He felt his skin prickle with discomfort and an upwelling of misery. People around him danced, twirling their stiff raised hands as they held imaginary sticks or scarves. He was only thirty-six, an engineer, a widower. There was no word for a father whose child was dead. Why was there no word, like *orphan*, like *widower*, for what he was?

. . . . .

Sam recited Imru al-Qays' *'Muallaqa'* as he always did, and they would have felt something was lacking if he didn't. Sam had once had 100 000 lines of poetry memorised, but now, no matter how hard he tried, he could only remember Imru al-Qays. *Stop and weep for the memory of the departed*, it began, but then was so vigorous and heroic as it progressed, that he enjoyed being in exile and the fact that he might as well shed tears for himself.

Then Rima, who was twenty-two and virtually a doctor, did something that hadn't been done before. She recited a *muwashshah*, an Andalusian love poem in both classical and colloquial Arabic, written in the tenth century, born of another clash of cultures. Everyone listened politely but without the profound stirring the pure and instantly recognised cadences of the great poet had evoked, and Rima's voice faded at the end and her face flushed red.

To cheer her up. Salah put a tape on the stereo and began a raucous song. His mother Ibtisam turned on him, clipped him over the ear and sent him to eject it. Rima laughed.

The women settled out at the edge, chattering and clanking dishes; the teenagers gravitated to the outside verandah, under the floodlit trunk of a lemon-scented gum; and the men pulled up chairs in the centre of the living room. Amin put a CD of Fayrouz's *Rajioun* on the stereo and some people sang along and others blew their noses. *We will return.* The bittersweet voice wound through the room. The clanging from the kitchen fell silent as the momentum of the *hafli* stilled and then slowly began spinning into the past. *We will return.* Some women gathered in closer on the periphery and the teenagers, sneering and smelling of cigarettes, filtered back into the room. The small children found laps and wove back into the centre of the circle.

. . . . .

Abd al-Rahman was reeling. These were the pleasures of exile, the happy tears and complacent grief that could one day be his. Levantine Arabic and the crisp and sibilant sounds of English filled his ears. He felt numb. All lament was remote and sweet, as removed as the dream of Australia. Then he saw his daughter Siham on a white gypsum floor, playing a Kleenex box like a drum, as if she were right in front of him. His heart burned and his scalp shrank against his skull. He stood up, thinking to take leave of his hospitable hosts, or at least to get outside. He couldn't breathe.

He stumbled out onto the verandah into a cloud of smoke hanging around three girls and four boys, all of whom straightened politely and exchanged glances as he leant over the balustrade and stared out. The Western cityscape glittered to the black velvet coast.

'You OK, Professor?' a tall boy said to him in clumsy broken Arabic.

'OK, OK', Abd al-Rahman said in English, but suddenly couldn't remember any more English words. He stared out at the city. For a moment it seemed as though he could reach out and touch it. Then it sped from him and settled into a middle and far distance, fixed and twinkling. Siham's drum-beat, the erratic patter of a child's hands on shallow cardboard, rustled and ratta-tatted in his ear. He thought he might vomit. He stood up and faced around, his back to the dizzying spangle. The girls had gone and the four boys stood ranged in a semicircle in front of him, silhouetted in the glow from the French doors. They said nothing. The curtains had dropped back into place and no one could see out. He felt the rough wood of the balustrade under his palms, and slowly, dimly, he felt himself begin to sweat. The boys' eyes glimmered in the swelling darkness. Why didn't they speak? They all looked familiar, homely, and he felt his heart thumping. The arched brows, fine, sculpted faces. The silence between them stiffened, thickened until it had gone beyond any possible exchange and into a meaningless, terrifying emptiness. It became part of the darkness that seemed to roil into the space between them. Siham would not leave him. She pounded the Kleenex box, battering it out of shape, then looked up at him and began to cry. He could not break, not now. Who were these strange boys? The strangeness of one with long hair. No moustaches. American haircuts. But achingly familiar. And yet he could not remember a single one of them from the round of introductions inside. Perhaps they really were strangers, who could run off into the night. He wanted to lift his arms but felt a pain pinning them to the wood, as if he had already been assaulted. The boys hadn't moved. He thought he was going to pass out. His chest was screaming with the pain that had driven him out of the light and into their realm. His jaw was aching, as if punched. They hadn't moved. Why was he afraid of four boys? Why didn't they speak?

Then, just as he felt himself slipping down, felt his body moving without his will, they all moved too. He thought he might scream from the terror of their approach, but pain punched him back into speechless, breathless silence. They moved in to catch him, and as their arms, screams and exclamations crashed in around him, the light flooded from the house, blinding him in whiteness. Warm arms of smelly, real boys wrapped about him, catching, lifting, crying out in English in panicked, shocked voices. Arabic fluttered in the background, distressed and helpless. English bounced back and forth between his boys and the men and women who rushed slowly out of the house to the verandah. He had the warmth of sweaty human skin against his ankles, and arms wrapped about his groin and chest. The long-haired boy held his head and stroked his brow as they carried him in. Then the boy leant in close and murmured in strange sweet Arabic into Abd al-Rahman's ear, 'Gently, Uncle, gently, all shall be well.'

Abd al-Rahman could smell aftershave. He smiled. He hoped they would never let him go. He wanted to laugh from happiness when Zein cuffed two boys and wedged her warm breasts up against his body too.

. . . .

Padre Nostro, Who Art in Heaven

JOSEPHINE VRACA

The rosary. Her Mamma makes her say it daily, in memory of her grandmother, who has just died back in Italy. While the other girls in her group are watching The Sullivans, *she is telling her beads. Until she can't take it any more. A small rebellion, but it highlights how a youthful generation abandons the traditions of the one that came before it.*

I hid them for a whole day. And a night. It was the only time I'd dared. But we'd been at it so long, threading the uneven silver beads through our fingers until we were numb and my hands were stiff. *Padre nostro che è nel'cielo.* Mamma would make me sound it quietly in English, so that I could be more like the other girls – *Our Father who art in Heaven* – but I didn't have the heart to tell her that the other girls were watching *The Sullivans*, not reciting the rosary night after night with their mothers. And I didn't tell her that the other girls didn't have votive candles at their bedsides with the face of Jesus delicately painted on the glass. Maybe they had a picture of Greg Brady or The Bay City Rollers. But I didn't dare tell her that.

· · · · ·

We had come back on the day that Elvis died. Papà was at the airport with the orange Falcon with the black racing stripes. His hair, dark like fermented wine, was flat and the curl that normally sat boldly on his forehead, like Dean Martin's, was limp and uncombed, as though he'd forgotten the Brylcreem. The skin around his eyes was the colour of pomegranates and puffed below his dewy eyelashes. He'd just heard, he said. Mamma rested her head on his neck and they touched each other like it had been months, which it had. And I sat on top of the luggage, dipping my fingers into the packet of Wizz Fizz that had become lumpy with moisture.

I wasn't sure if they wept because of Elvis or because of Nonna. Papà had called us while we were still in Italy, just days before Nonna had died, called to tell Mamma he was sorry and that he wished he could be there but the farm couldn't manage itself – he didn't trust any of the Turks to look after it. I would think of him there in that rusty tin house in the middle of nowhere. It rattled against the wind that could probably rip off its corrugated roof. I imagined him with the TV tray, the one with the paddle-steamer and the old-time travellers looking so festive. He'd be sitting in front of the dusty fireplace eating a bowl of spaghetti and watching the news, hopeful that something would filter through about the Mother Country. Anything. Sometimes, I would watch him from the doorway when he thought he was alone and see oil trailing down his chin but he'd be too tired to notice, too lonely to care.

On the other side of the world, Mamma slowly peeked into an old trunk. She lifted the thick damask and inhaled deeply. *What is it, Mamma?* I asked. *Lemons*, she replied. To me, it just smelled damp.

The rain pelted our heads as we bolted onto the train on our way to catch the plane back home, back to Papà. Mamma held her head and arms over the window and waved at her sister, like she knew it would be the last time. They locked their fingers together until the train moved with a jerk off the platform. The tears rolled onto Mamma's satin shirt. *You can never get tears out of satin.* Or was it silk? So many lessons.

She didn't have the energy to warm the kitchen on those first few days we were back. She stayed in bed in the room that faced the empty paddock and would cry out occasionally, *oh Mamma*, as though the words were like oxygen for the dead. I couldn't endure her pleas, so I left her with a glass of water and some Aspros and took the dogs for a run, stopping by the Turks' house and motioning through the door to the boy, careful that nobody should see me.

In the channel, the yabbies were jumping with joy into our dirty black buckets as the yellow nylon rope cut into our hands when we pulled against the current. The wind wound its way through the loquat tree and it seemed to talk, only it spoke words that only Mamma could understand – *go put a jacket on, the rain's coming*. But I never heard the words because it didn't speak to me.

After the boy went home, I sat on the edge of the murky channel where the river snakes slipped through making S's with their rubbery bodies and the cows mooed me into a restful sleep that lately seemed to evade me at night – the sounds that came from the dark wardrobe would drive me into an inescapable insomnia that would find me running for the school bus in the morning, hoping that I could keep my breakfast down, the taste of Vegemite thick on my tongue.

· · · · ·

I took them after the third month. By this time I'd committed each of the Mysteries to memory and my skin had been scorched by the embers that jumped from the fireplace each night – exploding redbacks, Mamma said. We would press each of the beads as we repeated prayer after prayer, watching the sun disappear after another day. They were the silver ones; the ones that she had brought with her and that she kept in a small square jewellery box with the name of the jeweller embossed in gold on the lid.

It was the sort of cloudy day in November when the sun gropes you with fingers so leaden that it leaves the inevitable red ring at the edges of your sleeves and a flush on your cheeks. I hid down the side paddock, the one next to the haystack and with grass so tall and green and filled with sweet dew. I knew that nobody would ever find me. I left a trail as wide as my outstretched arms, flattening the thin blades with my weight as I crawled through.

I peeked over the grass at old Mario Lentini who sat in the gutted-out Torana with a transistor on the dashboard. His legs hung through the shattered windscreen, and he was tapping them with a heavy hand. He sang high into the sky, and from the side he looked like he was howling. Fancied himself a bit of a rocker, with a curl that hung low over his brow, black and shiny like a rooster's comb. They said he sounded like Frank Sinatra but to me he sounded like he was singing in slow motion.

I lay on my back and made animals out of the clouds. I counted the number of beads on the rosary but lost track. Smaller than the ones I had hanging from my bedpost. I had big plans – one day soon, maybe when I was thirteen, I would pull them off the bedpost and replace them with a stuffed toy, Humphrey or Fat Cat. The rosary beads hung close to my head at night, each bead the size of a dry chickpea, heavy with repentance. I ran my fingers over them and they were uneven, all coarse edges, marking my palms. Like scars.

I chewed on a lemon flower and wondered if a dog had peed on it, like Mamma always warned, but it tasted good anyway. Despite the heavy rains early in winter that Papà had often told us about when he'd rung, much of the earth was already scorched. *Nothing like home*, Mamma would remind me. This place was all still so new to them and they were still indelibly connected to things I'd never even heard of – almond milk, yellow brioche dipped in tart but saccharine-sweet granita for breakfast and school notebooks with little grids instead of lines. Papà told me stories about walking the streets in summer without sunglasses because the sun was not so cruel, his eyes would be wide open and the air would smell like open fires and fresh milk – not the sort of fresh milk that came in a bottle, but straight from a sleepy cow and into a grey pail.

I wrapped the rosary around my fist and punched the air like a boxer, pressing the crucifix in my palm. *Our Father who art in Heaven...* Each of the Mysteries of the rosary imprinted just like the seven times table. *Seven times seven is forty-nine.* Sister Margaret was fond of slapping the times tables into us wog girls – slapped the backs of our calves with the wooden ruler until they glowed like sunburn. I still remember the seven times table. And I can still remember the prayers of the rosary. I can still remember redemption but I don't believe so much any more – like all good Catholic girls.

I climbed over the fence, where the cow had been gutted recently and the flies hummed melodies with the cicadas. Trails of intestines lay delicately over the stones like Mamma's stockings on the Hill's Hoist. I sniffed the air and drew the stench of death deep into my lungs, heavy and fearful like the dog when Papà came home late at night.

I opened the gate quietly, worried that the rickety, rusted hinges would sound out their alarm to Mamma and I would be found out. She was still filled with guilt that she had been so distant when her mother fell ill, but she had enough vigour left to pursue me with the splintered spoon she kept near the laundry door ready to punish untold transgressions. I latched the gate carefully and ran quickly to the chicken coop, watchful for the slithering gold bands of the tiger snake. I held the beads close in the pocket of my ruffled skirt, which caught against the dry scrub. My socks were thick with burrs that scratched my skin. But there was no time to stop to pick them off.

Shadows in the chicken coop. The red hen fluffed its feathers at me as I wandered through the gate. *Filomena.* Mamma had named her after the nun who used to teach her to embroider the thick sheets that were itchy against my legs at night. *Filomena, qua-qua*, she would call out, and the hen would immediately vacate her nest to display a small pile of creamy eggs, clean as though she had polished them.

But today, Filomena didn't move from her perch. It was the wrong time of the day for that. I watched her closely, fearful of her sharp beak as I approached the back corner of the coop. Cool against my fingers, I tucked the beads next to the crumpled packet of Benson & Hedges and a near-empty box of matches in the hole and replaced the wooden shingle and covered it with straw for good measure.

I ran back to the house as though I was running quickly over summer bitumen. Mamma was in the windowless kitchen pushing a piece of wood into the stove. The room smelled of yeast, and smoke came from the oven. *Bread.* My eyes burned from the roasted chillies that clung to the dampness. When she turned to me, her eyes were swollen. She wiped her arm across her nose and fished a jewellery box from her apron and opened it. A wad of cotton wool sat in the plastic box but it was empty. Mamma held out her hands, like she did when she wanted me to know that she was telling the truth. *Gone*, she mouthed, gone. *It must have been that boy.* She pointed at the Turks' house. She put the box back into her pocket and turned away to watch the burning wood.

Heaviness. Like the solar eclipse on my Communion day when we took cover beneath the fig tree for fear that the sky was falling. The weight of my mother's loss enclosed me and hummed slowly the tunes with words I no longer recognised. Sinless. And me, at eight, I wrapped her in my arms and allowed her to press her fingers deeply into my flesh, making purple marks. And I felt warm droplets on my neck, which washed it all away.

. . . .

HOSTILITIES

Dingle the Fool

ELIZABETH JOLLEY

Dingle, who is simple, lives happily in the attic of the old family house, above his two married sisters, Deirdre and Joanna, who start to quarrel. Joanna wants to sell the house but Deirdre, for Dingle's sake, does not. Then the dilemma is unexpectedly resolved, with Jolley's feeling for character everywhere evident.

'No one can tell what is taken up from the earth by a lemon tree.' Deirdre's mother said it didn't matter where the roots of the tree were, the lemons would take what they needed.

'What if they are in the drain?' Deirdre asked.

'What if they are?' her mother replied. 'Can you see drains on any of them lemons? Can you?'

Deirdre stood under the tree. It was fragrant with flower and fruit at the same time, she liked to be sent to fetch a lemon.

When Deirdre took off the cushion covers to wash them before Christmas, roses and peacocks from her childhood spilled out, frayed, from the worn covers underneath, reminding her of the tranquillity in that expectation of happiness as she and her sister Joanna, years ago, sat on the back verandah twisting tinsel and making red and green paper chains.

Now Deirdre remembered her mother most around Christmas. At that time of the year the sisters stole mulberries from the tree in the garden next to theirs and their mother, approving, made pies.

'Take Dingle to the river while I'm baking.' Mother called to them, so they took their brother out with them. They called him Dingle, it was his own name for himself.

'Dingle!' Mother called him softly smiling at his gentle face. 'Always look after Dingle,' she told the girls. 'Remember, people will say he is a fool and will try to take away anything he's got. And he will give them everything.'

He loved the river. He shouted on the shore and waded into the brackish water, waving his thin arms and following the other children, he wanted to play with them. The other children swam and Dingle followed them, unable to swim. He waded deeper and the gentle waves slapped his knees and then caressed his waist and he held up his arms as he went deeper and then the water was round his neck and over his face and his round mouth gasped as the water closed and parted, rippling over his shorn head.

'Dingle!' Deirdre shouted and ran into the river and grabbed him. She had to carry him home, her dress sopping wet, embarrassed because she was big and her breasts showed up round and heavy under the wet clinging material.

After the death of their mother the three of them lived on in the old weatherboard and iron house. And, for the time being, after they were married the sisters continued to share the house. Dingle had the two attics in the gable of the house, a cramped spaciousness all his own. They could hear him moving about up there for he was a heavy man and they often could hear his thick voice mumbling to and fro as he talked to the secret people in his secret world in the roof.

The sisters spent their time looking after their babies which had been born within a few weeks of each other. Every day when they had bathed the babies and were washed themselves and dressed in freshly ironed clothes – they were always washing and ironing – they went out from the dark ring of trees around the house into the sunshine and, crossing the road, they walked, brushing against hibiscus and lantana with their hips and thighs, up the hill to the shops. Joanna had a little pram but Deirdre carried her son, his dark fuzzy head nestled against the creamy skin of her plump neck. The sisters gazed at the things in the shops and they met people they had known all their lives and they showed off their lovely babies.

Everything was peaceful in the household except when the conversation turned, as it often did, to land prices and whether they should sell the house and the land. All round them the old houses had been sold and blocks of flats and two-story townhouses with car parks instead of gardens were being built. Joanna longed for a modern house on one of the estates. She had magazines full of glossy pictures and often sat looking at them.

'Look at this electric kitchen, Deirdre,' she would say. 'Just look at all these cupboards fitting in to the walls!' But Deirdre wanted to stay in the house; as well as being fond of the place where she had always lived, she had a deep wish to go on with a continuation of something started years ago. Sometimes she pictured to herself the people who first built the house and she thought of them planting trees and making paths and as she trod the paths she rested on these thoughts. And of course the house with the big tangled garden was the only world Dingle could have. And the house did belong to all three of them.

'The value of the land's gone up again!' Joanna said at breakfast. 'Why don't we sell now and build? Oh, do let's!' Deirdre moved the milk jug and pushed aside the bread. 'I want to stay here,' she said.

How would Dingle be on a new housing estate where no one knew or understood him? She imagined him pressing the old tennis ball, which he thought contained happiness, on complete strangers. It was all right at the bowling club where he went sometimes to trim the lawns, they knew him there and would take the dirty old ball and thank him and then give it back. Sometimes Dingle lost his ball and Deirdre and Joanna, scolding, had to leave their housework and help him search for it in the fallen leaves beneath the overgrown pomegranates, and in the fragrance of the long white bells of the datura, they parted stems and flowers searching for happiness for Dingle.

'What about Dingle?' Deirdre asked, her voice trembled. She was afraid Freddy, Joanna's neat quick husband, would insist they have a place of their own. Freddy and Joanna had more money, and in any case Joanna was entitled to her share of the house and land.

'There would be enough from the sale,' Spiro, Deirdre's husband said. He spoke slowly with a good-natured heaviness. They had to wait while he slowly chewed another mouthful. 'With his share, your fool of a brother could be very comfortable in some nice home.' Spiro did not mean to be unkind, Deirdre knew this, but she could not bear what he said. She felt they were all against her. More than anything she wanted to stay in the house and she wanted Dingle to be able to stay but she and Spiro had no money with which to pay Joanna and Freddy their share. So Deirdre said nothing, she got up from the table and started to go about her work and the talk was dropped for the time being.

Their lives went on as usual and the two sisters were kept busy with their babies.

One day Spiro came home in the middle of the afternoon. He walked straight through the kitchen and into the room which was their bedroom and he shut the door. The two sisters looked at each other and Deirdre put her baby down in his basket and went after her husband.

'He's not feeling well,' she said, coming back after a few minutes.

'Why? What's wrong?'

'Nothing much, but I think he's had words with the Boss. He's going to have a sleep.' Joanna shrugged.

'There's nothing like a good sleep,' she said. 'We'd better keep quiet.'

'Yes, a good sleep,' Deirdre agreed. Mostly the two sisters agreed. Their mother, too, had been an agreeable woman; hard working and thrifty, she had wisdom too.

'Sisters give things to each other,' she said when Joanna wanted to sell her sequined party bag to Deirdre.

'Give the bag,' Mother said. 'Sisters don't buy and sell with each other. They share things. Sisters share.'

And she had left them the house to share, Dingle included, of course. But when Deirdre thought about it, how could she expect Joanna to give her her share of the house.

Deirdre's husband continued to stay at home. He seemed to step on plastic toys and lemons and he was bored with all the washing and ironing and the disorder brought about by the two babies. For though the sisters kept the shabby house clean, there was a certain untidiness which was comfortable, but Deirdre, as Spiro stumbled crossly, began to see squalor everywhere. The verandahs needed sweeping every day, paint peeled and fell in flakes and there were rusty marks. For some reason wheat was growing wild in the rough laundry tubs and they had to wash clothes in the bathroom. Joanna worked hard too but she complained and kept on wishing for a modern house. She reproached Deirdre.

Deirdre felt annoyed with Spiro for being at home all the time when she wanted to clean the house. As well as being annoyed she was worried that he might not have any work, and then how would they manage. She avoided her husband.

And then the two sisters began to quarrel over small things.

'If you don't want to make your bed,' Deirdre shouted at Joanna, 'at least close your door so the whole world needn't see what a pigsty your room is.'

'Who cares! Bossy Boots!' Joanna tossed her head, and their voices rose as they flung sharp words at each other. They moved saucepans noisily and scraped chairs and there was no harmony in their movements when they prepared the dinner.

Joanna began to do things for Deirdre's husband. She made tea for him in the middle of the long hot afternoon. She sat talking to him, her pretty head turned to one side as she gazed attentively while he replied in his slow speech. Deirdre saw that she sat there with her blouse still unfastened after feeding her baby. And it seemed to Deirdre that Spiro was watching Joanna and looking with admiration at her small white breasts which were delicately veined and firm with the fullness of milk.

Deirdre went out shopping alone.

'I'm leaving Robbie,' she called out to her husband. 'Watch him when he wakes, will you.'

She had several things to buy from the supermarket. It would have been wiser to ask Spiro to go with her. She took upon herself the burden of the shopping and in her present unhappiness she thought she wouldn't buy a Christmas tree.

The two sisters had taken some time to find husbands. Deirdre, nine years older than Joanna and with her straight cut dull hair and sullen expression, had taken somewhat longer. Spiro had come just in time into Deirdre's life for the two sisters to be married on the same day.

Deirdre wished she could be alone with Spiro and persuade him to go back to his work before Christmas, even if only for half a day to make everything all right for after the holiday. But she knew he was a quiet man and proud, and besides, he was enjoying a kind of new discovery in her sister. Nothing like this had ever happened in the household before. Joanna's husband was deeply in love with his wife. He was always kind to Dingle and roguishly polite to Deirdre, admired her baby and her cooking, but really he only cared about Joanna and their own baby daughter. Joanna took all his love, basking, cherished, she seemed to glow more every day with the love she had from Freddy and now here she was trying to attract her own sister's husband, as if she wanted both men to pay every attention to her.

Unhappiness and jealousy rose in Deirdre and she trembled as she put packages in her bag and she thought again she wouldn't bother to have a tree this year. But on the way home she passed a watered heap of Christmas trees sheltered from the sun by a canvas screen.

'How much are the trees?' she asked the boy.

'Dollar fifty,' he looked at her hopefully.

'I'll take one,' she said, sparing the money from her purse, wondering whether she should.

'Which'll you want?' He reached into the heap and shook out one tree after another till she chose one with a long enough stem. Slowly she dragged it home.

They put the tree in the hall, it seemed the best place for it though they had to squeeze by. It seemed to Deirdre when the tree was decorated with the little glittering treasures saved from their childhood that there was an atmosphere of peace in the tranquil depths of the branches, and, as she brushed against it, a fragrance which seemed to come from previous years soothed her. The corners of the rooms and the woodwork seemed as if smoothed and rounded, the brown linoleum and the furniture, polished for so many years, were mellow and pleasant to look upon because of this fragrance from the tree. She felt better and wondered why she had been so unhappy.

'I think I can smell rain,' she said, smiling as she stepped on to the back verandah. 'It must be raining somewhere.'

'Yes, there's weather coming up,' Freddy agreed and they paused to breathe in the sharp fragrance of rain-laden air. Later they played table tennis; the old boards creaked and the house seemed to shake but the contented babies and Dingle the Fool slept in spite of the noise.

For some reason Joanna had put on a stupid frock. It had no shoulder straps or sleeves and she kept missing the ball and spoiling the game because she kept tugging up her frock saying it was slipping down. And every time she missed the ball she dissolved into laughter and the two men laughed too and Deirdre noticed how her husband only looked at Joanna. Usually he was impatient if anyone played badly but tonight he was laughing with Joanna.

'Oh, I'm too tired to play any more.' Deidre put her bat down suddenly.

'I'll take on the two men then,' Joanna cried. Deirdre wanted to shake Joanna, but she tried to control her anger, her voice trembled.

'No, Joanna,' she said as quietly as she could. 'I want to talk about the house.'

'Oh, Deirdre!' Joanna said. 'The agent was here again

this morning while you were out, they're going to start building on the block next door quite soon. He promised us a really good price if only we'll sell!'

'Be quiet, Joanna!' Deirdre said. 'I want to say how a house has such history, such meaning. Places, especially houses are important, they matter.' Somehow she couldn't go on, she kept thinking about Dingle.

They had to wait, Spiro was speaking, his broken English more noticeable.

'It's what a person really wants that has meaning,' Spiro said slowly. 'For you Deirdre, this house. For Joanna, it is new house,' he shrugged his shoulders lazily. 'It is the wanting that matters,' he said. Deirdre's sallow face flushed a dull red.

'I know you and Freddy want a modern home of your own,' she said. 'We'll sell this place,' she forced out the words; she had been preparing them all evening.

'Oh, Deirdre!' Joanna hugged her sister. 'Shall we really!' She was shrill with excitement. 'Mr Rusk, you know, the agent, said our two acres could be a gold mine if only we'd sell now!'

'Oh, be quiet, Joanna!' Deirdre said, she couldn't stop thinking of Dingle. 'There's no more to be said,' she snapped. 'Sisters share,' her mother had said. Deirdre couldn't share Spiro with Joanna.

'We'll sell,' she made herself say again.

'Oh, Deirdre!' Joanna hitched up her frock. 'Oh, we'll go on Sunday and look at the show houses on the Greenlawns Estate. Do let's!'

'Perhaps,' Deirdre said shortly. Joanna got out her magazines. 'Look at these kitchens.' She was showing her treasures to the two men long after Deirdre had gone, sleepless, to bed.

. . . . .

The two sisters sat together in the humid heat.

'I hope it'll be cooler on Christmas Day,' Joanna said. They fed their babies and drank cold water, greedily taking turns to drink from a big white jug while their babies sucked.

Spiro was out. Deirdre felt comforted. He was driving a load of baled lucerne hay, it was only work for one day, but it was something. She leaned over to smile at Joanna's baby.

The air was heavy with the over-ripe mulberries fermenting and dropping, replenishing the earth. Soon the tree next door would be gone, the house had already been pulled down.

Dingle the Fool came in, his hands and face stained red.

'Oh, let us get some mulberries too!' Joanna laid her baby in her basket and Deirdre put her little son down quickly.

Soon the three of them were lost and laughing in the great tree, it was as big as a house itself.

They pushed in between the gnarled branches and twigs, climbing higher and deeper into the tree, pausing one after the other on the big forked branch where Dingle often slept on hot nights. All round them were green leaves, green light and green shade. For every ripe berry Deirdre picked, three more fell through her fingers. Splashing her face and shoulders, they dropped, lost to the earth. She felt restored in the tree, as if she could go on through the thick leaves and emerge suddenly in some magic place beyond. And, as she picked and ate the berries one after the other, she wondered why she had let things worry her so much.

'Here's a beauty!' Joanna cried. 'If only I could get it.' She leaned, cracking twigs, 'Oh, I missed it! Here's another. Oh beauty!' The tree was full of their voices.

'Here's another!' Deirdre heard Joanna just above her and then Dingle slithered laughing beside her, smearing her white bare legs with the red juice. From above Joanna showered them both with berries and soon they were having a mulberry fight as they did when they were children together. Dingle could lose what little wits he had for joy.

Breathless and laughing they stood at last on the ground, stained all over with the stolen fruit.

'Anyone for a swim?' Spiro was back, he had the truck till the next day. His face widened with his good-natured smile as he saw them.

'Oh, I can't,' Deirdre said. And he remembered the mysterious things about the women after their childbirths and he was about to go off on his own.

'Wait for me! I'll come!' Joanna cried. 'Watch Angela for me, Deirdre, we'll not be long. Wait, Spiro! I'm coming!'

In the kitchen Deirdre stuck cloves into an onion and an orange. Slowly and heavily she began preparations for the Christmas cooking tomorrow. Reluctantly she greased a pudding basin. Sadness began again to envelop her. Joanna had scrambled up so quickly beside Spiro in the cabin of the truck. Deirdre tried to think of the mulberry fight instead.

Dingle came in, he had washed himself and flattened his colourless hair with water. He picked things up from the table and put them down, he examined the orange and the onion, he pulled out a clove and chewed it noisily.

'Oh, Dingle don't!' Impatiently Deirdre snatched them from him.

So then he began striking matches, one match after another. He watched the brief little flame with pleasure.

'Oh, Dingle, don't keep on wasting matches. Stop it!' Deirdre spoke sharply and then she tried to explain to him about the house being sold but he didn't seem to understand.

'You'll sleep in the doctor's nice bed,' she told him and tears came into her eyes as she spoke. Dingle came over to the table.

'Here,' he said to Deirdre. 'You have this.' He held out the old tennis ball to his sister.

'No, no, Dingle,' Deirdre was impatient. 'Try and listen, we are selling the house – No! I don't want your old ball!'

'Go on!' Dingle interrupted. 'You have it, there's happiness inside.' He bounced the ball and gave it to her. She took it, her hand covered in flour.

'Thank you,' and she tried to give it back to him.

'No, you have it, keep it,' he insisted, his voice was thick and indistinct but Deirdre always knew what he said. She refused to keep the ball. Flour fell on the floor.

Dingle drew a chair up to the table close to where she was working, he took her vegetable knife and began to cut the ball in half.

'No, Dingle, you fool. Don't!' Deirdre cried out and she tried to take the knife, but Dingle had strength and he held on to the knife and began working it right into the ball.

'Dingle, you don't understand!'

'I understand,' he muttered, 'I understand, half each, you have half.'

He cut the ball and stared at the two empty halves of it. He looked at Deirdre and he looked at the two halves and, perplexed, he shook his head. He sat shaking his head and, as he realised the emptiness of the ball, his face crumpled and he cried, sobbing like a child except that he had white hair and a man's voice.

Deirdre had not seen him cry for years, she saw his mouth all square as he cried and it reminded her of Joanna's mouth when she cried and she could hardly bear to be reminded like this.

'Don't cry, Dingle. Please don't cry.' She spoke softly trying to comfort him. But it seemed there was nothing she could do.

. . . . .

In the night Joanna was thirsty and she got up to go for water. The hall was full of smoke.

'There's a fire!' she called, terrified in the smoke-filled darkness. 'The Christmas tree's burning! Deirdre! Quick! The house is on fire. Freddy! Spiro!'

The whole house seemed full of smoke and they couldn't tell which part was burning the most. They saved their babies and most of their clothes.

'Where is Dingle?' Deirdre hardly had breath to call out. Her eyes were blind with pain from smoke.

Spiro tried to rush up to the attic but the heat and the burning timber falling forced him back out into the garden.

There was nothing anyone could do to save Dingle and nothing to do to save the house. They stood in the ring of trees. The Norfolk pines, the cape lilacs, the jacarandas and the kurrajong and the great mulberry tree in the next garden were all lit up in the hot light of the flames. The noise of the fire seemed to make a storm in the trees. They stood, helpless little people, beside the big fire, their bare feet seeking out the coolness of fallen hibiscus flowers which had curled up slowly in their damp sad ragged dying on the grass.

There was nothing they could do to save Dingle. 'He will have suffocated from the smoke before the fire could reach him,' Spiro spoke slowly, he tried to comfort them. Deirdre saw his hands bursting with the burns he had received and she saw how he was hardly able to bear the pain of them and she persuaded him to go with a neighbour to have them bandaged. They all allowed themselves to be looked after, quietly, as if they couldn't understand what had happened.

And later, Deirdre, wandering in the half light of dawn while the others slept on the vinyl cushions in the lounge of the bowling club, went back to the smouldering soaked remains of the house. She half hoped her brother would be dead but how could she hope for him to be burned to death. In her unhappiness she felt the burden of his life. His life was too much for her but the pain of wishing him burned in the fire was even worse. She felt she must search in the remains of the house and was afraid of what she might find. It would be easier if he had slept on and on in the smoke as Spiro said he had.

She thought she saw him in the forked branch of the mulberry tree. She paused, shivering, and hoped it was only his old washed-out shirt that was there, left behind after the mulberry fight. Dingle sometimes forgot his clothes and Deirdre often went about last thing at night gathering up his shoes and things.

She stood now and tried to see what was in the fork of the tree. She began, with hope and with fear to climb into the quiet branches, the cool damp leaves brushed her face and her arms and legs.

It was not just his shirt up there. Gently she woke him, empty match boxes fell as she shook him.

'Dingle, wake up!' He was asleep in the tree after all. Dingle the Fool stretched himself along the friendly branch. His face was as if stained with red tears. Deirdre hugged her brother clumsily, crying and kissing him. How could she have wished him dead?

'Another mulberry fight?' Dingle asked in his strange thick voice and he made a noise and Deirdre was unable to tell whether he was laughing or crying.

. . . . .

They thought they might as well choose a motel right on the sea front. They had only a short time to wait for their new houses to be ready. So every day they lay on the sand, even the babies sunbathed in their baskets.

'The quick brown fox,' Deirdre thought to herself as she watched Freddy put up the beach umbrella to make the best shade for Spiro who was still unwell after his burns.

Lazily they spent the days talking about nothing in particular and swimming and eating. They bought fried chicken and hamburgers to eat while watching television in the motel. There wasn't any point in wondering about the fire so they didn't talk about it.

Deirdre couldn't help thinking about Dingle. When she took him to the hospital he sat so awkwardly on the edge of the white bed. She wondered whatever could he do there. She went to the window.

'You can watch the road from here,' she said. Dingle got up and came to the window and obediently looked out at the corner of the road. There were no grass plots. Deirdre wished there was some grass and she could have asked if he could trim the edges. It was something he always enjoyed. She thought about him watching the empty street. What would he be doing now, Deirdre wondered. She watched Joanna and Freddy laughing in the sea. Joanna looked so happy, the green water curled handsomely round her lovely body. Deirdre envied Joanna, she envied her sister's innocence.

'The land's more valuable than ever with the house and

sheds gone and on top there's all the insurance!' Deirdre seemed to hear Joanna's excited voice ringing, she envied her happiness but more enviable was her innocence. Joanna had never wished her brother burned to death.

'Where's that fool of a brother of yours?' Spiro often asked this question when he came in, sometimes he had something for Dingle, a cake or some apples, sometimes he wanted Dingle to help him move a heavy box or shift the load in his truck with him.

Everyone called Dingle a fool, their mother said he would give everything he had and people would take it.

Deirdre had taken everything from him, she had made him give everything. Freddy and Joanna seemed hilarious in the water and Spiro, sitting with both hands bandaged, was laughing and laughing and all the time he watched Joanna.

'It's the wanting that really matters,' Spiro had said it himself.

Deirdre longed to talk about Dingle. She wanted to ask Spiro if he thought Dingle would be all right. She wanted comfort and reassurance but did not ask.

Near them on the beach was a bread-carter woman eating her lunch. She looked so carefree and sunburned and strong, Deirdre almost spoke to her.

'I have a brother –' but she didn't. In a little while the bread carter would eat her last mouthful and be gone, taking with her her strength and vitality.

Deirdre lay back, she heard the sea come up the sand with a little sigh. Tears welled up under her closed eyelids. Joanna and Freddy came running from the water and Deirdre turned her face away so that they shouldn't see the tears spill over her cheeks.

. . . .

The Hair and The Teeth

CARMEL BIRD

What is crucial about this story is the tone of voice of the narrator. It's detached, and strangely remote. This woman's house has been burgled, but it sounds as if she's been robbed before, emotionally. She's a single mother, and it appears as if life is about to overwhelm her.

People broke into the house one time when we were out at the supermarket. I suppose we were gone for about an hour and a half. The older children were at school, but I had the two little ones with me. They were only three and two when this happened, and so whatever we did, we did it fairly slowly.

You drive to the shopping centre and park the car in the basement. Then you take the children out of their car seats and get to the lift that takes you up to the level where the supermarket is. You have to get the children past the toyshop with the Humphrey Bear that will sing and dance if you put money in the slot, past the pink elephant ride, past the Coke machine. If you put the children in the trolley at the supermarket there won't be enough room for the stuff you have to get, but if you don't put them in the trolley you have to be prepared to move very, very slowly. So you move slowly. You get the music, the lights, the smell of disinfectant, and all the colours. Everything shimmers in the supermarket.

(I find the music and the lights and so on very tiring and I am inclined to be irritable.)

You fill up the trolley and stand in the queue. The queue moves very slowly. Every trolley in front of you has things in it that need to have their prices checked. The music shifts from the Ascot Gavotte to the Easter Parade, and you cannot be soothed. You want to just grab the children and leave the full trolley where it is. But you wait and you pay and you wheel the trolley to the lift, to the car. You pack the car, strap the children in, park the trolley, drive to the exit, pay to get out, drive home. It is dusk now. When you get home you put your key in the back door but the door won't open because the burglars (what is the correct word here? Is it robber, intruder, thief, crook, bugger?) the burglars have bolted it from the inside.

As soon as the door would not open, I knew pretty well what had happened. I left the children and the shopping in the car and went round to the front of the house. The window was wide open and the curtain was flapping, in fact billowing out, like a miserable bride or a cheerful ghost. One of the children had started to cry. I went back to the car, took two packets of biscuits from the shopping and gave a packet to each child.

'You can eat these,' I said, tearing open the packets and handing them to the children. The crying stopped and both children looked a bit surprised but they obeyed. I locked them in the car and went around to the front door. This door has no bolt. I opened it, put my hand in to turn on the light, and stood for a few moments listening and looking into the hallway. On the floor at the foot of the stairs was an earring, and halfway between the stairs and the front door was the lid of a jewellery box. The phone is on a table near the front door. I rang the police.

People tell me it takes a long time for the police to come to a break-in, break-ins being so common and policemen so rare, but these police seemed to be there by the time I had put down the phone. Possibly, because of the shock of the whole business, my sense of time was distorted. Anyway, the huge (it seemed to be huge) white car with blue writing and blue lights zoomed up the street and slid (really) in beside the kerb and two police, a man and a woman, jumped (true) out and were suddenly standing beside me. The first thing I thought about was how healthy they looked. They looked just very, very healthy. He was big and young and smiling and sweet. And she was little and young and smiling and sweet. They had hats. They looked very clean – in blue, sky blue and navy. They both smelt of nice soap.

They searched the house for hidden people while I got first the shopping then the children from the car. The children had finished the biscuits. I gave them some chips. By this time the ice-cream was beginning to melt and blood was dripping out of a plastic bag in which there was a chicken.

'Can you leave the kids with a neighbour while we get on with things?' asked the policeman. So I took them in next door. Luckily someone was home and the children were quite happy to stay there watching television.

We went all over the house, the police and I, finding evidence of what they said was the 'work of a real professional'. We sat at the kitchen table and made a list of what was missing.

I used to keep jewellery in the top left-hand drawer of a chest of drawers. They must have emptied the drawer onto the bedspread and then rolled up the bedspread and used it as a sack. I imagine two rat-like little men, real professionals, wearing masks, tiptoeing swiftly down the stairs, one with the sack over his shoulder, the other with an armful of leather coats. I start giving the policeman a list of things that have been taken: coral necklace, princess ring. He writes it all down carefully. The kitchen light seems to be too harsh, the paper the man is writing on too white. The clean strong police faces seem sympathetic but as helpless as the babies we have sent next door. I offer them biscuits and coffee but they say no. Jade ring, silver bracelet with lapis lazuli. They have stolen a basket of firewood. The police cannot explain this. Suddenly I remember that among the sentimental treasures in the drawer were the locks of hair and the baby teeth of the other children. Then my voice starts to waver and I think I am going to cry.

(I had wrapped the teeth in a piece of silk and put them in a tin from a machine in the Paris Metro. Snow was falling. The Metro was warm. I put the money in the machine and got an oval tin of lollies with a wreath of violets on the lid. The lollies inside the tin rattled. They were dusted with sugar.)

Will I tell the police about the teeth and hair? Will I say in my litany:

'Two tortoise-shell combs (Spanish), four ivory bangles (African), nine deciduous teeth (human), and two locks of human hair (golden)'?

They look at me kindly as I sit weeping at the kitchen table. I drink coffee and whisky. They keep writing. Periwinkle necklace, gipsy keeper (garnet).

I ask whether they think I will get any of the things back and they say that, in a case of this nature, it is unlikely we will recover any of the missing items.

I put in the insurance claim and a woman from the insurance company came to interview me. She had a briefcase under her arm and a shrewd look in her eye. She was a bit fat but graceful with a black dress and a fur jacket and beauty parlour make-up, hairdo and fingernails. She was wearing Chanel, and her shoes were Italian. She stood on the doormat with the blue sky behind her and she could have been an advertisement for something, probably wine or, now I come to think of it, insurance. Or funerals.

'Mrs Halliwell from Phoenix. I rang,' she said, and I took her into the sitting room. You couldn't discuss the basket of firewood and the jewellery in the bedspread with Mrs Halliwell in the kitchen. I offered her coffee but she didn't want it. The ordinary rules of hospitality do not apply to the police or to women from the insurance company. She had a typed list of all the things that were stolen. As she sat down, the sofa suddenly looked very shabby. A plastic fire-engine lay just near Mrs Halliwell's left foot.

'I will need more detailed descriptions of some of the items reported missing,' she said, looking up at me over her glasses. 'You will have to be more specific. A princess ring means nothing to me. What is a princess ring?' We came to the coral necklace which I said was made from round beads of coral, pale pink and smooth.

'Polished?' said Mrs Halliwell.

I said I supposed they were polished. 'Angel skin,' she wrote without speaking. Then she asked how long the necklace was, and when I told her she wrote, 'Opera length.' Satisfied, she then said aloud, 'Opera length polished angel skin,' and she almost smiled. 'Is there any other item you have omitted to report missing? This is your final opportunity to claim.' I tried to think of something, as if I needed to please her. Then I thought of saying half the things I had just told her were lies. Then I remembered the hair and the teeth, and all I said at last was no. She said we would have to put in an alarm system, arrange for a security patrol, get security doors and windows, or else get a reliable watchdog. I asked her for the name of somebody who puts in security doors and windows, but she said I would have to look in the

Yellow Pages. Then she said 'reliable watchdog' again as she tucked her briefcase under her arm. I showed her out.

'And a peephole and a security phone on the door,' she said as she walked away.

. . . . .

The next day a man came to measure the doors and windows for bars. He handed me his card at the door. On the card was a picture of a shark behind wire mesh.

'Jack McClaren,' he said, 'from Shark.' He looked around the garden and said, 'Nice large block you've got here. Surprising in this postal district.'

When he had finished measuring, and when we had discussed the quality of the optional one-way mesh and the need for the tri-safe locking system with the three-point deadlocking and antipick lock, he had a cup of coffee in the kitchen. We had some shortbread and a cigarette and I told him about the robbery. He said I was lucky and told me about people who had been completely cleaned out. 'Nothing left standing except the electric light. Lucky you weren't here when they came. Then they'd have done it with violence. There's a terrible lot of it these days. Armed robbery with violence. It's on the increase. I see all the statistics, of course.'

So then I told him about the hair and the teeth, and he said that was the worst.

'And the mongrels would just chuck those things away, you know. They'd just chuck the babies' curls into the gutter. I went to a lady's place where they'd taken nearly everything. And all these photos of her son that was killed in the war. You know they just let the photos blow away in the street, in the rain. And weeks later the lady was still finding the remains of her photos in the weeds by the side of the road. She never got over it.'

As he talked I remembered something else that must have been in the drawer with the jewellery. Something else that had been stolen. It was a small wax doll. I first saw her one night in the lighted window of a shop. She was a naked little girl with blue glass eyes and a wig made from real hair. The next day I went back to the shop when it was open. I thought the doll was very expensive, but I bought her.

. . . .

The Vampire's Assistant at the 157 Steps

MICHAEL WILDING

Life is hard enough for a neurotic living alone in an unheated fibro cottage halfway down a cliff. But when Dexter moves in, it gets worse. High-altitude comedy from Michael Wilding, the prose laureate of paranoia.

Dexter phones me to get him a woman. Not in the usual sense; not in the sense of get me a woman to screw. A woman to pose for *Vampire Vamp*. Though maybe ultimately it is in the usual sense; he plans to play the part of a young vampire in the book himself. Does that mean he gets to screw the woman?

'I need someone with a certain sort of teeth. Do you know any women vampires?'

My blood has been drained by them. My throat is a necklace of small incisions, like an exotic tattoo from Niugini.

She has to be beautiful and look like a vampire. I thought of Valda but I didn't want her tits and cunt exposed to any more men. There were some books I would prefer to close. Not reissued in runs of 10,000 copies.

'I need a vampire and three guys who get bitten by the vampire. And I need a coffin. Where would I get a coffin from? I only want to borrow one, they can have it back, I'll only need it for three days.'

I suggest he tries an undertaker.

'They won't be in it. They have this thing about the sanctity of death. I guess they're worried about people using them for black masses.'

. . . . .

Dexter needs somewhere to live while he shoots *Vampire Vamp*. He comes to stay with me. Each night he descends the 157 steps down the cliff face, wearing his vampire assistant's make-up, lighting his way with a candle. The dogs in the neighbourhood howl. The possums look down in terror from the gums. At the bottom of the steps, halfway down the cliff, he climbs in through the kitchen window of the fibro house and drags the covers off my bed. There are not enough bedclothes for both of us. Nor is there a duplicate key. When we divide the bedclothes, neither of us is warm enough. He offers to share my bed. I refuse. 'I don't want to fuck you, I just want to sleep in comfort,' he says. I don't trust him. Nor do I want vampire make-up all over the sheets. He refuses to wash it off. Sometimes he says he is too tired. Sometimes he says it saves having to make-up again the next morning. I do not believe either explanation.

Dexter takes the eiderdown and leaves me the blankets. I shiver all night. But it is colder still at Valda's, some sort of swamp having collected under her house owing to bad land drainage which makes the house like a tomb. I pile all her clothes on top of the blankets, coats and sweaters and scarves, but they always fall off in the night and I wake up. The bed slopes to one side. She refuses to believe that. She denies that that is the reason I cannot sleep. She says there are deeper reasons. Sometimes she says there are shallower reasons, reasons that are perfectly visible. But it is never the fault of her bed. As for sleeping at Faith's, that is cold too; she has to keep a window open for her asthma. She also refuses to draw the curtains, so that the light can wake her at seven to get ready for work at nine. Then I have to leave. She does not like leaving me in the apartment alone.

Dexter climbs in through the window and takes the

eiderdown about two am. He leaves about seven thirty. But at least I don't have to fuck him. I can get back to sleep after he finishes squeezing his fruit juice and making phone calls to his models and his photographer.

. . . . .

'I don't need sleep any more,' Dexter says. 'I sleep for two or three hours but I don't even need that. Alcohol doesn't affect me. I still enjoy it, but I don't get drunk. Dope too. I can smoke dope and then I can carry on working. I stopped eating for three weeks. Just drank water and fruit juice occasionally. You don't need all these things.'

He gets up at three am when his alarm rings. My alarm. He has taken the alarm clock so he wakes up. It isn't that he needs it. It is merely a precaution. He switches it off immediately because he is already awake. He gets up and squeezes some fruit juice and begins to make phone calls. He has to start shooting by the dawn light. I call out to him to bring me the eiderdown back if he is finished with it. He isn't. He has it wrapped round him while he makes the phone calls. He expresses surprise at my being awake. 'It's only three o'clock,' he says.

. . . . .

The timber frame house is at the bottom of 157 steps, surrounded by eucalyptus. Another 157 steps further is the water of the bay. The cliff face is nearly vertical. The eucalyptus trees are caught up with the high tension electricity cables, and the branches have frayed the insulation off them. At night I wake up screaming that the wires have been lowered through the roof onto me in bed, that the cliff face has collapsed and the ground is alive with fallen cables. I leap out of bed and switch on the light and look for the cables across the blankets. I get back into bed and realise how dangerous an act that was. Next time I lie there rigid, waiting for the moon to seep through the blinds to reveal where the cables have fallen. With the slightest move I could be fried. Splat.

. . . . .

The lights illuminating the 157 steps suddenly do not work. I descend the vertical cliff face in fear, holding on to twigs and rocks, alert for lizards, snakes, spiders, as I clutch onto things. I stop at every second or third step and look upwards for the cables, but the night is so black I can see nothing. If the lights are not working then the cables must have been rubbed right through by the eucalypts and will now be lying across the steps. I look out to see where they have fallen. I listen for an electric hissing, I watch out for sparks, I wait to die like a flying-fox, spread across two high tension cables.

. . . . .

Dexter tells me the Electricity Board have been. They came to check the safety of the cables. They have checked the wrong cables, the good ones, the ones that light the 157 steps. They have condemned them as unsafe. They have removed some vital link. We must now descend the steps in darkness. We hear the high tension cables still rubbing unchecked against the eucalypts as we walk beneath them.

. . . . .

It is hard to light your way down 157 steps of bush with matches. This is not because they blow out, though sometimes they do blow out. Nor is it because of the danger of bushfire. This could be a danger in bushfire weather. But this is not bushfire weather. The rain drips off every leaf. The moss spreads across every step. The difficulty is not because of bushfires. The difficulty is knowing where to hold the match so that it illuminates the steps. If you hold the match in front of you it illuminates the steps for beetles and bull ants and lizards lodged in the rocks and tree roots. But your eyes are blinded by the light of the match and you cannot see the steps. If you try the obvious reversal and hold the match behind you, where you have been is illuminated but where you have to go is blocked by your shadow. Your shadow makes it very dark. The steps descend vertically. They are slippery with rain and moss and crushed snails. You grab onto a branch and water showers down from the trees and ticks lodge in your head and neck. You reach out for the other side and there is nothing. Eventually you learn to stand a little to one side of the light. There is an optimum angle, height, distance at which to hold the lighted match. You learn to memorise the steps immediately in front of you before the match burns out. That way you save matches. If you can walk four steps into the imprinted, illuminated image after the match goes out, you save a lot of matches.

It is better to descend the 157 steps by candlelight, but Dexter has the only candle. Better still, to descend them by daylight. But then you have to take in supplies because descending by daylight in those short subtropical days you would not have eaten an evening meal, not while it was still daylight. So descending by daylight you end up getting hungry in the long cold evenings. Then you might even have to ascend the steps by matchlight. In order to purchase supplies. It is like living in a state of siege here, without supplies; or in a state of curfew, without light. 'I recognise all this,' Dexter says. 'What a depressing sight it is. When my last woman left me I lived like this for two months.' Without supplies, without curtains, without crockery or cutlery, without all those indefinable things whose absence creates the bareness. I have in fact two curtains left, though the room Dexter sleeps in has bare windows. I have some crockery and cutlery. I have two fridges. One works. The other I guess no one wanted to carry up to the top of the 157 steps when it stopped working. It used to be used to store vegetables. I do not buy vegetables, nor use those remaining. It seems now full of potatoes and onions and other root and tuber crops sprouting in the darkness of its closed doors. Inside it is shining white which is odd when you see the long wavy shoots that have sprouted from the root and tuber crops. But with the door shut it must be very dark. I now feel guilty about those potatoes and onions and things. I feel I should have planted them to let the life they have drawn from themselves spread into the soil and flourish. They are doomed in that old fridge. They are probably dead altogether now, rotted, mouldered. But for a while they drew on their stored life and sprouted in that whitewalled darkness.

. . . . .

In winter it is cold here. The sun shines on the other cliff across the bay; this cliff remains damp and shaded all day. Once in the house there is nothing to do but sleep. There is no television; it is too steep to carry a set down. It is too cold to read.

I come home early to sleep. It has become impossible to sleep at night without blankets, and with Dexter making phone calls. I find Dexter lying on the floor, across the doorways to his room and to my room. The doorways are close to each other. He has the electric radiator on, the one bar of it that works. The lights are off. His head rests on a pillow, and he is covered by the eiderdown. His shoulders sticking out above the eiderdown are clad in his duffle coat. He doesn't answer when I say hello. I step over him and switch on a light. I step back. He still does not move. I am shocked by the way he has aged, I feel a deep physical shock at the lines round his eyes, the dark hollows beneath them, the black dead flesh. He looks centuries old.

'Why are you lying there like that?' I ask. 'Why don't you go to bed if you're so tired?'

'I'm all right like this,' he says.

'It can't be comfortable.'

'I'm going to make a phone call.'

'Why don't you make it then and go to bed?'

'Not yet.'

'The phone won't move, you don't have to lie on guard by it.'

He wriggles into his eiderdown but does not open his eyes.

. . . . .

I lie in bed. The glow of the electric radiator comes through the doorway. I have come home early to sleep and I cannot sleep. I tell myself that it is not age on Dexter's face. We are not that near to death. It is the work of a brilliantly gifted make-up artist. It is very hard to sleep when someone who could be a vampire is lying across the doorway to your room. Even a trainee vampire. When the doorway has no door. When you don't have an eiderdown to wrap protectively round your throat. Apart from the additional fear of fire, that he might roll onto the electric radiator and ignite the eiderdown and himself and yourself; myself. Like Nosferatu in the first rays of dawn. What if he forgot his phone call and lay there all night in his duffle coat and eiderdown and eye make-up and the rosy fingers stretched across Middle Harbour and gently touched him? Pow.

. . . . .

This suburb that looks over the harbour must once have been a place for weekenders. Now the city has caught up with it and absorbed it and gone on way past it. But once it was a place to put little shacks up and to come away to for the fishing. The house is of prefabricated fibro. The materials decay yet never blend. A timber house yearns back to the growing trees around it. But the hard edges of this fibro stay forever hard, the metal window frames rust but never soften; they flake, they chip away, they support cobwebs. Lianas hang from the trees, lizards and insects scurry, possums leap on the corrugated iron roof. The house stays there, this cold, hard unbending cube. It asserts the origins of its manufacture in this flux of the bush. It is functional, minimal, technological. It provided quick and cheap happiness where there might not have been happiness: but when the happiness faded it could not sustain it. It is prefabricated and temporary: it will collapse but not decay. Like a Mayan temple overgrown in the jungle, it is a monument to a creed; it is a statue to loss of faith. The sun sets across the bay and its last rays reach the windows; the moon rises and lights them too. We sit there listening to the radio and smoking dope. We sit close to the window and do not see the houses around us, back of us. We sit in folding deck chairs because no other chairs have been carried down the steps.

. . . . .

Some nights when the moon is late rising Dexter shows me his transparencies. He shows me Chained in which a beautiful woman is immured in a deserted castle. She is naked and chained by her wrists to the wall of the dungeon. Each day her captor comes to whip her. He is the only person she sees. In her loneliness she looks forward to his brief visits. The whipping becomes the joy of her life.

. . . . .

The fridge that works is overfreezing. The cartons of milk go solid overnight. To make tea you have to scoop out solid milk. It strikes me as a possible new way of packaging: quick frozen milk cubes. They could be condensed and flavoured. Chocolate, coffee, malt, vanilla, lemon, herbal.

My pyjamas have a thick congealed substance on them. It is not frozen milk, otherwise it would have melted. I wonder what discharge this is. I usually examine my prick for discharges. I wonder if some come in the night. I wonder if when I masturbate strange new pusses emerge that I am unaware of. I carry this fear with me through the days that follow. I later decide I must have sat on the kitchen table where Dexter has spilt hot candle wax, climbing through the window. I take my pyjamas to the laundry and the symptoms never recur.

As I climb up the 157 steps and come in sight of the road, I see an old chair on the pathway. The steps wind up the vertical cliff and I see angle after angle of the wooden chair. Its odd construction reveals it to be a commode. I do not want an old chair full of shit blocking the way out of the house. I do not want to touch it. Old, forgotten diseases might lurk in it. I wonder why it has been dumped on my steps. I did not think my neighbours had the imagination.

They have not previously gone beyond sitting at their window with a rifle and threatening to shoot guests at my party.

It could accidentally have been dumped there. Yet why on my steps? Why not just sit it on the side of the road? I do not like to think of all those sick and aged people who have shitted into it. Though it does not seem to have been used recently. The wood appears to be distinctly weathered. It seems to have been exposed to the sun and rain for some time. I carry it across the road and wipe my hands on the grass.

When I come home at night it is back on the steps. I pick it up with one hand and carry it across the road from my steps again and dump it in the bush there. All evening I feel this anxiety. I cannot interpret the old commode on the steps. I cannot find its signification. I go round the house and secure all the doors and windows; except for the kitchen window which I have to leave open for Dexter. I do not like leaving the kitchen window open but there is nothing else I can do.

In the morning the chair is back on the steps.

In the evening Dexter says: 'You know there's something funny going on round here. The old commode, someone keeps moving it around.'

'Yes,' I say. I hadn't wanted to talk about it. I had hoped it was an hallucination. I would prefer to be mentally sick than have someone persecute me with an old commode.

'I found it on this tip when we were shooting *Garbo Girl* and I thought what a tremendous prop. But I didn't want to bring it right down the stairs and have to carry it back up when I go.' At least he still has the concept of going.

The next morning there is a circular in the letterbox. 'Dear Neighbour, One of our neighbour's daughters has been raped in this street. We are calling a meeting to arrange for more police protection in this area. We invite you to attend.'

I do not ask Dexter if he can explain that mystery too. I am afraid the neighbours will burn the house down if they work out he is living here. We are such natural suspects, such natural victims.

The next morning I find that someone has shitted at the top of the steps, and the commode has gone altogether.

. . . .

The Death of Sardanapalus

BARRY OAKLEY

This story is set in the nineteen seventies, when the young were rebelling against the proprieties of their elders. But when middle-class Mrs Ryan tries to do the same, the result is dramatic – and disastrous.

Teresa Ryan was a great believer in mental telepathy, and on Monday mornings she willed. She willed when she woke up, then there was a lapse while she cut lunches, but when the kids had gone and Jim was in the shower the willing began again, and when he drove off to work it started in earnest: PLEASE RING, it said, and as she knelt at the bed to tuck in the blankets the message came from her like a prayer, soaring out of Camberwell, speeding round the river and homing in on a decrepit terrace in Fitzroy where Bob Tantau, her tutor in English, maybe sat at that moment reading the *Age*.

It was a fine September morning and the sun had waited at the windows then gently moved in – finger-paints on one wall flashed and glowed, and in the kitchen the clutter of abandoned breakfast dishes seemed predetermined, as if suspended in floating dust-motes forever. A world of promise irradiated the house: it was the sun that ripened, brought things out, it was the sun that would bring to a head something that had started back in those first tutorials in March when she'd sit, an elderly fresher of thirty-five temporarily freed from motherhood, and take in young, impressive Mr Tantau.

He was bearded and looked as though he'd slept in his clothes, his pirate's hair was pigtailed back, there were bangles of steel on his right wrist, his sunglasses curved round his head like car fenders, and when you looked at them all you saw was yourself. Bob Tantau gave some kind of meaning to her great escape, her first year back in the real world. He was different, a mumbler, morose as Marlon Brando, oblivious of essays, timetables, punctuality – all the things that made the other lecturers belong so disappointingly to a world like her own.

Bob Tantau had only been at Monash University that year himself, arriving with a slightly American accent from areas undisclosed. His rudeness and indifference were impressive, but the most spectacular thing about him was his pants – things of wonder, starting with a frill of yellow tassels, rising through rich patchworks of blue and green and purple to a kind of crescendo at the crotch, where a ruby red heart was embroidered on a rich golden ground. He was what she went there for, a casual nosepicker and roller of joints, totally outside her own world of double garages and solicitors' wives.

The others in the tutorial disliked him, and week by week they fell away. At the first he said motherfucker, and a nun got to her feet at once. At the second he said the bank manager was the hyena of capitalism, and a man who looked like one rose up angrily and departed. Soon they were down to six, but the more the others succumbed, the more she held her ground. When the mumbling rose at the end and they realised that was his way of asking a question, the others looked away – only Teresa Ryan tried to answer. He'd train his reflectors on her, smile, and do his best to put her down. The more he attacked, the more she had to defend – middle-class morals, the motor car, the Saturday book pages, even the university itself – 'You attack it, yet you live off it.' 'Bite the hand that feeds you ma'am, that's my motto.'

TAKE UP THE PHONE AND RING. In the steam of the dishwasher he appeared before her, showering – broader and darker than Jim, almost a gipsy. Underneath his cool there was an intensity that rose up to the surface quickly, grabbed at something, then submerged again – 'Am I to understand ma'am that you're defending the capitalist system? I mean, this ain't the fifties' – then, looking over their heads to the endless red tile of suburbia – 'or is it?' Yes, he was showering, his first for a long time, the hair on his chest all matted, the ruby red heart of his crotch replaced by a white cumulus of lather.

DRY YOURSELF AND PHONE TERESA. She'd stayed on after a tutorial two weeks ago and discussed John Donne, and she'd never known him to keep his head up for so long. The room was dark, his shades were off, and he actually *looked* at her – cool, appraising, testing her out – and she'd looked back. And so they'd stared, for unbelievable seconds, and it was he that broke first, turning his gaze to the window, pausing, and then, remarkably, asking them over to his place for a meal.

'A meal? With him? You know I hate academics.' 'But that's the point, he isn't one.' 'Counter culturals I hate even more.' 'Nonsense, he'll do you good.' He didn't. The Tantaus had gone to no trouble at all. The front-door glass of their dank little terrace was smashed, she caught her foot in a broken floorboard, clothes were in heaps everywhere as though the cupboard had not yet been invented, the smell of burning incense brought on Jim's hayfever, and he sneezed his way through the meal in a halfsize children's chair that left his head almost level with the table.

Wholemeal spaghetti, yoghurt from the carton, and cask red. Its ordinariness mocked the Ryans' whole social style –

dinner parties with candles and placemats suddenly seemed absurd, and she resolved to invite people to tea instead of dinner from now on. She'd warned Jim that pot might be produced, but he refused it with such alacrity that for her to have accepted would have seemed a betrayal. To cap the night, Jim got into an argument with Marcia, Tantau's woman, a tall thin blonde girl from one of his classes whose nipples were pointedly visible through her blouse. He called the students who'd occupied the Monash administration building spoilt kids, while she regarded them as the last hope of society. They got heated with one another, Bob Tantau blankly watching Jim get redder and redder, then secretly slipping his hand into hers.

PICK UP THAT PHONE, O GIPSY ONE. Poor Jim. Provoked and pricked by Marcia's assurance, he'd stood up suddenly and said he was going. 'Suit yourself man,' said Bob, letting go of her hand. As they picked their way down the dark hall, the evening a disaster, she felt his hand again, this time on her behind. A little drunk, she'd slowed a little so that they came into gentle collision. 'Ring me baby,' he whispered, 'ring me soon.' 'You do the ringing,' she whispered back, before catching up with Jim.

And now, two days later, on this sunny Monday morning, it was ten o'clock and she knew it would have to be soon or not at all. Either it's been on his mind all weekend or it hasn't. As she inspected her face, the mirror caught a corner of the back garden through the open bathroom door: her face, the landscape – today everything fitted and the bull would be tempted into the garden. Or was it all her imagination? Suddenly losing heart, she declined to the lavatory, beaming a last message, with her head in her hands. And the phone rang.

'Hello?'

'Hi, mind if I come and see you?'

'What'd you want to see me for?'

'Let's say, ah, to return your essay. The one on Donne.'

'I'm not dressed.'

'All the better. Here he comes – the big bad wolf.'

God, what was happening? Had she sounded reluctant enough? Fifteen years a wife and mum and now this. She undressed, showered, lathered herself in her best body lotion, then posed in the mirror with her arms crossed, her breasts pushing up and out. Would it be bed, or intense rapping through the smoke of burning grass?

Artifice, what did he say about it in that tutorial on Pope? Okay if done with style. Rape of the Lock. Heroic couplet: white pants, white lycra bra. Promenading now in the dark bedroom and deciding – black tank top, sexy and tight, Indian skirt of filmy blues. Tidy up living room? No. Uncleanliness next to godliness in his scale of things. And for the coffee table, Kurt Vonnegut and yes, R. D. Laing.

Peeping out the window and there as she feared is old Doctor Bush pruning his roses and Miss Warden at her hydrangeas in an enormous sun hat – her two life interests about to coincide, gossip and gardening. She heard his motorbike before she saw it, and turned at once from the window, spotting and concealing a *Woman's Day* just in time. The noise grew louder, deafening, then stopped: the moon-man has come to Camberwell and there's no stopping him now: the front gate gives its sombre vibration, and he's at the front door. 'Hi.' 'Howdy.' The greeting was country and western, to go with his studded jeans and black cowboy shirt.

'Well, well, well,' he said. 'Teresa Ryan at home.'

'I know, the middle-class lady trapped in her habitat.'

'Corner her here and she's got nowhere to go.'

He walked right up to her, and she retreated to the kitchen for coffee. The drapes and plushes of the living room were embarrassing enough, but now she felt herself going back further into falsity.

'Well, here it is. Floral wallpaper and formica dressed up as wood.'

'You sound as if you're ashamed.'

'Too late for that now – I'm buried with my possessions, like the ancient Egyptians.'

As she turned to set the cups she heard his boots squeak. He came right up behind her, almost touching. She moved sideways and turned around. He moved too, and pressed against her, hard enough for her to feel the studs round the top of his pants.

'Pinned against the laminex – her last retreat.'

'I don't think tutors should do that.'

'I'm not your tutor any more.'

He kissed her, an ambush of beard, garlic, and stale booze.

'The prof. checked on my credentials. I haven't got any. I'm not employed there any more.'

She sparred on coolly, knowing he hoped to shock.

'Phonies aren't confined to the middle class then.'

'I thought you liked me because I wasn't academic.'

'I'm not sure whether I like you at all.'

Disturbed, disappointed, excited, afraid, she freed herself and slid further along the bench to make some coffee, while he retired to the breakfast nook to roll a cigarette, working the paper back and forth on the tobacco slowly, and at the same time hammering something out in his head.

'There's a battle going on Mrs Ryan. Ever since that first tutorial.'

'At least in those days I knew who I was fighting. If you're not my tutor, who the hell are you?'

'Accompany me to the bedroom and find out.'

'I think I'd rather accompany you to the gate.'

'You're offended. I've been too – direct. In Camberwell that's a form of discourtesy.'

'You've been – disappointing. Stop following me around.'

But what had she hoped for? Explorations, understandings, intensities. All he did was plod about after her like a slow-motion assassin.

'What, because I don't have a degree?'

'No – because you don't have imagination.'

'I have a very vivid imagination, Mrs Ryan. I am imagining right now what you look like without clothes. You can't even imagine me without degrees.'

'This morning, making the beds, I thought I imagined you. But you're not it. And now, if you don't mind, I have the housework.'

For no obvious reason she went to go out the back door, and he blocked her path.

'This morning, while I breakfasted, I imagined you – and you're just what I imagined, exactly.'

'So why'd you come then?'

'To take off my clothes, Mrs Ryan. I came here to take off my clothes.'

He took off his shirt, and he took off his shoes. As he stood there shirtless, balancing on one leg, she rushed past him, and got to the phone. But who the hell could she ring? Jim? The police? Impossible. By this time, he stood in the doorway in his briefs.

'You're scared, Mrs Ryan. But you're not scared enough to ring Jim. Poor old red-faced conservative Jim.'

'Please go. Please.'

'Okay, I will.'

'Not like that. Not in your underpants.'

'I'm going, Mrs Ryan. You asked me to go and I'm going.'

'Please put on your pants.'

'I'll put mine on if you take yours off.'

'Why? Why are you doing this to me?'

'It's the death of Sardanapalus Mrs Ryan. When Sardanapalus, the barbaric Asian despot, was dying, he ordered that all his slaves, his horses, and his women be put to death before his eyes. I'm leaving this world too. My job's gone, Marcia's about to go and in two days I'll be going as well – to Los Angeles. Know what I did on Friday? Sardanapalus punched the professor – actually punched a professor. He's like you – he took it. People like you'll do anything. as long as there's no scandal, no scene. Now take off your clothes and I'll put mine on.'

'You promise.'

'I promise. I'm a disappointment I know, but I keep my promises.'

So she did. As her skirt came off, his pants went on. Her tank top, his shirt. In pants and bra, defenceless, she stopped.

'For pity's sake.'

'Sardanapalus has no pity. Come on, then I'll go.'

So she took them off, first her bra, then her pants, and stood there, with her arms folded across her body to cover her breasts, shivering. She felt cold, humiliated, angry, afraid.

'Like I said, Mrs Ryan, it's a battle. I'm leaving you your essay, Mrs Ryan. D Minus. Love, poetry and Jack Donne – you just don't understand.'

He went over to her. For a second she thought she was going to be attacked, but all he did was hand her her essay, forcing her to release an arm from a breast to take it. Then he pushed open the flywire door and went. She heard the gate give its familiar bass vibration, and the explosion of his bike. Then, still naked, she sat down at the table and cried.

. . . .

MORTALITIES

Nails of Love, Nails of Death

JAMES MCQUEEN

The story of Carlo the gardener, and the mystery girl in the sunless flat nearby, who seems to be wasting away. What's her secret? Carlo has to know. It might have been better if he never found out. Two characters, skilfully counterpointed and acutely observed.

He was hunkered down beside the newly turned earth of the garden bed when the battered old VW swung in through the narrow gate and slid to a skewed stop at the head of the steps. He paused, watching, as the driver's door opened and the girl got out. For a moment she stood, her body hidden from him by the dented red body of the car, an arm laid on the rusty curve of the roof, looking out over the sprawl of the city, the distant windings of the river. The light wind stirred her lank black hair, and she lifted one pale hand to brush a long strand from her eyes.

When she moved he lost sight of her for a moment as she passed behind the car. Then she reappeared at the top of the steps, started down. She stooped a little to avoid the low branches of the apple tree, and he realised that she was nearly as tall as he was. But much thinner.

She stopped beside him on the narrow concrete path, a plastic carry-bag in each hand. The sleeves of her grey cardigan reached almost to her knuckles, and pale-pink apple petals were caught in her hair, hair as black as his own. But she was pale, the skin of her face almost translucent. He felt, in his stocky tanned body, suddenly thick and clumsy. Her eyes were a deep and sleepy blue.

'Hullo,' she said, standing flat-footed in her cheap thongs, the breeze pressing the thin folds of the long green dress against the backs of her thighs. Fine wisps of hair drifted about her face; a face pale, high cheek-boned, a little too square.

'Hullo,' he said, watching the wide vulnerable mouth.

'I'm looking for number three,' she said, her voice low, as tenuous and insubstantial as the wind.

He stood up, flexed his knees, jerked his head towards the corner. 'Just round there.'

She nodded, moved away, drifted round the edge of the building.

Number three was the lowest, the deepest, of the twelve flats, tucked away at the bottom level of the square three-storey block. It had been empty for nearly a month. No one stayed there long – it was too dark, too airless, too cold; its windows caught little sunlight, even in summer.

He went back to his planting.

Within a few minutes she was back. He heard her footsteps, heard them pause, sensed her waiting, immobile, behind him. He glanced over his shoulder.

The eyes, he saw, were really less sleepy than vacant. No, not that either; but engaged, their vision turned inward, closed and private.

He raised his eyebrows at her.

'I've got some stuff in the car,' she said. 'Do you think you could give me a hand?'

'Sure.' He got to his feet, followed her up the steps to the carpark, brushing aside the new leaves bursting from the rough knots of the grapevine, dodging under the overhang of the apple tree.

The car was crammed with cardboard cartons, paper parcels, plastic bags. He began to unload, carrying them down to the flat. There was less than he had thought, and it took only a few minutes. Inside the dim flat her few possessions seemed lost, swallowed up in the small cramped emptiness: a stack of records, a player, stained books, unpressed clothes, a few groceries.

He stood for a moment in the dim mustiness of the passage.

'Anything else? Can I help with anything?'

She stood in the doorway of the tiny kitchen. A little bright afternoon sunshine, filtered through the leaves of the peach tree, found its way into the room; against the vibrant green of the light her body, shadowed, took on a two-dimensional aspect, flat, anonymous.

She shook her head. 'No thanks.' Then, 'You're not Australian, are you?'

He smiled a little, almost shyly. 'No, Spanish. My name's Carlo.'

'Mine's Helen.'

'Well …'

'Thanks …'

He left her, still standing in the doorway, and returned stolidly to his flowerbeds.

. . . . .

She came out again a little later, when the sun was edging down towards the distant sawtooth hills, sat on the low concrete wall watching him, smoking a cigarette in sharp quick puffs. He looked at her once, briefly, noting again the paleness, the translucency of her skin, the angular slightness of the body. She wasn't pretty, he decided, wouldn't be even if she were less thin. But there was an openness about her face, an innocent quality that made him think of the faces of young children; an openness denied by the veiled barrier of her eyes.

'You speak good English,' she said. 'Was it hard to learn?'

He laughed. 'No,' he said. 'I've been out here since I was a kid. We speak Spanish at home, but ...' He shrugged.

'What are those?' She nodded at the plants in the bed, arranged in their neat rows like some small orderly army of grey-green spiders. 'I don't know anything about gardening. What sort are they?'

'Carnations,' he said.

'Oh.'

She seemed almost indifferent, as if her interest was a kind of obligation. She took a quick puff at her cigarette. 'What do you call them in Spanish?'

'*Clavel*,' he said, '*los claveles*.' He grinned at her, white teeth sudden against his dark unhandsome face. '*Clavos de amor, clavos de muerte.*'

With some effort she summoned another question. 'What's that? What's it mean?'

He laughed, turning to face her, squatting on his heels. 'It's a kind of play on words,' he said. '*Clavel* is a carnation, *clavelon* is a marigold. *Clavo* is a nail ... so '*clavos de amor, clavos de muerte*' ... nails of love, nails of death ... carnations, marigolds ...'

Her eyes seemed to wake a little in genuine puzzlement. 'Why? What does it mean?'

'I don't know,' he said apologetically. 'Just a saying, you know, maybe nothing ...'

'Oh.'

'Just a saying ...'

She shivered. 'I'd better go in.'

He looked up at the sun, down at the shadows. 'Yeah,' he said. 'Nearly time to knock off.' He picked up the hose, turned the tap, and began to spray the small plants lightly. 'See you next week, maybe.'

'You come once a week, do you? Every week?'

He nodded. 'That's me, regular rounds. Here Tuesdays, over at Norwood Wednesdays, all over the place the rest of the week.' He smiled. 'If you want a hand any time ... you know ... odd jobs ... just give us a shout. The landlord doesn't mind.'

'Oh ... thanks.' Then she was gone, and the sun dipped below the top of the big quince tree at the bottom of the garden. Carlo began to gather his tools, load them into his old utility.

. . . . .

He didn't see her when he came to work the next week, although the shabby VW still stood crookedly in the carpark. Through the day he worked methodically, planting, weeding, watering, mowing; passing and repassing her green-painted door. But it remained closed, the opaque glass panel dark and blank.

'She's a quiet one,' said Mrs Sykes from number two, bringing out her garbage in the late afternoon. 'Hardly ever see hide nor hair ...'

'Doesn't she go to work?' asked Carlo.

Mrs Sykes shrugged, the pale bee-sting of her mouth indifferent in her puffy middle-aged face. Wriggling a finger under the towelling turban she scratched her scalp. 'Never seen her.' She stalked back towards her door. 'I think she's been sick ...'

Carlo began to trim the edges of the lawn with sharp precise strokes.

. . . . .

On the next Tuesday he had been working for several hours, repairing the grape trellis, training the passionfruit vine along the fence, when he heard her voice calling to him from the doorway.

'Would you like a cup of tea?'

He turned quickly. 'Sure.'

She was standing, hunched a little despite the warmth of the morning, the same shapeless grey cardigan pulled up about her throat, drawn down over her wrists. 'Come on then,' she said, and turned away.

He paused for a moment; he had expected that she would bring the tea out into the garden. There seemed to him a certain impropriety in social visits to the tenants' flats. But, all the same, he followed her into the dimness, along the corridor, and into the kitchen. The sudden coolness of the flat struck at the bare skin of his arms and shoulders, chilled the dampness of his sweaty singlet.

He sat at the tiny hinged table, fiddled with a cigarette, while she lit the gas, filled the kettle, spooned tea into a cheap aluminium pot. He looked idly about the room. It seemed still anonymous, bare. There was little evidence of her occupancy; odd plastic canisters, a few cheap jars, a small transistor radio, a couple of threadbare tea-towels.

She poured the tea, fetched the milk from the tiny refrigerator, opened a screw-capped jar half-filled with lumpy sugar.

He sipped, relaxing a little, aware of some impending break in the wall of her indifference. But he sensed, too, a struggle in her, a hint of that effort he had felt before, the effort she seemed to find necessary to admit outsiders to the private world behind her eyes.

Before he had half-finished his tea, hot and weak, she spoke. She looked, not at him, but down at her own cup, chaliced in her thin hands. Carlo noticed, with a sudden stab of something like tenderness, that the two little fingers were slightly curved, bowed, a curious parenthesis.

'Listen,' she said, 'you told me if there was anything ...'

The pause lengthened.

'Yes?' he said at last, curious.

'Well,' she said, 'it's not a job or anything ...' She raised her eyes suddenly to his, and before she looked down again he caught the quick tremor of some desperate urgency. 'The thing is, I'm a bit light on for the rent. I wondered, could you lend me ten bucks? I'd pay you back next week for certain ...'

'Sure.' He was taken aback, embarrassed at her need and somehow disappointed. He reached quickly into the hip pocket of his shorts, found nothing there. 'My wallet's in the ute ... I'll get it.' He stood up quickly, and walked out into the warmth and light of the morning. In the parking lot he reached through the window into his coat pocket, opened his wallet, pulled out a note. Turning, he was surprised to find her standing close behind him, and he almost bumped into her. He fumbled the money into her hand.

'Thanks,' she said. 'Next week ... for sure.'

'No worries. On the dole?'

She nodded quickly and turned to go, hesitated. 'You want some more tea?'

He was sure she expected, hoped for, a refusal. And with some relief he shook his head. 'I better get on with it.'

Her sneakers made no sound as she drifted across the concrete and down the steps, out of sight.

It was three days to rent day, he knew. No mates, he thought, and she must be nervous.

A little later, burning rubbish in the far corner of the garden, he saw her hurry up the steps, climb into the VW;

heard the engine grind reluctantly to life. The car reversed into the street, narrowly missing the gatepost, and disappeared. He listened as its uncertain cough slowly faded.

At lunchtime he went to a pub half a mile away for a beer. When he returned he saw that the VW was back in its place. There was no sign of the girl. But towards evening, when the sun was striking deeply into the tiny box of her porch she came out and sat on the concrete floor, back against the wall, legs stretched straight in front of her. As he passed, going towards his utility, sweat cooling and drying, he saw that her eyes were closed. They opened slowly as he passed, and he saw that they were somehow different; less darkness in them, lighter, wider. She smiled at him, said nothing, just smiled, easily, gently. He noticed that, despite the late-afternoon warmth, the grey cardigan was still drawn tightly up to her throat, the ends of the ragged sleeves tucked into her loosely clenched fists. She closed her eyes again, her face open as a flower in the late sun.

Driving away, it occurred to him suddenly that the next Tuesday was a long way off.

. . . . .

The next week the door to number three was closed again, dark and blank as ever. Mrs Sykes, on her way to the supermarket, saw him looking at it.

'Won't see *her* yet a while,' she said, a thin scornful edge to her voice.

'Oh?'

'Resting up, I reckon. Doesn't look too strong, you know, I s'pose all the night work's taking it out of her ...'

'Got a job, then, has she?'

Mrs Sykes gave him a single pitying glance as she

straightened a pink plastic curler and swung away up the steps. 'More like a profession, I'd say...'

Carlo watched her go, frowning a little, then began unloading trays of petunias.

An hour later Mrs Sykes was back. 'Come and have a cuppa,' she called to him as she passed. 'No cooking today, that bastard Charlie's taking me out to eat tonight, even if he doesn't know it yet ...'

He sat on the steps that led to her chrome and Laminex kitchen, a kitchen crammed with gadgetry indulgences. Eating sweet biscuits and drinking tea, he half-listened to her easy chatter. But all the time he was wondering about the closed door of number three. When he was released by Mrs Skyes he felt relieved, and went quickly back to work, finding a place from which he could observe the door. It's the ten dollars, he thought; I'm not getting done for a tenner just because she lays those big sad eyes on me. But he had a habit of honesty; and knew quite well that there was more to it than that.

He did not see her that day, nor the next week.

. . . . .

On the following Tuesday he considered knocking on her door. But if he did, and she hadn't the money, they would both be embarrassed. And even if she had it, he realised, they would still be embarrassed. So he waited, glancing almost furtively at the door from time to time, aware of growing tension and uneasiness inside himself. It wasn't the money at all, he accepted that now. He had faced that fact, had written it off, discounted it in his mind, weeks ago.

And had almost given up hope of seeing her again. Only the sight of the red VW in the carpark reassured him of her continuing presence in the closed flat.

So he was surprised when, early on a Tuesday morning a month later, she ran, a little breathless, from her door. It was summer, now, and in the full heat and glare she seemed frailer than ever, a wraith floating in her strange long dress and thread-bare cardigan. Her paleness was startling beside his deepening tan.

Quickly she pushed a note into his hands.

'I'm sorry,' she said. 'Sorry I was so long about it.'

'That's all right.' He felt awkward, wanting suddenly to touch her, to run a single blunt finger over the fine skin of her cheek. But she had retreated, stood a safe three paces away, watching him with eyes brighter, bluer, livelier, than he remembered.

'Come and have some tea,' she said. 'Later, after I've been shopping.'

'OK.'

She backed away, smiling, then turned and ran lightly towards the dark tunnel of her doorway.

A little later he saw her again, moving quickly up the steps to the carpark. She waved at him, and he raised a hand.

He ate his lunch in the carpark, reluctant to leave in case he missed her return; then went back thirsty to work. The afternoon dragged on interminably as he went about the garden chores, waiting. Finally he took the shears and went to work on the west side of the building, out of sight of the car-park, a conscious rebellion against his new and disturbing dependence. But all the time his ears strained for the sound of the returning VW. It didn't come, and at last he gave up. At five o'clock he packed his tools and left, driving out of the car-park feeling hurt and let down, and angry at himself because of it.

But he waited for several minutes at the corner in the vain hope of seeing her return.

. . . . .

The weeks passed, the solstice and its celebrations came and went, the heat grew, white dust drifted in from the road and settled on the parching leaves of the peach, the apple trees, the quince. Fruit ripened, the ground grew dry and powdery and Carlo spent more time watering, weeding, mulching. Sometimes on very hot days, he came in the evenings, to water the beds. The carnations were in full bloom now, filling the air with their cinnamon scent.

Carlo watched, but saw her only once. She came, late one evening, when the fading day was returning shadow and colour to the garden. He heard the old car lurch through the gate, and saw the familiar battered bonnet quiver to a stop. She was halfway down the steps before she saw him. For a brief moment she paused, then went on, hunching her shoulders a little, looking downward at the hot concrete where her sneakers scattered whispers of dust.

'Hi,' he said.

'Hi …' She raised one hand a little, a half-wave, and kept going. He watched the door close behind her, and turned away.

She seemed thinner, he thought, as if she were being somehow drained.

. . . . . .

The summer crept slowly over the land like a slow bright cloud, leaching the colour from the trees, the sky. Only the fruit, the flowers, grew daily brighter. And as the season faded, so, thought Carlo, did the girl. He caught only brief glimpses of her, now; she seemed intent on avoiding him, and when she could not avoid his presence, avoided the open concern in his eyes. On the few occasions when they met she scurried like some frightened animal to the dark shelter of her flat.

. . . . .

At last, on a day of heat and lowering cloud, he conquered his common sense, and knocked on the glass panel of the door. She was there, he knew; the VW was in the carpark.

But the sound of his knocking echoed emptily, again and again, beyond the door.

He almost turned away, but at the last moment, in a panic of resolution, he twisted the knob … and the door opened.

Inside, the passage was as dim as ever, as musty, an oppression of thick stale air.

He walked slowly past the kitchen, past the bedroom with its unmade bed and untidy scattering of clothes; found her in the living room at the end of the corridor. The blinds were drawn, and she lay on the shabby vinyl sofa by the left wall, facing him. He stopped in the doorway, motionless, looking at her.

. . . . .

'Go away,' she said, 'please.'

He walked to the sofa, stood looking down at her. She was shivering a little, her nostrils red and raw, her eyes swimming and dark in bruised valleys. He sat down beside her on the edge of the sofa, feeling the slight weight of her hips against him. Despite the heat she wore the old grey cardigan. Slowly he reached out and picked up her left hand, the one that lay nearest him. She tried to pull away, a movement so weak that it seemed a hardly discernible reflex. Only in her eyes was there a firm strength to her resistance.

'Please,' she said.

With the other hand he slipped the sleeve of her cardigan up her arm until it was above the elbow. For a long moment he looked at the dead-white skin, then gently drew down the sleeve again to cover the needle marks. When he looked back at her eyes again he could see nothing there but pain; and wasn't sure whose pain it was – hers, or his own, reflected in the dark hollows.

'What is it?' he said. 'Smack?'

She lay silent, her eyes fixed blankly beyond him.

'Word games,' he said. 'Funny, we talked about word games once. *El clavo*, remember? It means something else too … a bummer, you, a bad trip, something that gives you the shits …' Shit, he thought without humour, up to your eyeballs in it …

Still she said nothing. He watched the faint veins throbbing gently in her naked throat.

'Go away,' she said at last, her voice small and very tired. 'Please.'

He stood up, went out into the bathroom. It wasn't there; nor in the bedroom. He found it, at last, in the kitchen; an old chocolate tin hidden clumsily in the cutlery drawer. Inside it lay the deadliness of the wasp-sharp hypodermic, the tie, the discoloured spoon. There was nothing else – no bag, not even an empty one. He put the tin back in its place, returned to the living room. She hadn't moved.

'Can't you score?' he asked.

She moved her head, a slow side–to–side motion of almost indifferent hopelessness.

He sat down again beside her, lifted her hand, held it

clasped between his large calloused palms. She made no move to withdraw it, lay staring tiredly up at the cracked map of the ceiling.

'You haven't got a job,' he said. 'And you're not tough enough to be ripping stuff off. So you're hawking it, right?'

She said nothing, lifted her other hand to wipe her nose.

'Doesn't have to be like this, you know,' he said.

For a moment she dropped her eyes, looked at him, and he saw in them a curious emptiness that frightened him. But he ploughed on. 'You *can* get off it, you know …'

'How would you know?'

He was surprised at the coldness, the immense bitterness, in a voice so faint and distanced.

'Ever tried?' he asked. 'Cold turkey?'

After a long pause she shook her head.

'I'll tell you something,' he said. 'It never killed anyone yet. It's bloody awful, I know … But it never killed anyone.'

She sighed then, deeply, tiredly. 'Please,' she said 'just fuck off, will you? I know you're a nice bloke, but please fuck off …'

For what seemed a long time he sat beside her, cupping her palm, gently stroking the soft skin of her wrist with his thumbs, as if trying to massage a little of his rude strength into the ruin of her flesh.

'If you want,' he said, 'we could try.' And realised in a sudden swooping that was close to nausea, the enormity of his commitment. 'I could come every day. In the mornings, at lunchtime, at night. At the weekends.' He paused. 'That's all it would take. A week. I'd bring you some flagons of wine … it's a help … you could make it … I know.'

Slowly she closed her eyes. 'Go away now,' she said. 'Please. I really want you to go now …'

For a moment he thought that he felt a slight pressure, a warmth, in her fingers. He waited, but there was only the faint pulse of her blood.

'All right.' He stood up, releasing her fingers. 'But ... if you change your mind, just tell me. Any time.'

She nodded faintly.

For one more long and clumsy moment he stood there, his limbs seeming to grow strangely larger, more gross and useless. Then he wheeled quickly away and plunged out through the door, back down the narrow passage towards the heaviness of the hot grey day that lay waiting for him.

Mrs Sykes, pegging out her washing, gave him a thin glance as he clumped past her.

Wordlessly, he began grubbing out fading plants from the dry soil.

. . . . .

The weeks dragged slowly for him. In the evenings, on his way home from work, he often found himself going out of his way to drive past the flats. Sometimes the VW was in the carpark, sometimes not. He never stopped.

And, on Tuesdays, he never went near the closed door again. But it seemed to him that a kind of ache bled through the plain green panels of the door, the dark pebbled glass, stirring a dull answering pain inside him.

He never saw her, and there was no sign, no appeal.

But he waited.

. . . . .

In the coolness of a morning at the beginning of autumn he set out the trays of plants, dug and raked the bed, preparing. The sunlight, even at mid-morning, was cooler now on his naked back. Soon it would be time for a shirt again.

'Did you hear?' asked Mrs Sykes, leaning from her window, nibbling at a Chocolate Royal. 'About her?' She jerked the bright paisley of her rayon turban in the direction of number three.

Carlo stared blankly at her, shook his head.

'Found her on the weekend, they did.' She pursed her lips around crumbs of sticky chocolate. 'On drugs, they said. You know, heroin or something …'

'Where is she?'

'Gone,' said Mrs Sykes. 'Dead. You know, an overdose …'

Carlo lowered himself slowly to his knees, rested his knuckles gently on the gritty soil, looking downward at the sudden strangeness of his blunt hands so that she would not see his face.

'Why do they do it?' said Mrs Sykes, reaching behind her for another biscuit. 'They must know it'll kill them …'

'I don't know,' said Carlo, watching his fingers crumble small clods of soil. A surge of grief and pity swept over him, an almost unbearable weight of darkness that seemed to suffocate him. Yet under the grief, the pity, he felt the beginning of a sickness start in his belly and rise towards his throat, a sickness at the unspeakable guilt of his own relief. For some charge had been taken from him. He felt suddenly light-headed and dizzy at the immensity of his betrayal.

He reached blindly into the tray beside him and dug out a cluster of plants.

'What are you planting?' asked Mrs Sykes.

'French marigolds,' said Carlo, staring down at the tiny plants. 'For the winter.'

'That's nice,' said Mrs Sykes. 'A little bit of colour for the dull days.' She swallowed the last of her biscuit, withdrew her head and closed the window.

Carlo began to scoop small holes for the marigolds, spacing the plants neatly a hand's-breadth apart in the waiting earth.

. . . .

The Wheelbarrow

PATRICK CULLEN

A dying father, an angry mother, a quietly observant young son, through whose innocent but knowing eyes the tragedy is captured. A vivid opening paragraph takes us to the doorstep of a simple but deeply felt story.

Mum's rougher on the gears than Dad ever was and she's driving too fast. It's the middle of the night and we're riding the hills out of town like a rollercoaster. The car leans over on the bends and my face pushes against the glass. I know that the clouds are up there somewhere in the black sky and I know that they're heavy with rain that just can't find a way out. It's all stuck in there. The clouds are hanging on to their tears just like I'm hanging on to mine.

I'm hanging on to my seatbelt too because Mum's still got her foot down hard and bare. She kicked off her shoes when we left the carpark at the hospital and now they're on the floor in front of me. I'm sitting cross-legged on the vinyl benchseat looking from the space between us to her shoes on the floor. I'm sure the heels on her shoes have been getting shorter each day we go to the hospital. Maybe we're all wearing thin.

Mum's squinting out at the road and her lips are tight like she's chewing them inside out. She's angry but I know it's not at me because she'd have already given me the *what-why-when* ten times over if it was. She hasn't said anything but I know she's angry, and I know it's because she wants to leave town, get right away from the hospital and back to the farm. I know that's what she's thinking even though she hasn't said it because I'm thinking the same thing and I'm not talking either.

I can't think of anything good to say. Couldn't if I tried, so I'm thinking of something Dad might say to make sense of a mess like this. He's never run out of words but now his telling takes longer and his stories don't make as much sense as they should. His own punchlines knock him around now, leave him sucking in air to do some decent laughing with. Then the laughs turn to coughs and it ends with us all back inside our fear.

. . . . .

'We can't do it on our own,' Mum said as we followed the ambulance into town the day she said she'd had enough. 'He can't breathe out here. It'll be better for him in hospital,' she told herself and me.

We've been to see him every day this week. We come straight to the hospital now, Mum's not stopping at the church any more and she's looking a bit mixed up like she's letting go and hanging on too tight at the same time. A bit like the way Dad's breath fights its way in and out of him.

Dad's got his own room. It's at the end of a dog-legged corridor, close to the back door. The door's got an alarm that screams at me every time I try to sneak out. 'There's no escape,' Dad said. Then he couldn't even work up the breath to laugh at himself. Or, maybe like Mum and me, he wasn't in the mood for doing much laughing.

Dad would be screwing up his face if he heard the whingeing Mum's dragging out of the EH as we slow down for the gate. This night is all a dream until we hit the cattle grid and that knocks some sense back into me and the world is all too real again. As we shoot down the driveway, the hustle of the car stirs ducks from around the dam and they slap across the water together and break up in the darkness like fragments of a ghost.

When we pull into the yard, the headlights fumble through the yard until they pin the wheelbarrow to the shed wall. It's propped up there where Dad left it, on its nose with the handles nesting in the corrugated iron. It looks like a gravestone waiting to be heaved into place. 'Do you remember when –' I stop myself because even the thought of saying it hurts too much, and it begins to rain.

· · · · ·

On any other day the wheelbarrow would be hanging on to a load of dirt or sand or chookshit, but when Dad got hungry for yabbies, he'd hose it roughly out, toss in a Milo tin of layer pellets and a tangle of netting, and head off across the paddock toward the dam. Mum would hear him go and she'd cringe at the complaint of the wheelbarrow's axle until its pleading fell beyond earshot.

I go with him sometimes and when I do I see him do the same things the same way every time. He parks the wheelbarrow up at the top of the dam wall and puts a finger to his lips to press me further inside the silence I'm already in.

Then he goes once around the dam empty-handed to decide where to make a start. Second time round, he leaves a trail of layer pellets an arm's length out into the murky water. Then he'd take up a spot under the willow and stop for a smoke. And to wait. The smoke that came off the end of his cigarette drifted off like Catholics' incense and the coils of it were a blessing when they weren't so thick they took the place of your breath and left you deep in prayer. One day I thought I saw Dad praying, down on his knees like people do in church. He said he wasn't though. 'Just coughing my lungs up,' he said. 'Too many cigarettes over too many years and no amount of prayer and promises are going to fix a fate like that.'

He told me that people only ever kneel down in church to give their bums a rest and that you only ever got a sore bum for two reasons: you were either sitting on it for too long or you'd been given the hiding you probably deserved. 'That's Catholics for you,' Dad said, in a way that was supposed to make sense. I thought that even if people prayed for reasons other than to save their bums, I couldn't believe anyone, even Dad, could take this yabbying business seriously enough to bother to call on Him for help.

To end it all, Dad would drag the netting through the shallows and he'd reef up armfuls of ferocious crustaceans. He'd be a flurry of legs, slipping and sliding as he scuttled up the dam wall toward me, reeling them all in, and I'd be backing away, laughing, getting the hell out of his way so I wouldn't be swept up in the chaos.

'We reap what we sow,' he'd wink at me as he trotted back across the paddock, through the broom-end stubble with his kicking and bucking cargo. 'We reap what we sow.'

Mum would already be out on the verandah with the flyscreen pinned back against the wall, waiting for the return of her triumphant hunter. He'd *thump, thump* up the stairs backward, peck her on the cheek, and head down the hallway. Dad knew that the wheelbarrow should never have been in the house, let alone the kitchen, but he'd trundle it in anyway and he'd stand there barefoot and grinning on the lino. In the wheelbarrow, the scrabble of yabbies would be fighting against each other and the fate of them all. They were a writhing, clambering mass of futility.

Dad would set about preparing the feast: purging the yabbies in a sink of fresh water for almost long enough, and whispering intangibles to each of them as he transferred them with great ceremony into the pot water's boil.

When Mum talks about those days she still seems surprised at the way he turned those yabbies into a feast. There were never any recipes. Dad ran on instinct and luck, and the only sure thing was that we'd be well fed. Dad's harvest kept us fed on *dam prawns* for three days, and it was always a sad time when we held the final spoonfuls to our noses and decided whether to keep going. 'Better not risk it.' Dad would make the call.

I'd lay awake and hear him head out across the yard to dump the leftover bits and pieces. There'd be a thud as Dad tried to sneak the wheelbarrow down the stairs and then the sound of the hose in the wheelbarrow, sloshing out the mess. When I looked out from my window I couldn't see all of him. Just his cigarette burning down between his lips. In the morning, the wheelbarrow would be propped up against the shed ready to go again.

. . . . .

There's a pile of dirt halfway between the house and the dam. It's about the size and shape of an upturned wheelbarrow and the grass grows deep and relentless. This midden of yabbie peelings lies there like a shallow grave and it represents the cumulative fragments of our lives. All of those bits and pieces are as much a memory as they are a fact. It is where Dad first taught me about the reality of death and decay, and it was the thing that came back to me as I watched Dad decaying before my eyes.

His lungs gave up in the end. In the final days of the

cancer's devouring of him, he whispered to Mum, 'The wheelbarrow – After they've finished with all the ashes to ashes, dust to dust stuff, wheel me out of the church in it and dump me in the dam.'

'What?' Mum shrieked and squawked. 'What?'

'We reap what we sow,' he grinned and sighed. 'We reap what we sow.'

. . . .

A Pawpaw All The Way from Queensland

BEVERLEY FARMER

An ailing, wheelchaired widow and her two failed sons, one of whom, resentfully, has to care for her. The temptation for Jessie to end it all with the pills she's saved is always there, until the problem is taken out of her hands. Farmer's story seems unrelenting, yet it is illuminated by an inner sympathy for her characters.

The newspaper with its yellow splashes of pawpaw and broken glass was still spread out all over the lino. She folded it into the bin somehow and made real coffee in the saucepan, trundling from the sink to the gas stove, leaning out over the arms of the wheelchair. She spilt some, straining the dark grounds, and sipped the rest luxuriously. She wasn't allowed to use the stove. Still, rules were made to be broken and in this case it was after midnight and Alan still wasn't home. He was ashamed. You've been a good son to me, she wanted to say to him. You, not Billy. You've looked after me. I know it's been heavy going. It doesn't matter. Forget it.

I always liked a rainy night, she thought. I was always one to go skimming over bright puddles, the raindrops throbbing down on the taut black veil of my umbrella, rolling and glowing there. Cars slid by in their lamplit steam. Jessie, good God, woman! You smell like a wet spaniel, Jack always said. I roasted my legs by the fireside while he made coffee and poured us a whisky. Poor Jack, the whisky killed him. Six years ago already. Yes, I was fifty-eight last birthday. He being an older man, retirement's the killer. The whisky on top of the diabetes, and then his heart. It's my turn now.

At about nine o'clock when Alan walked out the rain was so heavy the windows looked as if they had shattered into crystals. Later the drizzle set in. A grey skin of mist grew on the closed panes. These days she felt unsafe with a window open, as if she might float out. She kept inside by a radiator with two red bars and a fan heater that breathed warmth: together they were almost a fire. From room to room she wheeled herself, lamp to lamp. She always had at least two burning day and night, the stooped, white-cowled reading lamp, Alan's really, and her mother's porcelain one with the red silk shade that glowed in the polish of the sideboard like a pagoda on a lake. A street lamp flickered on the front windows. The glass doors of the sitting-room always held some light, red, white or gold. Within the sphere of this or that lamp hour after hour her hands made shadows on her empty skirts and on the pages of the book in her lap. Not that she read any more. She remembered as much as she wanted to of her books. Besides, drops or no drops, her eyes were bad. The same with the television Alan rented. She made a show of watching for his sake, while her mind wandered. Nothing on it could hold her interest for five minutes together. Alan would read to me once in a while, she thought, if I asked. He's hard to talk to. A man of few words. Worse since his marriage broke up. And what he *did* say …! Well, he flew off the handle and no wonder.

My poor sad boy, she said aloud. Come home soon. It doesn't matter. How can I make you see?

Her back ached. She sighed. No use getting upset about the aches and pains. Bodies are like cats and dogs, they have a will of their own. They get slow and stiff, cranky. Think of old Smoky at the end. Pamper them, humour them, do what you like, the day will come when they turn on you. Make messes. Get sick and die and break your heart. Smoky, so fat and sulky, the way he kept rubbing his plushy old head on my legs with this creaky little meow, meow, he knew – what would he make of me these days? He'd take my having no legs as a personal insult. I think I've wet myself, she thought, but never mind. It's warm. Bodies are like the Irishman's dog, one word from me and he does what he likes. Cuddling Jack one night when his manhood had let him down, I told him about the Irishman's dog. You make fun of me, woman, he snarled, and you'll live to regret it. Oh, a morose man. Alan's the image of him. Oldest sons are. Those three years made all the difference. Look at Billy. Nothing throws Billy. He behaved so badly today. He goaded Alan. That's why Alan turned on me and said. Said what he said.

A ring at the door at six o'clock, she remembered, and who should be there but Billy and Wendy, back from two weeks hitchhiking up the coast to Queensland, panting and dusty, all laughter, hugs and kisses. No sooner in the door than Billy was dragging clothes and towels out of his rucksack. He peeled a football, orange-gold and blotchy, out of a tangle of singlets and rolled it over to her chair.

'Good heavens,' she gasped, leaning over to peer, 'whatever's this?'

'A pawpaw, of course!'

'What?'

When she meant why. He bent and picked it up. 'Beauty, eh? It better be,' he crowed. 'We've humped it all the way from Queensland.'

'They sell them in Melbourne,' Alan said.

'This is the real thing, but. Picked ripe from the sun. Have a smell, Mum.'

She put on a great show of delight, made him bend down for a big kiss and thanked him for bothering. Billy, do you or don't you know I'm hanging on by a thread? she wanted to say. First the legs and now the kidneys, how long can I go on dragging this out? I want to do away with myself. No use saying, and she just smiled while Billy, of course, had to set about cutting the thing that very minute. Wash it first, she said. It must have been years since she tasted pawpaw. It was all for her, Billy said, knowing how fond of it she was. Nonsense, she insisted, look at the size of it! They would all have a share. So he sliced it in four, scooped out the glossy round seeds that lay in rows on their beds of flesh like spawn, gunmetal grey – how I used to love crunching those seeds that tasted of capers, of peppercorns! she suddenly remembered – and sprinkled each shell with lemon and sugar. No sugar for me, she said weakly, and at that he grabbed hers, rinsed it under the tap and tried again with plain lemon juice. She ate what she could. It had a bitter aftertaste, or it was the tablets she was on. The blotch on the skin was slimy and had a fur on the outside. She said how delicious, of course, rolling her eyes for him like when they were little after one of her treats. Billy and Wendy gobbled and chattered on about Queensland. They made coffee. All this time Alan had not moved.

'Hey, eat up, Al,' said Billy. 'What's the matter?'

'No, thanks.'

'Come on!'

'Thanks, I don't happen to like pawpaw.'

'Don't know till you've tried it, do you?'

'I have. Tastes like cold boiled pumpkin to me.'

'Oh! It does not! Does it, Mum?'

'It's lovely, dear.'

Billy was watching her eagerly. Foolishly, she couldn't move, transfixed with sadness, and why she didn't know but tears were dribbling down her nose. Billy, ever helpful, grabbed the spoon from her hand. 'Open wide,' he said. He dug out a bright yellow chunk and crammed it between her shuddering gums.

'She doesn't want it. You can see that,' Alan said.

'She's my mother too, you know.'

'So help look after her why don't you?'

'I wish I could.'

'Oh yes, *you're* married. I forgot. Sorry.'

'I happen to put in a sixty-hour week.'

'Oh right. In between hitchhiking.'

'That's you all over,' Billy said. 'God. Always the martyr, Saint Alan.'

Alan walked out of the room. 'God,' Billy spat after him.

'Good heavens, aren't you *brown*, you two! Come here and let me see. You're *burnt*! Better watch out you don't peel!' She was babbling anything she could think of to fill the silence. 'Did you get as far as Townsville? I was born there, you know, dear.' Grinning at Wendy who grinned tremulously back. 'My happiest, earliest memories. I met Billy's father there. We sailed back on our honeymoon on the old *Kanimbla*.' That got them chattering on and on. They had no money left. What was the point of a sixty-hour week at that rate? They seemed to think they could carry on like this forever. Why get married then? Because they had to, of course, why else: or he thought they did. A boy of nineteen. Well, he's twenty-one now and off my hands. The lamplight dazed her and her eyes kept closing, but at last they were packing up the rucksacks, looking up train times, calling out taut goodbyes to Alan, who didn't answer. He came back in after they had gone. His wedge of pawpaw was still glistening on the table.

'Where do you want this?'

'In the fridge, I suppose, thanks, lovey.'

'Can't you eat it and be done with it?'

'Oh dear.' She was too tired for this. 'I couldn't. Tomorrow.'

'It won't keep.'

'Oh, we can't just throw it out, can we? Not when they carried it back all the way from Queensland?'

'It was off. They got it cheap. You'll end up with the runs before you know it.'

'I'll end up before you know it anyway,' she said, and heard with a pang of shame – and alarm too – the quaver of injury in her voice. Self-pity. Alan had spread a newspaper on the lino to wrap the peels and the coffee grounds. Now he slammed the bowl of pawpaw face down so hard that it smashed. He sat on his heels glaring up in defiance, livid, her jealous little Alan of a thousand tantrums. 'Oh, Alan, dear,' she sighed, smiling.

'Oh Alan dear,' he simpered. He stood over the wheelchair, head down and snarling in her face. 'What does that bloody well mean, "Oh Alan dear"?'

'Oh, don't.' She closed her eyes.

'Don't what? God damn you to hell; bitch,' he shouted then. 'What are you waiting for? Die and be done with it. Is that what you want? What the fuck's stopping you?'

Before she could say a word he had dashed out and slammed the front door. Rain was falling in a white rush round the street lamp. There was no sign of him. She had drawn all the curtains and sat among her warm lamps for ages. She rolled up closer to the mantel clock. Could that be right, half past two? She must have dozed off. The fan heater fluttered her empty skirt. Where was he? He never stayed out all night. So dreary, this long grey rain.

Perhaps, it occurred to her, he was home all the time. He might have found her in here asleep and still been angry enough to leave her be and go straight to bed. Alan, she called out softly. Alan, and then thought better of it. He needed the sleep. Carefully she rolled down the passage and turned the handle of his door. No, his bed was made, more or less, the covers pulled up in lumps and wrinkles, still empty.

Surly Alan with his black moods, she thought, and rowdy greedy silly Billy, how I loved them once! They're heavy weather the pair of them, now they're grown men. Alan who's clammed up since his wife walked out and can't stand self-pity. No, that's his preserve. And Billy who was the ant's pants, he got well and truly caught, a false alarm, the oldest trick in the book and he falls for it. If you ask me, she really is expecting now, though, which should bring him down to earth with a thud. No, as men they were a disappointment, only real when she caught a glimpse of their childhood selves. Did they feel the same? Most likely. Who's the old bag, then? The cripple with the goggle-eyed face under a tangle of veins, leaking into her chair? Not me, not the real Jessie. Some old baglady has got in under the skin of the real Jessie, the buxom and bustling younger Jessie who loved her little boys. I take myself by surprise, she thought, as the sight of these stumps of thighs and my arms as the Sister sponges them, the flesh loose and yellow on the bone like overcooked chicken. When did it happen? Time was thin and vague now, the after as lost and out of reach as the long before. It might be the tablets. All the months when ulcers ate at the grey flesh of her legs and she sat up night after night clenched all over to keep so much as a whimper from waking Alan – even those times were washing away. Dozing off, she was this and that other Jessie, young Jessies with long legs. Which only went to show that the truth still hadn't sunk in after all this time, not into every fibre of her being that the helpless old bag of bruised and aching flesh here, in and out of hospital, gangrened and lopped and gangrened and lopped all over again, was the real and last, one and only Jessie. While it lasted.

She wheeled over to the window and rubbed a space in its cold mist. Was he down on the beach? On the day he moved back in when he spent hours trying to tell her his marriage was a failure and could he come home – for hours that day he kept her hobbling up and down on the beach in just such a soft rain, the grey waves slowly beating, pitted. Their faces were wet. Raindrops glowed in his hair. Her legs were so bad he had to prop her up. In fact she had the artificial leg by then. When was the first operation? – she was on one leg. The dry sand was hopeless so he kept to the firm sand, the wave line, higher and higher, so that now and then a cold, fine cloth of water would be thrown up as they went, and go flattening and frilling around their shoes. He never even noticed.

He only got married because Billy was. That's all, deep down. Spite. They're as bad as each other, it's just that it takes them differently. Neither boy can face facts. Alan goes into his shell and as for Billy, look at him – Billy's all glitter. Night was falling by the time we struggled home, she remembered, for coffee and pancakes. By way of consolation. Oh, Alan, dear, always coming home for consolation! We had a whisky, just like the old days, which I shouldn't have, I know, but life isn't worth living if you can't break a rule when needs must. We had our guzzle of whisky in the lamplight and at last we could hug, and laugh and cry. None of that now. I still had the one leg. My one wet foot I could feel, the wash of the water and sand between my toes. I'm not allowed to cook any more. Or laugh, or cry.

Oh, Alan, dear! A cup of coffee would be nice. They bring me Meals on Wheels, bless their hearts, and Alan dishes me up his little treats of a night. I can't complain. Even oysters he bought me the other day as a surprise, shiny and grey on their crinkled half-shells, my favourite food. I'd forgotten how delicious. It's all soft foods since my upper plate broke. I used to like cooking. Banana pancakes, that was Alan's favourite. The boys had pancake races. Let's see who can eat the most. Usually Billy won; not that he was that keen on them, which is Billy all over. Me in the kitchen, not knowing till too late. We had pancake picnics in the ti-tree along the foreshore of a summer night. Fed the seagulls. I stare out at a seagull now as if the beach was a world away.

How ironic life can be, she thought. No longer caring if she slept or not, she had saved up more than enough tablets to bring on an easy death. *Easeful* death: that was in some poem. Alan would never know. The Sister or Doctor Smith might, but even so they would never let on. But now that Alan had said *that!* He'd blame himself. He'd have this hanging over him for the rest of his life. *Die and be done with it.* How could she take them after that, no matter how desperate she was, even if he wanted – which he didn't. She shook her head. You're getting morbid, my lass, she thought. You'll go in good time. You and your tablets. Wait for nature. Because in a few hours, when the first bird woke with a hoarse chirrup at the window, wouldn't she feel ashamed to show a poorer spirit than birds and snails and avid unfolding green plants? Another day. Snooze and roll about the house, be sponged and dressed and fed and jabbed and dosed again.

She trundled into the dark kitchen. A blown leaf – a mouse? – rustled across the lino. She leaned over the sink to fill the saucepan, measured ground coffee into it and, carefully tucking up her sleeves, lit the gas ring. The coffee frothed up. She strained and sipped it black and strong. Woman, you don't boil coffee! Jack, shouting. You'll ruin it! Poor Jack. At least with the heart you go quicker. She smiled. Oh, the fireside nights and Jack, far gone in whisky. All gone now. It'll be morning soon. Oh, Alan, look, I understand. How can I make it better?

Pancakes! she thought. And when he comes in – Look, I can say. Alan, look what we've got for breakfast – pancakes!

She crouched rummaging in the cupboards for flour. In the white glare of the fridge she found an egg and half a bottle of milk. No bananas in the house. We get the giant pawpaw lugged home in person and yes, we have no bananas. Well, then, lemon and sugar. No lemon: it all went on the pawpaw. Never mind, jam will do. Hugging the bowl, she mixed and beat, mixed and beat. Flour settled on her lap and sleeves and in her coffee, which she gulped down. The batter should be left to stand. No time for that. She had a feeling he would walk in any minute. She had better be quick or her surprise would be spoilt. *Look, Alan:* smiling, she pulled out the black iron frying pan, rubbed a butter paper over it and relit the gas. A curl of smoke soon rose from the pan. With a tea towel she grasped the hot handle and raised the bowl to pour some batter down into the middle. Her hand shook and, afraid it would spill, she jerked both hands sharply up to save it. The little crown of flames, catching at the tea towel sprang roaring up her sleeve. Flames glared into her eyes, clawing her, and she beat at them with seared hands. Flames tore her other sleeve. There where she sat, her hair and her hanging skirt flared. Fire covered her.

. . . .

From *Beverley Farmer: Collected Stories*, UQP, 1996

The Car Keys

PETER GOLDSWORTHY

In moments, Barbara's erotic escapade turns into nightmare – made even worse because it has overtones of farce. It's not easy to keep two such disparate elements in balance, but Goldsworthy succeeds through his skilful control of tone.

1

Later, Barbara remembered a platitude she had read somewhere: that an orgasm was a kind of death, a little death. A death-throe.

At the time, lost in her own death-throes – not so little – she failed to comprehend her lover's strange, exaggerated moaning. He was outside the high walls of her own pleasure; she half heard him, but thought it – *half* thought it – some sort of joke. From the start there had been moments of irreverence, of clowning, in their relationship: an antidote perhaps to the illicit lust, extremely serious, that fuelled it.

His noisy groaning might have been a self-parody at first, a cartoon-come, but the sudden chill in his skin, the cold clammy sweat, shocked her. She was instantly alert, dragged back from a charged erotic world, where pain sometimes meant its opposite, into an actual world where pain meant nothing but pain.

'Luke? What's the matter? Is something the matter?'

She realised – an even sharper instant of terror – that he couldn't answer. He no longer had the breath to inflate the words; he stared up at her from the floor with mute terror. He was in agony.

'Oh shit!' she screamed, and lifted herself free of him and ran to the phone.

She riffled, fingers trembling, through the teledex for the emergency number, stammered her address into the phone. The operator wanted more information; she was too agitated to answer, straining away from the receiver, trying to glimpse her lover lying in the hall, wanting to get back to him.

'What does it *matter* how old he is, for Christ's sake? Just get here!'

What next? She sat on the floor, cradling his head in her lap, helpless, waiting for the ambulance. He sucked laboriously at the air, dragging the stuff into his lungs as if it were treacle. His limbs flailed weakly – some kind of semaphore, perhaps, which she couldn't read. They were both still naked, their clothes scattered over the length of the hall. He had rung earlier from his office, begging to see her, to *touch* her, unable, he claimed, to wait till Thursday; she had opened the front door to him a few minutes later, and allowed him, for the first time, into the sanctuary of her house. Her husband's house. The momentum of his embrace had carried them towards the bedroom, her husband's bedroom; some last scruple had made her bring him gently to ground on the carpet in the doorway, his feet in the hall, his head and shoulders in the bedroom. She had permitted him halfway into her life, halfway into her private world, but no further. Guilt might be inescapable, but there were degrees of guilt: guilts that could be lived with, or tolerated.

'Please don't die,' she whispered, 'please.'

The wailing of the approaching ambulance shocked some sort of sense, of self-awareness, into her brain. She slipped a pillow beneath his head, pulled on her sweater and jeans, then tried, urging him to help, to clothe him. His movements were ineffectual, even pointless. She slid his jocks on, despite his dripping, still half-tumescent state. Tears blurred her vision, her movements were panicky and confused. She pulled his trousers roughly up over his legs; he seemed to shift his weight to help automatically, a reflex movement. There was no time for his shirt: the siren was dying in the street outside. She shouted in his ear, 'I won't be long, Luke. The ambulance …'

No answer. His eyes had glazed over; it seemed his breathing had almost stopped. She touched his white face; it felt as cold as stone. An Easter Island face, she had once told him, jokingly, tracing with her finger the long nose and narrow crown. It was closer now to those impassive stone statues than it had ever been.

She rose, jerked open the front door and ran to the gate. 'Help! Please!'

The ambulance was crawling along the kerb, its driver – a young woman, almost a girl – scanning house numbers. She spotted Barbara waving frantically, and slewed the vehicle into the gutter; an older, green-overalled woman jumped from the passenger side and ran towards the house, carrying a large box and canister of oxygen.

'Where is he?'

'This way. Quickly. I think it's a heart attack.'

The woman knelt at Luke's side, felt briefly for a pulse in his neck, then turned and spoke calmly to her younger colleague, the driver, who was pushing a collapsible stretcher down the hall.

'It's an arrest, Emma.'

She rolled Luke flat onto his back, pressed a facemask to his pale, sweaty face and began squeezing an air-bag, rhythmically. The younger woman, Emma, dropped her stretcher and began pressing the heels of her palms into his chest, up and down, a slightly faster rhythm.

Barbara watched: helpless, distraught.

'We've got a pulse,' the older woman announced, and turned to Barbara. 'Here, squeeze the bag.'

'Me? But I can't. I don't know *how* ...'

'Like this.' The voice was firm, calm, controlled. The air-bag was pushed into Barbara's right hand, her left was clamped over the face-mask and chin. She held tightly with one hand, squeezed with the other.

'A little slower. Perfect. Listen – is your husband on any medication?'

'Uh – no. I don't think so.'

The younger woman glanced at her sharply. 'You don't *think* so?'

'He's not my husband.' This did not seem adequate; she hurried on, 'Luke is ... a close friend of my husband.'

Was there anything more stupid she could have said? Her lover had never *met* her husband. The phrase seemed to leap from her mouth with its eyes closed, compounding the guilt.

The younger woman watched her for a moment – stared at her, openly curious – then turned back to her work, pressing Luke's chest. The older, unperturbed, was pushing a needle into the crook of his elbow. Her manner was been-there-done-that, unshockable.

'You want to ride in the ambulance?'

Barbara hesitated. Their professional calm was infectious, she at last seemed able to think more clearly.

'I'll follow in the car. I need to make some phone calls first.'

2

Who to call? First instincts said Gerry – to prepare the ground, fit together the ribs of a plausible story. She rebuked herself: Luke's kin had the prior claim, surely. But where were they? *Who* were they? She realised how little she knew of him. They had first met only a few weeks before: swapping Royal Family sarcasms across a magazine rack in a newsagent, followed by a cappuccino in a café next door, the jokey laughter suddenly more nervous, at least on her side. She was aware that merely by accepting his invitation to coffee she had crossed a new boundary.

This much he had told her: he was a solicitor, but business was slow, he was under-employed. Often unemployed. His self-deprecating manner, however well-practised, charmed her. She visited his apartment a few days later – heart pounding – unable to refuse his phone demands any longer. *I want to get to know you better. I can't seem to get you out of my mind. Please visit – just once. If you want to leave …*

He had seldom spoken of his ex-wife, although he occasionally boasted of his small son. Framed portraits of a single smiling infant abounded in an otherwise minimally decorated apartment.

He had silenced her when she had attempted to speak of her own children.

'I don't even want to know their names. That's your other life. Different compartment. It has nothing to do with this.'

Even as they undressed each other at that first assignation he was quick to establish these ground rules. Too quick, she decided afterwards. Too … cold blooded.

'We won't do this again,' she assured him, pulling on her clothes, overcome with regret, wanting only to be safely home as quickly as possible. 'Not ever. It's not right.'

He was sitting naked in bed, propped on pillows, watching as she hastily covered herself.

'It might not be right, but it can be made civilised.'

'What do you mean?'

That impassive Easter Island head. 'There are ways of doing things, Barbara.'

'Not for me. Never again.'

Her resolve lasted a week, although she was drawn back to him as much by confusion as by desire: by a need to settle her disturbed state of mind, one way or another. Also by the need to talk about it – there was no one else she could talk with. She still felt uneasy the second time, afterwards – but felt also, absurdly, that it would be, well, *rude* to rush off again so quickly.

'There are rules for war,' he murmured into her ear as they lay together. 'A Geneva convention. War is wrong – but it happens. It will always happen. It's in our nature. We can only attempt to limit the damage.'

For the first time she felt comfortable enough to tease him. 'You sound like a lawyer.'

'Perhaps there should be rules for adultery,' he suggested. 'Laws of adultery.'

Her pulse flared at the sound of the word. Adultery. A small thrill of torment passed through her each time she heard it. Or even, in the coming days, read it: suddenly there seemed to be any number of adultery stories in the newspapers; the word kept finding her eye, jumping off the pages as if set in bold type, or embossed upon the flat page.

She had announced her own laws the following week. One: she loved her husband. Two: she would never leave him. Three: he must never, ever, *ever* know.

Her conviction on this point seemed, oddly, to reassure her lover: a safety net had been stretched beneath their difficult trapeze act, protecting him, perhaps, as much as her.

'He won't *want* to know,' he reassured her.

She was not convinced. 'I read somewhere that they

always know. Within a few hours. They read the signals.'

'Wives know,' he told her. 'Men aren't so … sensitive.'

Relieved, she found this easy to accept. 'Gerry doesn't notice small things. He's so bound up in his work. He …'

Her lover pressed his fingertips against her lips. 'I don't even want to hear his name.'

'You're right. It's not fair. To him.'

For the first time she sensed that Luke had been here before, more times than once, that he was allowing her to discover these excuses, these rationalisations: the rules and procedures, if such were possible, of adultery. The etiquette of betrayal. At times his answers to her worries would come too easily, too glibly: a frictionless gear change. But she was grateful even for this. At other times, more subtly, he would deflect her questions back at her, allowing her to uncover answers that he only hinted at.

He had pursued her relentlessly from their first meeting; but slowly, after talking it through – gnawing together at the same bone, obsessively – it had come to seem an equal responsibility.

'What if I talk in my sleep?' she asked him once.

'*Do* you talk in your sleep?'

'It might burst out of me. I've never lied to him.'

He seemed more pensive that usual, his answer taking time to emerge. 'The worst thing you can do is make a confession.'

'You sound as if you're talking from experience.'

He averted his face. It was the nearest he had come to autobiography, to providing clues to the fate of his own marriage.

And now, here, today, as the ambulance siren faded into the general noise horizon of morning traffic, Barbara realised that she had never once heard his ex-wife's name.

3

She tugged the *Yellow Pages* from a shelf and searched under 'Solicitors' for his work number. She had rung him several times at his office – a small suburban shop-front – but had not yet committed the digits to memory. To memorise such detail would have been to grant the affair some sort of permanency.

'Is that Luke Pascoe's office?'

A butter-voiced secretary assured her that Mr Pascoe was 'out with a client'.

Barbara interposed, bluntly, 'He's in hospital with a suspected heart attack.'

The voice at the other end of the line was suddenly higher-pitched and panicky. 'But he can't be! He was here – just an hour ago.'

'I'm sorry. It looks, um, serious. I wondered – if you could contact his family ... He's been taken to the Queen Adelaide.'

Barbara was given no opportunity to lie as the voice raced on terrified, tearful. 'Give him my love. Please. Tell him Sandra sends her love. I'll be right there.'

As she hung up Barbara realised, stunned, that she had opened at least one bulkhead, inadvertently – a hatch that led into another of Luke's compartments: a dark crawl space she had no desire to enter.

She gathered her purse and car keys, stepped out of the house, locked the front door. Preoccupied, she had climbed into her car, started the engine and begun reversing before turning to check the drive.

Luke's car – a red sports coupé, a car that always looked more like a cliché than a car – was parked behind hers, blocking the exit.

She braked inches from the front fender, climbed out and peered through the driver's window. The doors were locked, the ignition empty. With a sinking feeling she re-entered the house, and spent some minutes searching the hall and bedroom carpet on hands and knees. The search was as futile as she had dreaded: Luke's keys were surely in his trouser pocket, speeding towards hospital.

She rang a taxi with trembling fingers, then waited, fidgeting, restless, outside in the street. Luke's car glinted in the sun, incandescent red, drawing the entire world's attention to itself: Exhibit A. Her predicament overwhelmed her; the desire she had felt for him, the frightened thrill of those secret visits, was suddenly beyond her comprehension. What *had* she been doing? This immovable object, parked in her drive, filled her thoughts to the exclusion of all else – even her worry over whether Luke was still alive.

She had two hours, perhaps three, before Gerry arrived home from work. A taxi turned the corner. She stepped down into the road and waved both her arms above her head, desperately.

. . . . .

'Are you his wife?'

'No, just a friend. How is he?'

The nursing sister – a young, thin man, his hair gripped tightly in a ponytail – watched from behind the desk.

He half rose and gestured to a chair, 'Perhaps you'd better sit down.'

Barbara remained standing in the door of the office, knowing immediately that his words were a formula, an explanation in themselves; they had nothing to do with the act of sitting.

He shrugged, and sat again himself. 'He died a few minutes ago. I'm very sorry.'

She blinked, and swallowed. 'Could I see him?'

He glanced down, pretending to scan some notes on his desk. 'We need to contact his family first. Next-of-kin. Perhaps you can help us?'

'No. I'm sorry … But his secretary will be here soon. Sandra somebody. I'm sure she can help.'

Her legs felt weak. She finally sat on the offered chair; hating herself for what she had to do, for the selfish premeditation of it: a further betrayal. And yet it seemed a lesser betrayal: Luke was beyond help; her first loyalty must now be to the living. Among whom she included herself.

'Look, um, Sister. I have a small problem. I think my car keys are in his pocket.'

'I can look,' he offered, and rose, and slipped past her through the door. The office was glass partitioned, she watched him disappear behind the curtain of a nearby cubicle, allowing her no glimpse of whatever that curtain concealed. He re-emerged almost immediately, carrying a small cardboard box, a shoebox labelled in black felt-tip scrawl: PASCOE, LUCAS.

'His personal effects.'

He eased free the thick rubber band which bound the box and lifted the lid. It contained a watch, a black leather wallet, a miscellany of coins – and the missing keys, a key-ring attached to a plastic chequered flag, poignantly jaunty.

Barbara reached across the desk, but the nurse slid the box out of reach.

His tone was apologetic but firm, 'I'm sorry, I should have explained. Personal effects are the property of the coroner's office. We can't release them. Not yet.'

Her hand remained frozen above the desk, as stiff as the arm of a gramophone. 'But I have to move the car.'

He watched her intently: he seemed to be examining her. She realised, suddenly, that he had been in this position before.

'Okay,' she confessed. 'It's his car. But it's blocking my drive.'

'I'm very sorry,' he said. 'Really. If it were up to me …' He shrugged. 'But there are procedures we must follow – by law. Until the coroner determines the cause of death and releases the body.'

She could feel the panic growing in her. 'When will that be?'

'After the autopsy. In fact, you might be able to help, Ms…?'

'Mrs Browning.'

'Mrs Browning. I gather you were present when he first became ill.'

She sat, saying nothing, admitting nothing.

'Perhaps if you could describe the symptoms?'

A crazy thought crossed her mind: to strike some sort of deal. A swap.

'I just want to move a car,' she said.

'Mrs Browning – please. I can't help. But if you were a witness I think the doctor would like a word with you.'

'I wasn't there. I don't know anything. Please give me the keys.'

'Perhaps you could call a locksmith.'

'That might take hours! I need to shift it now.'

Tears welled in Barbara's eyes, but they were not tears of grief – whatever grief she felt had been deferred, under pressure of greater, more immediate emotions. What was she to do? What were the rules, the procedures? What subsection of Luke's absurd Geneva Convention dealt with this? She felt an overpowering, irrational urge to enter the curtained cubicle and angrily demand answers from the dead body, the dead lawyer who was filed there, discreetly out of sight. *What now? What do I do now? Tell me the precedents.*

On the other side of the desk the nurse fitted the cardboard lid carefully over the shoebox of personal effects, stretched the thick rubber band about both, and released it with a soft snap.

Rage overwhelmed Barbara: rage at this man who had died in her house, on her carpet, who had thoughtlessly, carelessly, left his ridiculous sports-car blocking her drive. She reached across the desk and grabbed the shoebox from the nurse's hands with such force that he could only watch, stunned. She jerked off the lid, and extracted the keys.

'I'll return these later,' she said.

And she rose and walked rapidly from the cubicle and down the corridor, those stolen keys grasped tightly in her hand, the nursing sister still sitting behind his desk, watching her leave, paralysed by surprise.

. . . .

NOTES ON THE AUTHORS

Jessica Anderson has written three collections of short stories and seven novels including *Tirra Lirra by the River* and *One of the Wattle Birds*.

David Astle is the author of two novels – *Marzipan Plan* and *The Book of Miles*. His current project, due for release in early 2005, is a curiosity guide to Australia.

Larissa Behrendt is professor of law and indigenous studies at Sydney's University of Technology. *Home*, published in 2004, is her first novel.

Gretta Beveridge's short stories have been published in *Meanjin*, *Overland*, *Westerly* and *Island* magazines and have been broadcast on ABC Radio National.

Carmel Bird's most recent novel is *Cape Grimm*, the last in a trilogy. She has edited several anthologies.

Lily Brett is a New York-based Australian writer. She has published two collections of short stories: *Things Could be Worse* and *What God Wants* and a novel, *Too Many Men*.

Marshall Browne has written ten works of fiction, including the popular Inspector Anders mystery series. His short story collection, *Point of Departure, Point of Return* was published in 2003.

Bill Collopy is a Melbourne-based writer and social policy researcher. His stories have appeared in many Australian magazines.

Patrick Cullen lives on a property in the Hunter Valley. His writing has received a number of prizes. He is currently completing a collection of short stories and a novel.

Liam Davison's novels include *Soundings*, *The White Woman* and *The Betrayal*. He has also published two volumes of short fiction. He lives in Melbourne.

NOTES ON THE AUTHORS

Nick Earls has written short story collections, children's books and six novels, including *Zigzag Street*, *Perfect Skin*, *World of Chickens* and *The Thompson Gunner*.

Beverley Farmer's books include three short story collections – *Milk*, *Home Time* and *Collected Stories* – and the novels *The Seal Woman* and *The House in the Light*.

John Gascoigne, who has worked as a journalist in Sydney, Melbourne and Bendigo, has had a collection of his short stories published in *Nuggets: Golden and Human*.

Peter Goldsworthy's novels, poetry and short stories have won numerous literary prizes. His most recent novel, *Three Dog Night*, won the Christina Stead Award. *The List of All Answers*, a collection of his short stories, was published in 2004.

Miles Hitchcock won the *Age* Short Story Competition in 2003. He has written a suite of stories on the theme of 'Generation X trying to grow up'.

Janette Turner Hospital, a Melbourne-born writer, has spent much of her life in Canada and USA. She has written several novels and short story collections including *Dislocations* and *Isobars*.

Elizabeth Jolley, born in England's industrial Midlands, has lived in Perth since 1959. Her published work includes four collections of stories, fifteen novels, poetry and radio plays.

Cate Kennedy's short stories have won several awards. 'A Pitch Too High for the Human Ear' was first published in the University of Canberra's magazine *Redoubt*.

Anthony Lynch's fiction and poetry have appeared in journals in Australia, USA and UK. In late 2003 he was awarded an Australia Council grant to complete a collection of short stories.

James McQueen, who was born in Tasmania, wrote five novels and six collections of short stories, winning national and international awards for short fiction. He died in 1998.

David Malouf has written a collection of short stories *Dream Stuff* and several poetry anthologies. His novels include *Remembering Babylon*, which won the first Dublin International IMPAC Prize. He has won many Australian awards.

Barry Oakley is the author of five novels, the most recent of which is *Don't Leave Me*. He has also written numerous plays, stories and columns, and has published a selection from his diaries entitled *Minitudes*. He was the *Australian*'s literary editor.

Desmond O'Grady, an Australian author who lives in Rome, has written thirteen books, including two collections of short stories, *A Long Way from Home* and *Valid for All Countries*.

Paddy O'Reilly writes fiction and screenplays. Her work has been published widely and has won a number of awards including the Glen Eira *My Brother Jack* National Short Story Prize in 2003.

Eva Sallis was born in Bendigo, Victoria. She has a PhD in comparative literature, Arabic and English. Her books include *Hiam*, *The City of Sealions*, *Mahjar* and *Fire, Fire*.

Steve J. Spears is the author of the classic Australian play *The Elocution of Benjamin Franklin*. He now works full-time as a novelist and essayist. He most recent work is a blackly comic crime novel *Murder at the Fortnight*.

Josephine Vraca came to Australia from Sicily when she was two. She spent several years as a music and film writer for the *Age* and *Rolling Stone*. She is currently working on the final draft of her first novel.

Sari Wawn lives in north-eastern Victoria. Over the last ten years she has kept a journal documenting the interactions between life and place. She has had several short stories published.

Michael Wilding's novels include *Living Together*, *Pacific Highway* and *Academia Nuts*. He has written several collections of short stories including *The Man of Slow Feeling, Great Climate, This is for You* and *Somewhere New*.

Tim Winton's novels include *Cloudstreet, The Riders, Blueback* and *Dirt Music*. He has written three collections of short stories, *Scission, Minimum of Two* and *Blood and Water*, and won many Australian literary awards.